Novels by Marc Curtis Little

Don't Blink When God Calls (The Curt Felton Series)

Angels in the Midst (The Curt Felton Series)

After Obama (The Curt Felton Series)

Magnificent Redemption

Faithful Servants

A Novel

COLLECTOR'S
EDITION

Marc Curtis Little

USA
2019

MLPR Books
7707 Merrill Road
Unit 8244
Jacksonville, Florida 32239
www.MarcLittleWrites.com

Printed in the United States of America

Library of Congress Control Number: 2017907491

Faithful Servants: a novel / Marc Curtis Little

pages cm

ISBN: 978-0-578-44795-7

Summary: "A star black athlete and his nationally celebrated Jewish coach are caught in a battle of cultures in post-1967 riot America, while discontent escalates between African Americans and Jewish Americans."

Provided by the publisher.

1. Civil Rights 2. African Americans 3. Jewish Americans 4. Newark, NJ History 5. Riots 6. High School Basketball 7. Philip Roth 8. The 1960s 9. Faith 10. Progressives 11. Rebellions 12. American History 13. Racial Tensions 14. Police Brutality 15. Disparate Community 16. Black Power 17. Negro 18. The Great Migration

Editing by Beth Kallman Werner, Author Connections LLC
Interior Design and Cover by 1106 Design
Photo Courtesy of Expressions by Karen Waters

IN MEMORIAM
Matthew Major Little

June 16, 1925–November 9, 2018

"Mission Accomplished, Assignment Fulfilled"

A True Faithful Servant

To Zaundria Mapson Little,
Thank you for letting 'yes' be an important word in your vocabulary.

Dedicated to the memory of Clara Eleazer Little (1925–2009)
Your strength continues to fuel my passion.
"I waited patiently for the Lord; He inclined to me and heard my cry."
Psalm 40:1

THERE WAS AN AIR OF superiority floating around Alabama's largest city. The conflict was regarding a high school basketball clash; Birmingham was the site of the first official high school basketball game between a predominantly black school from the north and a predominantly white school from the south.

Southern sports media anchors spouted opinions about a convincing victory over the invading force from New Jersey—dreams of the South rising again. Even the *Birmingham News*, owned by New York-based Advance Publications, dismissed the chance that Weequahic High School of Newark, New Jersey might defeat the nation's second-ranked Woodlawn High School of Birmingham. One sportswriter actually claimed that because of the racial makeup of the Alabama team and the fact that it was coached by a white man, Woodlawn was more intellectually prepared to defeat the perceived less cerebral Weequahic, coached by a black man. While some in the city opened their arms to the visitors from Newark, others looked forward to, "chasing them back to the urban jungle," as one columnist opined.

Each team's captain—Beau McCracken of Woodlawn and Nehemiah Garvey of Weequahic—met the referees at center court before the opening tip-off. The officials, both white, went over the ground rules, but neglected to have the two captains shake hands. McCracken surprised Garvey by extending his right hand. As they shook, Birmingham's

McCracken told Newark's Garvey that he had heard about Garvey's achievements in Newark after the 1967 riot, remarking, "I'm proud of your work."

Many in Newark's Jewish community joined a number of black citizens in criticizing the decision to play a game in Birmingham, mainly because they felt it unsafe for the players and fans who traveled to the city once dubbed 'Bombingham' because of racial violence there in the early '60s. But to supporters of the move, it was standard operating procedure for a team whose mission was to shine a positive light on a city determined to rebuild its physical and social infrastructure after the fiery rebellion of 1967. Weequahic's basketball team used its surprising success during the 1967–68 season to prove that a group of young people from diverse backgrounds could help solve the racial animus that was threatening the security of the world's most powerful country.

Neither Newark nor Birmingham knew the checkered future that awaited their citizens over the next fifty years, but something happened on that February night at the end of Weequahic's upset victory over Woodlawn. Players and coaches from both teams met on the court and kneeled. A prayer was led by Nehemiah Garvey and Woodlawn's Beau McCracken. Players and coaches from both teams met on the court, and not only did the young men show the world they could compete against each other in brotherhood, but they were also capable of kneeling together to praise a higher being.

Chapter 1

"Negroes have proceeded from a premise that equality means what it says, and they have taken white Americans at their word when they talked of it as an objective. But most whites in America in 1967, including many persons of goodwill, proceed from a premise that equality is a loose expression for improvement. White America is not even psychologically organized to close the gap—essentially it seeks only to make it less painful and less obvious but, in most respects, to retain it. Most of the abrasions between Negroes and liberal whites arise from this fact."

~ DR. MARTIN LUTHER KING JR., IN HIS LAST BOOK,
WHERE DO WE GO FROM HERE: CHAOS OR COMMUNITY? IN 1967

A FRIGHTENED WOMAN RAN UP to two policemen, complaining that a tall black man was giving her a menacing stare.

"Did he touch you in any way?" one of the officers asked.

"Why are you asking her that? The only thing we need to know is that a white woman feels threatened by a Negro's presence. Whenever something like this happens down south, they just bring 'em in, no questions asked. Let's go get him."

"We're not down south. I thought we did things differently up here?" the other officer asked.

"These people are the same, whether they're in Alabama, Mississippi, Louisiana, or New York, New Jersey or even Washington D.C. We don't need to treat them decently. What are they gonna do about it, fight back?"

This kind of attitude was standard operating procedure in America's inner cities during the 1960s.

RIPPEL FIELD, THE BLACKTOP playground across the street from South Side High School in Newark, New Jersey, was teeming with the usual throng of neighborhood youngsters. A variety of ages were involved in activities typical of any public recreational setting in urban America during the mid-sixties: highly competitive three-on-three games on both ends of the basketball court, the melodic cadence of French-style—also known as Double Dutch—rope jumping, the strategy of hotly contested checker matches. Not to be left out was the gathering of individuals who bantered endlessly about practically nothing, better known as talking trash. This is one of the meeting habitats in a section of some cities; the section once called *the ghetto*.

"Yeah, I told those damn state troopers they better not shoot out any more windows on Bergen Street," one of the young men who had just lost a game on the basketball court said.

"Aw, motherfucka', you ain't got that kind of heart. You ain't nothin' but a punk ass nigger," another older teen in the crowd called out.

As the two were jawing back and forth, Nehemiah Garvey was leaving the court with one of his teammates.

"There's Fuzzy, talkin' that shit again. That flake ass nigger was probably hidin' in his basement during the riot," Jimmy Trawick, Nehemiah's best friend said. Jimmy playfully slapped Nehemiah on the back.

"From what I heard, he was right down the street on Bergen and Custer when Gerald Watkins got shot in broad daylight," Nehemiah said with a tinge of anger. "They say it was a bunch of state police officers who killed Gerald."

"That dude didn't deserve to die like that. He was goin' to his grandmother's house when he accidentally walked up on some policemen robbin' Jo Rae's. The policemen told Gerald to leave before the state police came, but he got stopped by the troopers before he could walk away. People who saw the shootin' from their apartment windows said Gerald was on his knees beggin' for his life. I'm glad you were away when this place was goin' up in smoke."

Nehemiah had been working at an upstate New York country club during the riots in Newark; washing dishes during the day and playing in a basketball league every evening for three weeks. The facility was owned by a group of Jewish businessmen who had become friends with pro sports stars and A-list celebrities. The entertainment complex gave high rollers a place to play in private, where they could do nearly anything they wanted without fear of public scrutiny. For his part, Nehemiah had accepted the opportunity to play against some of the best high school and college basketball players in the country during his few weeks at the club.

Nehemiah Garvey—also known as "Nee" by close friends and family—was a 15-year old star athlete at Weequahic High School in Newark, New Jersey. He earned varsity letters in football and baseball, but basketball was his main sport. Nehemiah earned a varsity letter as a sophomore, after playing quite a bit for the state championship team, which was rated number one in the country during the 1966–67 season. By his junior year, he was considered one of the best athletes in New Jersey.

It was a plus to his personality that Nehemiah was also a deep thinker, whose views about the world were vast and growing clearer with each passing year. This was due, in no small part, to Nehemiah's father, Samuel, who had been born in 1905 to a teenaged white girl and a young black man in Kingston, Jamaica. The girl's parents had been afraid the child would have dark skin, so they took the daughter to a midwife, an older black woman, instead of a hospital. The grandparents gave the baby boy to the midwife after she delivered him. She named him Samuel, and taught him to read, write, and do basic arithmetic; his training had started by the time he could talk extremely well at only eighteen months old.

When Samuel was five, his birth mother married and took him back from the midwife who had raised him since infancy. His birth mother's husband wanted to place Samuel as hired help to rich, white families, who would pay the stepfather while Samuel would get nothing in return for his labor; he was only a young boy. To save him from the certain doom of such a life, the midwife helped Samuel run away from his birth mother's home. Because Jamaican laws did not treat black children fairly, his birth mother and stepfather would be able to find him and force him to return, so he was no longer able to stay with the midwife. Though he lived mostly on the streets, the woman helped and took care of him when she could, but it wasn't much. Samuel survived by working odd jobs and eating and sleeping wherever he could.

When he was only nine, the brainy and perceptive Samuel became enamored with Marcus Garvey's Universal Negro Improvement Association (UNIA), a black nationalist organization founded in 1914, in Jamaica. In 1916, Samuel stowed away on the same ship that brought Garvey to the United States, passing himself off as a Garvey relative. Once he arrived in New York, Samuel assumed the Garvey name and found his way to the Harlem community. He worked for several years as a delivery boy for Stephanie Saint-Clair, a notorious numbers runner in Harlem, and in various capacities at restaurants and nightclubs owned by gamblers and other unsavory characters.

Though he diligently followed the UNIA for several years in response to its call for black economic empowerment, Samuel became disenchanted with a number of the organization's tactics in attracting new members. He migrated to Newark, New Jersey in 1925, where he started leaning toward the teachings of the Moorish Science Temple of America, founded in 1913 by Timothy Drew, who later became Noble Drew Ali. Samuel became a street corner orator for the temple, which placed him in front of many people on a daily basis.

Tall and muscular with a tan complexion, the young preacher caught the adoring eyes of many women in Newark while doing his work, and he did not shrink from the lavish attention. The temple frowned upon his perceived immoral behavior, which created a distance between him and the organization shortly after Drew's death in 1929. Samuel fervently embraced Christianity a few years later when he joined First Samuel Missionary Baptist Church, pastored by Frederick Jeremiah Wade, in Newark's Central Ward. Wade's mentor was Pastor Adam Clayton Powell Sr., of Harlem's Abyssinian Baptist Church. Powell Sr. was the father of the legendary Congressman, Adam Clayton Powell Jr., a pivotal figure in national politics during the Civil Rights era. Over time, Samuel became a prominent member in First Samuel, eventually rising to Chairman of the Deacon Board, and a trustee.

Nehemiah's mother, Eva Jean, was born in Prosperity, South Carolina in 1923 to Lula Mae and Abraham Eleazer. When Eva Jean was 13, she moved with her mother and eight siblings to Newark in 1936. The willowy, brown-skinned Eva Jean met Samuel shortly after her family arrived in Newark, and quickly developed a crush on the young man with big dreams and old-fashioned manners.

She graduated from high school in 1938 at fifteen years old and was immediately sent back to Prosperity, to live with her maternal grandparents and attend Benedict College in nearby Columbia, South Carolina. Benedict College was an institution built by white Baptists in 1870 to educate black students. Eva Jean completed her studies in just three years, earning a degree in teaching. She was ready to return to Newark to work. Too young to teach in the New Jersey public school system when she returned, Eva Jean began working at her mother's beauty parlor and beauty school. Lula Mae's establishment was thriving in its location, the former home of one of the richest businessmen in America—a three-story, forty-room mansion on High Street.

Samuel drove a delivery truck for a meat packing company for several years, and when he had saved enough money, he opened a restaurant in 1945. He and Eva Jean started dating shortly after and married in 1948. Nehemiah was born three years later.

The family lived with Lula Mae and some of Eva Jean's other siblings in the large three-story home that Lula Mae had purchased when they first came to Newark. But Samuel was too proud to continue living in his mother-in-law's home, so he focused on moving into the blue-collar, working class section of the city called the Valley, where a small number of black families resided; not too far from the predominantly Jewish section of Newark, where Weequahic High School was located.

In 1955, Samuel and Eva Jean purchased a two-family dwelling across from the Peshine Avenue School not far from Bergen Street, where a half-mile stretch ran across the city almost into Newark's North Ward, featuring a large number of Jewish-owned businesses. The young couple rented the downstairs apartment in their home to a Jamaican family that had moved from New York, which helped pay the mortgage for a number of years.

The neighborhood was comprised of only three black families and a mixture of whites of German Jewish, Eastern European Jewish, and Irish descent, when the Garveys moved to the area. The community rapidly transitioned to predominantly black over the next several years due to a practice by lending institutions commonly known as *redlining,* which accelerated the flight by white families from areas that became attractive to potential black homeowners.

Tragedy struck the Garvey household in 1965, when Samuel came up missing after leaving the restaurant one night. He was never found and his disappearance was filed as a missing person in police records. Law enforcement authorities throughout the country often ignored such cases when they involved black people.

Nehemiah was slowly dribbling a basketball on the pavement while he talked to Jimmy Trawick. "Yeah, I was gettin' an education while I worked at the country club durin' the day and played ball every night. One of the college guys who worked there taught me about makin' money honestly aside from my dishwashin' job," Nehemiah said. "On mornings before I started work, I shined the shoes and ironed the shirts of the men whose families rented the suites at the club. I made a lot of extra money and I learned a lot about business from listening to the men whose shoes I shined and shirts I ironed. My father always told me to listen when white men talked."

Suddenly, Nehemiah and Trawick encountered a group of boys who blocked their path on the sidewalk.

"Nee Garvey," Harold Jones said as he mocked Nehemiah's bouncing of the basketball, "the star of Weequahic." Jones was also known as Bumpy because of his pock-marked facial complexion. He was one of the best street boxers in the city. "Nee, you're the man with the plan. Fastest hands in Newark. At least until it comes to me."

"I already took you out on the court, Bumpy, and whipped your butt. So, you need to get in somebody else's face," Nehemiah spoke while slamming his hand against the playground fence. "You know I'm not scared of you, right?"

"Man, you know I'm just messin' with you. You play for the number one high school team in America and you gonna win the state championship again this year. I won a lotta money bettin' on Weequahic last season," Jones said. "I heard you got sharper playin' against them jokers in upstate New York. Somebody said you played against Wilt Chamberlain and Oscar Robertson up there."

"Nah, that didn't happen. But, dig it, I did see a lotta pros play. Saw Lew Alcindor too. He's a bad dude."

"Nehemiah is goin' over to play in the Rucker tournament in Harlem and show them New York chumps what Newark basketball is all about," Trawick said. "Bumpy, while you're out here boxin' on the corners, Nehemiah is gonna be seen by college scouts from all over the country. He'll be playin' for the Knicks one day."

"Slow down Jimmy. It ain't like that," Nehemiah said in his normal measured tone. "I was sent up there to work and nothin' else. Playin' basketball was not the only reason. And Bumpy, we're not number one in the country…not just yet anyway."

"C'mon, Nee. Stop bein' shy," Trawick said. "You gave up football and baseball to concentrate on playin' basketball this season. Mr. Marcus wants to be number one in the country again and you gonna be the man to help Weequahic do it."

Trawick was talking about Michael Marcus, also known as Mickey, the celebrated coach now in his 20th year at Weequahic High School in Newark's South Ward. He had already won fourteen state championships, eleven county championships and the renowned Newark City League title thirteen times. Mickey had won more than twenty games every single season he coached Weequahic and never lost a game by more than twelve points during his tenure. Close to one hundred players from Weequahic earned college scholarships and ten players went on to play in the National Basketball Association over that 19-year span.

Weequahic was the seventh public high school built in Newark, opening its doors in 1933. Though few people ever admitted it, the stately appointed edifice with New Deal-era artwork on the walls of its entrance was built to accommodate Jewish parents who did not want their children attending school with large numbers of African American children at nearby South Side High School. The neighborhoods surrounding the once predominantly Jewish school were steadily being inhabited by black families who were moving from the economically depressed Central Ward. Ironically, the Central Ward was replete with Jewish families at the beginning of the 20th century but dramatically transposed over roughly thirty years starting in 1910.

The Central Ward was considered a black entertainment mecca— similar to Harlem in uptown Manhattan, Shaw in Washington DC, South Street West in Philadelphia, Bronzeville in Chicago, and Paradise Valley in Detroit. The area boasted vaudeville houses, jazz/blues clubs and upscale drinking joints owned by African American entrepreneurs. At the same time, most white landlords charged black tenants high rents for poorly maintained apartments and rooming houses in the area.

In the meantime, large numbers of Jewish households began planting themselves in the South Ward, many opting for the better neighborhoods of the Weequahic district on the extreme south end, while maintaining business presences in their former neighborhoods with African Americans as their loyal customers. Newark was an interesting blend of populations throughout its five wards, and from the early 1900s through the 20th century, that diversity would prove to be the bane of the city's long and storied history.

"Can you believe that just five weeks ago this playground had military vehicles parked here, with soldiers and cops being dispatched from this very spot throughout the city to stop lootin'?" Trawick said to Nehemiah.

"Man, how long are we gonna replay the riot? I'm gettin' sick of the word riot," Nehemiah said. "It was a rebellion, if people are really honest." Just as he finished, a couple of good-looking girls in shorts were walking past. Nehemiah's attention shifted their way.

"Girl's all right with me, you know the girl's all right." Nehemiah sang a refrain from a well-known song by The Temptations, a popular black singing group known for its superb harmony and synchronized dance steps. He also did a quick bow, a standard thank-you created by the group.

"Hi Nee," one of the girls said in a melodic voice to Nehemiah.

"Hi Lena. You know you can wear those shorts." One of the girls began frowning.

"Oh, he speakin' to you now, girl, since that witch of his ain't around," the girl said with total disregard for Nehemiah's sincerity.

"Aw Sharon, you just jealous because ain't nobody talkin' to you," Trawick said, nearly stopping Nehemiah's adversary in mid-sentence. "You need to zip your lips." As the two of them began shouting back and forth at each other, Nehemiah and Lena found a secluded spot to conduct their own conversation.

"Nee, I've been knowing you since we were little and you were living with your grandmother," Lena said. "I thought your father was going to find a home for your family in this neighborhood and we would be going to the same schools. But he moved the family away, closer to Weequahic."

"Yeah, some of the boys I played with when I was little thought I was gonna live with my grandmother so I could go to Miller Street

School and South Side," Nehemiah said. "But my mother wanted me to go to Peshine Avenue School and then Weequahic. She felt those schools were better. You know, Lena, I'm takin' a real chance comin' over here now. You know you South Side Bulldogs don't like me."

"Uh, uh, you got it wrong, Mr. Weequahic Indian," Lena said. "We like you when we're not playing against you."

As the action in the playground continued and the intense discussions of various kinds ensued, a group of well-dressed young men with finely groomed, low-cut hair were holding verbal court outside the gates with a captive throng hanging on their every word. One of the young men called out to Nehemiah.

"Hey, church boy, you got your copy of the paper? All so-called Negroes like you need to know what the prophet is teaching." The assemblage in the playground yelled "Oooh" at the remark. "What, you waitin' for permission from your Jew boy coach Mickey Marcus?"

Nehemiah, dressed in his t-shirt with khaki pants and black canvas Converse All-Star low top basketball shoes, began a slow, deliberate walk toward the young men, who were resplendent in their gray sharkskin suits, white shirts and black bow ties. Trawick ran over to his friend.

"Don't let 'em get to you, man. They ain't worth it." The six-foot three, 195-pound tightly muscled Nehemiah did not break his stride, only pausing slightly to turn his head and give his nemesis a menacing stare.

"Why are y'all so uptight?" Nehemiah asked. "Maybe you should take it easy and eat a tasty, grilled pork chop from my mother's restaurant." The crowd started laughing.

"Oh, you supposed to be a street corner comedian, huh, dip ass nigger? People like you pushin' up daisies with talk like that." The speaker was Michael Herring, a 17-year old high school dropout who had converted to Islam while confined at the New Jersey State Home for Boys, better known as Jamesburg because of the town in which it was located. Herring had a reputation for fighting—and beating—older boys and in some cases, grown men felt his wrath. He viewed the younger Nehemiah as easy prey.

"Michael, you know there ain't no punk in me, so whatever you wanna do, bring it. Dig it?" Nehemiah said while maintaining his fiery gaze at the shorter but equally muscular Herring. As the two of them were preparing to square off, several black men ran from down the street.

"Brothers, brothers, what's up with this?" John Harrison said. Harrison, at 19, was eligible to be drafted into the Army and possibly go to fight in Vietnam. "I can't believe that after everything white people have done to us this summer, you two young black brothers are gonna fight? While y'all buggin' out?"

"That nigger ain't no good. He ain't nothin' but a fuckin' Uncle Tom," Herring said.

"Nah, that ain't it. You wanna tell me what to believe and I ain't havin' that," Nehemiah said. His reply was loud enough for people inside the playground to hear. The crowd swelled around the two boys with Harrison squarely between them.

"Okay, alright, Michael. I understand your point and I respect it," Harrison said. "Nehemiah, you need to understand that it's nation time. In other words, the world we once knew is changin' and we need to be ready for the revolution that is comin'."

"Revolution? What are you talkin' about, John?" Nehemiah asked.

"Newark and Detroit this summer. Watts just a few years ago. Harlem, Plainfield. All those places were in flames over what the white man is doin' to our neighborhoods and to our people. Black people who no longer believe in the white Jesus are doin' somethin' about it, and the Black Panthers are doin' big things, stretchin' out from Oakland to LA and other cities. Black power is takin' over and you need to be with the people. Like the Impressions sing, 'People get ready, there's a train a comin', you don't need no ticket, just get on board'.

"I know you're a ballplayer and you think none of this affects you, but you're wrong, Nehemiah. Look here, there's a brother, Harry Edwards, in California talkin' about black athletes boycottin' the Olympics next year. He plans to use sports to get the message of black power out in the public. I know you love your coach Mickey Marcus, but he's old news. We don't need some white boy to look after us. We can take care of ourselves."

Nehemiah's eyes scanned the suddenly quiet multitude that was paying rapt attention to Harrison's perceived well-researched dissertation. Nevertheless, he wasn't impressed.

"There was no stronger revolutionary than my father, who believed in most of what Marcus Garvey advocated a long time ago. He also believed that black people could succeed beyond any hurdle that the white man put in front of us. He purchased his own home when most black people in Newark were still rentin'. He opened his restaurant when the most legitimate businesses owned by black people were small nightclubs and gamblin' rackets, and those were mainly frontin' for white gangsters. And my father was smart enough to teach my mother how to run the business, so it didn't close when he disappeared. It's still open and doin' well to this day.

"My father showed his nation time credentials with his deeds, not his mouth. He employed black people in his restaurant, he used black lawyers for his legal work, and he only bought supplies from companies that employed black people. My mother is still doin' the same thing today. How many of y'all fed families that couldn't get food during the rebellion? My mother did. I don't need an education from any of y'all about being black. I had the best teacher in my father, and I continue to have a great teacher in my mother."

"Yeah, that's why your father left you and your mother," Herring said. "Probably sold out to some white boys, talkin' that religion crap with them Jesus lovin' preachers. And you said black instead of Negro. I'm surprised that you understand the difference, Judas." Nehemiah began to narrow the space between him and Herring.

"That's not good for a brother to leave his African queen. The black man has got to be strong to grow his black family," Harrison said. He stretched his arms to keep the two other boys apart. "If we're going to build a black nation through black power, we have to stick together.

And that means Mickey Marcus is going to have to leave Weequahic this year. You with us on that, Nee?"

Trawick and the rest of Nehemiah's friends walked toward their best friend, flanking him on both sides. "All of you brothers can talk that talk, but where's the walk?" Trawick said. "We know what we have in Nee. Y'all talkin' that black power, separatin' from the white man and all that stuff, but somethin' ain't right with all that, especially when we all know how y'all really livin'."

Herring sneered at Trawick. "Whatcha tryin' to say, motherfucka?"

"I'm not tryin' to say somethin', I'm sayin' it," Trawick retorted. "You ain't nothin' but a so-called black. You and your boys are just tryin' to pimp black people in the name of your religion. Nee is a real brother who got a great education from his father and mother about how to survive. Mr. Marcus is Nehemiah's ticket to a future that none of y'all can see. He would be crazy to mess that up just because y'all don't like Jews."

"Okay, we'll see what happens," Herring said. "Newark is a black city and it needs to be run by black people. The rebellion proved that white devils like Mickey Marcus and those crooked Italians will only get in our way."

"Newark will go down the toilet with your kind of thinkin'," Nehemiah said. "Let me tell you this, Michael. You might curse me, but I'm blessed. You might persecute me, but I will endure. And when you slander me, I will answer kindly. First Corinthians, fourth chapter, twelfth verse."

Chapter 2

"In short, the haters, both white and non-white, are now operating on the same wave length. They both want to resegregate the country. They both want to replace the extended hand of friendship with a slap in the face."

~ Clarence Mitchell, director of the Washington, DC NAACP, speaking at the National Beauty Culturists' League convention, about white segregationists and black nationalists, in 1967

Sunday afternoon dinner was a special day in the Garvey family. The custom had been started by Nehemiah's great-great maternal grandfather in the 1870s. The current location was the home that Nehemiah's maternal grandmother had purchased when she brought her fatherless family of five girls and three boys to Newark in the mid-1930s. Though a majestic dwelling, it was in one of the lower income neighborhoods of the school district that encompassed South Side High School. The area was popularly called the Valley.

"Eva Jean, I pray that you made enough of that good potato salad, girl," Elizabeth Sarah Vandiver said to her youngest sister.

"You know I did, sister." The doorbell rang. "Nehemiah, please get the door, honey," Eva Jean said to her son.

All of the eight Eleazer children were offspring of Lula Mae and her husband Abraham. Lula Mae herself was the youngest of fifteen children

14

reared by a Baptist minister and a mother who worked alongside her husband in the church. The family was well-respected by blacks and whites alike in Prosperity.

Abraham's family was prominent in the church, though Abraham himself had a dubious reputation. He and Lula Mae had been smitten with each other since they were nine-year old children in the one-room church schoolhouse, funded by a white philanthropist from Chicago. While she was an outstanding student who showed a stunning aptitude for mathematics and English grammar, Abraham was talkative; he found reading and studying as boring as watching paint dry. Still, he worked hard on the farm that his extended family had owned since the end of the Civil War.

Few people left Prosperity for college in those days, and Lula Mae and Abraham were no different. They married in 1906 at age 16 and brought Elizabeth into the world a year later. The rest of the children came in rapid succession after that, with Eva Jean born in 1923. Abraham took his growing family from living on the Eleazer farm and built his own home on a piece of property his father gave him when he turned eighteen.

Abraham started working for a white man who sold dry goods in Newberry and Little Mountain, both of which were roughly eight miles east and west from Prosperity. The work was steady but dangerous because the two men had to travel alone on roads late at night. None of this fazed Abraham because he did not fear any man. When the work became less steady at the onset of the Great Depression in 1929, Abraham began looking elsewhere. He caught the attention of a moonshine dealer who needed someone to sell his illegal liquor to blacks in parts of South Carolina. Abraham quickly learned the mechanics of the lawless trade and soon began earning a lot of money.

It was during this time that Lula Mae opened a beauty parlor for black women in Prosperity, which brought in customers from throughout the county and made it an overnight success. She built her business using and selling products developed for black women by Madame C.J.

Walker, the woman who was reputed to be the nation's first female self-made millionaire.

Because Lula Mae and Abraham lived on the land given to them by the Eleazer family, they were able to save a large portion of their earnings. Abraham also became a popular figure in illegitimate gambling circles around parts of South Carolina during the early 1930s, which along with his work in the bootleg liquor business, added to the family's collective wealth. Much to their credit, Lula Mae and Abraham eschewed the high-class lifestyle, avoided the spotlight from the local populace and quietly amassed a tidy sum of money over a number of years in tiny Newberry County.

Things began to change in 1933, when the federal government repealed the Eighteenth Amendment to the U.S. Constitution, which lifted the ban of selling liquor in the United States. Outsiders, mainly from the North, began to cultivate the South as a lucrative market for legal alcohol sales. Blacks who unlawfully sold moonshine and other forms of liquor became an endangered species and Abraham was included in that number. He was viewed as a major competitor by the liquor sellers from the North.

One night in 1936 a group of white men caught Abraham by himself on one of his cash pickups and attempted to rob him. He nearly killed three of them and got away after the others fled. Abraham had to leave Prosperity immediately, before law enforcement authorities caught him. He never said goodbye to his family; Lula Mae and their eight children were left by themselves. Because whites suspected that Lula Mae knew her husband's whereabouts and questioned her endlessly, she became irritated and decided to take the children up North where she had friends in the hair industry.

Fortunately, Lula Mae didn't leave Prosperity broke and destitute; far from it. She took thousands of dollars that she had earned and stored in a private place, along with all of the money Abraham had left behind. The Eleazers had already been moving on up in Prosperity when Newark,

New Jersey suddenly became their unexpected destination. They were part of the historic Great Migration.

Nehemiah opened the inside door, then pulled open the vestibule door that led to the porch.

"There's my good lookin' nephew. Ain't he fine, sisters?" Mary Deborah Bryant said to her twin sisters Martha Hannah Richardson and Naomi Marian Carter.

"Fine and spoiled, thanks to all of us," Martha said.

"And his grandmother," a voice said from inside the house, "and she ain't ashamed."

The words came from Nehemiah's grandmother, Lula Mae Eleazer. Strikingly tall, she had jet-black hair streaked with gray highlights and a smooth, brown face. Lula Mae was 77-years old, quick-witted, and possessed a scrappy demeanor that had developed as a result of her seemingly genteel Southern upbringing mixed with Northern brash. One might think that she had manipulated her children's chromosomes, because they all by and large possessed her physical characteristics, along with a smattering of her take-no-prisoners attitude.

Ms. Mae, as she was called in the neighborhood, lived in the gracefully appointed home with her oldest daughter, Elizabeth, whose husband, son and daughter-in-law were killed in a 1960 factory explosion. Elizabeth was awarded custody of her granddaughter, Denise, shortly after the accident. Denise had come to live with Nehemiah and Eva Jean because Elizabeth wanted her to attend Peshine Avenue School in the neighborhood where her sister resided.

"Y'all need to leave my grandson alone," Lula Mae said. "Now let's get this table ready because Reverend Wade will be here soon."

"It looks like it'll be just us for a while; our husbands are still counting money from this morning's service," Naomi said as she walked in from the back of the house.

"All right, all right, all right," a sharp, baritone voice said at the front door of Lula Mae's home. It was Reverend Frederick J. Wade, longtime pastor of the First Samuel Missionary Baptist Church in Newark. Lula Mae's father had contacted Reverend Wade when Lula Mae and her children were on their way to Newark. The family joined the church thirty-one years ago, when they arrived by train from Prosperity, and remained members as the community grew into the largest black congregation in New Jersey over three decades.

"Come on in, Reverend Wade," Nehemiah said. "You and the first lady are always welcome here."

"Thank you, young man. Oh, by the way, I believe I saw your basketball coach sitting in his car outside. You can't miss that blue Cadillac on this street."

"You gotta be kiddin'. What is Mr. Marcus doin' here?" Nehemiah said.

Eva Jean spoke up. "I invited him after the two of us had a conversation at the restaurant while you were up in upstate New York at basketball camp. He came in with his wife one night to have dinner and we talked."

"He's walking toward the door. I'll let him in," Mary said.

Mickey Marcus was a tall, slim man—about six feet two and a few pounds shy of 180—with snow white hair, though he was only in his late 30s. He had grown up in Charleston, South Carolina in a Sephardic Jewish family, whose ancestors had come to America from the Netherlands more than fifty years before the Revolutionary War. While Mickey's forefathers were wealthy business owners during their longstanding history in Charleston, both of his parents were school teachers in the city's segregated public school system.

An only child, Mickey had been an outgoing young man with friends of all races. He had learned to play basketball by competing against his friends who lived in black neighborhoods, much to the consternation of other Charlestonians because of the racial segregation attitudes that prevailed in the city during those days. His affiliation worked out well—Marcus received a full scholarship for academics and athletics to the College of Charleston and played basketball during his four years.

After graduation, he went straight to the Charleston draft board and enlisted in the United States Army. Ironically, he signed up with several of his black friends.

"Coach Mickey Marcus, the legend, right here in Lula Mae Eleazer's home," Reverend Wade said as he waved his hands to the sky. Nehemiah looked embarrassed at Wade's gesture as he escorted Marcus inside.

"Mr. Marcus, I believe you've met my pastor," Eva Jean said.

"Oh yes. I went to First Samuel before I stepped foot in a synagogue when I first came to Newark," Marcus said.

"Mr. Marcus and I have developed a great relationship, though we never were public about it all these years. I believe some of his people might not have understood it in the early days."

"All right, everybody, time to get cleaned up for dinner," Lula Mae said. "The other children will be here in a few minutes and the men are on their way. We will have plenty of time to talk after we eat."

As expected, the meal was savored by all in attendance. Then, little by little, the majority of guests ate and ran, leaving only a few who stayed behind to help clean up. The conversations over dinner were lively—the terrible baseball season the New York Yankees were having while the New York Mets were still miserable, and the war in Vietnam never failed to come up—but no one talked about the Newark Riot. That conversation took longer to approach, but it was bound to occur before everyone departed.

"I wonder why the television reporters and newspapers keep calling them riots," Reverend Wade said as he walked in his pastoral stride with Marcus toward the expansive living room. "Riots are what happened in the north when the newly freed Negroes left the south after the Civil War and were attacked by white mobs. Negroes didn't start that stuff. What's happening these days is Negroes are the ones being defiant and figuratively throwing the first rocks. Seems like the disturbances we've seen over the past few years are more about Negroes violently rebelling against the whole system than having to defend themselves against white people."

Marcus began nodding his head as he sat down. "Reverend Wade, I can't disagree with you. There were riots in 1876 in South Carolina; in Charleston, Hamburg, Ellenton, Cainhoy, Edgefield, Beaufort, and Mount Pleasant, when whites from both the Democratic and Republican parties tried to keep Negroes from voting. The Negroes were only defending themselves as they were harassed and assaulted on their way to the polls. But a few weeks ago, the people in Newark seemed to be saying they were tired of being treated poorly and they weren't going to take it anymore."

"You're from Charleston, right?" Reverend Wade asked.

"Yes I am."

"Did your people participate in any of those riots?"

"Truthfully, Reverend Wade, I don't know. From what I heard when I talked to my grandparents, our people were too involved in making money that didn't require the enslavement of people. I guess they didn't see the need to revolt. But my father was involved in the Charleston riot during Red Summer in 1919."

This statement amazed Reverend Wade. "Oh really? You never told me that, Mickey."

"When many decorated Negro soldiers returned home from World War I, whites in cities across the country were not receptive to them, and this wasn't only in the South. There were four riots in Pennsylvania, two in New York, Arizona had one, and Connecticut," Marcus said. "Many of those riots saw a large number of deaths and injuries, but there were only five deaths and a few injuries in Charleston. It lasted a little over an hour and ended when the mayor and other authorities enlisted citizens to plead with the mobs to stop the violence. My father was one of those who got a call to help."

"Good for your father. I know the feeling. The mayor called me and many of my ministerial brothers to quell the violence during the rebellion here," Reverend Wade said. "All of us to a man told him he should have listened to us during those years when we complained about police brutality, the terrible living conditions for Negroes in the Central Ward, and the unequal education for our children. We knew the troubles were coming, but we helped anyway. I hate to think how many more would have died had we not convinced our people to stop looting."

"I had women in my beauty parlor who couldn't leave when the National Guard came into Newark on that Wednesday night," Lula Mae said. "If it wasn't for the men in the neighborhood those women might have gotten shot. They came to the shop and personally escorted the women to their homes. God bless those men."

Marcus began a slow grind of his teeth. "I was in Los Angeles getting my players ready to start college at the University of Southern California during that week. I was sick to my stomach when I read the stories in the newspaper out there. My guys were worried about their families, but they settled down once they called and found out they were okay."

"I had a hard time concentratin' on playin' basketball that first night at the country club," Nehemiah said.

"Yes, but once you heard my voice and Denise's on the phone, you were able to relax," Eva Jean said. "I must admit, I was on pins and needles during that time. We fed a lot of families at the restaurant after they had to evacuate their apartments during the sniper firing around Springfield Avenue and other places."

The diminutive Wade stared at Marcus. "I might be a small guy, but God has given me a big heart. You know Mickey, I played football in the twenties when the helmets had no face masks. Had plenty of bloody noses."

"What's your point, Reverend Wade?"

"That I have a head hard enough to withstand a lot of pressure," Wade said. "No, seriously, these are the times that try men's souls," Wade said, reciting by memory the first sentence from *The Crisis,* a popular essay written by Thomas Paine in 1776. "The summer soldier and the sunshine patriot will, in this crisis, shrink from the service of their country; but he that stands by it now, deserves the love and thanks of man and woman. Tyranny, like hell, is not easily conquered; yet we have this consolation with us, that the harder the conflict, the more glorious the triumph. What we obtain too cheap, we esteem too lightly;

it is dearness only that gives everything its value. Heaven knows how to put a proper price upon its goods; and it would be strange indeed if so celestial an article as freedom should not be highly rated."

"Mr. Marcus, you read this to us before we played Camden High School in the state championship game last year," Nehemiah said. "Thomas Paine wrote this when this country was fightin' against Great Britain for its freedom."

"I heard Reverend Wade recite this when he spoke at my synagogue during a community rally in 1963," Marcus said. "You were asking people to take a stand against prejudice in Newark's public housing system. Right after that, your church began raising money to purchase land in the neighborhood, to provide affordable housing for people in the area. You enlisted help from Rabbi Seligman in that effort."

"Yes, Brother Marcus, we bought that land and next month we will be breaking ground for the construction of those homes. You see, the only way we are going to keep Newark from going up in flames again is to give people hope. I am willing to do my part. What about you?"

Lula Mae sat up in her chair and looked at Marcus. Eva Jean and her sister Elizabeth walked in from the dining room, while Nehemiah began rubbing his hands together with a nervous repetition.

"I'm just a basketball coach who's been lucky for twenty years," Marcus said.

"The word is blessed, Brother Marcus, and you are more than a basketball coach. You are a man who has seen our community change in a mighty way and you wrapped your arms around that change. But your people have moved from Newark and only a few of them remain, and those few don't have a lot of good things to say about Newark."

"And your people are trying to kick me out because my complexion is different. I'm caught between a rock and a hard spot in spite of what I have been able to accomplish with some great young men from some great families. Let me ask, Reverend Wade, who is going to stay in Newark with these high taxes and property values going down the drain?"

"You're still here."

"I believe in Newark."

"And Newark believes in you. That's why we are going to do everything we can to keep you at Weequahic. Even if you're the only white coach left standing."

"Mr. Marcus, please tell 'em you're gonna fight for your job," a concerned Nehemiah said. "Weequahic brought great pride to Newark last season when we were number one in the country. We can do it again."

"Nehemiah, Newark is a different place these days," Marcus said. "The other schools in the city are trying to steal your teammates with this black power stuff, telling them that white coaches, especially Jewish ones, have taken advantage of them. Even if I come back, our team won't be competitive."

"Yes, we will," Nehemiah practically shouted. "You know we will."

"Mr. Marcus, you are not going to let my son down. You are not going to let his teammates down," Eva Jean said. "His father taught him some valuable life lessons and there is no better time than this for Nehemiah to use them. Samuel's wisdom has served me well for all of these years he's been gone, and my life has turned out pretty well. One of those lessons is loyalty."

"My daughter is right, Mr. Marcus. You are not going to let this boy down," Lula Mae said. "Nehemiah believes in you like he believed in his father. Samuel loved Newark and so does Nehemiah. He will do what he has to do to save it. We need you to have faith that Newark can be saved."

"Newark needs a faithful servant, Mickey," Wade said. "Now more than ever."

Chapter 3

"Regardless of the difference in my outlook, I insist upon my rights to pursue my livelihood in accordance with the same rights granted to other men and women who have disagreed with the policies of whatever administration was in power at the time. I am looking forward to immediately continuing my profession. As to the threat voiced by certain elements to strip me of my title, this is merely a continuation of the same artificially-induced prejudice and discrimination. I have the world heavyweight title, not because it was given to me, not because of my race and religion, but because I won it in the ring through my boxing ability. Those who want to take it and hold a series of auction-type bouts not only to do me a disservice, but actually disgrace themselves. I am certain that the sports fans and fair-minded people throughout America would never accept such a titleholder."

~ MUHAMMAD ALI, IN A WRITTEN STATEMENT AFTER
REFUSING TO BE INDUCTED INTO THE U.S. ARMY, IN 1967

NEWSPAPERS, MAGAZINES, TELEVISION and radio reporters across the country ran stories about the riots and racial unrest episodes in 159 cities in 1967. While uprisings have been part of the nation's history since its birth, these had a different tone—they looked more like reactions to injustice, where black people were rebelling against civic infrastructures designed to keep them in slave-like status. The thread of connection between this series of events and the ones in the past was thin, because this time it was black people hurling the first objects of discontent, unlike in the past when whites in the north and south normally initiated the acts of aggression, often putting blacks in a defensive mode.

"You got a nice game, my man," an older college player said to Nehemiah after competing against him during the Rucker Park basketball tournament in Harlem. "You one of those Newark boys, huh?"

"No doubt," Nehemiah said. "I play for Weequahic High School, number one team in America last year."

"Heard a lot about that team and the one in Georgia that also claimed to be number one. What do you think about that?"

"Yeah, Beach High School, down in Savannah. I know about 'em. *Sports Illustrated* rated them ahead of us last season but they didn't play the better disciplined teams we played up here. Plus, they didn't have the country's best high school coach, Mickey Marcus. Nor do they have one like him now."

"I hear you, man. Did you know that Newark has the reputation of having some of the best Jewish basketball players in the country?"

Nehemiah gave the man a startled look. "Get outta here. Really?"

"Oh yeah. Quite a few of them played in the NBA."

"Yeah, I know some of 'em, but I didn't know they got that kind of respect. Any of 'em ever play over here?"

"Nah, they played most of their ball at their own community centers in Newark and cities around Newark. Now, the Jewish boys from New York would play here and they held their own. There was no punk in any of 'em. But the Jewish boys from Newark, they were a rare breed."

Newark had a Young Men's Hebrew Association—also known as the "Y"—as did Hillside, Irvington and South Orange. The main center in the Weequahic neighborhood produced some of Mickey Marcus' best players. While the facility was called the YMHA, the activities were not limited to men and boys. The Y also had programs for girls in the Jersey towns of Belleville, Nutley, Kearny, Bloomfield and Montclair.

"Weequahic won a lotta championships when it was predominantly Jewish, but a lot of those families have left Newark. They will probably all be gone when school starts because of that damn riot," Nehemiah said.

"Happens that way, little brother. Negroes burn and loot, white people leave, cities are left in ashes. Happened like that here in Harlem, same thing in Watts, in LA. People get angry about stuff that affects their people negatively, like what's happenin' with Adam Clayton Powell."

"You talkin' about the Congress tryin' to make him leave office?"

"Man, you on top of things, young blood. Not only can you play ball, you got a workin' brain, too. Yeah, Republicans and Democrats are trying to kick him out. Seems to me that white people feel uncomfortable with Negroes in high positions, especially when they know how to think. The same thing is happenin' with Thurgood Marshall."

"But a white man is the one who wants Mr. Marshall on the Supreme Court," Nehemiah said. "The senators are holdin' up the vote, not President Johnson."

"Hey man, I never said that all white people are bad. I'm sure there are some who recognize and agree we are equals. Just a precious few though. But know this; people operate in ways that benefit them, that's human nature. So, the riots, or rebellions, whatever you want to call 'em, are causing the last of the white people to leave places like Newark. Even Negroes with a little money are leaving. That's the way it is."

"Man, I don't wanna see that in Newark. That's my home, that's the place I love," Nehemiah said. "Us being the number one team in America last year brought pride to Newark, and the white people in other parts of the city treated it as if it was nothin'. The Jewish people at Weequahic were proud, but they're leavin' the school anyway. We lost our best players from last year to graduation and some of the boys who could make a difference this year are transferrin' because the other schools have black coaches. And they're convincin' them to transfer by sayin' Mr. Marcus is not a good person."

The man stood up and started shooting the basketball from deep in the corner of the court.

"You wanna get those boys back? You wanna get some of those Jewish families to let their boys come back to Weequahic? You wanna make sure Mickey Marcus keeps his good name? You gonna have to convince the players that it's not a bad thing to play for a white coach in Newark. You have to tell the Jewish families that their sons and daughters will be safe at Weequahic, in spite of what they're hearin'. And you have to tell your coach to fight back against his enemies."

The man dribbled the basketball to the other end of the court, laid it into the basket off the backboard and yelled over his shoulder. "You need to make a plan to build some new pride at Weequahic, the kind that many people in the city can pick up on. Weequahic basketball and your coach have a nationwide reputation. The country has got to see that everybody at the school is gonna fight to keep that reputation. That alone can help Newark get rescued from the rebellion. Trust me on that."

"Me with a plan? You can't be serious. I'm just a fifteen-year old high school junior. What do I know?"

"You know more than you think you do. You're not givin' yourself enough credit. If you pursue that plan like I see you do on the basketball court, you can get it done. I believe that."

THE GOVERNOR'S SELECT COMMISSION on Civil Disorder for the State of New Jersey began its work in August 1967. A number of prominent men from Newark were appointed to the body. The governor's marching orders to the group were clear.

"What I am seeking, and what the people of New Jersey expect, is not a meaningless and detailed repetition of studies, but a realistic analysis of the disorders…and practical proposals which, hopefully, will prevent their recurrence in our State," the governor wrote in the opening statement of the report.

The group planned to pay special attention to the problems in Newark, which were the most complicated. The Commission also planned to delve into the festering controversy over bringing the New Jersey College of Medicine and Dentistry to Newark. That report was due at the end of 1967.

"MICKEY, YOU HAVE A TOUGH HILL to climb this season, but I believe you can do it." Marcus was talking to Solomon Brinn, an attorney who lived in South Orange and a member of the Weequahic graduating class of 1937. The two were having lunch at Brinn's office in Newark.

"Sol, all things being equal I would agree with you, but that's not the case," Marcus said. "There are people in this city who want me out for the mere reason that I will be the only white basketball coach left in Newark. Mort Levin left as Weequahic principal after the last school year to work at the central office of the Board of Education and our new principal seems too afraid to buck the black power crowd."

"Mickey, Mickey, don't worry about that. I've got people who can handle those people at the Board. I just need to know that you still have some fight in you. And what about your partnership in those nationwide gyms?"

Marcus interrupted. "Spas, Sol. They call them spas. Health spas to be exact. Now is that all you're concerned about? Me making money?"

"Okay, spas. And yes, I do worry about you making money. There are people are jealous of you because of your wealth. But that aside, I need to know that you have the backbone to stand up to the people who are trashing your reputation. It's all up to you."

"Look, Sol, you know I'm a fighter, but my weapons are limited to you and some of my other Jewish friends. I don't know if that's enough because my opponents are relentless. They're willing to throw the city down the sewer to prove a point. Look at what was said at the black power conference right here in Newark a couple of weeks ago. They talked about blacks controlling everything including City Hall, the school system, and the neighborhoods.

"I don't have a problem with working together to accomplish improvements for the city, but many of these people don't want me or anyone who looks like me in the room, much less with a seat at the table. Sol, I couldn't care less about the political crap. I just want to help the boys at Weequahic use their athletic skills to go to college, come out with degrees and make something of themselves. You know my track record. It should speak for itself."

"Yes, I do know your record, and so does the rest of the country. But Mickey, the riot has changed the dynamics in Newark. We need someone who can peacefully influence the movement. You need to be a force in this change, not watching from the sidelines. But we have to find someone who trusts you enough to join you; somebody who has the energy and the smarts to fight this battle."

"Oh, I know exactly who can do it," Marcus said. "I had the opportunity to dine with Reverend Wade a couple of weeks ago and we talked about the best person to help."

"Reverend Wade of First Samuel? He's a good friend of Rabbi Seligman. He's got the respect of many in this town. I don't know anybody, Negro or white, who doesn't like the good reverend. Mickey, you have a winner with Reverend Wade."

"Sol, you're going down the wrong street. I neglected to tell you I had dinner at Lula Mae Eleazer's home, with her daughter, Eva Jean Garvey, and Reverend Wade."

Brinn's mouth broke into a huge smile. "This is getting better and better. You have relationships with the pastor of the largest Negro church in New Jersey, the lady whose beauty parlor and beauty school serve hundreds of Negro women every week, and her daughter who just expanded her restaurant and moved it into the Weequahic section, where whites and Negroes have the opportunity to dine together. What did I get wrong, Mickey?"

"I'm not talking about any of them leading the effort," Marcus spoke with a confident tone. "I'm talking about Eva Jean's son, Nehemiah. *That's* who I'm talking about."

Fear spread across Brinn's face. "What? Your star player on this year's team? I know you have a lot of confidence in him as a leader on the court, but a high school kid to do the work of men? Mickey, I don't understand you."

"'And a little child shall lead them', Isaiah, eleven six," Marcus said. Brinn scrambled to get his Torah and began to read aloud. "'The Book of Yeshayahu. The wolf also shall dwell with the lamb, and the leopard shall lie down with the kid, and the calf and the young lion and the fatling together, and a little child shall lead them'."

"Sol, Nee Garvey is a brilliant young man. He has been on the honor roll since the first grade. All of his classes are advanced placement. He has a sincere passion for learning and pride in his heart for his hometown. Plus, he is as streetwise as any boy I've ever met. Nee told me that he wants to save Newark from going down any further because of the riot."

"So, you're saying he is motivated to do the heavy lifting to help you remain the coach at Weequahic?"

"No, Sol, this is not about me. It's about cleaning up the mess in Newark that started long before you and me; a mess that we've ignored for too long. And it didn't just start in July with the police brutalizing a war veteran. It's so much more than that. And by the way, Sol, I have as much confidence in Nee Garvey as I do in the taste of your wife's matzo ball soup."

DETROIT WAS CLEANING UP the wreckage from the July 23rd through July 27th rebellion on its streets. Forty-three people dead, 1,189 injured, more than 7,200 arrests, more than 2,000 buildings destroyed, and property damage estimated at 80 million dollars.

"The only genuine, long-range solution for what has happened lies in an attack, mounted at every level, upon the conditions that breed despair and violence. All of us know what those conditions are. Ignorance, discrimination, slums, poverty, disease, not enough jobs," President Lyndon Johnson said in an address to the nation on July 27, 1967, announcing the formation of the special Advisory Commission on Civil Disorders. "We should attack these conditions...not because we are frightened by conflict, but because we are fired by conscience. We should attack them because there is simply no other way to achieve a decent and orderly society in America."

There was a group of women sitting in Lula Mae Eleazer's beauty parlor, watching President Johnson give the speech on a 25-inch color television. "That country boy got a lot of courage," Lula Mae said. "He signed the Voting Rights Act, Civil Rights Act, Medicaid, Medicare, and all of it helped Negroes."

"Some of those boys who used to hang on the streets are in the Job Corps now," one of the women said. "The idle time they had that the devil was using for his workshop is now in a government program, thanks to Lyndon Johnson."

Another chimed in. "Yeah, all that's good. But that law controlling crime is just another reason for more police brutality in our neighborhoods. That's how that Army man got beat up the night the riot started."

"Please, y'all need to be quiet. I want to hear what the president is saying," Lula Mae said.

President Johnson continued. "This is not a time for angry reaction. It is a time for action, starting with legislative action to improve the life in our cities. The strength and promise of the law are the surest remedies for tragedy in the street. There is a danger that the worst toll of this tragedy will be counted in the hearts of Americans. In hatred, in insecurity, in fear, in heated words which will not end the conflict, but prolong it."

"That man is the reason President Kennedy got killed," one of the women shouted. "And the way he treated Daisy Bates and the Negroes from Mississippi at the Democratic convention in 1964 was shameful."

"Hush up. Let us hear this please," another lady said.

Johnson continued. "To those who are tempted by violence, I would say this. Think again. Who is really the loser when violence comes? Whose neighborhood is made a shambles? If you choose to tear down what other hands have built, you will not succeed. You will suffer most from your own crimes. You will learn that there are no victors in the aftermath of violence. The apostles of violence, with their ugly drumbeat of hatred, must know that they are now heading for disaster. And every man who really wants progress or justice or equality must stand against them and their miserable virus of hate.

"Let us resolve that this violence is going to stop and there will be no bonus to flow from it. We can stop it. We must stop it. We will stop it. And let us build something much more lasting. Faith between man and man, faith between race and race. Faith in each other and faith in the promise of a beautiful America."

One of the women in the shop was the president of the Parent-Teacher Association at Peshine Avenue School. She was also heavily involved with voting precinct work in the Weequahic neighborhoods. "Lula Mae, I know you like President Johnson, but I read in the newspaper that his administration is not appropriating any federal money for riot torn cities like Newark and Detroit to clean up the mess."

"And those are our so called Democratic friends saying that," one of the women said.

"We need to stop begging the white man to do what we should do for ourselves. *We* are going to have to clean up this mess. White folks are leaving Newark like cockroaches scatter when the lights come on," Lula Mae said. The women started laughing. "First thing we need to do is get with our Jewish friends who are still here. Like Mickey Marcus. I talked with him a couple of weeks ago and he told me about some people that are trying to run him out of town." The women nodded their heads as if they had rehearsed the motions.

"Marcus wasn't my son's coach at Central, but I know he helped some of his teammates get into college," another woman said. "He didn't just help the white boys at Weequahic, he helped the Negro kids too."

"And I know he wants to help Newark get back on its feet," Lula Mae said.

"Ladies, we did a pretty good job of figuring out this clean up thing. That makes me wonder why there are only men on President Johnson's commission and the governor's committee," the PTA president from Peshine Avenue School said. "We could probably do a better job if they had appointed some of us women."

Lula Mae laughed out loud. "Honey, don't hold your breath."

Chapter 4

"The Negro says now. Others say never. The voice of responsible Americans, the voice of those who died here and the great man who spoke here, their voices say together. There is no other way."

~ Remarks of Vice President Lyndon B. Johnson in Gettysburg, Pennsylvania; May 30, 1963

"I want to be the President who educated young children to the wonders of their world. I want to be the President who helped to feed the hungry and to prepare them to be taxpayers instead of tax eaters. I want to be the President who helped the poor to find their own way and who protected the right of every citizen to vote in every election. I want to be the President who helped to end hatred among his fellow men and who promoted love among the people of all races and all regions and all parties."

~ Special message from President Lyndon B. Johnson to the Congress, March 15, 1965

"In our time change has come to this nation, too. The American Negro, acting with impressive restraint, has peacefully protested and marched, entered the courtrooms and the seats of government, demanding a justice that has long been denied. The voice of the Negro was the call to

34

action. But it is a tribute to America that, once aroused,
the courts and the Congress, the President and most of the
people, have been allies of progress."

~ Commencement Address at Howard University
by President Lyndon B. Johnson, June 4, 1965

President Lyndon B. Johnson's Great Society initiatives in
1964 and 1965 pulled people at all levels of American life up from the
trash heap of society, much like President Franklin Roosevelt's New
Deal had done for the vast majority of the country between 1933 and
1940. The centerpieces of what Johnson crafted were the Civil Rights
Act of 1964 and the Voting Rights Act of 1965, both of which dramatically altered the racial landscape of the United States and influenced
governments worldwide.

While a number of the Great Society programs were designed to
adjust the attitudes of Americans toward their fellow citizens, others
were constructed to teach inner-city youngsters what it took to succeed
in the larger culture.

"How did you get that job teachin' at the Neighborhood Youth
Corps?" Nehemiah's teammate Danny Clark asked him.

"Somethin' called usin' marketable skills," Nehemiah bragged with
eloquence.

"Marketable? Man, you sound like a motherfuckin' white boy!"

"Watch your mouth Danny. My grandmother taught me that when
a person uses profanity, he has a limited vocabulary."

"Nee, you callin' me stupid?"

"Nah, man. Just askin' you to use your words wisely. Okay, let me
answer your question. Remember when we started workin' that summer
with the Neighborhood Youth Corps before we started high school in
'65? When we worked with the janitors cleanin' the bathrooms during
elementary summer school at Peshine? I used to go to my grandmother's
house after working those five hours and tell her how hard the work

was. She would say, 'If it's too hard, learn an easier job. Make sure you learn how to do the jobs correctly and then market your abilities to the right people'."

"Yeah, I remember that summer. That was some hard work."

"And what did I do after that?"

"I remember the next summer you worked with the crew that checked in the food for the cafeteria durin' summer school at Weequahic. That was easier work."

"That's because I used to go down to the cafeteria after workin' with the janitors and help the food service crew at Peshine. I saw how they checked in the food supplies. That was the easier job my grandmother told me to look for. I applied for that job the next summer when the youth corps counselor came around the neighborhood with the assignment list. I got the job I wanted at the Weequahic cafeteria and made more money for less work," Nehemiah said. "Then durin' that summer I talked to one of the guys about writin' resumes and fillin' out job applications, which I taught at the Youth Corps for a few weeks before I went to upstate New York and worked at the country club. Danny, I got the skills and then let the right people know I had 'em, like my grandmother told me to. That's how I got those easier jobs. I marketed myself."

THE SUMMER VACATION OF 1967 was winding down, but a week before Labor Day the physical heat still remained. Along with nearly 100 degrees outside every day, the human temperatures in the corridors of political power around Newark were rising to a boiling point.

"The colored people will finally get their way in Newark," a Newark city council member from the predominantly Italian North Ward said. He was meeting with a number of other city council members and a group of businessmen in an office building in downtown Newark.

"They aren't really getting anything after they burned down what might have been theirs. If they had just waited," one of the business owners remarked. "The property values in the Central Ward ain't worth a damn and now that the mayor can't control that colored council member representing the ward, anybody investing in that ward is a fool. I'm supporting the medical school getting built in that area so I can sell my property and get out."

"You mean you're not going to burn it up and get the insurance money?" someone from the back of the room said. "Like everybody else?"

"I can't say I wasn't tempted, but I have a different view. The city is going to be realigned in a major way, even more than what the Charter Commission did in '54, when they gave the office of the mayor all that power," another businessman said. "But just like we cut our deals before that, we found a way to continue to make money with this system after a while. We can do it again."

"Yeah, but the Negroes weren't too bright back then, so we could fool them without too much trouble. Their own people sold them down the river with our help," the council member from the West Ward said. "Now they got Negroes talking about black power and all that goes with it. They're smart; even thinking about having a Negro mayor, like in Cleveland."

"Okay, all that is just talk. They tried to get a Negro elected mayor in '66, but he lost. They couldn't even beat that crazy dude in the South Ward council race because they had too many Negroes running and split the vote. And even if they get a Negro in the mayor's office in the next election, with a Negro majority on the City Council, they won't have any power if we play our cards right," the West Ward council member said.

"The first thing we have to do is stop any good news from coming to Newark. We need to control the message. If we keep it bad, everything negative and scary, no one will want to live here except the colored people with no money. All they want are low paying jobs or work for the government anyway, and many of them don't want to live here. Then you have the ones who want to bring Africa to Newark, growing their hair in those Afros, wearing dashikis, speaking Swahili, whatever that language is. Then you have the Negroes who don't believe in Jesus, who want to have economic development by selling newspapers, bean pies and opening eateries called Steak and Take."

"You know those people, huh?"

"Look, they love to talk about their revolution, taking over from whitey and all that stuff," the North Ward councilman said. "While they're doing that, we'll control the expansion at Newark Airport through the Port Authority, this thing called Amtrak coming through Penn Station, both of which the feds are going to finance. We are also going to control the construction jobs on the federal highways coming through here. Even if we're not elected to political offices, we need to find a way to control who will sit on the boards that make the policies. We should just let the Negroes have their culture, their neighborhoods, and all that Pan African crap. As long as we control the money.

"The city is ours for the taking. Just like the Depression was good for the Mafia, the riots in Newark will be good for us in the long run. Organized crime benefited from a bad situation and so will we, you can bet on that. What was really good about the riot is that it chased the last of those Negro loving Jews out of Newark. Thank God."

THE TELEPHONE RANG at Eva Jean's restaurant.

"*Garvey's* Restaurant, may I help you please?" the cashier said.

"Hi, my name is Michael Marcus. May I speak to Mrs. Garvey?"

"Let me check to see if she's busy. Please hold on."

Eva Jean came to the phone within a few seconds. "Hi Mr. Marcus. Good to hear from you."

"Mrs. Garvey, you've been calling me Mr. Marcus all these years. You can call me Mickey, I don't mind."

"Okay, Mickey, if you will call me Eva Jean."

"That's a deal."

"So, Mickey, what's on your mind?"

"First, I know you're busy, so I'll be brief. I need Nehemiah to take the lead on what we talked about a couple of weeks ago, at your mother's home."

"You mean helping you to keep your job?"

"No, that's taken care of. In fact, the way it was done might be a problem, but I have friends who will work that out. I need Nehemiah for another part of the plan."

"Mickey, you're confusing me. If you're going to keep your job as basketball coach at Weequahic, why else would you need my son, other than to play for you?"

"I just found out that there are some very influential people who want to make Weequahic a private school, starting this year. In fact, the Board of Education is seriously considering it."

"And what about the students attending Weequahic now?" Eva Jean said as she slumped in her chair. Tears were welling in her eyes. "Weequahic, a private school?"

"Eva Jean, since the riot, many people are searching for easy answers to difficult problems that have existed in Newark for a long time. Making Weequahic a private school is one of the so-called solutions being pushed. Truth be told, if Weequahic becomes private, a number of Jewish families that no longer live in Newark would send their children back there, simply because of the great academic tradition at Weequahic; that's attractive to them. They wouldn't have to live in Newark and could still send their children to Weequahic, which they have always considered to be their school, even though it is a public school. They believe they could easily convince universities that Weequahic's high education standards are safe and maintained because the majority of the student population would be white."

"What about the smart Negro children? Would they remain?"

"If their parents could pay the tuition I'm sure they could. But to be quite honest, I get the feeling that most of the parents of those families don't care about what happens to the Negro students, even the smart ones. They feel the reason that Weequahic's reputation is going down is because of the Negro children.

"For the record, I'm not in favor of the change. I know that many of the children at Weequahic right now are good students and could be better if the teachers would take their jobs more seriously and work harder in the classroom. I'm sure if I don't endorse this silly idea, many Jewish people will have second thoughts about Weequahic being a private school."

"So, I assume you have a plan?"

"I do, and Nehemiah is a major part of it. Are you willing to listen?"

There was a long pause on the telephone.

"I'm all ears. Talk to me."

NEHEMIAH AND LENA GOT ON the 8 Lyons bus at Hawthorne Avenue and Bergen Street on their way to downtown Newark.

"I'm glad you not wearin' shorts today," Nehemiah said. "I'm not ready to be fightin' with any boys lookin' at you."

"I wouldn't let you fight over me. You're not that kind of boy," she said. Lena Ashby was the oldest daughter of two high school teachers. She was an honor roll senior at South Side High School. Lena was already accepted to Hampton Institute, a well-respected private college in Hampton, Virginia, mainly populated by black students.

The bus was in its normal condition—noisy and crowded. It was a nice August day, with the temperature in the low-70s and low humidity, perfect for a mid-afternoon walk downtown.

"It's the couple of the year, right here on the 8 Lyons," one young man on the bus yelled out. "That's cool, but it's strange. A South Side Bulldog with a Weequahic Indian? Ain't that peculiar, peculiar as can be," he finished, singing a piece from the Marvin Gaye song *Ain't That Peculiar*. Some of the riders laughed. Nehemiah gave the boy a cautionary stare, one that could have been construed as an invitation to fight. Lena sat down, while Nehemiah stood next to the seat.

"Nee, don't say anything. It's not worth it."

"I know. I have too much to lose if me and him get to fightin' on this bus."

"Honey, don't worry about that boy," an elderly woman who was sitting next to Lena said. "I know your family. Your father probably did something good for that boy and he don't even know it. Samuel Garvey was a good man. You don't want to mess up memories of him by fighting with that silly boy. You and this pretty girl ignore him and enjoy yourselves."

"Yes ma'am," Nehemiah said.

The bus rumbled down Broad Street to Market Street, where Nehemiah and Lena got off.

"Why did we get off the bus here if we're going to the museum?" Lena asked. "The museum is past Military Park on Washington Street."

"Well first we're goin' to Sam's Delicatessen for a pastrami sandwich, then we'll walk to the museum."

"Oh, this is a date. Thanks for telling me."

"No problem." Instead of going straight down Branford Place to Sam's, they walked down Market Street to Bamberger's department store to look around.

"Lena, what if I told you I'm thinkin' about leavin' Weequahic?" Nehemiah asked as they walked into the store. "Between you and me, St. Benedict's wants me. They remember when I played on their football field, when I was in the Pop Warner program with the Newark Bears. I can play football, basketball and baseball there."

"When you were in the seventh and eighth grade, right?"

"Yep. They've been following me since I've been at Weequahic, both in sports and the classroom."

"One thing for sure, you'll get a good education from teachers who are not just there for the paycheck. And you'll dominate the competition in all of the sports. And when you graduate, you could probably go to Notre Dame, or Boston College, or any of those religious schools. Because of how smart you are, you could do well."

"And I could go to any other college because of St. Benedict's reputation. Yale, Harvard, Princeton, you name it, I can go there."

"And have a great life. But you will be away from the people you love, and you'll have to be the man they want you to be. I don't think you want that, Nee. I think I know why you wanna leave."

"I'm sure you do." Nehemiah walked with great haste toward the elevator. Lena ran to catch up with him.

"Second floor please," Nehemiah told the operator.

"Nee, you can talk to me. Losing Mr. Marcus as coach is not the end of the world."

"How did you know about that?" Nehemiah said as his voice began to crack. "Oh, what am I talkin' about? Everybody in the state of New Jersey and the country probably knows what's happenin' with Mr. Marcus."

Lena locked her arm in his. He kept talking as they got off the elevator and walked across the second floor, heading toward the men's clothing department.

"Lena, my heart broke when I was in upstate New York workin' at the country club and the riot was goin' on. Then I came back and Mr. Marcus told me he might not be comin' back to Weequahic. If he doesn't return, the last great story about Newark is over. I don't want to be at Weequahic when that happens."

"Nee, Newark will come back from the riot and I believe you will be part of it. You've been told the stories about your father. How he helped people in this city. How he didn't know how to say 'no' to anyone in need. You are just like your father, Nee, and I'm not the only person who believes that."

"His favorite expression was 'Stand up', which to him meant be a man, even when everything around you is in a mess. When I think about him, I remember his toughness when times were bad. I was just gettin' to know him when he disappeared. I was only twelve."

"You should know this much. If he was here, he would tell you to do what you think is right. What is right is to stop thinking about leaving Weequahic. Then go to your mother and tell her that you want to help Mr. Marcus stay."

"I appreciate all this advice, Lena. You're a good friend. Is there anything else?"

Lena smiled. "Get on your knees and ask God to give you strength. You have a big job ahead of you. And please get me that pastrami sandwich. I'm hungry."

IT WAS FIRST SUNDAY AT First Samuel Missionary Baptist Church. Reverend Frederick Wade was in his customary seat at the pulpit. Wade had come to First Samuel back in 1932, his first pastoral assignment after graduating from Morehouse College in his hometown of Atlanta, Georgia. He was only 20 years old when he took over the tiny storefront church in Newark's Central Ward. Back then membership was mostly from a few neighborhoods that were predominantly black. The church moved twice after Wade became pastor; once to a slightly larger building that had previously housed a Pentecostal congregation in the Central Ward, and then to a newly built structure that was hailed as one of the finest examples of New Jersey architecture in the late 1950s.

Wade focused on the progress he had seen Reverend Adam Clayton Powell Sr. make at Abyssinian Baptist Church, in New York's Harlem community where Powell served from 1908 through 1936. Wade studied and used the Abyssinian blueprint to grow First Samuel into one of the most influential churches in New Jersey over the thirty-five years that he was its leader.

"This long hot summer is coming to an end, but our work to rebuild Newark must not cool down," Wade said after the church participated in Holy Communion, customary in most black churches on first Sunday. "There are some who will tell you that Jesus Christ is no longer relevant, that the gospels are to be ignored. But let me assure you that the same God of Abraham, Isaac and Jacob is your God. He is still on the throne and Jesus is sitting on His right side, interceding on your behalf.

"We now stand at a crossroad, a forced pause in moving forward. Our dilemma is that we can choose to progress in a way that benefits our communities within the framework of this country, or we can watch as other, misguided populations soldier on and roll over us. Our people are holding conferences and conventions and forums about who's going to be the black this and black that, but few people are talking about actually feeding the poor and clothing the naked. As I look around the church this morning, I'm thinking about who truly understands what the apostle Paul was saying in First Corinthians twelve about spiritual gifts. I can say with good conscience that many of us here at First Samuel do understand First Corinthians. I can also say this: There are some who fervently and constantly pray, and they have faith that their prayers will be answered. What makes my heart warm is when our young people understand the messages from the word of God, and I stand in support of them, especially those who want to lead.

"As that same Paul told Timothy in First Timothy four twelve, 'Let no one despise you for your youth, but set the believers an example in speech, in conduct, in love, in faith, in purity.' We have a mighty steep hill to climb in the coming days, but I believe that our children might be the ones with the energy to take up the task."

Chapter 5

"What I want to do is put the facts on the table without any cover-up because I think this is the time to do it…I think we are going to have to call a sharp halt to all of the camouflage that has gone on for the past ten, fifteen, and twenty years."

- Harold J. Ashby, president of the Newark Board of Education, testifying about the condition of Newark's public school system in front of the Governor's Select Commission on Civil Disorder, State of New Jersey, in 1967

A WELL-ESTABLISHED BLACK COMMUNITY with its own churches, social services and a desegregated public school system were several of the reasons why African Americans from the south migrated to Newark in the early 1920s. By the end of the decade, blacks accounted for close to ten per cent of the population in the city. According to many observers, the continuing exodus of middle-class whites during the second decade of the 20th century was attributed to the growing presence of black residents, which also was reportedly a major factor in the diminution of the tax base of Newark.

The Great Depression that started nationwide in 1929 exacerbated Newark's fiscal problems because close to thirty percent of the U.S. population was unemployed, more than 26,000 businesses had shut their doors, and nearly one billion dollars in deposits in as many as

1,400 banks were worthless. By 1931, thirty-one per cent of Newarkers were jobless. Nevertheless, many residents of the city during the '60s mistakenly believed Newark's problems had just started in the late 1950s.

"Man, I'm getting' tired of sittin' on these stoops," Percy Howard, one of Nehemiah's friends, said. Percy and several other neighborhood boys were talking on the front porch of the Garvey home. "This is the last day to be outta school; we need to take advantage of our freedom."

"Y'all ever listen to this cat on the radio, Frankie Crocker?" Nehemiah said. "I like that lady sayin' 'Frankie Crocker, the love man'. That's too cool. I listen to him every night."

"What about this part, Nee? I'm designed to put more dips in your hips, more cut in your strut, more glide in your stride," one of the boys, Slick Pep, said. "If you don't dig it, you got a hole in your soul and you don't eat chicken on Sunday. While other cats are laughin' and jokin', Slick Pep is takin' care of business, cookin' and smokin'."

"Dang, Slick, you got it down, man," a couple of the other boys shouted.

"Please don't encourage him," Nehemiah said.

"Ah, Nee, you just jealous because the ladies like my platter chatter. You ballplayers ain't the only ones who can get the women."

"Uh oh, here we go. Now he's gettin' ready to tell us about his good looks."

"Frankie Crocker must have been talkin' about me when he said this part," Slick Pep said. "Tall, tan, young and fly. Anytime you want me I'm your guy. Young and single and I love to mingle, can I mingle with you baby?"

"I told y'all he was gonna do that," Nee said while laughing. "Y'all had to put up with this when I was in upstate New York?"

"Pretty much," Jimmy Trawick said. He had a serious tone in his voice as he stepped from the porch and walked toward the street. "Slick Pep and some of the other boys kept our spirits up. Nee, you wasn't here during the riot. You don't remember when that National Guard jeep drove through here and the soldier told us to get off the stoops and into the house. I felt like I was in jail. You wasn't here, Nee, so you don't know."

"Yeah, but I been feelin' the effects with the way the police been tryin' to handle us since I got back. What about when we got stopped in Hillside that night and the cop told us they weren't gonna let what happened in Newark happen over there? I was here when that happened."

"And then they took our money. But you still wasn't here when we needed you, man. You wasn't here durin' the riot."

Nehemiah sprang to his feet. "You know what? This talk is gettin' too deep. We need to get off this porch before our minds blow up. Let's go walk on Bergen Street. C'mon Slick. We need you to help us laugh before we start cryin'."

Walking down a big street close to neighborhoods was a popular activity in most urban areas, and Newark was no different. Bergen Street, between Watson Avenue and Lyons Avenue close to where Nehemiah lived, attracted a lot of people—mostly black—during the mid '60s. At one time, though, it was the near exclusive province of whites. There was a high-end fur shop, a popular Jewish delicatessen, a bakery that experienced heavy customer traffic on a daily basis and a movie theater that consistently showed first-run productions.

"My mother bought shoes for my brothers and me in a buildin' that used to be over there," Fred Rashid, one of Nehemiah's teammates on Weequahic's basketball team, said as he pointed to a vacant lot.

"But after your feet grew so big she had to go to the grown man's shop at Bamberger's to get your shoes," one of the other boys yelled out.

"There were a lotta good places to shop on this block, but they left," Nehemiah said. "One of the reasons was because Jewish people moved from the area and more Negroes moved in. My father said that their customers went elsewhere, so they had to go where their customers went. Daddy actually said they did us a favor because there are now more Negro owned stores around here makin' money."

Jimmy Trawick chuckled at Nehemiah's comment. "Your mother moved her restaurant after a lotta her customers moved out of the Valley.

She followed the money, too. And oh yeah, Nee, the word is black, not Negro."

"Alright, Jimmy, black owned businesses. Still, it's on us blacks to keep these stores open by doin' business with 'em. That's what the Italians and Puerto Ricans do in north Newark, that's what the Portuguese do in Ironbound, and it's what Jewish people have always done all over America."

Nehemiah stopped in front of the delicatessen that was a nice place for African Americans to dine on any day of the week. "Look at this place. Four Star Deli, owned by a black couple. Good food, just like what was served when it was owned by Jewish people. My mother brings us pastrami sandwiches from here on some Saturday afternoons. Instead of goin' way up Lyons Avenue to get our records, there's a record shop right down there," Nehemiah said, pointing down the street.

"Nee Garvey, my man. Y'all gonna win state this year?" The deep voice came from a man who was walking behind the group. It was Al McCoy, who owned the newly-opened sporting goods store on Bergen Street. He had played on one of the state championship basketball teams at Weequahic, when the majority of players were Jewish. "I certainly hope so, because y'all will be wearin' uniforms from my shop."

"Really?"

"Mr. Marcus called me at home yesterday and said he would be orderin' the team uniforms from my store."

"You heard some people want him to quit, right?"

"I heard that bull and I ain't buyin' it. Mickey Marcus is the best thing to happen to Newark over the past twenty years and I'm sup-portin' him. Don't get me wrong, I believe in black power, but I also believe in people who believe in me. I would have never gone to college if it weren't for Mickey Marcus. It was because of Mickey Marcus that I got a job I got when I graduated from college, and it was because of him that I got the bank loan to open this store. Nee, Mickey Marcus is uptight and outa sight, for real."

Nehemiah and his friends continued their walk on Bergen Street.

"Nee, you think Mr. Marcus is gonna stay?" Fred Rashid asked.

"Why you askin'? You gonna transfer?"

"I'm thinkin' about it."

Nehemiah's temples began to throb. "You know what? I'm tired of hearin' all you crybabies worryin' about whether Mr. Marcus is leavin' or stayin'. If y'all wanna play for Weequahic, meet me for weight trainin' and runnin' in a few weeks so we can get ready for practice. And let me say this. Weequahic is gonna win city, county, and state, and we are gonna be number one in the country, again!"

WHITE FLIGHT FROM NEWARK continued and middle class black flight was rapidly increasing as public schools opened the Tuesday after Labor Day in 1967. The lack of student achievement had already been under intense scrutiny for several years. Low scores on standardized tests caused a number of colleges to second guess applications submitted by students from Newark. Weequahic, highly ranked nationally when it was predominantly attended by Jewish students, had fallen below many of the suburban high schools that surrounded it, though it was still Newark's top academic public school. Weequahic enrollment swelled due to more families moving into the area from across Newark, which meant Weequahic was over capacity.

The Star-Ledger, New Jersey's statewide newspaper, published an editorial about the school dilemma in Newark:

> School bells ring this morning all over our great state, and each district knows how it will operate as the young people walk through the doors. All districts, except Newark. New Jersey's most populous city is in the worst shape it has ever been in its long history, with teacher assignments still being made and student enrollment shifting like the sands that swirl around the Jersey shore in the winter. While the riot advanced white flight—which actually started increasing shortly after World War II—it accelerated the movement of the Negro middle class to those outlying suburbs whose

populace felt comfortable with mass entrance. The decay of the Central Ward brought the decimation of Springfield Avenue from Bergen Street to the Newark-Irvington border, and this will not be remedied overnight. Nor will destruction of the once-proud neighborhoods of the lower South Ward to the Weequahic section. Opportunists in the forms of absentee landowners, self-serving city officials—both elected and appointed—and community activists whose agendas seem to be more divisionary than inclusionary, all exhaust precious financial and human resources, keeping Newark in its place as one of the nation's poorest cities with some of the highest property tax rates in America.

All of this will affect the education of deserving students at public schools in a city that has potential for greatness with a seaport and airport connected to New York, and a mass transportation hub that stands among the best on the eastern seaboard. The issues facing Newark over the next several years will infect its classrooms with social viruses that will take a major effort to cure; the kind of effort that unfortunately does not currently exist within our borders. Witnessing the demise of Newark will be painful.

DAYLIGHT BEGAN TO PEEK through the window of Nehemiah's bedroom, waking him.

"Denise, it's time to get up for your first day of third grade," he yelled to his eight-year old cousin.

"Already up, sleepy head," Denise yelled back. She was in the kitchen helping Eva Jean cook breakfast. "This is my first day to cook and I'm scrambling *your* eggs."

Nehemiah hopped out of bed and walked quickly into the kitchen. "Ma, you're not lettin' Miss Junior Flip cook breakfast, are you?"

"And why not? Didn't you start cooking at this age?"

"Actually, it was before. I was seven when I used to do a little cookin' at the restaurant."

"How well do I know, especially when you almost set the place on fire when you tried to grill some steaks by yourself."

Denise began laughing uncontrollably, pointing at Nehemiah.

"Fire? Not you, Nee! I thought you could cook?" Nehemiah reached over and picked her up, tickling her under her arms.

"I'm not perfect, but I'm special to you," he said as he put her down and kissed her on the cheek. "I'm only kiddin'. I will gladly eat your cookin' any time, sweetie pie."

"Okay, Denise, fix your plate and eat. I'm going to walk you across the street to school so I can meet your teacher. Nehemiah, let's go in the living room. I need to talk to you for a minute."

Eva Jean walked ahead of her taller son, then sat down.

"I had a long conversation with Mr. Marcus about him leaving Weequahic." Nehemiah looked startled. "I should say, about him staying at Weequahic." On hearing this update to her statement, Nehemiah broke into a wide grin.

"Are you serious? You mean he's not gonna be forced to quit?"

"Come on Nehemiah, did you really think that man was going to leave you and the other boys? That was not going to happen. But he wants you to step up and take the lead in building the team. He wants you to be captain."

"Get outta here, Ma. I'm only a junior this year. Weequahic has never had a captain that wasn't a senior."

"Well, you're the first. And you will have more responsibilities than just being captain of the basketball team."

"What are you talkin' about, Ma?"

"Mr. Marcus will tell you today, when you get to school. It will be a lot of work, Nehemiah, but I believe you'll like it. To my mind, he couldn't have picked a better person."

"Ma, you're not tellin' me everything."

"Nehemiah, you know how much I miss your father," Eva Jean said. "He taught me a lot about life. He taught me how to be unselfish. He taught me how to be a wife and a mother. Most of all, he helped me become a woman of faith."

"Just like he was a man of faith?"

"Yes. And I need that faith every day when I think about where he might be since he mysteriously disappeared. Still, I have faith that he will come back, the same faith that Nehemiah exhibited when God called on him to help rebuild the walls of Jerusalem. God had a job for Nehemiah to perform, and he did it. God also gave your father a job on this earth and he is getting it done."

"So, you believe that my father isn't dead?"

"I am absolutely certain that Samuel Garvey is not dead, just like I'm sure you won't fail in this huge task that Mr. Marcus has in store for you, despite any criticism you might get."

"You're confusin' me, Ma. What are you really tryin' to say?"

"Lena came by here yesterday afternoon and told me about you nearly having a fight over at Rippel Field playground, behind South Side. She also told me what the boy said to you on the bus."

"Don't worry about that stuff, Ma. I can handle it."

"Nehemiah felt the same way," Eva Jean said. "He was doing a great job, but two men, Sanballat and Tobiah, were critical, and the Arabs, the Ammonites and the Ashdodites, were angry that the walls of Jerusalem were being rebuilt. They plotted against Nehemiah and caused confusion."

"Ma, save your breath. I know the story. His enemies were doing their best to convince the people that their strength was dwindlin', that they had no endurance to rebuild Jerusalem's walls. But a group of people came and pledged to guard Nehemiah and his people while they continued their work on the wall. It's right here in Nehemiah four, fourteenth verse." Nehemiah walked over to the table where a Bible lay and opened it to the scripture he was quoting.

"And I looked and arose and said to the nobles and to the officials and to the rest of the people, 'Do not be afraid of them. Remember the Lord who is great and awesome, and fight for your brothers, your sons, your daughters, your wives, and your homes'."

"And I can hear your father saying, 'If you dare to speak God's truth, or attempt to lead God's people, you are going to be attacked. Expect it and be tough.' Nehemiah, this is God sending you on this mission, not only Mr. Marcus. Remember that as you move through the task." Eva Jean then kissed her son on his forehead. "I love you."

Denise came into the room. "Auntie Eva Jean, I finished my breakfast and I even washed my own dishes. I'm ready to go to school."

Chapter 6

"There are no moderates in the cause of equal rights. No one calls for gradualism; no one counsels patience; no one thinks of compromise. What exists is militancy versus extremism, and that is really a question of responsibility versus irresponsibility, sanity versus insanity, building versus burning."

~ WHITNEY M. YOUNG JR., NATIONAL URBAN LEAGUE
EXECUTIVE DIRECTOR, AT THE ORGANIZATION'S
57TH ANNUAL CONFERENCE, IN 1967

THE YOUNG MEN'S HEBREW Association had a reputation for having some of the best athletes in Newark. In the 1930s and part of the '40s, a number of Jewish athletes played at South Side High School, but even more played for Weequahic in the '30s. However, as the city's population began to shift after the end of World War II in 1945, so did the makeup of the sports teams at the two high schools. Many African American families fled the overcrowded and poorly maintained neighborhoods in the Central Ward and moved into the section of the South Ward called the Valley. Smaller numbers relocated to an area called Clinton Hill. Both sectors were heavily populated by Jewish families that moved from the Central Ward before the war but could not afford to live in the wealthier Weequahic neighborhoods at that time.

54

As the 1960s approached, practically no Jewish families lived in the Valley and smaller numbers lived in Clinton Hill, which made it possible for more black families to occupy the vacated dwellings, some as homeowners and others as renters. The Weequahic area changed rapidly in the early '60s and by the time the riot occurred in 1967, Weequahic High School was predominantly African American.

"Gentlemen, we have a visitor to our hallowed halls this afternoon," Larry Gottlieb, the basketball coach at the Young Men's Hebrew Association said. This location of the "Y" had moved earlier in the decade to the same block as Weequahic High School, about five hundred feet away. "This visitor is someone we all know. Nehemiah Garvey of the Weequahic basketball team, the one currently without a coach."

"Leave him alone, Larry. Nee is a good guy." Billy Stern, the six-foot five, 210-pound captain of the "Y" basketball team had kindly come to Nehemiah's defense. In April, the Newark team won the YMHA national championship for the second consecutive year.

"I don't have a problem with Nee," Gottlieb said. "It's his coach who I don't give a damn about." Gottlieb had played on Weequahic's state championship team in 1958, went to New York University and was a starter for three years, and then played for four years in the National Basketball Association. "Now, Nee, what brings you over here to the Y today?"

"I invited him," Stern said. "He came here because I asked him to come."

"For what? He wants to play for us?"

"Nope. He wants some of us to play at Weequahic."

Gottlieb's eyes lit up in a fit of rage. "That no good S.O.B. Marcus is at it again. Recruiting players outside the school's district. Look, Nee, tell my Jewish brother ain't none of these boys playin' for him. Not now, not ever. Not a single one."

"Mr. Gottlieb, me and Billy got a little bet goin'," Nehemiah said. "He says I can't beat your startin' five if I play with the last five on your roster. I say I can."

"You mean you play with these freshmen and sophomores against my top five, the ones who led us to the national title the last two years? I know you Marcus boys are crazy and delusional, but this takes the cake. Billy, what is this stupid ass bet?"

"Nee says he can win all three twenty-point full court games playing against us with those boys. I say he can't. But if he gets lucky and wins, some of us will strongly consider going back to Weequahic."

"You got a lotta chutzpah, Nee," Gottlieb said. "You come in here and try to steal my players for your jackass coach. Look, I've watched you since you been at Weequahic, saw you play like an experienced high schooler in the summer league at Branch Brook Park and at the South Ward Boys' Club, both times when you were only in the eighth grade. I heard Marcus sent you to the country club in upstate New York to play against high school and college dudes from across the country this summer and you went over to New York to the Rucker tournament and turned it out against some of the best from D.C. to Boston, which improved your game. All that's good, but you ain't beatin' my boys three games in a row with those young boys. Ain't gonna happen."

The competition committee for the Newark City League was holding a special meeting at Barringer High School during the first week of school. The league was comprised of public school athletic teams in Newark, sanctioned by the New Jersey State Interscholastic Athletic Association.

"Now that all of you know I will be coaching Weequahic again this season, can we move to the next agenda item?" Mickey Marcus said. Marcus was a member of the committee, which oversaw the schedules of each member of the league and the eligibility of its players.

"Mickey, you must be feeling a little strange since your players are being recruited from Weequahic, just like you used to recruit players from other schools," one of the other coaches said.

Marcus reared back in his chair; he was in a relaxed mood. "How long are you going to keep telling that story? No one has ever been able to say that any of my players came to Weequahic in an illegal or unethical way. We've just been blessed with some talented boys from great families, who had terrific work ethics on the court and in the classroom. How many of your players came to me, to help get them into college because most of you ignored them after their seasons were over?"

"Let's settle down, gentlemen. No time for petty squabbles. We've got work to do," the committee chairman said. "Now, Mickey, you are petitioning the committee to let Weequahic play more games during the week than our by-laws allow, is that correct?"

"Yes, it is, Mr. Chairman."

"You realize that whenever we make a recommendation to the state association we are responsible for compiling all of the documentation that accompanies the request."

"I have everything this committee needs, along with a bound copy for each member," Marcus said while reaching into his briefcase.

One of the other committee members started laughing. "You must have been working on this since last season. Why do you want to play more games, Mickey? Auditioning for another job after you get your tails whipped this year?"

"Mickey, you gave me a copy of this request last week and I have been reading it with interest," the chairman said. "The main reason you are giving for needing more games is that you want Weequahic to be an ambassador for the city of Newark, that this summer's riots put a deep stain on the city, and you feel by displaying the Weequahic basketball program to the rest of the country you will be able to help remove the albatross that hangs over Newark's image and reputation right now. Your petition states that Weequahic will have the opportunity to play in some of the most prestigious tournaments in the country, against the top high schools. I must say, you make a good case." There was a bit of murmuring around the table.

"Sounds like an expensive proposition," another committee member said. "But that's right, we're talking about Weequahic. You Jewish people have all the money, especially with the outrageous rents your people charge for those rat-infested apartments in the Central Ward."

Another committee member interrupted. "You're out of line with that one. It's bad enough you talk about Negroes like they are second-class citizens, and now you're sounding like a member of the Third Reich. Mr. Chairman, after reading the executive summary you gave us prior to this meeting, I am in favor. Since all of our member schools can also do what Weequahic is proposing, it is equal across the board. I make a motion that we accept this petition and enthusiastically present it to the state association."

"All in favor of the motion as presented, please raise your hands," the chairman requested. The vote was unanimous.

"Gentlemen, this is a wise decision because all of our schools and hopefully the city will benefit from it," the chairman said to the group. "Mickey Marcus has been a faithful servant to Newark and a great member of this organization since its inception. He has earned our respect. Mickey, I throw my full endorsement behind this vote and all of us are behind you."

THE SOUND OF GRUNTING was loud in the Weequahic weight room. A number of football players were getting ready for their first game of the Newark City League season against Barringer High School.

"You heard that those north side boys tried to cancel the game right after the riot?"

"Yeah, that fat prejudiced, white boy over there was tryin' to keep Barringer from playin' us, South Side and Central. He wants them to get out of the City League, sayin' too many niggers play in the league. Those were his words, not mine."

"Hey Nee, whatcha think about that?" Nehemiah was in the corner, doing a set of pushups.

"Well, if he wants the City League to have fewer blacks, the league won't exist anymore. All the schools have black players on their basketball teams, with four of the seven with all black players. The football teams are a little more balanced, but there are still more blacks when you add 'em up," Nehemiah said through exhausted breath. The players began to walk toward him as he stood up, wiping sweat from his face with a small towel.

"There's a bigger issue with what he said. There are some people in this city who wanna take money from here and give it to people who don't live here. They wanna make Newark a bad place to live so they can rip off the money from the port, airport, and sell off the land downtown."

"Nee, how do you know this stuff?"

"I listen, and I read. My father kept a lot of newspaper clippins' about what was goin' on in Newark way back in the 1930s, up until he disappeared two years ago. He taught me about the history of this country when it comes to Negroes. He gave me a book called *The Miseducation of the Negro* by Carter Woodson when I was eleven and it's really good. I've been readin' a lot of magazines and I read newspapers every day, catchin' up on what we're not learnin' in school, and I listen to my pastor talk about Newark."

"Can what they're tryin' to do to Newark be called a conspiracy?"

"Damn right," Nehemiah said. "If you read that book my father gave me, you would see why I believe that. And we need to do somethin' about it."

"Nee, who is we? We ain't nothin' but a bunch of high school boys."

"I'm workin' on a plan and I'm gonna need y'all to help me. We need to work on Weequahic's reputation, get it back to the way it was when a lot of Jewish kids went here. If we do that, we help Newark's reputation."

"They have money. They have businesses. They work together. I don't think they're willing to stay in Newark and help us."

"And what are you sayin'? Isn't it possible for us to help ourselves? We might not have as much money as they have, but we have businesses, and we should be able to work together."

"C'mon Nee, my father's been talkin' about all these Negro groups working against each other to see who is gonna be mayor and on the

City Council in the next election. And then you have people who want to be called black instead of Negro, and if you don't wanna be called black, they wanna fight."

Another player said, "And you better buy a bean pie and a newspaper or else you might have to fight some more."

Nehemiah dropped the weight he was lifting on the floor, making a loud noise. "Alright, alright. I hear you. All those people have the right to push their programs and you have the right to say no. Just ignore 'em if you don't want to join 'em. But look, I have a plan and it can work. It's just gonna take us young people to make it happen. Not only athletes, but people who don't play sports, and some who are already in college. And not just black people.

"Y'all have to promise me that when you hear the plan, you'll work with me. There's a lotta value in Newark and we better not give it away without a fight. This is our home. Weequahic was already the number one high school team in the country once, and if we do it again it will bring serious notice to Newark, in a good way. And if the other schools do well, that will make it better. Can you imagine us winnin' state in our group, South Side win in their group and Central and the other City League schools do well in their groups? This has been Newark's decade in basketball, and if we continue, Newark's reputation will benefit. All of us young people need to stand up for Newark. Y'all ready to stand with me?"

Because of turmoil that resulted from the riot of 1967, the Newark public school system faced a number of student placement challenges when the new school year began. Many white families were moving to nearby cities, but some of their children who were 11th and 12th graders wanted to finish and graduate from the Newark schools in which they were enrolled. Conversely, highly talented athletes were being recruited to schools that had newly-hired African American basketball coaches.

"Nehemiah, I'm glad you came by this morning. Have a seat," Marcus told Nehemiah as he closed the door to his small office inside the school gymnasium. "I understand you've been pretty busy these days."

"Yes, I have, Mr. Marcus. Very busy these days. You know we're losin' three starters from this year's team."

"Yeah, I know. Two to South Side, one to Central."

"You know why that's happenin', right?"

"Oh yeah. They are being told they need to leave because of me. Because I'm a rich Jew and I am using them to make more money. There are some coaches who are telling the parents of some of these players that many of the buildings that were looted during the riot belonged to me and my wealthy Jewish friends, that I deserved to lose the players because I had been using Negroes for my own benefit."

Nehemiah cast a cautious glance at Marcus. "Well, compared to many families here you are rich, and yes, many of the dwellins' that were looted and destroyed are owned by some of your Jewish friends who have a lotta money," Nehemiah said. "Aren't you embarrassed by that?"

"I really don't know how to answer that question, Nehemiah. I'm not happy about some of the things that are happening, but I am not sorry that those people are my friends, or that they happen to own property."

"Okay, Mr. Marcus. Your wealth and your friends' wealth are not the issues. It's how are we gonna rescue Newark from the rebellion that happened this summer, and how can we keep it from happenin' again."

"Rebellion? Nehemiah, that was not a rebellion. It was a riot. The whole world is calling it that."

"With all respect, Mr. Marcus, the whole world doesn't live in Newark. The world didn't see the bad stuff that was happenin' in Newark earlier this year, or 1966, or 1965, or the years before that. The world ignores the police brutality that's been happenin' to people like me all over the country, the world ignores the rat problem where black people live, the world ignores the overpriced slum dwellins in the Central Ward and places like that all over America." Nehemiah's anger began to rise as he spoke.

"Many of the people who took to the streets in July were sick of the mess that was happenin' here in Newark, just like what happened in Watts, in Harlem, in Cleveland, and the other 160 cities over the last three summers. Those people were rebellin' against the system,

Mr. Marcus, plain and simple. To call them all riots makes it comfortable for this unjust governmental system to thrive."

"Why are you yelling at me, Nehemiah?"

"Because I'm mad!" Nehemiah screamed as tears streamed down his cheeks.

Marcus reached across his desk, offering to shake Nehemiah's hand.

"Nehemiah, this is the passion I was hoping to see from you for a long time, especially when we talk about the rebellion. Your intensity, your energy and intelligent voice are what we need to rescue this city. I am aware that we might disagree over what is a rebellion and what is a riot, but I don't disagree that you are the person who needs to lead the charge to rescue Newark."

"Mr. Marcus, I know I can handle my end of the bargain. My mother told me what you want me to do. I know a lotta people are not gonna like me because of how I feel about Newark, but that's too bad. My father was a tough man and his blood flows through my veins. He moved into this section of the city because he wanted me to go to Weequahic, to prove that a Negro…excuse me, a black man, could compete in the classroom with other children from any background at this great high school. You know that I have not only competed but consistently excelled in both the classroom and on the athletic field, but what I don't think you believe is that there are others like me."

"Nehemiah, how can you say that when I have sent so many boys before you to college and the pros?"

"This group of young men is way different from the ones you met in your first fifteen years. Some of them don't stand for the National Anthem, and others refuse to pledge allegiance to the American flag. The country is changing, Newark has changed and Weequahic has changed, and you will have to change, too. God sent me to change you. That's why my mother is so confident that I will be successful with your plan of attack."

"You don't have any fear of what you're facing, do you?"

"None whatsoever. Watch me."

Chapter 7

"Confusion may be defined as the act of creating tensions, stirring anger, bitterness, and animosity out of which one hopes may come constructive solutions to the evils of present day society. Race riots, the burning and destruction of property, looting cannot in any way build an ordered society."

~ DR. J.H. JACKSON, PRESIDENT OF THE
NATIONAL BAPTIST CONVENTION, FROM HIS BOOK,
UNHOLY SHADOWS AND FREEDOM'S HOLY LIGHT, IN 1967

A CROWD OF PEOPLE WAS huddled on the corner of Bergen Street and Renner Avenue, in front of the nightclub, Spot 977. Most of the contingent was trying to get in, to listen to one of Newark's best singing groups, Harold and the Marvelous Men.

"Nee, ain't nobody gonna play for that Jew, no matter how hard you try," an older black man told Nehemiah a few steps from the club's front door. "It's black power today, brother, and nobody is feelin' a groove for Weequahic. It ain't nothin' but a school for Jews."

"Man, y'all act like there ain't nobody black at Weequahic," Nehemiah said with a voice loud enough that could be heard on all four corners.

"You know the history of Weequahic, that the Jewish people built it to get away from the blacks who were movin' into the Valley from the Central Ward. And now, they're tryin' to make it a private school for white kids because too many blacks are there."

"Weequahic was built in 1933, when every other high school in Newark had more whites than blacks. South Ward had a lotta blacks livin' there and Jewish families were tryin' to get away and they moved from the Valley," Nehemiah said. "But neither one of us was around then, so we don't know why it was built. But I do know this much. If this black power we're talkin' about is for us blacks to control each other, the white people who have been rippin' Newark off for all these years will continue to rip the city off and then take the money out of town. None of those people are black, and no black person in Newark has the power to keep up with them while they continue takin' the money. And by the way, that private school thing ain't nothin' but a rumor."

"So, you think gettin' behind Mickey Marcus is the way to go?"

"I would rather get behind somebody I know than get with somebody I don't know. I trust Mr. Marcus because I know guys who played for him and they trust him."

"Nee, I knew your father. He was a man who believed in black people ownin' property and ownin' businesses. I honestly believe that he would call you, his own son, an Uncle Tom for what you're sayin'. White people like Mickey Marcus are the reason Newark is like it is. But since the rebellion, we know how we can take it back."

"My mother knew my father when she was a little girl going to First Samuel Baptist Church, when she lived in the Valley. She married him at a young age and they had me a few years after. My mother knew my father better than anyone. She tells me I'm just like him, so I would take her word over yours any day. I'm sure he would support me and not call me an Uncle Tom."

"Nee, you got a lotta work to do. You are goin' against a well-known musician and writer, a bunch of college-educated politicians, preachers, teachers, and a whole group of black people who wanna take over Newark. But you know what? I got a lotta respect for your courage."

Nehemiah walked down the street to a house party where he encountered a couple of friends.

"I saw you up on Bergen talkin' to that old cat," Jimmy Trawick said. "Looked like you were gettin' mad."

"Nah, I'm just gettin' a little tired of tryin' to convince these fools that Newark ain't goin' nowhere without workin' with people that are not black. I'll be honest with you. I wouldn't be surprised if some of these black people who don't like me are workin' with white people who wanna get Mr. Marcus out of the way."

"Nee, you better be careful talkin' like that. You know how some of these old cats think. They might try to take you out," Jimmy said.

"Man, let's stop talkin' about all this serious crap. I just saw some thick girls walk in that house party. I need to do some dancin' to release this tension."

Jimmy laughed. "What about Lena?"

"Oh, she's probably got her head in some book, which I respect. She's still my girl no matter what."

NEWARK'S MAYOR WON re-election in 1966 in a campaign against the man who was mayor for eight years until he lost in 1962. A black candidate got into the campaign late and still received more than 17,000 votes, mainly from the Jewish and black communities. The current mayor kept many of his Italian and Polish supporters, and got enough black votes to take him over the top.

"I asked you gentlemen and ladies to this meeting to discuss the future of Newark," Reverend Frederick J. Wade said. The meeting was held in Pastor Wade's expansive, stately conference room at the church.

"Beg your pardon, Pastor Wade, but we already have a blueprint for the future of Newark," a representative of a Chicago-based civil rights organization said. The statement set off a flurry of partly incoherent whispers around the room.

"That paper has not been reviewed by our group." That statement came from a member of the Newark branch of a national civil rights organization.

"We don't need out-of-towners telling us how to solve our problems." This was from a man who had been a resident of Newark for less than five years. His comment got an "amen" from a woman who lived in nearby East Orange. The bickering continued for nearly a minute.

"Please, my friends, there needs to be some courtesy in your comments," Wade said as he attempted to quiet the gathering. "Your language should respect the dwelling in which we sit."

"Pastor Wade, as the sole community development expert in this meeting, I apologize for the manner in which my collective brethren are speaking," Gene Oldham said. Oldham was a native of Georgia, who had a reputation within Newark for being a problem solver.

"With due respect, you don't have enough experience in the political arena around here, so you need to be a spectator," Herbert Evans, a former Essex County Freeholder said.

"Brother Herbert, you don't qualify who does what in this meeting," Wade said. "It was called by me, so I make that decision. Gene, you have equal standing here at First Samuel. Now, I repeat my desire to discuss the future of our city after that nasty episode we experienced a few months ago. None of us will disagree that it has been coming for a number of years before the young man who just came back from Vietnam was beaten by the police. One of my most prominent members, and a faithful servant of Newark, has been missing since 1965. Chances are that he might have been brutalized by the Newark Police, perhaps even murdered by some out of control officer."

"There is no respect for the positions of Negroes in this city," Evans said. "The mayor has looked the other way as neighborhoods deteriorate, and it will get worse with the highway coming through the South Ward and the medical center being built in the Central Ward."

"Don't forget the mess about the white man with only a high school diploma who could be appointed to a top position at the Newark Board of Education, over the Negro who is a public accountant with a Master's degree from Cornell University, and working as budget director for the city," one of the women shouted, pointing her finger in the air.

"As a matter of fact, the mayor is supporting that appointment. That is disrespectful to Negroes in Newark." A few others started shouting to be heard.

"Alright, I will get to everybody, but let me say this," Wade said. "Some of you in this room got in the way of getting a Negro elected to the City Council last year, because you got on the ballot with another Negro, which split the Negro vote."

Evans interrupted. "But Reverend Wade, you don't understand."

"Pardon me, Brother Evans. What is there to understand? I live in the South Ward where this happened; I have members who were involved in that election, and I was involved as well. All of us know that you were on the ballot, so please don't tell me I don't understand. Now, Brother Williamson, you've been going back and forth with the Democrats and Republicans about them paying you to deliver the Negro vote. How has your method worked?" Wade was talking to Perry Williamson, the area's current representative in the New Jersey Assembly.

"That's not the way it happened, Reverend Wade."

"Young man, I didn't just fall off the watermelon truck. I know what you've been doing because the people that you have been talking with have contacted me. And Brother Evans, I know why you joined the South Ward election for City Council last year. Both you and Brother Williamson are hungry for power, and nothing will stop either of you until you get it, and the money that goes with it."

"Reverend Wade, are you calling me a crook?" Evans said.

"Wear the tie around your neck if it fits, and pray that it doesn't choke you, Brother Evans. Now, let me get this straight. I called all of you into this meeting to understand your desires to build a new Newark. I know that many of you think we need to drive all the white people out of the city. Let us not be stupid, that is not a solution.

"Newark has a lot of valuable resources. Port Newark, Penn Station, and the airport all give us visibility across the country. Downtown has a lot of potential. Let's be honest, none of those white people are going to completely leave Newark and leave all that. They might have moved away, but they will continue to lurk around and try to get their hands on whatever they can. Similarly, some of you have exhibited a level of personal motivation that borders on the same kind of greed and manipulation.

"I am not going to join your efforts, nor those of any of these groups that are claiming black power in one way or another. Much of that is just ways of controlling the Negro community; I will not be a partner in such an action.

"Our church has started building homes around this neighborhood without needing to claim some kind of movement, and we have other community restoration projects on the books. There are people who aren't Negroes helping us and I don't plan to refuse the help. Now, I will join in the effort to save Newark and I will encourage my members to do the same, but all that black power stuff is nothing but apostasy. That is not something I am interested in. I don't trust the motives of the people who are involved."

"So, I guess we'll have to add you to the list of people we are going to call 'Uncle Toms'," Evans said.

"It won't be the first time you attempted to label somebody with a bad name. You did it to Sam Garvey, but he ignored you. I'll do the same thing, ignore you; but unlike Sam Garvey, I'll do more than act as if you don't exist. If you come around this neighborhood looking for protection money from my members, I have friends by the names of Smith and Wesson waiting for you and your black power thugs. All my people have to do is let me know if they are being bothered and I will take action. You can count on that."

Gene Oldham stared at both Wade and Evans from his deep-set eyes. "Gentlemen, this meeting shouldn't be going like this."

Evans' voice was tense. "Yeah, I thought preachers were supposed to be non-violent. You need to call Martin Luther King, Reverend Wade."

Reverend Wade stood up and focused his gaze intently on Evans. "Brother Evans, you need to read the Old Testament," Pastor Wade said as he strummed his fingers on the desk and shook his head. "Even the tough guys loved the Lord."

N EHEMIAH AND HIS COUSIN, Denise, were walking into his mother's restaurant.

"Auntie Eva Jean, you said I could eat at *Garvey's* if my grades were good this cycle," Denise said as she placed her books on the table in Eva Jean's office.

"That is correct."

"Well, what does all A's get?"

Eva Jean walked to Denise and held her close. "I don't have any dish special enough for that outstanding accomplishment, honey. I guess Nehemiah and I will have to figure something out. Go wash your hands and sit down at our favorite table. We'll be right there." Eva Jean walked toward the back of her office.

"How are you doing with the plan?" Eva Jean asked as she placed papers in the file cabinet.

"It's goin' in slow motion, but it's goin'," Nehemiah said. "I didn't think my own people would be fightin' me, though."

"The same thing happened to your father. He started talking about buying stores and other property in the neighborhood. There were some people who followed him, but many didn't. He bought a small store when he first came to Newark, built it up for almost fifteen years, then sold it to the man who worked for him while he drove the delivery truck during the day. He used the money from selling the store to buy this restaurant, and he continued his work on the delivery truck while I managed the restaurant. He used the money from the delivery job to buy the house, so none of that money went to the restaurant.

"We were doing business in the Valley at the time. In the beginning, most of our customers were Negroes who lived in the neighborhood, then Negroes from different sections of Newark started coming. The word began to spread, and then we started seeing customers from other cities in New Jersey, some of them were white. Even people from New York were coming. There were some Negroes who said we were uppity, that we thought we were better than others because we were successful."

"Did Daddy get mad about all that?"

"No, he didn't. He just kept working on the delivery truck and saving his money until he started working in the restaurant full time, which gave me more time to take care of you and then Denise, when she came to live with us. Your father didn't listen to the criticism, he just kept pressing on.

"Nehemiah, don't listen to those people who are trying to keep you from your passion. You believe that Newark can be saved and you have to take your plan to the people in the street, the real people. People who have been faithful servants to God, who said in the 25th chapter of Matthew, verse 21, 'You were faithful with a few things, I will put you in charge of many things. Enter into the joy of the master'. You are a blessing to many people and the Lord is watching. Do not be dismayed or discouraged, son. It will all work out."

Chapter 8

"We would have suggested that a twenty-cent bus ride through any black ghetto in America with the window open would give any Congressman, Senator, aide, or social scientist all the evidence he would need to find out why the riots came and why they will continue."

~ DEL SHIELDS, EXECUTIVE VICE PRESIDENT OF THE PREDOMINANTLY BLACK NATIONAL ASSOCIATION OF RADIO AND TELEVISION ANNOUNCERS, CRITICIZING THE DECISION TO SPEND FEDERAL TAX DOLLARS ON STUDYING THE CAUSES OF RIOTS, IN 1967

THE BASKETBALL SCHEDULE for the schools in the Newark City League was being finalized. The motivation of the coaches held few surprises.

"Looks like South Side and Central are going to try to match our schedule with the competition they're booking," Mickey Marcus said to Caleb Frazier, his African American assistant coach. Frazier had been hired by the Newark school system in 1966, after he left his Durham, North Carolina hometown. The six-foot four Frazier had played college basketball at Charlotte's Johnson C. Smith University with Newark high school basketball legend Leon Stone, who was a National Basketball Association first round draft choice after he graduated from college. Stone had played at South Side High School, participating in some memorable games against Weequahic in the mid-1950s. Marcus was able to bring Frazier to Weequahic because he could fill an open position that required a Master's degree in health education. Stone helped Frazier get the job.

"They can try all they want, but they won't get close to the teams we'll be playing this year," Frazier said. "The schools we're playing are from LA, Detroit, Cleveland, New Haven, and those are just a few. All of those schools won state championships last season and they are just as competitive this year. Nobody else in Newark can boast about playing that level of challengers."

"Caleb, is it ironic that most of the cities to which we'll be traveling to play are ones that had riots over the past few years?"

"Mickey, there's always a method to my madness. But I have to be honest, that was Nehemiah's idea. He convinced me when he quoted Hebrews, the tenth chapter, thirty ninth verse in the Bible. 'But we are not of those who shrink back and are destroyed, but of those who have faith and preserve their souls.' What he was saying to me, to my mind, was that in order for us to show the strength of Newark high school basketball, we have to play the best in the country from the most desperate of situations. Similar to what we face in Newark."

"Being the man of faith you are, I'm not surprised that you received his message," Marcus said.

"That young man could sell ice to Eskimos and dirt to farmers, he's that good. Now Mickey, here's the question. Are we going to have enough talent to handle this competition? The new Negro coaches in Newark are trying to take as many of our players as they can, and that includes Nehemiah. Problem is none of them can coach as well as you, and the boys who are leaving will eventually find that out."

"Well, if they are having second thoughts about their decisions and want to play for us they'll have to be enrolled at Weequahic by next week. That's the deadline."

"You know the other schools aren't telling their players that they can come back to Weequahic, and we can't talk to them if they aren't at our school. That would be recruiting and the state of New Jersey has rules against that."

"Caleb, Leon Stone is holding a fall basketball league at Branch Brook Park right now. I know Nehemiah might be playing on a team with some boys from the Valley. I don't think you or I should show up over there, but we do have a friend who is very involved with the league."

"I think I know what's working inside that mind of yours." Caleb laughed as he walked out of Marcus' office. "Leon Stone is our ace in the hole."

"WHERE'S NEE?" JIMMY TRAWICK asked the other students who were running around the track at Untermann Field behind Weequahic.

"He better show up before Mr. Frazier gets here to take attendance," Fred Rashid said. After the group jogged past the front entrance to the field, Nehemiah was in the grandstands, walking toward the other boys. Caleb Frazier was several steps behind him.

"Well alright, there is Nehemiah Garvey with...is that Billy Stern from the Jewish Y?" Trawick said.

Nehemiah was at the field with three of the starters from the Newark Young Men's Hebrew Association basketball team, winners of the YMHA national championship in the spring of 1967. "Hey Nee, what you doin' with that crowd? They don't go to Weequahic no more."

"Wrong about that, Jimmy," Stern yelled.

"Welcome to Weequahic's newest students," Nehemiah said with a haughty tone. "And perhaps our new teammates."

"Enough of the talk, son. Let's hit that track," Frazier said to Nehemiah. "Loose lips sink ships. Remember that."

"What's Mr. Frazier talkin' about, Nee?" Rashid asked.

"My big mouth, that's all I can say."

"Aw c'mon, Nee. Is Billy Stern comin' back to Weequahic?" one of the other runners whispered.

"You have to ask Mr. Frazier."

"Mr. Frazier ain't sayin' nothin'. You know he can keep a secret."

"Billy, I'm surprised Gottlieb let you boys come back to Weequahic," Frazier said to Stern as they began to jog together around the track. "You know there's no love lost between him and Mr. Marcus."

"It wasn't that simple, Mr. Frazier. Nehemiah came to the Y almost two months ago, and challenged our starting five to three games. Full court."

"Who did he bring with him? Jimmy, Danny, some of the other boys he hangs around with?"

"No, it was just him. He told Mr. Gottlieb that he wanted to play with the young boys from our team, the ones who sat on the bench for most of last season. He said he and those boys could beat us, the starting five from the national championship team. I told him that if that happened, some of us might come back to Weequahic."

"And?"

"We're here."

"You mean to tell me that Nehemiah Garvey basically singlehandedly beat the national champ Y team on their own court? With players who were benchwarmers? Get outta here!"

"Yep. And here's the hurting part. They beat us in all three games by more than five points, in games of twenty. You wanna know what else, Mr. Frazier? Are you ready for this?"

"Try me."

Stern stopped running and positioned himself as though he was jumping.

"He dunked on me, Mr. Frazier. Six foot five me! He dunked on me. Three times!"

THE PRINCIPAL OF WEEQUAHIC, Max Steinberg, was in his office with the door closed. He was meeting with the football coach, David Holloman.

"David, you are only bringing this up because you have been angry since Nehemiah said he wouldn't play football this year. He wants to concentrate on basketball," the diminutive Steinberg said, as he threw his wire-framed glasses against the wall.

"Max, the only reason you are not taking it seriously is because you Jews stick together."

"David Holloman, I don't believe those words just came from your mouth. You sound like the group blaming the problems of Newark on Jewish businessmen." A crowd of teachers began to form outside of Steinberg's office, listening to the fierce conversation. "Nehemiah not playing football has nothing to do with his eligibility in the advanced placement program."

Rumors were spreading that several teachers at Weequahic had gone to the superintendent to get Nehemiah removed from advanced placement courses because they felt he was not smart enough. The prevailing notion was that Mickey Marcus had orchestrated Nehemiah's entry into the Advanced Placement Program.

There was a light knock on Steinberg's door. "Who the hell is it?" Steinberg said.

"Michael Kowalski."

"Come in." Kowalski was Nehemiah's homeroom teacher since he came to Weequahic in 1965, the same year the boy's father had disappeared. Kowalski was also the varsity baseball coach. He'd hesitated after the invitation, as if he was being ushered in front of a firing squad by trained sharpshooters.

"Dammit, Mike, just walk in. There are no land mines in here. Just an angry and unreasonable man who is being influenced by current events."

"Max, you just got here," Holloman said. "Mort Levin was afraid of Mickey Marcus and he let him do what he wanted. A lot of people thought Marcus was principal, not Levin. I thought you would be different."

"David, I have been supportive of everybody at this school. You and I met during the summer, right after the riot, to discuss the possibility of losing players from the football team. I don't remember ever telling you 'no' on anything you wanted. I even went with you to talk to the families of players who were thinking about leaving. You and I took the time to discuss with them the merits of those young men staying at Weequahic, and they ended up not leaving. I am working with you to make sure the boys are not in over their heads with their classes. But I am not going to join you and others in endorsing the removal of Nehemiah from the Advanced Placement Program."

"Max, Nehemiah Garvey is not only a credit to Weequahic, but to Newark and New Jersey," Kowalski said. "I met him when both of us started here in '65 and he has gained my utmost respect. I cannot tell you how hurt he was when he found out about this situation."

The telephone rang in Steinberg's office. It was the central office of the Newark Board of Education.

"Yes, this is Max Steinberg. I will hold on for the assistant to the superintendent." He cupped his hand over the mouthpiece. "I need the two of you to leave while I take this call. Don't go too far."

"David, how could you be the person leading this effort against Nehemiah?" Kowalski said to Holloman as they walked into the hallway.

"I have been told that he is not academically qualified to be in the Advanced Placement Program. It's that simple."

"So, you're the person who drew up the petition, got the signatures, and then delivered it to the Board? Without discussing it with Mr. Steinberg? How is that right, David?"

"It is right because I said it's right, Kowalski," Holloman said. "You white people have elevated Nehemiah Garvey to God like status since he walked into this school. I'm tired of that boy. You're only coming to his rescue because he's your star baseball player."

"David, you'll use any excuse to justify what you did. Let me ask you this. Is this the same Nehemiah Garvey who was going to be the captain of your football team this season? Is this the same Nehemiah Garvey who has been playing varsity football since he was a freshman? The same young man who never missed a game or practice in football, basketball, or baseball? I think some of this is based on your resentment of Nehemiah, simply because he decided to concentrate on basketball instead of playing football this year."

"Kowalski, none of this has anything to do with sports. I question his commitment to academics."

"David, this young man has never missed a day of school since he started at Peshine Avenue School in kindergarten. He is respected by his fellow students, Negro and white, whether those students are his age or older. His mother faithfully serves on the PTA at this school and at Peshine, and she contributes her time and effort to all of the schools in the South Ward. The Garvey family, which includes his grandmother Lula Mae Eleazer, is committed to education and the community." Steinberg stuck his head outside the door of his office and motioned for Holloman and Kowalski to return.

"Well, David, you got your way. The central office wants Nehemiah to test in all of the Advanced Placement courses in which he is enrolled. I hope you're happy. For the record, I seriously believe this stems from Nehemiah's desire to unify this city through this high school, and some people don't like it. I've been hearing that you're part of that crowd, the folks who want to assign blame on Jews for the problems that plague Newark. Nevertheless, I refuse to stoop to your level. I support you and will continue to support your efforts with the football team, but on this issue, I vehemently disagree with you. You will look mighty bad when Nehemiah passes those tests with flying colors. Gentlemen, you are dismissed. I have work to do down here, and you both have classes to teach."

NEHEMIAH AND EVA JEAN arrived at the Newark Board of Education's testing office a few days after the meeting in Max Steinberg's office.

"Honey, don't let these people make you nervous," Eva Jean said as they sat together in the waiting room.

"Ma, I'm Samuel Garvey's son. We don't know the meaning of nervous."

Tears welled in her eyes, turning them pale pink. "Your father helped me get through college. I considered not going back to Benedict after my freshman year, because I was losing confidence in myself. I had a few bad grades. But Samuel told me I was homesick and that was the reason I was having a hard time. He spent the summer after my freshman year helping me build my confidence. When I went back that fall I became the top student in my class and graduated in only three years."

"So, Daddy just talked to you and that made the difference?"

"That and writing me almost every week for that next school year, sending encouraging quotes by famous people and Biblical scripture."

"Speakin' about the Bible, I've been meanin' to ask you somethin'. Why didn't you name me Moses, or David, or Samuel Jr.? Why Nehemiah?"

Eva Jean smiled. "You haven't asked that question since you were in the second grade, when a little boy teased you about your name. Your father loved the Biblical story of Nehemiah, how he ignored the opposition to rebuilding Jerusalem's walls and built them anyway. But your father's admiration of Nehemiah went further than that. Nehemiah stopped the oppression of the poor people who were working in the vineyards and the olive orchards. He was generous with his own money by feeding those same workers. Much of this is described in the fifth chapter of Nehemiah, which Samuel read to me when he started talking about naming you."

"Are you Nehemiah Garvey?" It was a woman who entered the waiting room to call his name, interrupting their conversation.

"Yes ma'am, I would be him. And this is my mother, Mrs. Eva Jean Garvey."

"I am quite familiar with your family, Nehemiah," the woman said. "I met your father when he delivered product to my family's meat market on Bergen Street back in the late forties. He talked to my father endlessly about the benefits of living in Newark, and how he hoped to one day have a son who would be a leader in the city. Your father came to our store after he opened his restaurant and bought product from us.

He told my father that he admired him because we had Negroes working in the market. Please tell him you met me and ask him to come by to see my brother and father when he gets the opportunity."

"My husband disappeared over two years ago. We have not heard from him," Eva Jean said.

"Oh, my God, I'm sorry to hear that."

"We appreciate your sympathy, ma'am," Nehemiah said. "My father's memory lives with us. He's just missin'. He'll be back one day."

"Just from this conversation I believe there's a lot of your father in you," the woman said. "I came in here to bring you back to the room where you will be interviewed by several teachers. Mrs. Garvey, you will not be able to accompany your son, but you are welcome to wait in a more comfortable office."

"Thank you so much," Eva Jean said. She then hugged Nehemiah. "Give it your best. Everybody will be proud of you no matter how it turns out."

"Don't worry, Ma. I already have the victory."

Chapter 9

"You don't make progress by standing on the sidelines, whimpering and complaining. You make progress by implementing ideas."

~ Shirley Chisholm, member of the U.S. House of
Representatives from New York 1969–1983,
first African American woman elected to Congress

Fall was in full bloom as First Samuel Missionary Baptist Church celebrated its 75th anniversary on an October afternoon.

"God has granted this glorious church three quarters of a century of leading people to His word," Reverend Frederick J. Wade said from the pulpit. "I am also thanking God for blessing me to be your shepherd for the last thirty-five years." Shouts of amen and hallelujah could be heard throughout the majestic 3,000-seat edifice that was built in the Clinton Hill section of Newark in 1959.

Wade continued speaking to the crowd that filled every seat in the church. "Our congregation has lived through so much during these seventy-five years. God had His hand on us and helped us deal with adversity in each of our three locations, and we are thankful. God has blessed the migration of millions of Negroes from the south to our city and hundreds of other cities across the country. God has blessed us through the Great Depression, two World Wars and with the continuing denial of equal opportunity.

"Our church did not sit idly by and watch these events. We found a way to make a difference. We were on the front line with protesting unequal treatment, when Rosa Parks refused to give up her seat on the bus to a white man in Alabama. We were present and accounted for during the Freedom Rides, the March on Washington, when President Johnson signed the Civil Rights bill and the Voting Rights bill. I personally attended the Supreme Court confirmation hearings for Thurgood Marshall. First Samuel was on the front lines for Negro progress in Newark all those years and this church will always occupy that space, so long as I am here.

"But I don't want to take this precious time to talk about the past, I want to focus on the future. Lena Ashby, please come to the front of the pulpit." Nehemiah's friend since their pre-school years walked from the back of the church.

"As Lena makes her way to the microphone, I want to say that few people in this church are prouder of this young lady than I am. When we began the signing of the petition supporting the nomination of Thurgood Marshall, Lena got more signatures than any single member of First Samuel. When there was a citywide debate between high schools on the Newark public radio station about the possible removal of Congressman Adam Clayton Powell from the House of Representatives, Lena was stupendous with her performance. And may I remind you that she has been teaching Sunday school here since she was in the eighth grade.

"I am proud to announce that our Lena will be graduating from South Side High School next June after only three years, and she has already been accepted by Hampton Institute. Let us all say Amen for this bright young lady who holds so much promise. She is the future of our country, no matter how much some of our unenlightened brethren might try to deny her sterling aptitude. And please sit still, because I have many more names to call. My brothers and sisters, please pray that the United States of America will fully embrace the contributions of our Negro children who will change this country in the years to come."

Caleb Frazier was teaching one of his classes when he noticed someone peering through the clear window panel on the classroom door.

"Mr. Holloman, I'm surprised to see you," Frazier said as he stepped into the hallway. "You know, Mickey has gone downtown to the Board, to discuss getting Nehemiah back into the Advanced Placement Program. You and I need to talk about that."

"We can talk about that later. There's something I need for you to see in the gym right now."

"What, another plot against the basketball team? Against Nee maybe?"

"Caleb, you don't know the whole story. If you did, you wouldn't feel the way you do. But c'mon, we need to get to the gym."

"Man, y'all need to get up on that white boy before he shoot y'all out the gym!" the boys with high-pitched voices echoed in the tiny gymnasium that was nicknamed The Indians Den.

"They can't stop him! Look at him with those moves!" The boys' gym was extremely loud with catcalls and laughter from the crowd in the bleachers during Mr. Holloman's gym class.

"David, what's going on in there?" Frazier asked.

"You'll see," as Holloman opened the door to the gym. A dark-haired white boy, about five-foot six, dribbled down the court, shot the basketball from about twenty feet, and made it.

"Whoa! Where did he come from?" Frazier said.

"He's been doing that since they started playing this period." The warning bell rang and the boys ran to the locker room.

"Hey you, hey young man," Frazier said.

The boy yelled back. "Are you talkin' to me?"

"Yes I am. My name is Mr. Frazier. What's yours?"

"Tommy Caruso."

"I want you to come to my classroom after school. Room 222."

"Mr. Marcus, we appreciate your concern about this situation with Nehemiah Garvey," the testing clerk at the Newark Board of Education said. "I realize this took some time, but it's worth it because it could impact his college prospects."

"I'm more concerned about why and how this happened," Marcus said. "Can you give me the names of the people who started the petition?"

"Well, you already know that David Holloman circulated the petition at your school, but it didn't originate there. I was concerned about it because I'm a Weequahic graduate from the old days, when the school had the reputation of being the best high school for academics in New Jersey, and one of the best in the country."

"You said it didn't originate at Weequahic?"

"That is right. Now, you can't say anything, but I saw the file. This happened to several Negro students at other schools, as if some people around Newark didn't want Negro children to be enrolled in Advanced Placement classes."

"Sounds like a conspiracy to me," Marcus said.

"I'm not surprised," the clerk said. "I've been reading stories about school systems all over the North that are trying to manipulate formation of their districts and return to segregation. One of the ways is to place Negro children, especially boys, in remedial courses and not expose them to advanced education, which many colleges want among their ranks. I also read that many people believe that only those in the South were upset with the Brown versus Board of Education decision. That's not exactly accurate."

"You're right. I know there were people here in Newark who hated that decision," Marcus said. "In fact, I know some teachers in Newark who only come to work for the money and don't really teach, using the excuse that Negro children can't be taught. I appreciate everything you've told me. This is some helpful information."

"Here are Nehemiah's test results. You will be pleased. At least we know that Nehemiah won't be manipulated by this system."

"Yeah, I hope we'll be able to keep this from happening to other Negro children. Well, I have to get back to school. Thanks again for your time."

THE BUZZER SOUNDED, ending the championship game of the Leon Stone Fall Basketball League. Nehemiah's team, comprised of players from the Valley who attended Weequahic and South Side, won the title with an undefeated record.

"For some reason, I believe this will be part of the Weequahic basketball team for the '67–'68 season." Leon Stone was speaking about the team Nehemiah organized for the league.

"Mr. Stone, I would agree with you if I knew that some of these boys would be comin' to Weequahic," Nehemiah said. "You know we lost some players to South Side, and Central. They were good junior varsity players last year and were gonna play important roles on our varsity this season."

"From what I understand, Weequahic won't need them," Stone said. "I heard that some new players will be coming to the school this week."

"You know some people are going to say that is part of the legendary Mickey Marcus recruitin' scheme."

"Mickey Marcus doesn't have to recruit any damn players. Understand that young man," Stone said, slamming his closed right hand into his open left hand. Several people looked toward Nehemiah and Stone. Stone calmed his tone. "Nehemiah, Mickey Marcus is the best basketball coach that ever walked this earth. I stake my reputation on that statement. That includes college and professional. Now, I know if someone heard me say that they would probably send me to the crazy house, but that's the way I feel. I have known him since I played against those great teams he had in the fifties, when I was at South Side. I actually tried to transfer to Weequahic by taking Latin as my foreign language requirement because it wasn't offered at South Side. Marcus told me I could come, but he wouldn't let me play basketball because I didn't live in the Weequahic district. I told him I wanted to play basketball for him and that's why I wanted to come to Weequahic. He said no, and that was final. Marcus is not a cheater and he still wins."

"What are you tellin' me, Mr. Stone?"

"That Weequahic is going to get some outstanding players this week when practice starts. And this will be the greatest coaching year of Mr. Marcus' career."

Nehemiah nearly shook his head off his neck. "What? Mr. Stone, I know you are one of the greatest players to ever come out of New Jersey, and you were legendary down at Johnson C. Smith, especially when you beat some of those white players in pickup games at the University of North Carolina gym, even though blacks weren't allowed to play at the college because of segregation. But that doesn't make you an expert. How can you say that after all of the championships and the players who went to college and the pros in the past because of Mr. Marcus, this will be his greatest year?"

"Nehemiah, listen to me. Mickey's job was made difficult because of everything that resulted after the riot. Many people have been challenging him, not because of competitive reasons, but because of his race. Even some of his own Jewish friends are turning their backs on him because he won't desert you and the team. Boys from Weequahic are transferring to other schools. But still, Mickey Marcus is coaching as if none of this is going on.

"Weequahic just might be the number one team in the country again. You and Mickey Marcus are a combination that is world class, trust me. I heard about what you did this summer at Kutsher's Country Club in the Catskill Mountains in New York, and remember, I saw you play at the Rucker tournament against those high school seniors and college boys. You're ready, Nehemiah. In fact, you were ready after you came home the summer before last, from that Five-Star Camp that was run by a friend of Mickey's. I know who's coming to the school this week and they're ready. Last and most of all, Weequahic has Mickey Marcus, and I know he's ready. I saw his work firsthand, when I attended his summer basketball camps, when he had some of the best high school players in the nation, tutored by many of his coaching friends across the country. There were boys whose families couldn't pay for camp, but were able to catch the eyes of college coaches because Mickey Marcus allowed them to come for free. I was one of those boys. You are with a man who is committed to helping people, which makes his coaching better. That's why I said what I said. And I mean it, young man."

THE DEADLINE FOR TRANSFERRING to public schools in Newark was rapidly approaching. Weequahic had a student waiting list, but only a few of them played basketball, which seemed to be a problem for Mickey Marcus. The dilemma was not lost on Lula Mae Eleazer.

"I have been keeping up with all the issues about Weequahic and the basketball team," Lula Mae said to her daughters; Elizabeth, Mary, Martha and Naomi, while they sat in her office at the beauty parlor.

"I talked to Eva Jean and she is thinking about letting one of the new players move in with her and Nehemiah," Elizabeth said. "I asked her how well did she know the boy."

"How well *does* she know him?" Martha asked in her normal skeptical tone.

"She knows what Nehemiah told her about him," Elizabeth said, "and you know how much she trusts her son."

"Martha, Eva Jean doesn't do stupid things," Mary said. "I'm sure she has a good reason for taking this boy into her home, especially after she talked to Nehemiah." Naomi nodded in agreement.

"Girls, all of us were at my house when Mickey Marcus talked about possibly losing his job because he was not a Negro," Lula Mae said. "I have a problem with that."

"Mama, that might not be so bad," Martha said, waving her finger in the air. "People like Mickey Marcus have been running things in Newark for a long time and maybe they need to give it up."

"Martha, please. This is not only about Mickey Marcus. It's about a handful of whites and their Uncle Tom Negroes wanting to take over the city and do exactly what the mayor is doing right now. Nothing!" Mary said.

"I agree with Mary, Mama," Naomi said. "I'm suspicious of those people who want black power to rule Newark and using the excuse that Mickey Marcus and his supporters are controlling the money in Newark."

"So is Reverend Wade," Lula Mae said. "He told me about some meetings he's had with Gene Oldham, Herbert Evans, Perry Williamson and several other so-called Negro leaders, and he said they tried to get him to support their ideas. Reverend Wade told them to their faces that he didn't trust them. I have also spoken with many ladies here in the shop, and they support Mickey Marcus because he has helped many of our boys get into college, even the ones who didn't play for Weequahic."

"Let's get back to that other subject, the one about the boy moving into Eva Jean's home. Are we going to stand behind our baby sister and tell her that we support her letting the young man live at her house?" Elizabeth asked.

"Yes," Naomi said, as she reached over to grasp Elizabeth's hand.

"Yes," Mary said, touching Naomi's knee.

"I don't know about that," Martha said. "I need to talk to Eva Jean." The other sisters started shouting at Martha.

"Calm down, girls," Lula Mae said. "We all knew that Nervous Nellie, better known as Martha, was not going to give her approval without hesitation. Did we expect anything else?"

"Mama, that's not fair," Martha said. "I'm not nervous, I'm just cautious. What's wrong with that?"

Lula Mae let out a hearty laugh. "Nothing. Nothing at all, honey. We still love you, baby. I'll call Eva Jean and let her know that the whole family is with her." At that point, the sisters and Lula Mae embraced in a group hug.

Chapter 10

Mickey Marcus ushered nearly fifty young men off the basketball court into the bleachers immediately after the first tryout for the varsity and junior varsity basketball teams.

"Nee, I appreciate your mother for lettin' me live with you while I go to Weequahic this year," Tommy Caruso said to Nehemiah.

"No problem, brother. After we talked in Mr. Frazier's office, I knew you needed a friend."

"I *really* needed a friend. I couldn't believe that my mother and father just packed up and left Newark without me during the riot. I was lucky that my grandmother let me live with her for a while. And then I met you and I am now a proud Weequahic Indian. Nee, you are a blessin'."

"Tommy, who said you could call me Nee? You didn't get my permission. Only my friends call me by that name."

"I'm sorry. I guess I have to call you Nehemiah from now on."

Nehemiah broke into a laugh, and then said, "Man, you can call me Nee."

Mickey Marcus started bouncing two basketballs, one in each hand. "Men, that was an amazing first phase workout," Marcus told the group of prospective players from all four grades—freshmen, sophomores, juniors and seniors. "Now we get to phase two."

The gym door swung open as Marcus was getting ready to blow his whistle. In walked Billy Stern, Lenny Rosenberg and Stuart Greenblatt, all members of the starting five from the 1967 national champion Young Men's Hebrew Association basketball team.

"Okay, let's line up for wind sprints with the twenty-pound weighted vests," Marcus said, never losing the focus of his talk despite the sudden intrusion. "You three boys who just walked in, you need to talk with Mr. Frazier before you can participate."

"Nee, who are those guys?" Caruso asked Nehemiah.

"You'll find out soon enough. They might be the keys to Weequahic being number one in the country again."

Frazier went into Marcus' office and sat on the desk. "I didn't think you boys were ever going to register for classes," he said as the three of them found places to sit in the miniscule space.

"Mr. Frazier, we got a lot of grief from some people in the Jewish community over coming back to Weequahic," Stern said. "My grandmother has been seriously thinking about leaving Newark since the riot. She was particularly upset over a white reporter getting beaten up at the black power conference that was held here a week after the riots. A lot of people are telling her that the students at Weequahic don't want any Jewish kids."

"My father doesn't like being called a white devil, especially by people he's been trying to help for a long time," Rosenberg said. "He's been teaching in the Newark schools for almost twenty years, and he was one of the white people who went to the March on Washington."

"My family is worried about me gettin' into fights with some of the Negro boys who blame the riots on white people," Greenblatt said, "and my father wouldn't like me backin' down from nobody that gets in my face."

"Okay, save that energy for the basketball court, Stuie," Frazier said. "I am in charge of you boys at Weequahic and I guarantee that nothing will happen to you."

"Mr. Frazier, we don't want special treatment," Stern said. "We're coming here because we want to be part of the team, a team that could be number one in the country. We can handle ourselves."

"Uh, Mr. Frazier, I'm not worried about anybody messin' with me 'cause one of my uncles is part of the Jewish mafia in Jersey and New York. He's tough," Greenblatt said.

"Man, Stuie, why don't you stop that?" Stern said. "Mr. Frazier, this boy has been into this Elliot Ness, *Untouchables* thing for a long time. He acts like he's on a bad trip, listening to that beatnik music and all that stuff."

"Stu, no alcohol or drug smoking, right?" Frazier said.

"Uh, uh, all that's a drag, Mr. Frazier. I'm too good of a ballplayer to be doin' that."

"Alright, that's enough," Frazier said. "Mr. Marcus and I are glad to have you boys with the team. The two of us appreciate your courage. We know your move back to Weequahic doesn't come easily and can't be taken lightly, but we all believe with your help we can take this team to number one. Now we need to get back to practice with the rest of the boys."

THE WORD BEGAN TO SPREAD about a coalition of black leaders in Newark that was drawing up a campaign ticket for the city-wide elections in 1970. The organization's choice for mayor was leaning in the direction of the same black candidate who ran in 1966 and forced a runoff between the same men who ran against each other in 1962. He received the majority of the black vote and a good share of the Jewish vote, both of which helped him get 20 percent of the total vote.

"The city might look a lot different in three years with all of this black power talk," *The Star-Ledger* managing editor Walt Peters said. "You're going to cover the Negro beat for the newspaper starting today." He was talking to a young black man sitting in his office.

"Is that because I'm competent, or because I'm black?" Ralph Edmondson said.

"Why would you question my motives?"

"Because I know you didn't make this decision alone. If it was left up to you I would still be writing obituaries. How much of a raise in pay am I going to get for this new assignment?"

"More money? I would expect you would be honored to cover your people during such an important time."

"Walt, you know that I know you cannot send a white boy into any of those meetings, caucuses, or whatever programs dealing with black people we need to cover. The people at the black power convention threw white reporters out of their meetings and I'm sure the organizers putting this black voting ticket together for 1970 will do the same to any *Ledger* reporter who isn't black. That means this newspaper won't have adequate coverage of a historic event if it sends anyone who isn't black to their meetings. Which means you need me. Now, what about the money?"

"Write down your figure on a piece of paper and I'll take it to the powers that be this afternoon. There's a Negro coalition meeting tomorrow night to discuss a recall election in the South Ward. I expect you to be there."

"Walt, I like being at the *Ledger*. After all, I'm a Newarker and it's nice to be working at my hometown paper; but make no mistake, there are some nice options out here since the rebellions across the country. A lot of magazines, other newspapers, radio and television stations are looking for blacks to join their ranks, and my eyes aren't closed. So, bring back the offer first, and then I'll be at tomorrow night's meeting with my *Star-Ledger* press card. If no offer comes from you, I'll be looking elsewhere. You can bet on that."

"Ralph, you've become more and more outspoken over the past several months. What gives?"

"There's a reason slave owners didn't want slaves to learn how to read and write. You know why?"

"No. Tell me."

"A little education goes a long way. Aristotle said 'It is the mark of an educated mind to be able to entertain a thought without accepting it.' My four-year degree from Rutgers has prepared me quite well, but my schooling on the streets of Newark has made me a shrewd Negro. And, by the way, I'll be using black instead of Negro in my stories."

> When you read the name 'Hy Silverman', you know it's probably somebody Jewish. So, in case you didn't know who I am after all these years as sports columnist at this newspaper, now you know. I thought I would tell you, since today's column is about a school that has long been regarded as the exclusive province for educating Jewish students, a virtual private school financed by tax dollars.
>
> The school is now heavily attended by Negroes, much to the chagrin of some of its alumni. But the focus on educational achievement is still highlighted when you talk to the man who replaced the legendary Mort Levin as principal, Max Steinberg. Kudos to Steinberg, who seems to believe that all children deserve a quality education no matter what their surroundings might be, or what their circumstances might entail, or whatever the color of their skin. Still, there is only one figure who has consistently typified the spirit of brotherhood at Weequahic High School in both academics and athletics. His name is Mickey Marcus. Since 1947, Mickey

has been the most successful high school basketball coach in America in one of the country's basketball hotbeds. Not only has this roundball genius sent hundreds of young men from high schools all over Newark to college, but many of his own players are also captains of industry and leaders in academia throughout the country because of their scholastic prowess. Over the years, Weequahic has been imitated but never duplicated. Now, the story begins to look different.

This past summer's riots shed a bright but negative light on problems that have existed in Newark for nearly 40 years, and now the Grim Reaper is knocking on the door of New Jersey's most populated city. Marcus and this year's Weequahic basketball players are stubbornly refusing to bow to the negativity surrounding Newark. Thanks to one of Weequahic's most talented student-athletes, Nehemiah Garvey, the South Ward school is not only on target to be a major force in state basketball, but to also compete for the crown of the number one team in the USA; a distinction it held with the tall, talented and disciplined Indians that laid claim to be Weequahic's greatest basketball squad in its 34-year history last season.

There is a difference, however, in this team's mission. After spending a number of days talking to Marcus, his assistant coach, Caleb Frazier and their players, I got the notion that this scrappy squad wants to lift the image of Newark off the ground, to a place it has never been. Weequahic returned Garvey and a number of capable, junior varsity players to its group. Nothing to write home about, but it was able to attract three starters that led the Newark Young Men's Hebrew Association to the national championship in the highly competitive YMHA national basketball tournament, a player from the North Ward whose parents deserted him during the riot, a couple of transfers from South Side, and a promising athlete whose family moved from the Bahamas to Newark this past summer.

While this team is nothing like last year's unbeaten crew that boasted three high school All-Americans, it has a competitive schedule that creates more opportunity to show the country that Newark is better than what the riot displayed during those five days in July.

I must admit, this honorable mission pleases me for two reasons: one, because it shows that sports can be a great racial equalizer; and two, because it shines a light on the Newark City League, which deserves respect for its determination to bring together players from various walks of life. Regardless of socio-economic status, the competition is designed to prepare them for life's ups and downs. I also carry a measure of pride because this calling emanates from Weequahic, the school in which I was a member of the first graduating class in 1937.

Hallelujah.

— Hy Silverman, sports columnist, *The Star-Ledger*

"Well, what do you boys think about that?" Mickey Marcus asked the basketball team during the annual pre-season dinner he and his wife hosted at their home. He had just read *The Star-Ledger* column to the players and their parents after they finished their meal.

"I say we should give a round of applause to our captain, Nehemiah Garvey," Billy Stern announced to the group. Everyone in the huge dining room cheered for Nehemiah. Shouts of "speech," "speech," "speech," followed.

Nehemiah rose from his seat and raised his hand, asking for quiet.

"Please allow me to pause for a moment, to say thank you to my Lord and Savior Jesus Christ," Nehemiah said, "for without Him none of this would be possible. I do this in the presence of both my pastor, Reverend Frederick Wade, and the highly-respected Rabbi David

Seligman, whose commitment to civil rights is known nationally and internationally. I rise to humbly speak to my teammates, their parents, Mr. Frazier and his wife Carol, and our gracious hosts, Mr. Marcus and his wife, Esther.

"Mrs. Marcus, thank you for this meal that you prepared with some help from my grandmother, Lula Mae Eleazer. I need to let everybody know that none of the desserts have sugar in them thanks to Mrs. Marcus, and the vegetables are fresh from my grandmother's backyard garden. Nutrition, exercise, and plenty of sleep are the recipes for success for all of Mr. Marcus' teams, and all those victories and championships are indications that they work.

"As captain of this current Weequahic basketball team, I want to thank our parents, for supporting us. When Mr. Marcus told me what was happening among the coaches in Newark regarding race, that many people wanted him to leave Weequahic because he is white, I got angry. I still can't believe that people in our city wanted to hide behind black power, only to limit the ability of someone like Mr. Marcus who helps young men go to college and better themselves, to obtain the power of education, not the power of a lot of talk. As Mr. Marcus told us earlier, we have a team of men, not boys. Men who stood up to the challenges of some people in our community who believe in separating people by color, letting them know that bringing pride to Newark through teamwork, exceptional ability and sportsmanship are going to be our priorities."

The people in the room gave Nehemiah a sustained round of applause, mixed in with Amen, Hallelujah and Hallelu et-shem Adonai. His teammates stood up and cheered.

Nehemiah concluded. "This team has a Garvey, a Stern, a Caruso, Rashid, Martinez, Greenblatt, and Cambridge. We also have a Clark, a Lewis, a Howard, and a Williams. What a great way to show America that Newark is rescuing itself from the rebellion. Thank you."

"Mr. and Mrs. Marcus, thank you for your hospitality this evening," said Reverend Wade as he rose to speak. "I also thank all of you for your presence, which affirms your desire to be in fellowship with all peoples, to be faithful servants in the effort to salvage our land.

"Rabbi Seligman, please stand with me as we pray with this group. I ask that everyone hold a hand.

"Lord, we want to be an instrument used by You to help others grow in their walk with You. Grow us in our talk and then also place us near others to disciple in Your way. In the name of our Lord and Savior, Amen."

Chapter 11

> "These Americans suffer something more acute than poverty of the purse. They suffer an active and intense frustration that comes from watching the other America at work and play on the television and knowing that it is beyond their reach."
>
>

~ Vice-President Hubert Humphrey, on the condition of African Americans, in 1967

Cleveland, Ohio elected the first African American mayor of a major northeastern U.S. city and predominantly white municipality on November 7, 1967. The election of Carl Stokes paralleled victories of more than 30 major officials in Mississippi, Maryland, Kentucky, and Louisiana, as well as countless others in the South. These accomplishments spurred talk of organizing coalitions to elect mayors in other large cities across the country.

"We're way ahead of the game here in Newark," Herbert Evans, one-time Freeholder and unsuccessful candidate for Newark City Council in 1966 said. "We'll probably have a Negro mayor before New York, Philly, Chicago and Detroit, even LA. All of these cities had riots just like us, but I believe we learned more from ours."

"Our brother for mayor shook things up by getting all those Negro votes in the election in '66, and getting so many Jewish votes," community development specialist Gene Oldham said. "We would have had more representation on the council if you and Perry Williamson didn't compete against each other last year and let that slick-talkin' Mark Chernoff get re-elected. Y'all split the vote, and it helped him win. Now he isn't doin' a damn thing for the South Ward."

"Don't worry about that, Gene. The community organizations are working to get him out of office next year."

"I heard about that, but I also hear they're pushin' Reverend Wade over at First Samuel to run against Chernoff in a special election."

Evans peered over his glasses with a grave look. "Gene, the last thing we need is a Negro preacher on the city council."

"THERE'S WORD THAT THIS IS your last year as coach at Weequahic," *The Star-Ledger* reporter Ralph Edmondson said to Mickey Marcus in his office. "Can I get a confirmation from you on the record about that?"

"You won't get that on or off the record for that matter. What do you think, I'm crazy? I have had a hard enough time trying to get this season off the ground, get some of these boys in college, and help save the reputation of this city without having to deal with something that might appear in your newspaper in the wrong way."

"Well, that brings me to my second question, since you brought up Newark's future. How true is the scuttlebutt across the state that you are going to run for mayor in 1970, and by leaving this job after this season, you can start organizing a campaign? I hear Lula Mae Eleazer and her daughter, Eva Jean Garvey, are two of your biggest supporters."

"Ralph, I don't smell alcohol on your breath, and I'm sure you don't smoke grass, so where is all this coming from?"

"It's out there in the street."

"Get outta here. First, there is supposed to be a movement to remove me as coach at Weequahic, and now people are talking about me as leading from City Hall. Everyone around here knows I'm just a basketball coach. That's all I want to be."

"Yeah, a legend with the highest winning percentage of any high school basketball coach in the country, and more state championships than anybody else. C'mon, Mr. Marcus, give me something to write about."

"Ok, write this. Mickey Marcus predicts this year's Weequahic team will be number one in the country again."

"That's a sports story. I'm writing a feature story."

"Seriously, Ralph, I want this to be a special year in Newark. Let me paint this picture for you. The city of Newark philosophically burned down during the riot last summer, with people fleeing to other cities and leaving this town like roaches running when the lights are turned on in the room."

"Are you sure you want to say roaches?"

"Oh hell, Ralph, you know I don't mean roaches literally. Anyway, Newark is consumed with racial pride and racial hatred from various quarters. Negroes, Jews of different stripes, Italians, Puerto Ricans, you name it, competing in the worst possible ways with each other. Politicians are jockeying for position. Preachers, rabbis, priests, and black Muslim imams, all closing ranks and working in their narrow corners of the city. Opportunists abound from everywhere, with no unity in the community. Are you following me?"

"Yes, I am," Edmondson said as he furiously scribbled on his note pad.

"And then there is this group of young men—not boys, but young men—who are determined to leave their mark on the country by rescuing their hometown from a rebellion that was forced on them. They are basketball players, but they are also faithful servants with a cause, on a mission. These guys are inspired right now by something bigger than they are, and they have an opportunity to put that passion into others. I'm just trying to do all I can to help them. That's it in a nutshell, Ralph."

Edmondson leaned back in his chair. "Mr. Marcus, I thought I knew you. But now it's clear to me that I really didn't. That was great. Is there more?"

"Get comfortable."

THE YOUNG MEN'S Christian Association—also known as the "Y"—in downtown Newark was lively as usual for the Thursday night high school party. Lining the walls around the large room were young men in leather front shirts, colorful knits, and alpaca sweaters. The young ladies were looking good with their slingback shoes, fishnet stockings, and miniskirts. The weekly events were made possible by a Newark school teacher who convinced the Y's leadership that young people 16 through 18 needed a place to enjoy themselves that doesn't serve alcohol or cater to adults. Admission to the dances required each teen to show a flyer, which was handed out at Newark high schools.

"You heard about those Jew boys going back to Weequahic?" a student from South Side High said to a Central High student.

"I heard Mickey Marcus paid Larry Gottlieb at the Jewish Y to convince those players to come to the school," another student said.

"Did y'all hear about this guy Cecil Cambridge from the Bahamas?" one of the students said. "His family moved to Newark in June and he suddenly ends up at Weequahic. He's six-foot-five. How did Marcus do that?"

"I heard he can't play."

"That's what they said about Larry Dennis when he came to Weequahic from New York, but he was six-eleven, 225 pounds, and strong. Marcus must have taught him somethin' about basketball because he was all city, all county, all state, and all America with two state championships; undefeated in both seasons. Man, he was shootin' better hook shots than Lew Alcindor. If this dude Cambridge is half that good, Weequahic is gonna be tough to beat."

The dance floor was full as the disc jockey was playing *Cold Sweat* by James Brown. Cheryl Johnson had caught Nehemiah's attention as soon as he walked downstairs into the dance area. He immediately wanted to get to know her.

"I didn't know people from Roselle knew about Thursday nights at the Y," Nehemiah said as they danced.

"Brothers and sisters from Newark have this idea that they're the only people with soul in Jersey," Cheryl said. "You do know there are black people in Roselle, Linden, and Elizabeth."

"And East Orange, Montclair, Irvington, Orange, Bloomfield," Nehemiah said. "But a lot of those families started right here in good old Newark."

"I'm not sure about that, but we can debate it another time. Speaking of Newark, I've been hearing about what you're doing to help the city. Using young people is right on. How can I help?"

The music changed from fast to slow, with the disc jockey playing *Natural Woman* by Aretha Franklin.

"You mind dancin' to this one while I explain what you can do to help?"

"With that velvet voice sounding like that, who wouldn't accept such an offer?"

"Well you know, gettin' a Douglass College sophomore who graduated from a private all-girls' high school to listen to a young high school junior from the ghetto ain't easy."

"You're just asking me to dance."

"And tellin' you about savin' Newark."

Cheryl grabbed Nehemiah's arm and placed it around her waist. A few girls from Weequahic observed them.

"Wow, Nee, you goin' for the old girls these days. I guess high school is too slow for you." Then, to Cheryl: "Sister, he's only fifteen."

"Don't listen to them. I turned sixteen three weeks ago," Nehemiah assured Cheryl.

"I am not paying those heifers any mind, my brother. Now how is getting those Jewish boys on the basketball team going to help?"

"For one, they're good. Second, they're good. And third, they're really good. In other words, it doesn't matter what color their skin is, or their religion. They are talented enough to help us win."

"Nehemiah, you're talkin' to a sister whose father is a Wall Street lawyer. My brother is a tax accountant. The two of them deal with slick people every day," Cheryl said. She wrapped her arms around Nehemiah's neck. "You remind me of them. What's goin' on in that mind of yours, brother?"

"I'm solid, my sister. As a matter of fact, havin' the Jewish boys gives the team more notice from the newspapers. We already got a story by Hy Silverman in *The Star-Ledger*.

"Who's Hy Silverman?"

"Silverman is a Jewish sportswriter, a graduate of Weequahic, and a big fan of Mr. Marcus. Jewish people support each other and that's not a bad thing, especially when it works for Weequahic."

"I also heard that Ralph Edmondson is working on a feature story about Mickey Marcus for this Sunday's 'Around New Jersey' section in the *Star-Ledger*," Cheryl said. "I assume you are the architect of all of this?"

"No, I didn't say that. But I honestly feel that God chose me for this assignment." The song ended and the two of them walked off the dance floor.

"Why would God pick you?

"Why not?"

"Nehemiah, I must say, I'm glad I met you. I've heard a lot about you before tonight and you seem to be as advertised."

"What does that mean?"

"It means that what people are saying about you is true. Listen, I gotta go. Can you walk me to my car?"

As they walked toward the door leading to the street, two boys stopped them.

"Nehemiah Garvey. We'll be seeing you on Tuesday at our gym. It will be your first loss in forty-five games. By the time we finish with you Indians, this fine sister will be cheerin' for us." Nehemiah started to answer, but Cheryl got between him and the boys from Central High.

"You're right, I *will* be cheering for you. And I'll be cheering for *this* brother. I'll be cheering for both of you, all of you, including the Jewish boys on Weequahic's team. I'll be cheering that you play to win and may the best team be victorious. I'll also cheer for Newark's young men to show the best of themselves. That's most important to me."

"Man, Nee, you got a winner there. I like how she thinks. And how she looks." The boys walked back into the Y.

"Now to you, Mr. Garvey. It's your thing, do what you wanna do, but please do it right. If you ever need me, here's my phone number." Cheryl pressed a piece of paper into his hand. "And by the way, youngster, you have a sweet way of dancing. You've got potential. I might be thinking about you after tonight. Oh, to get the record straight, I'm a *senior* at Douglass." She kissed him on his cheek as they walked toward her car.

"Pop, our first game is Tuesday. Think you'll make it?" Billy Stern asked his grandfather.

Yussel Stern walked past his grandson without even a casual remark.

"So now you ignore me?"

"Billy, you know how I feel about sports. There are more Negroes playing and no room for Jews."

"Pop, you sound prejudiced, like you don't like Negroes."

"I like them, but I don't trust," the older Stern said. "The pursuit of sports made your father leave his home and he never made it to the pros to make money. He should have played baseball, where Jews have done well. Hank Greenberg, Sandy Koufax, Moe Berg. Basketball? No."

"Dad was a great high school basketball player and did okay in college, but he wasn't ready for the pros, Pop."

"What about the Heyman kid and that boy who played for North Carolina who stopped Chamberlain in the championship game? They were outstanding players, but they couldn't play in the pros because of all the Negro boys."

"Pop, Pop, c'mon. I'm just asking you to come to the game on Tuesday. I'm not asking you to be a crusader for civil rights."

"Billy, your coach didn't keep you on the team before, because he had so many Negro boys."

"Yeah, and they won the state championship two years in a row and became number one in the country. I'll be okay; my friend Nehemiah Garvey is captain."

"Oy vey, another Negro kid. Billy, those people are not even loyal to their own. Look what they do to Martin Luther King? He spoke out against the Vietnam War and his preacher friends are turning their backs on him."

"Pop, I'm gonna be alright. Look, Rabbi Seligman is friends with Nehemiah's pastor, Reverend Wade. He's keeping an eye on everything at Weequahic."

The much shorter grandfather reached up and touched his grandson's face.

"I don't want to lose you like I lost your father. I ran him away. I promise I won't do the same with you. You make a good case to play at Weequahic, and your grandmother and I will support you. You have a chance to do well. You go and make the Stern name proud."

Chapter 12

"The press has too long basked in a white world looking out of it, if at all, with white men's eyes and white perspective."

"Our nation is moving toward two societies, one black, one white—separate and unequal."

~ Two major conclusions of The National Advisory Commission on Civil Disorders, known as the Kerner Commission, and named after its chair, Governor Otto Kerner Jr. of Illinois. The 11-member commission was established on July 28, 1967 by President Lyndon B. Johnson, to investigate the causes of the 1967 race riots in the U.S. The commission released its report on February 29, 1968.

"I'm the big basketball star, the weekend hero, everybody's All-American. Well, last summer I was almost killed by a racist cop shooting at a black dude in Harlem. He was shooting on the street—where masses of people were standing around or just taking a walk. But he didn't care. After all we were just niggers. I found out last summer that we don't catch hell because we aren't basketball stars or because we don't have money. We catch hell because we are black."

~ Kareem Abdul-Jabbar, once known as Lew Alcindor, on boycotting the 1968 Olympic Games, in 1967

Weequahic High School's Indians began the 1967–68 basketball season with seven straight victories, beating three of their main Newark rivals—South Side, Central and West Side—each by more than 20 points—as well as easily defeating schools in nearby East Orange, Elizabeth, Linden and Plainfield. At the same time, Pittsburgh's Schenley High School, Los Angeles' Fremont High School and New Haven's Wilbur Cross High School in Connecticut were sitting atop the *Scholastic Magazine* national rankings after each of them won their first ten games.

"Well fellas, are we there yet? Are we the best team that we can be?" Mickey Marcus asked his team, which was assembled in a classroom to view film of their last game. "I say we have to improve in many areas, but it is my belief that improving is striving for excellence. I'm looking around and I don't see Nehemiah. Where is he?"

"Here I am," Nehemiah said as he rolled a cart with a cake on it into the room.

"Congratulations Mr. Marcus, on winning five hundred games," the players shouted.

"How did you do it, Mr. Marcus?" Billy Stern said as he stood up. "We want a speech."

As Marcus began to speak, his wife walked into the room and stood next to him.

"Because of this young lady's dedication to me since my first year of coaching twenty years ago," Marcus said as he kissed his wife on the cheek, "and because of boys like all of you, this great school has won all of these games in such a short period of time. There's the speech. Now let's get to work."

The decorations that adorned downtown Newark for Christmas and the holiday celebration were in full bloom in December 1967. Tournaments were being staged across America, and Weequahic was preparing to face national competition, as were several other teams in the city. All of this, however, was a mere backdrop to the drama across the country as the Vietnam War raged on.

"And that's how we looked against South Side, men," Caleb Frazier said after the game film ended. "That was as close to a perfect game as we have played this season. Let's keep it up. Now talk with the student managers who will give you the details of our trip to LA for the Watts Roundball Classic. Nehemiah, I need to talk to you," Frazier said as he began to walk toward the back of the room.

"Who is Cheryl Johnson?" Frazier asked, launching into the conversation with a quiet tone.

Nehemiah stuttered. "Uh, she's this girl I met at the Y."

"Which time?"

"I don't know what you mean."

"Nehemiah, I know I'm speaking English. You've been with this Cheryl Johnson girl a few times, and not only at the Y. Somebody saw the two of you at the movies on Bergen Street. Now, who is she?"

Nehemiah rolled his eyes toward the ceiling. "What, I can't go see a movie with a girl? Why the questions, Mr. Frazier?"

"There are some people who are worried about your friendship with her. Those people include your mother. And by the way, you went to see a movie for adults only and you could only get into the theater with somebody over twenty-one."

"What does my mother have to do with this? And, by the way sir, it was *The Graduate*. It wasn't a dirty movie."

"Don't try to change the subject, son. What about the telephone calls to your mother's house from this girl, calls to her restaurant from this girl, looking for you? That doesn't include the time you spend talking to her on your mother's telephone at the house. Some other worried people are your good friends, like Lena Ashby. I have heard that you went to a nightclub in Harlem with this girl."

"Mr. Frazier, are you working for Perry Mason now? I guess my missing father is worried too." Frazier edged closer to Nehemiah with anger dominating his body language. From across the room Mickey Marcus stared at Frazier with a bewildered expression. Frazier tapped his chest, indicating to Marcus that he was in control of the situation.

"Don't get sassy with me, young man. Your mother asked me to talk to you about this Cheryl girl. She knows she's a senior in college and she wonders why she would be interested in a high school junior."

"My mother should have asked me."

"I'm asking you."

"Mr. Frazier, she's just a girl who came up to me at one of the high school night dances at the Y. She said she wants to help me save Newark. That's all."

"You don't think it's strange that she just showed up out of the blue?"

"She said she heard about my crusade to keep Newark from gettin' negative headlines. She said she wanted to help change that."

"Nehemiah, I'll take your word that she's just a girl with honest intentions, at least from your point of view. But I have my suspicions. Now, I have been noticing that your energy level has not been the same lately, especially in practice. I'm not going to keep bothering you, but know that I am keeping my eyes on you and if you continue to slip, I will let you know. This tournament in LA is important for us and I am not going to let everybody's work be in vain because you are infatuated with a college girl. Nehemiah, I am watching you."

"Grandma, am I going to the tournament in California?" Denise Vandiver asked her grandmother, Elizabeth, Eva Jean Garvey's oldest sister.

"Yes, you are, along with Aunt Eva Jean, Big Mama, Reverend Wade, and some other church members." The doorbell rang. Denise ran to the door.

"Who is it?"

"It's Lena."

"Hi Lena," Denise said as she opened the door. "Guess what? I'm goin' to California to see Nehemiah play."

"Guess what? I'm going too."

"So, your parents are letting you go to LA?" Elizabeth said. "That's good. Weequahic is going to have a great cheering section out there."

"When my parents heard that Reverend Wade and some of the other members of the church are going, they decided to go. I also heard he's going to preach at a church out there."

"Reverend Wade sees this as a chance to talk about how Newark is going to be a better city despite the riot," Elizabeth said. "He wants to see what the churches out there are doing in their recovery from the 1965 riot in Watts, and I'm sure there will be ministers from the other cities. I'm looking forward to the trip because I have never been so far away from Newark."

"Miss Elizabeth, this is a big step for Nehemiah and his desire to showcase Newark. I am really happy for him," Lena said.

"Even though he's been hanging around that college girl?"

Denise had a confused look on her face. "I thought Nehemiah was your boyfriend, Lena?"

"Girl, get out of other people's business and go in the living room and do your homework," Elizabeth said. Denise ran out of the kitchen as fast as she could.

"I like Nehemiah as a friend, not a boyfriend, so I'm not upset about that girl," Lena said to Elizabeth. "But I don't think she really likes him."

"So, what do you think is going on?"

"I think somebody is trying to start problems with the Weequahic team and that girl is supposed to distract him."

"That sounds like something from that television show, *Mission Impossible*. You really think it's like that? You think it's going to work?"

"Miss Elizabeth, that's your nephew, you know him better than I do. But I know how boys my age think about older girls, especially ones in college. No tellin' what she's doin', but everybody better keep their eyes on Nehemiah so he doesn't take a wrong turn with her."

"Are you going to keep an eye on him, honey?"

"Especially me."

THE NONSTOP FLIGHT FROM Newark to Los Angeles seemed to take a lifetime. The players, though, were entertained by the humor and human-interest stories of Mickey Marcus and Caleb Frazier. Marcus told jokes about his former teams, about opposing coaches and some of the interesting things that happened on and off the court. Frazier shared his accounts of segregation in the South and how it shaped his attitude toward education, as well as his interaction with non-blacks in the North. The team's plane landed on a Monday morning, one week before Christmas, while the plane that carried other people from Newark was approximately one hour behind them.

"I ain't never ate food from a shoebox before," Tommy Caruso said to Nehemiah, who was sitting next to him. Caruso was talking about some meals that were prepared for the team so they wouldn't be hungry on the long flight. "I knew your mother could cook, but I didn't expect it to taste this good."

"There's some history about shoebox food," Nehemiah told him. "When black people began to migrate from down south to the north in the 1920s, they brought food in shoeboxes to eat on the train. Normally, there were a couple of pieces of fried chicken, a few slices of white bread, and a hard-boiled egg."

"Don't forget the cake," Caleb Frazier said, laughing out loud. "My grandmother would pack a slice of her world-famous pound cake in my shoebox when I traveled."

"Listen up, boys, we are going to disembark the plane together and we are going to walk through the terminal as a team," Mickey Marcus said.

"What's disembark mean, Mr. Marcus?"

"It means to go out through the back door," Billy Stern yelled. Everybody laughed.

"THIS PANEL DISCUSSION HAS got to achieve the purpose of disrupting the cause of this basketball team. I talked to our brothers in Newark and they tell me that this Nehemiah boy and that team could upset our plans back East," Amir Jali, leader of a Los Angeles-based group that espoused black power and Black Nationalism said.

"Brother Amir, how can some sixteen-year old child stop the inevitable revolution that started with the rebellion here in '65 and continued in Newark and Detroit this year?"

"I understand he comes from good stock. According to what I heard, his father was part of brother Marcus Garvey's family and followed them from Jamaica when they came to America. This boy supposedly has a revolutionary mind similar to that of his father, only he's using it to further the cause of the oppressors. They say he is a Jew lover. Our people in Jersey say he is dangerous. He needs to be stopped."

"So how does this panel discussion stop him?"

"The organizers of the tournament are brothers who believe in our cause. They were students in my Pan African class at Los Angeles City College when I first started the organization. When I heard that they were organizing a high school basketball tournament that would feature a number of schools from riot torn cities, I saw an opportunity to get some media attention for what we are doing across the country.

"Our followers are forming operations nationwide, especially on college campuses. The organization in New Jersey has a committed sister at Douglass College and she is right on. Most of our people are just like her."

"All of that is good, but you still haven't said how this discussion will embarrass him," one of the women in the group said.

"We will stack the audience with our followers to ensure that their questions will put this boy on the spot. The pressure will be too difficult for him to handle."

"What if his coach won't let him participate?"

"This Mickey Marcus guy has a lot on the line in this tournament. He is one of the country's most successful high school coaches and he is being coveted for a number of coaching jobs at major colleges. He is a partner with a group of wealthy white people who are opening health clubs across the country, and I heard that he is working to develop a health beverage for athletes. Nehemiah Garvey gives Marcus cover with many black people in Newark. Marcus will want Garvey to participate in this discussion, to make him look good for his coaching legacy and his business interests."

"You've got it all figured out, don't you?"

"You better believe it. Over the next five to ten years, black people will control the major cities in America, and I plan to be part of the revolution. In order to do that we must stop people like Nehemiah Garvey."

THE STATELY CENTRAL CITY Baptist Church in Los Angeles had a history similar to First Samuel Baptist Church in Newark. Both had charismatic pastors who elevated their respective churches to prominence through local community activism and throughout the United States due to their linkage with church associations and dynamic nationwide religious leaders.

"Only what you do for Christ will last," Reverend Wade said to the congregation that packed the church in the section of Los Angeles that was affected by the Watts Riot in 1965. "The choir sang the words from the great writer Raymond Rasberry's composition so well. "...'you may build great cathedrals large or small, you can build skyscrapers grand and tall, you may conquer all the failures of the past, but only what you do for Christ will last.' Hallelujah." Wade walked down the steps, away from the pulpit, holding his hands toward the sky. "Remember, only what you do for Christ will last. Remember, only what you do for Christ will last, only what you do for Him will be counted at the end. Only what you do for Christ will last.

"My brothers and sisters, I am thankful for being given this opportunity to preach in this ordained structure. The presence of the Holy Spirit is here, and oh how we need it," Wade said as he began the end of his Tuesday evening sermon with a rousing crescendo that electrified the mixed audience of blacks and whites, overwhelmingly true believers in God's grace and mercy. Rabbi David Seligman from Newark was among those in attendance.

"We came here to Los Angeles to support our young men in a contest that will test their athletic skill and intellectual prowess in a thinking man's game. We are also sharing ideas about how to change the fortunes of all the cities torn asunder by centuries of festering misunderstandings. We have witnessed first-hand the repudiation of American values. We can no longer allow or enable the digression of rights given by God through his grace.

"Our coming together tonight will set the stage and tone of our meeting in the morning—a gathering intended to ferret out the fears of impending change, so we can safely and comfortably embrace the diversity that makes our wonderful country a place for all people to live.

"As the choir sang tonight, 'though your song and prayers are heard and praised by man, they've no meaning unless you've been born again. Sinner, heed these words, don't let this harvest pass, for only what you do for Christ will last.'

"Let us embrace one another in brotherhood. Amen."

Chapter 13

"A moderate Negro must prevail over those who seek solutions to their problems through violence. It is the moderate who will get the job done while rioters will become the victims of their own violence."

~ NEWARK, NEW JERSEY CITY COUNCILMAN CALVIN WEST,
AT XAVIER UNIVERSITY (CINCINNATI, OHIO), IN 1967

THE INFLUENCE GAINED BY President Lyndon B. Johnson's Great Society platform came from monumental victories in shrewdly crafted legislation, but all levels of government were threatened due to violence in the streets during the turbulent mid-1960s. Groups with different agendas sought membership from blacks who nonetheless felt disenfranchised. In spite of striking achievements in civil rights, voting rights, equal opportunity by affirmative action, early education through Head Start, health care for seniors and poor people through Medicare and Medicaid, plus assistance for urban areas within the Model Cities program, hot-button terms such as Black Power, Pan Africanism, Black Nationalism, and Self Determination dominated conversations among blacks in America.

"LENA, I CAN'T BELIEVE I'm going to Disneyland," Denise Vandiver said.

"Thank God you have been doing well in school and you were allowed to take this trip," Lena said. It had been a stroke of good fortune that the Watts Roundball Classic committee was able to secure Disneyland group tickets for fans attending from out of town. "I'm looking forward to meeting people here for the tournament from other cities." Eva Jean Garvey was eavesdropping on the conversation.

"This is a good idea, to bring everybody together. We should do something like this in Newark."

"Miss Eva Jean, I thought you were going to the meeting with the ministers this morning," Lena said.

"No, honey, only men are invited to that meeting. I guess women don't have anything constructive to say about improving the community, though many of the women on this trip own businesses where they live, including my mother and me in Newark."

"I hope that women will be getting more respect when I finish college and start working," Lena said.

"Honey, Aretha Franklin said it right, R-E-S-P-E-C-T, find out what it means to me. Things are changing and you'll be all right. Maybe you might be the woman who pushes her way into these kinds of men-only sessions. I'm just praying that these men will come up with some good ideas while they're meeting this morning to improve the conditions in these cities."

"Uh, Aunt Eva Jean, it's time to meet the bus to Disneyland," Denise said with a curt tone. "I'm ready to go."

WEEQUAHIC WAS FINISHING ITS practice session at the Los Angeles Sports Arena, which was home to the Los Angeles Lakers of the National Basketball Association until they moved into the Fabulous Forum in Inglewood, California in 1967.

"So, this is what it's like to play on a basketball court made for major college and professional teams," one Weequahic player said to Billy Stern.

"I'm not trying to brag, but our Jewish center team played on a few legendary basketball courts during our national championship run last spring," Stern said.

"How did you feel when you first went on the court?"

"Just like you probably felt this morning when you first went out to practice in this place; somewhat intimidated thinking about who played there before. I thought about Bill Russell, Sam Jones, and Tommy Heinsohn, and those other Celtics when we were in the Boston Garden. In Philadelphia at the Palestra, I felt a rush in my spirit thinking of that place as the cathedral of college basketball. But once you're out here for a while, all of that stuff vanishes and you have to get down to business like we will tomorrow."

Seven teams in the *Scholastic Magazine* high school basketball poll were playing in the Watts Roundball Classic, including the top three—Schenley of Pittsburgh, Fremont of Los Angeles, and Wilbur Cross of New Haven, which was Weequahic's opponent in their first game on Thursday.

"I thought a lot about this panel discussion that's happenin' this afternoon," Nehemiah told Caleb Frazier as they were walking off the court after practice. "I think it would help with the theme about savin' Newark."

"You know there's going to be a lot of those black power advocates in that room. As a young black man, they might try to make you feel like you're an Uncle Tom with your opinion about blacks and whites working together. Think you can handle that pressure?"

"I know I can. I'm sure they think they can run all over a sixteen-year-old crazy boy who believes in savin' a city that has been in ruins for almost forty years."

"I'm listening to you, Nehemiah, and I'm impressed with your courage, but I'm not surprised. You've overcome a lot, especially the disappearance of a father you loved very much. You dealt with that Advanced Placement Program issue like a real man. Now, are you sure you can focus on winning this tournament, even with the likely distraction of that panel discussion?"

"Sure, I can. No matter what, the tournament comes first. I'll also say this: Weequahic will be the talk of the country when we walk off this basketball court Saturday night. And it will not only be because we win the next three games. Something else will happen."

"We want our people flanking me, sitting at the head table. I will be at the podium, right in the center," Amir Jali said. "The people who oppose our points of view will be seated at the end of the table." Jali was the moderator for the panel discussion centered on black power advocacy. His Los Angeles-based group was sponsoring the event. "By placing them on the end, the audience will have to strain to see them, which will impede their focus on what is being said. And make sure that boy, Nehemiah, gets the most uncomfortable chair you can find."

"What about our supporters sittin' in the audience?" asked one of the members. "How will their voices be heard?"

"They will be seated in the first three rows, right in front of the podium. They need to be vocal, aggressive, and intimidating, which should distract the panelists."

"I'm guessin' you want them to be aggressive enough to have Nehemiah Garvey feel the pressure."

"I don't have to strategize this meeting in an effort to avoid a kid who has no clue about nation time," Jali said, slamming a chair to the floor. "I won't lose any sleep thinking about that boy."

"Your body language is sayin' somethin' else."

"What are you, a damn psychoanalyst? Give me a break. My greatest joy was accomplished with the rebellions in Detroit, Newark, Tampa this year, and the ones in Harlem and here in Watts the last few years. They fueled smaller insurrections in other cities, which help undermine these Jesus-loving niggers and Jew elitists. Just think, a lot of the blame is being heaped on a bunch of patty boy white liberals. Now, do you think that some chump nigger from Newark is going to get in my way? Don't hold your breath."

"I don't know. Those dudes from Newark are a tough bunch. I know some brothers from Harlem who don't even get in their way."

"Well, we'll see what this Newark boy is made of today."

THE SMALL AUDITORIUM in the community center was filled to capacity. The fact that this event was taking place in the area where most of the Watts Riot had occurred was drawing extra attention, and a slew of reporters from regional and national news outlets stood along the walls of the facility. The chairs on the stage were occupied by each participant, except the one reserved for Nehemiah.

"I want to thank you all for attending this panel discussion titled, *Where Do We Go From Here?* All but one of our invited guests have arrived," Amir Jali said at the podium. Suddenly, a group of people erupted into a loud cheer at the back of the room as Nehemiah Garvey walked down the middle aisle toward the stage.

"I guess I was somewhat hasty about announcing your absence, Mr. Garvey," Jali said. The group's applause, led by Nehemiah's grandmother, Lula Mae Eleazer, continued while Jali spoke. "Ladies and gentlemen in the back, we appreciate your enthusiasm, but we have an agenda for this afternoon and your cheers are holding us up."

"Grandma, Ma, everybody, you can stop cheerin'. Thank you. I think they get your point," Nehemiah said as he took his seat at the end of the table. "And by the way, Mr. Jali, thanks for the end seat. I'm able to stretch my weary legs after that long practice Mr. Marcus put us through this morning."

"To get us started, please refer to the handout each of you received when you came in," Jali said. "It will take too long to introduce each member of our panel, but their information is on the session material.

"The first question to all of you is, 'What comes to mind when you hear the title of this discussion?' I will select each respondent."

Nehemiah immediately stood up, without being recognized by the moderator.

"It reminds me of Reverend Martin Luther King's book of the same name, which has been criticized by many people, but is a work of deep, reflective thought." Nehemiah's six-foot three frame towered over the audience from the elevated stage. A noticeable hush invaded the room as he continued. "It's interesting that you, Mr. Jali, and the organizers of this discussion, are advocates of black power, which Reverend King praised in the book as a call to black people to amass the political and economic strength to achieve their legitimate goals.

"But he also surmised in the book that black power is an implied rejection of interracial coalitions and a call for retaliatory violence, which prevents non-violent resistance from having the substance and influence to become the basic strategy for the civil rights movement. I am surprised that this group would use the title of Reverend King's book as a disguise to discuss something that he absolutely does not fully endorse."

The other panelists were shifting in their seats as if a pack of flesh-biting, red ants had been released underneath their feet. The crowd that had lapsed into a moment of stoicism now started to murmur in a growing frenzy.

"Please, everyone, please calm down," Jali said. "I don't know about your intention, Brother Garvey, but your assertion seems to be misplaced."

"I don't think so, Brother Jali. I have done my research on your organization, and I know about its rise after the Watts riots in '65. I have done background work on you, as well."

Jali's face signified his barely contained shock and anger. "You are disrupting this discussion with your implied accusations, my brother. I am a tenured university professor with an academic background in urban studies, which makes me a far more qualified expert on black folk than a high school basketball player with visions of grandeur. This sounds like a planned attack, most likely orchestrated by a group of rich, white oppressors bent on keeping the black masses on the slave plantation. Mickey Marcus, I lay this outburst from this misguided ingrate at your feet."

Marcus stood up. "I'm just an observer, Mr. Jali. I had no discussion with Nehemiah about this event. You sound a bit paranoid."

"I don't need anyone to tell me how to think, Brother Jali," Nehemiah said, "I have been blessed with that ability by my God who art in heaven."

What had been planned as a panel discussion about the impact of the riots—called rebellions by many—had erupted into a battle of wills between the revolutionary-minded, formally educated Jali and the seemingly naïve, sixteen-year old Nehemiah.

Another person in the audience rose from his seat. It was Al McCoy, the Newark resident who owned a sporting goods store on Bergen Street in Newark. McCoy was also a graduate of Weequahic who had played basketball for Mickey Marcus.

"This is a travesty, Mr. Jali. You have made a mockery out of a good idea."

"And who might you be?" Jali asked.

"Someone who believes in the kind of black power that utilizes moderation and judiciousness combined with constructive engagement with those persons trying to build coalitions. That's where this young man is trying to lead his team, and in the long run, we should all be praying that people in Newark will follow."

"Be not silent, O God of my praise. For the wicked and deceitful mouths are opened against me, speaking against me with lying tongues. They encircle me with words of hate, and attack me without cause," Nehemiah said, reading from a piece of paper, quoting the first three verses of Psalm 109 from the Bible.

Jali laughed hysterically. "There you go with prayer to the white Jesus, on your knees begging and pleading for grace and mercy from your invisible cosmic father." Just as Jali finished speaking, the panelists began leaving the stage. The attendees started walking out.

"Well brother, looks like your so-called discussion on resurrection through rebellion has met an untimely end," McCoy said. "God don't like ugly."

"What's God got to do with it?" Jali wanted to know.

"Everything," McCoy replied. "He will not be mocked."

Nehemiah walked toward the exit, to mingle with some people leaving the auditorium.

"Thank you, everyone, for supporting this effort," he said. "It was a step in the right direction, only the motivation was wrong. I look forward to seeing all of you tomorrow at the tournament."

Eva Jean walked up to her son.

"For several minutes, I thought I was watching your father when you stood up to that man. You looked just like him. I'm proud of you, Nehemiah."

"No tears, Ma. You need that energy to cheer us to win these next three games. Okay?"

THE OPENING ROUND pairings for the Watts Roundball Classic pitted Weequahic against the nation's third-ranked team, Wilbur Cross High School of New Haven, while second-ranked Fremont of Los Angeles and top-ranked Schenley of Pittsburgh drew opposition from fifth-ranked Dunbar of Washington, D.C. and eighth-ranked Highland Park of Detroit, respectively. Both Schenley and Fremont easily won, but Weequahic, the only unranked team in the tournament, struggled in their upset victory. Center Billy Stern, along with guards Tommy Caruso and Jimmy Trawick, were the standouts, while Nehemiah, playing at forward, had an off night.

"I hope all of this outside activity is not affecting your play," Mickey Marcus said to Nehemiah during the morning practice on Friday. "That episode with the black power group the day before the game seemed to have an effect." Weequahic was playing the host school, Fremont, in the last game that night, with the winner going to the championship game on Saturday.

"I had a good night's rest after the game. I'm ready for the LA boys tonight," Nehemiah said as he sank a long jump shot. Marcus smiled.

"Yeah, boy, that's what I'm talkin' about," Jimmy Trawick said as he watched Nehemiah's shot swish through the net. "Somethin' tells me that we got Fremont's number tonight." Billy Stern was standing on the sideline talking to Caleb Frazier.

"Billy, they got some big boys underneath. Makes me think of our team from the last two years," Frazier said. "Their three frontcourt guys are six-five, six-six, and six-nine."

"Those guys from New Haven had a six-ten guy and two who were six-four. We handled them. Even though Nehemiah didn't score a lot, he grabbed some big rebounds over those guys and I know you remember that blocked shot he got on the tallest guy when they were making a comeback. We could probably say that Nehemiah saved us in the end."

Marcus blew his whistle, indicating the end of the intense workout.

"Alright boys, it's the host school tonight. They set it up for us to lose this tournament. We played the number three team in the country last night, we play the number two team tonight, and we could possibly be playing the country's top team tomorrow," he said.

"And we're not even ranked!" Nehemiah yelled out, "…but it makes no difference, because we have the best coach in the country and he put together a plan that will give us the two victories we need to win this tournament. After the dust clears, *we* will be number one in the country!"

Chapter 14

> "Abraham Lincoln was not the Great Emancipator. There is abundant evidence to indicate that the Emancipation Proclamation is not what people think it is and that Lincoln issued it with external misgivings and reservations."
>
>

~ Historian and nationally prominent author Lerone Bennett Jr., citing his research on race relations and the Negro in America, in 1967

WHILE THE COUNTRY DID its best to celebrate the birth of Jesus Christ and Hanukkah in 1967, times were tumultuous. President Lyndon B. Johnson was besieged with criticism over the Vietnam War, and the majority of Americans were largely in denial over the messages sent through the previous summer's riots in underserved communities. Dismissive attitudes in elected officials neglected legislation designed to improve conditions for working class populations; revolutionary messages rang loudly in economically deprived, ethnic provinces; and subversive elements lurked on college campuses, threatening the social fabric of the national status quo.

The image of Newark took a quantum leap last week when Weequahic High School won the championship at the Watts Roundball Classic in Los Angeles. The Indians narrowly defeated the nation's third ranked team, Wilbur Cross from

New Haven, Connecticut, in the first game; then soundly whipped the second-ranked team, Fremont of Los Angeles; and finally, crushed America's top-ranked high school basketball team as polled by *Scholastic Magazine,* Schenley of Pittsburgh, for the title. From the stories being written by reporters in the cities that participated, the prevailing consensus is that the coaching job by Weequahic's legendary Mickey Marcus was nearly perfect. But if you think this story will be a rehash of another high school basketball victory, think again. The sports section of this newspaper has already detailed the game quite well. It is the back story that has become front page news.

The much-heralded junior star of Weequahic, Nehemiah Garvey, has been on a crusade to rescue Newark from the rebellion that left the city in ruins barely six months ago. Newark, along with New York, Los Angeles, Cleveland, and Detroit, are subjects of a nationwide report on urban disturbances commissioned by President Lyndon B. Johnson. Unlike those other cities, though, Newark is not large, if you count big businesses, eccentric celebrities, and major league sports teams within your zip codes as the definition of a sizeable place. One would think that Newark's prominence would be on a smaller scale, making Garvey's task seem improbable, if not impossible. But it didn't stop him.

Nehemiah's first task was to convince his coach to fight to keep his job at Weequahic. This was after a group of influential people in Newark tried to convince Marcus to resign, because white coaches at predominantly black high schools were becoming as popular as using the word "Negro" when referring to black people. But the coach stayed.

Garvey's next task was to help Marcus lobby the Newark City League officials, pushing them to allow member schools to schedule more out of town games in order for Newark to get more exposure.

It worked. In fact, several other school districts in New Jersey did the same thing and were successful in bringing more attention to their cities. Garvey has not been as successful in persuading students not to transfer from Weequahic, especially white pupils. But he has not given up.

Nehemiah's most sterling accomplishment thus far was during a black power debate in Los Angeles. Amir Jali, a nationally-known advocate of the theory of Pan Africanism and college professor there, organized a panel discussion entitled "Where Do We Go from Here?" The panel program was set to commence the day before the start of the tournament, in a community center not far from where the Watts Riot took place in 1965.

Garvey was invited to participate and he did just that, clearly stating his doubts about the motivation of the discussion's organizers. When he stood up to answer a question about the program's title, a contentious debate ensued between Jali and Garvey which caused the other panelists to leave, quietly and abruptly. Shortly after, the overflowing crowd followed.

The reporter from the *Los Angeles Times* wrote, "The young basketball star proved that he is nobody's dumb jock, especially in the arena of black activism, when he went toe-to-toe with a skillful, experienced debater like Jali."

A national magazine columnist opined that Garvey, "showed grit that few knew could come from a young Negro who lived in a small, impoverished hamlet such as Newark, New Jersey."

Though the story from the weekend before Christmas was the surprising performance of the Weequahic basketball team, what Nehemiah Garvey accomplished in less than an

hour at a local LA community center spoke volumes about
his desire to help Newark rise from the rebellion of 1967.
—Editorial from *The Star-Ledger*

Issues of *The Star-Ledger* were passed out at the morning pep rally before Weequahic's afternoon game against Vailsburg. The details of Nehemiah's confrontation with Amir Jali were also chronicled in a story by the newspaper's Ralph Edmondson.

"Ladies and gentlemen, please give me your attention." Max Steinberg, the principal of Weequahic, was addressing the student body and teachers in the school auditorium. "I think that all of you would agree with me that our basketball team has been busy over the holiday." The crowd yelled "Yes!"

"I think that you would also agree with me that because they beat the top three high schools in the country, way out in California, they should be the nation's top ranked team after this afternoon's game." The crowd again yelled "Yes!" The Weequahic cheerleaders ran into the facility with the team—led by Nehemiah—running behind them.

"My fellow students, are you ready for Weequahic to be number one in the country?" Nehemiah yelled from the microphone at the stage. The crowd began chanting, "Indians…Indians…Indians."

"So are we, so come on out this afternoon and cheer as loud as you can. Today's upcoming victory against Vailsburg will be number eleven on our road to the city, county and state championships. And number one in the United States of America!"

TWO BLACK MEN WALKED UP the steps of the renovated mansion where Lula Mae Eleazer's beauty parlor and beauty school were located. The address was the former home of a wealthy real estate mogul who owned large parcels of downtown Newark property.

"I can't believe this woman made us come here of all places to meet her," Herbert Evans said. "We could have met in my office. It's more professional."

"Herb, you're the one who wanted to meet, not her," Gene Oldham said. "She's a shrewd woman. She wanted to conduct this gathering on her terms. She likes control."

"Gene, you think I'm going to let a woman handle me? You can't be serious."

"Don't underestimate her. That would be a mistake."

The two college-educated, politically connected men reached the door and walked into the salon.

"Hello, gentlemen. Welcome to my establishment," Lula Mae said. "Lucille, please bring these men some coffee and danish."

"Thank you, Mrs. Eleazer," Evans said in an unfamiliar, syrupy tone. The sound of this unexpected voice surprised Oldham.

"No need to be so formal, Herbert. Especially when you don't mean it," Lula Mae said contemptuously.

"Now, Mrs. Eleazer, please don't treat me like a red-headed stepchild. I come in peace. I want to talk to you about your radical grandson."

"And you're coming in peace, to talk bad about my Nehemiah? I can't promise peace with your attitude about my little man, Herbert," Lula Mae said.

"Nehemiah embarrassed all of us out in LA, and it made national headlines," Evans said.

"Really, Herbert? Gene, is that your opinion?"

"Don't answer that, Gene. She's looking for someone to agree with her."

"I don't need no damn agreement, Herbert," Lula Mae said as she pointed her finger at Evans. "I am the daughter of a Baptist preacher who raised a proud family in the backwoods of South Carolina. My daddy compromised nothing in the face of great moral challenge from a group of shameless peckerwoods who hid behind the phony exterior of patriotism as they committed racist acts. He didn't need a partner then and taught me to walk on my own steam as long as I prayed for the Lord to light my path."

Both Oldham and Lucille began to chuckle.

"Excuse me, you two. My comments are not part of a comedy show," Lula Mae said. "If you want to stay in this room you need to act like wallpaper and just hang. Understand? Now, Herbert, what do you have to say about my courageous, intelligent grandson?"

Evans exhaled. "Uh, Nehemiah's actions at the panel discussion were consistent with a child. He was extremely disrespectful to a college professor who organized a forward-looking event intended to define the purpose of the disturbances of last summer."

"Is that your rehearsed way of saying that Nehemiah made a mistake in saying that man was wrong for using the title of Reverend King's book to name that meeting? And by the way, Herbert, Nehemiah is a teenager who is enrolled in all Advanced Placement high school courses. I think he is able to understand motivations."

"He should have been quiet until he was called upon to speak."

"You mean quiet like in, 'children should be seen and not heard'? Does that apply to women, too?"

"Well, that's why you have us! Men in position to make the right choices. Women can trust that we will do the right thing."

"Um, like the men in Congress made the right choice by failing to approve funding to help eliminate the rat problem in cities like Newark? Like the men in this city who made the right choice to misspend government money intended for neighborhood development? No, Herbert, children and women must be heard, and men must listen, for three good reasons. First, women brought men into this world. Second, we taught them how to communicate with this world; and third, women are powerful allies in helping adult men deal with this world.

"Children, boys and girls, are the future. And when people like you and Gene leave this world, these children have to be prepared to lead."

"You know I don't agree with you, right?"

"It doesn't make a difference, Herbert. But I would ask that you use your head for more than a hat rack. The simple fact is that Negroes need some fresh ideas. They can't come from people who are taking money from the political parties and selling us out. And the ideas can't come from people like that man in LA, who only wants to replace the old ideas with this black power nonsense. Young leaders like Nehemiah are smart enough to see through all of you, and that means they are a problem for you."

"So, that means you aren't going to stop your grandson from being so outspoken?"

"Not only will I not stop him; I am going to encourage him to continue. And I will organize people to work with him, including women. As Reverend King says in his book, *that's where we are going from here.*' Now, gentlemen, I have a busy day with my customers. We can talk another time."

"Mrs. Garvey, we need to talk right now," Oldham said. "I am sure my friend will be more respectful to you."

"Gene, neither you nor Herbert move me, nor do either of you groove me," Lula Mae said. "If the two of you and men like you were so instrumental to these government people in Trenton and Washington, there would be more women, *Negro* women, on these committees that are investigating the causes of riots. Instead of being corny ass, Negro men who keep talking loud and saying nothing, you should be training more young Negro boys to control their destinies by buying property and opening businesses. Herbert, you bore me with your slick ways."

"Gene, I'm tired of this woman talking to me like I'm some kind of fool." Evans started walking toward the door, but Oldham grabbed his arm.

"Herb, I think you are taking this more personally than you should."

"Let him go, Gene. He and I have nothing else to say to each other. But I will leave this thought with both of you... Proverbs thirteen sixteen says, 'all who are prudent act with knowledge, but fools expose their folly'. You two have a blessed day."

WHEN WEEQUAHIC HIGH SCHOOL opened in 1933, rumors had circulated that it was constructed to educate Jewish children whose families were moving from the Valley section of Newark, as African

American families left Newark's mostly black Central Ward in the late '40s to reside in the vicinity of South Side High School. Then history repeated itself in the mid-1960s as more African American students than ever before started attending Weequahic when the majority of elementary schools that fed the high school became predominantly black. Still, the Jewish alumni of Weequahic were reluctant to cut the umbilical cord to the school.

"Mickey, the perception is that Weequahic is a school for the Negro middle class," Max Steinberg, principal of Weequahic said. "Nehemiah Garvey's activism in his determination to save the reputation of Newark is driving that mindset. Many of my Jewish friends are not happy, especially those who graduated from Weequahic."

"Does that include you, Max?"

"I am a proud alumnus of Weequahic; so yes, it includes me."

"Nehemiah loves Newark, as I do. That's why neither of our families have left," Marcus said. "Eva Jean Garvey could have been like a lot of middle class people and left Newark many years ago. She could leave now. She certainly has the money to do so. And you know my family could be like so many of our friends and take off to the suburbs."

"Are you trying to say that Jewish people are running from Newark?"

"C'mon Max, when's the last time you had a Newark address?"

Steinberg turned his chair around to face the window in his office, looking away from Marcus.

"Max, I don't mean to impugn your integrity by saying you abandoned Newark for dubious reasons. I know you want to improve the lives of students here, but you can't deny that many of the white teachers at this school are only here for the paycheck."

"Mickey, that is a slanderous statement and it is beneath you."

"Just telling the truth, Max. Just telling the truth."

"I know I can't do anything to stop Nehemiah Garvey from his crusade. It has now gone nationwide. But I will tell you that I won't do anything to help him. Weequahic is not going to be like South Side;

I will make sure of that. And you better be careful in your support of what Nehemiah is doing."

"Or what, Max? I'll be called names like nigger lover? Why, because I hired a Negro as my assistant coach when many people wanted me to continue with a Jewish guy on the bench with me, a guy who a lot of Jewish people liked, but was too busy trying to get my job to be effective as junior varsity coach? Or because Nehemiah convinced some good Jewish players to come back to Weequahic and not play for Gottlieb at the Jewish Y? What's the problem, Max?"

"Mickey, I am only looking out for your good."

"I'm a big boy, Max. I don't need your help, unless it's to help me with getting these kids at Weequahic and other parts of Newark their high school diplomas, so they can receive good college educations and become productive members of society. That's always been my only goal. It still is. As for the name calling, it's been going on since the first Negro kid put on a Weequahic uniform, and I have lived with that. But I do know this. Winning cured all of that then, and it will again this time. Trust me."

Chapter 15

"The techniques included basically the techniques of the mafia and the concepts of the Black mafia, whereby a person's life is threatened if they did not carry out the work of the Student Non-Violent Coordinating Committee workers. Isolating H. Rap Brown and SNCC from the U.S. OEO operations is unquestionably called for. Rap Brown has given up on the American system and is opposed to it, and therefore anti-poverty people have no options except to regard him as on the opposite side."

~ Maurice Dawkins, Associate Director for Civil Rights of the Office of Economic Opportunity, on including Black Power groups to receive funding to develop neighborhood programs in urban areas, in 1967

The term 'Uncle Tom' became more prevalent in the mid to late 1960s than during any other time in the history of the United States. It was used to describe African Americans who did not agree with all tenets of the Black Power ideology during that era. Ironically, the term allegedly came from the book, *Uncle Tom's Cabin*, written by Harriet Beecher Stowe in 1852 and widely credited with strengthening the fight to abolish slavery. In fact, it was reported that when President Abraham Lincoln met Stowe just after the start of the Civil War, he said to her, "So this is the little lady who started this great war."

THE *SCHOLASTIC MAGAZINE* NATIONAL rankings for high school basketball were released two weeks after the holidays. Weequahic had won three games since that time, giving the team an undefeated record in thirteen games, which included wins over the three top teams in the rankings at the end of 1967.

"Nee, you have a phone call," Nehemiah's eight-year old cousin Denise yelled out. Nehemiah ran to her and grabbed the receiver before she could say anything else.

"Stop bein' so loud, girl," Nehemiah said.

"I just wanted to tell you it's that girl who calls all the time and won't leave a message."

"Okay, I got it. Now go somewhere else so I can talk in private."

"Private? What do you have to say on the telephone that's so private?" Eva Jean had just walked into the living room. "It must be a girl."

"Yeah, Auntie Eva Jean. It's that girl who always calls him."

"The girl in my history class who I've been studyin' with."

"Hmm, I'm wondering about that. You know Mr. Frazier and I have talked about that girl from Roselle. Is that her?"

"Uh, not really. Yeah, he told me about it. Can I finish talkin' and then we can talk about that?"

"I'll let you decide when you want to talk to me about her. You're a man and I trust you to make up your mind." Eva Jean left the room, shaking her head.

"Haven't heard from you in a while, Miss Johnson. You callin' to laugh at me about the ranking?" Nehemiah said to Cheryl.

"I heard about Weequahic not making the top ten, and Camden is number seven. Sorry about that."

"Doesn't make any difference. We can beat Camden like we did the last two years in the state championship. Them bein' in the top ten is no big deal. We will be state champs again and then number one in the country will be within our reach."

"Nehemiah, Weequahic had a great team the past two years, that's why you beat Camden. But this year, they've been beatin' good teams and by a lot of points. Weequahic has been inconsistent and lucky. Sure, you beat the top ranked teams in the country out in LA, but you played lousy against sorry teams around here. Y'all barely beat Vailsburg and East Side the last two weeks and both of them only won two games apiece this season. That's probably why Weequahic isn't ranked."

"You sure know a lot about this high school basketball stuff. Why would a college girl pay so much attention to high school sports?"

"I need to know about it because my child's father is involved." Nehemiah suddenly gripped the phone until his knuckles nearly turned white.

"You got a baby? Is it somebody's in Roselle?"

"No, I don't have a baby now, but I'm pregnant, and it's by someone you know."

"Somebody I know? Oh no, you and Mr. Frazier? I know he's been talkin' about my involvement with you, but I hope he wouldn't mess around with somebody your age." Cheryl started laughing.

"Nehemiah, I haven't had my period since the two of us were together before you went to LA."

"What?"

"Yep. You are going to be a daddy."

"Get outta here. Are you sure it's mine?"

"Yes, I know. And you'll know in about seven months. Are you really serious about that question? Of course, it's you. Oh, I guess you're worried about your so-called reputation in Newark, especially when your name has been in newspapers across the country. Are you concerned about what the people in your high and mighty church might say?"

"C'mon Cheryl. That's not what I'm thinkin'. I'm tryin' to figure out what I'm gonna do."

"Nehemiah, you don't have to do anything. You can be just like your father and walk away."

"Wait a minute. This has nothin' to do with my father. Plus, nobody knows what happened to him."

"Oh yes we do. Is he at home with you? Is he sleeping with your mother every night? Is he paying any bills for your family? Hell no!"

"What's wrong with you, Cheryl? I'm only tryin' to get over the shock of what's happenin'. You just laid some heavy stuff on me."

"Alright, while you get over the shock, little boy, I'll just deal with vomiting every morning, the headaches all day, and wondering what I'm going to tell my parents in the next three weeks. I don't have time for juvenile delinquents from Newark. I gotta go."

"Wait a minute," Nehemiah said, but he heard her telephone slam down.

1968 WAS ONLY A MONTH OLD when many in the United States witnessed the Tet Offensive on television. It was the largest campaign of the Vietnam War, waged by the forces of the Viet Cong and the North Vietnamese People's Army of Vietnam against the armies of South Vietnam, the United States, and its allies. The siege came after the U.S. public was told by the Johnson administration that the enemy was not capable of launching such a massive effort, which caused the loss of many key cities and towns to North Vietnam.

Meanwhile, elected officials in the U.S. House of Representatives and Senate practically ignored legislation focused on improving housing conditions and strengthening the Equal Employment Opportunity Commission. This was in spite of President Johnson's plan to highlight protection of federal rights, jury trials, and fair housing in his State of the Union speech.

"One year ago, on this very date, *The Star-Ledger* reported about the progress in Newark, predicting where the city could be in the year 1985," Reverend Wade said during a Sunday service at First Samuel Missionary Baptist Church. "This was according to the prognosticators, those who prophesy and predict the future. Though many middle-class Negro families are expected to be moving from Newark into the Essex County suburbs over the next ten years, the anticipated growing economy and ease of transportation is expected to bring others to Newark. Well, we all know where we stand today," Wade said as he moved from side to side at the pulpit.

Silence from the largely black congregation intersected with the pastor's rhetoric.

"My sisters and brothers, as of this moment we are in dire straits. A mere five days in July brought the issues of disrepair, despair, and disgust to a blinding light, and the whole world was a witness. Add to that a total lack of will by our leaders in the nation's capital to do anything tangible. They seem either incapable, or uninterested in seizing an opportunity to foster dramatic change.

"The Senate dragged its feet to place Thurgood Marshall on the Supreme Court; the House of Representatives is cutting dollars for urban initiatives, and wasting time battling with Adam Clayton Powell over the right to represent his Harlem district in Congress; and President Johnson is spending precious tax dollars from hard working Americans to wage a war that is killing our young men in record numbers. Even Reverend Martin Luther King is becoming frustrated, organizing a civil disobedience campaign with more than three thousand demonstrators across the country. Here in Newark we have factions disputing whether to work with those who want to be our friends, or to slap the hand of friendship and segregate within our ranks.

"But, there is good news," Wade said with a distinguishable lift in his voice. "Our level-headed brethren in New Jersey have negotiated with the State Assembly to pass a resolution to include Negro history in our public schools." The audience cheered and Amens rang through the sanctuary. "That is truly great news, because those who don't know their history are doomed to repeat it. And here's some more encouraging news... there are white preachers in our state who are heeding the call to be more active in the fight for civil rights, even risking their positions at their home churches. I know I sounded a tone of pessimism a few minutes ago, but I am encouraged. Psalm 46:10 says, 'Be still and know that I am God. I will be exalted among the nations. I will be exalted in the earth.' No matter what man wants, this is still God's earth and it will be fortified," Wade said, exciting the congregation. Hundreds stood and applauded loudly for close to a minute.

"God is great, and He is worthy to be praised," Wade said. Then he invited those who wanted to join the church to come to the altar.

Wade gave the benediction and much of the large crowd began to leave the church.

"Thank you, Pastor. We needed that word this morning," one attendee said while shaking Reverend Wade's hand. Others stood in line to talk to him.

"I noticed you were moved by the pastor's sermon," Eva Mae Garvey said to her son as they were preparing to leave the church. "Do you want to say something to Reverend Wade?"

"Yes, ma'am. You can go home without me."

"You know we have dinner at your grandmother's and you know she doesn't like latecomers."

"I know," Nehemiah said as he hastily moved to the front of the church. "I'll be on time." He got to the back of the line waiting to speak with Reverend Wade.

"Ah, my hero, Nehemiah Garvey," Wade said as he gripped Nehemiah's hand. Nehemiah's response was tepid.

"Nehemiah, that is not the handshake of a confident man. Something is troubling you."

"Can we talk in your office?"

"Certainly. Just wait until I finish speaking to these other people, alright?" Nehemiah stepped to the side. Lena Ashby walked up.

"Hi Nee. My father and brother are gonna be watchin' the Celtics and the Lakers later on. You wanna come over?"

"I don't know. I'll be at my grandmother's house for dinner, and then I have some homework. I'll see how much time I have after that."

"You're gonna miss watching the Lakers and the Celtics with my brother? Are you okay, Nee? You look worried."

"I'm going through some changes. Nothin' I can't work out by myself. I'll be alright. Thanks for askin'.

"You know you are one of my best friends and you can talk to me about anything. Okay?" Nehemiah nodded as Lena walked away.

"We can go to my office now," Reverend Wade said. Nehemiah's walk from the sanctuary was slow and unsteady, almost as if he was under the influence of drugs or alcohol. His condition did not go unnoticed. "Are you high, young man?" Wade asked.

Nehemiah stumbled into the pastor's office, fell on the floor, and started to cry.

"My God, what is wrong, son?"

"I didn't mean to do it, Reverend Wade. I didn't mean to do it."

Wade helped Nehemiah to his feet. "Come, sit on the couch. I'll get you a glass of water."

"I should have listened to my mother, and to Mr. Frazier. They both knew what they were talkin' about. I should have listened."

Wade gave Nehemiah the glass of water and then sat next to him on the couch.

"Let's talk, young man. What is going on in your life that has brought you to tears?"

"I got a girl…pregnant," Nehemiah confided.

Wade's eyes looked around the room and then settled their gaze on the trembling young man.

"It isn't Lena Ashby, is it?"

"Oh, no," Nehemiah answered in a snap. "Absolutely not."

"Good. Do I know the young lady?"

"I don't believe so, but then again, you know a lot of people. Her name is Cheryl Johnson. She's from Roselle. She's in college. Her father is a lawyer. I think he works on Wall Street."

"I don't know her, but I do know her father and I know their pastor. Her father is heavily involved in civil rights in the state. He's a board member of the New Jersey NAACP. Now, tell me. Are you sure you're the one who got her pregnant?"

Tears began to form again in Nehemiah's eyes.

"We had sex several times without any protection. She told me that her period is late and she's been vomitin' a lot, and havin' a lotta headaches."

"First, you need to stop crying. Men don't cry. You lay down with a woman and now there's a possibility that a life will be brought into this world as a result. I share some of the responsibility for this."

"You? Why?"

"Because I promised your father that I would watch over you if something was to happen to him. And if what you're telling me is true, I let him down. I really let him down. But I'll take it from here."

"Do you have to tell my mother and grandmother?"

"Yes, they will have to know, Nehemiah—if you indeed are the father."

"Reverend Wade, I am truly sorry. I keep asking God for forgiveness."

"Nehemiah, you are in the public eye now, and many people will be looking to tear you down. I am not saying this is necessarily the case with this young lady, but anything can happen. I will ask the Lord to guide me and I pray that I will get the information I need to help you."

"Can you tell me what you're gonna do? I don't know what to do. She was pretty angry when we talked on the phone."

"Don't worry about what I am going to do. You keep working hard in the classroom and doing a great job on the basketball court. Give me your hand, son. You know about Job and his great trials. Here's what he said to one of his friends, who said God was angry with him. 'But if I go to the east, He is not there; if I go to the west, I do not find Him. When He is at work in the north, I do not see Him; when He turns to the south, I catch no glimpse of Him. But He knows the way that I take; when He has tested me, I will come forth as gold. My feet have closely followed His steps; I have kept to His way without turning aside. I have not departed from the commands of His lips; I have treasured the words of His mouth more than my daily bread.'

"Don't stop praying to God and praising Jesus Christ. You might not believe me right now, but God is with you. Hebrews fourteen six says 'Let us therefore come boldly unto the throne of grace, that we may obtain mercy, and find grace to help in time of need.' "There is an old poem that was sung by the old saints as a hymn," Wade said. "Please listen to these words.

'Lead kindly light, amid the encircling gloom, lead me on! The night is dark, and I am far from home, lead me on! Keep thou feet, I do not ask to see the distant scene, one step enough for me.'" Nehemiah began to cry again as Wade finished singing.

"Go ahead and let your tears flow, my son. There is a reason for this, but only God knows what that reason is. Please stay prayed up. We have a big mountain to climb."

Chapter 16

"We need to be thinking about ways to organize votes and strategies to help ourselves at the city and state level. Young Negroes are tired of political hand-me-downs, behind the scenes compromising and begging for a few appointments. They want politics to produce the action that demonstrations do. Too much of our strength is diluted by organizations waging campaigns to register and then use the Negro vote for their own interest—labor, industry and individual political parties. We must harness our own voting power and use it to elevate ourselves."

~ CLARENCE TOWNES, SPECIAL ASSISTANT, REPUBLICAN
NATIONAL COMMITTEE, AT A NEGRO ELECTED
OFFICIALS CONFERENCE IN CHICAGO, IN 1967

INACTION BY HIGH-LEVEL Democratic lawmakers in Washington, D.C. left legislation affecting urban areas sorely lacking. This gave license to many prominent blacks to seriously consider supporting Republicans during the 1968 presidential election year. While Robert Kennedy, Eugene McCarthy, and Vice-President Hubert Humphrey took the tried and true Democratic Party path in campaigning heavily in black neighborhoods, Republicans Richard Nixon and New York Governor, Nelson Rockefeller, were treated cordially by many black Democrats in their quests to win support for their campaigns. African Americans were registering as Republicans in similar numbers as what occurred after the Civil War and during Reconstruction.

At the same time, Dr. Martin Luther King Jr. and the Southern Christian Leadership Conference ignored protests from the National Association for the Advancement of Colored People (NAACP), the National Urban League, President Johnson, and the leaders in the Democratic National Committee, as they planned the Poor People's March on Washington, scheduled for mid-April 1968. The march was designed to disrupt activity in the nation's capital in order to bring attention to the plight of America's underserved communities.

One major finding in the report of the President's Commission on Civil Disorders, was that the cities of New Orleans, Richmond (Virginia), Baltimore, Gary, Cleveland, Jacksonville (Florida), St. Louis, Detroit, Oakland, Philadelphia, and Chicago would have predominantly black populations by 1984, much like Newark and Washington, DC already had.

NEHEMIAH AND TWO OF HIS friends were sitting on his porch after playing basketball in the Peshine Avenue School gym.

"Nee, I don't know nobody in this neighborhood that reads as much as you," Jimmy Trawick said.

"Yeah, man, I remember you used to go to the library almost every day when we were in elementary school," Danny Clark said. "Your mother made me go with you because she didn't want anything to happen to you on the way."

Nehemiah held up a copy of *Jet* magazine. "My father started readin' this from the first day it was published, which was November 1, 1951. He said God gave me this gift when I was born."

"My parents won't let me read *Jet*, *Ebony*, or any of those black magazines," Trawick said. "I have to come over your house to read 'em."

"My father keeps them in his barber shop. He calls *Jet* the Negro authority. He won't allow any white magazines in the shop," Clark said.

"Look, where else will you find out what Reverend Martin Luther King and Stokely Carmichael talked about after the riots? What about the blacks that are joinin' the Republican Party?" Nehemiah said. "Right there in *Jet*."

"What about it, Jew lover?" a voice said from across the street. It was Michael Herring, the tough guy high school dropout who had recently served time at Jamesburg, the New Jersey State Home for Boys. "Your father was one of those Republicans supportin' that no-good Nixon, wasn't he?"

"Nee, don't get into it with him," Clark said. Herring approached the porch with three of his friends in tow.

"Shut up, nigger," Herring said, "ain't nobody talkin' to you."

"Danny is sittin' on my porch and he can say whatever he wants," Nehemiah bellowed.

"Oh, the high school basketball star playin' for Jew-boy Mickey Marcus, who is rippin' off our people, Uncle Tom can talk," Herring said. He and Nehemiah had almost come to blows when Michael came home from Jamesburg right after the riot. "Whatcha have to say, motherfucka'?"

Nehemiah stepped off the porch to confront Michael. "I guess we're back to where we were last summer. I'm just as ready to deal with you now as I was then."

Herring began to take off his trench coat and leather snap cap, only leaving on his expensive, multi-colored Alpaca sweater and finely creased mohair pants. He wore a pair of black alligator skin shoes.

"Man, I'm not even gonna take off my sweater and shoes to kick your ass, nigger. Alright, throw up your hands."

As Nehemiah was taking off his Navy pea coat, Michael rushed him, taking a swing at his head. Nehemiah ducked and backed up while getting out of his coat. Trawick and Clark laughed.

"Uh huh, tried to cold cock my boy and he slipped it," Clark yelled. "Yeah!"

Nehemiah, the taller and bigger of the two, walked up on Herring and landed two punches to his head, knocking the older boy to the ground. At that point one of Herring's friends pulled a machete knife from under his coat.

"Oh, hell no you won't," William Fore yelled as he ran toward the melee. Fore, whose nickname was Billy Boy, was one of the older boys in the Peshine neighborhood. He was brandishing a large wooden baseball bat. "If you swing that at Nehemiah, I'll drop you like a bad habit, boy." Everybody practically froze in their tracks, as if on cue from the director of a movie.

"Whatcha doin' Billy? You one of the original Condors. I can't believe you comin' to this punk nigger's side. He ain't nothin' but a Uncle Tom, sellin' out to white boys," Herring said.

"I don't mind a fair fight, but your boy was gonna cut my man when he had his back turned," Fore said. "Can't have that. That's a punk move. If you fight him man to man, I'm solid with that. It ain't gonna happen otherwise."

"Ah, man, I ain't got time to fight this nigger. C'mon boys, let's chalk this up," Herring said as he put on his coat and cap. "Hey, Jew lover, this won't be the last time you see me." The three boys walked down the street without looking back.

"Thanks, Billy Boy," Nehemiah said. "You saved my life."

"Yeah man, if that dude had hit Nee's neck with that machete, he would have bled to death," Clark said. "Yeah, Billy Boy. Gimme some skin!"

Fore pushed Clark's hand away, and then angrily grabbed Nehemiah by his coat collar.

"What in the hell is wrong with you, man? Why would you stoop to fightin' that hoodlum? He ain't got nothin' to lose and you ain't got nothin' to win."

"I ain't no punk."

"I know that, you know that, everybody that knows you knows that," Fore said. "Nee, a lot of people are tryin' to tear you down because you are doing somethin' that a lot of them don't want to happen. You are keepin' the spotlight on Newark while there are some people that wanna do their stuff in the dark and rip Newark off while nobody's watchin'. That goes for whites and blacks alike."

"Billy Boy is right, Nee," Trawick said.

"Nee, you are a carbon copy of your father. He was a smart man, way ahead of his time when it came to controllin' his destiny," Fore said. "He bought property, opened the restaurant, and was drawin' up plans to open a bank on Bergen Street, which would have helped people in this community get loans to buy their own homes and start businesses. Then, all of a sudden, he was gone. Disappeared into thin air. Now, we need someone to continue that momentum and that person could be you. But not if you get in the gutter with somebody like Michael Herring."

"You really think I'm like my father? How?"

"He had a deep love for Newark, like you do. He had an intense love for God and His son, Jesus Christ. But most of all, he was workin' the plan by organizin' people around this area and committin' to his church. I've been watchin' what you been doin' with the basketball team, and the good things you're doin' at First Samuel. Just like him."

"What was Michael talkin' about you and the Condors?" Clark said. "I thought they were a gang."

"We were back then, but Mr. Garvey turned us around after we almost had a gang war with the Aztecs. Most of our members came from Peshine, while they got their members from Bergen Street School, Clinton Place Junior High, Avon Avenue School and Belmont-Runyon School. They fought the Paragons, who mainly came from Hawthorne Avenue School, in a fight around Hawthorne Avenue and Osborne Terrace. After the Aztecs won the battle, they brought the Paragons into their ranks, and they were comin' our way to take us over. We were tryin' to get some more members so we could hold off the Aztecs, but everybody thought we were tough enough for the Aztecs, even if they had the Paragons so they wouldn't join us. Remember that Saturday when the gang war was supposed to happen?"

"Yeah, I remember that. I was in the eighth grade. I was playin' the pinball machine at Mickey's and Ruth's candy store when I heard you talkin' about gettin' ready for the fight," Nehemiah said. "Man, a lot of us little guys were scared to come outside that day."

"Well, every night that week before the big fight, I was plannin' the strategy with the other Condors while working. Then one night, when your father came in for a loaf of bread and his copy of the *New York Daily News*, he overheard our conversation. After they left, he pulled me aside and told me to get the Condors together and meet at his restaurant the next day."

"What did he talk about? Did he yell at y'all?"

"Nope. When we got there, he had the Aztecs, the Paragons, the Tip Tops from the Central Ward, and the Undertakers from the Valley around South Side in his office. Mr. Garvey was really cool with his conversation, and he gave us hamburgers and French fries. He talked about the problems in Newark, how the politicians were not really workin' to help the community, and how we young guys were wastin' our time tryin' to be tough. Instead, he said we had to make a plan for changin' Newark, because Newark would be changin' one day. That was in the Spring of '65. He disappeared that summer. But he gave us somethin' to think about. I was in the eleventh grade then and I got the message. I decided that I would commit to excellence after that. No more membership in a gang, no more fightin' in the streets. If you remember, there was no gang war on that Saturday."

"What does that have to do with what happened tonight?"

"You don't need to get involved with people that ain't goin' nowhere, like Michael Herring. Nee, you're a future leader of Newark and you need to stay clean so nobody can keep you from makin' progress. Look, I graduated from Weequahic last year and I had the chance to go to a lot of colleges away from here. I decided to stay and go to Rutgers in Newark. By goin' to school every day and comin' home in the afternoon I don't spend money to live on campus, and I don't need a car to travel to classes. I still have my job at the store, I'm savin' money, and I know what's happenin' in Newark. I want to get my name known around here because I'm gonna be a leader in this city. Newark is ripe for guys like us and I want your help with leading this city in the future. I can't count on you if you're in the youth house or down in Jamesburg, or worse, Rahway State Prison."

Nehemiah dropped his eyes to the ground. "What about if we have some personal problems?"

"Nee, there is no problem too big for God. King David had some serious issues, but his heart for God was pure. Each time he messed up, he confessed his sin and asked the Lord for forgiveness. God is always available for His children. That means you."

"I wanna talk to you some more about my father's vision and what he wanted to do for Newark. And I want to thank you again for savin' my life tonight."

"No problem, man. We'll talk about that real soon. And guys, avoid people like that damn Michael Herring. God told me to tell you that."

It was a quiet Saturday morning in northern New Jersey. A light February snow left a pretty white mist under the sunny sky. Mickey Marcus and Caleb Frazier were sitting at a booth in a Montclair diner.

"Well, Caleb, Nehemiah's mission is starting to take place. Newark is getting recognition across the country, and I got the national rankings early this morning," Marcus said.

"You mean to tell me you couldn't call me to give me the good news before we got here?"

"How do you know it's good news?"

"Because I got a call about the rankings last night, and I know it's good news."

"So, you know that we're tenth in the country?"

"I sure do. And I also know that Camden is number five and undefeated, just like us. We're on a collision course for another state matchup."

"Caleb, let's not get ahead of ourselves. We still have to meet South Side, West Side, and Central before the county tournament, and we might face either in the tournament. And we could even meet Central in the state tournament, like we have the past two years."

"Mickey, I know you are always cautious around this time of the year, but why do I think there are other things on your mind?"

"I was thinking about when we really got to know each other. Do you remember?

"I had been at Weequahic for two years before we actually met outside of school. You invited me to watch Texas Western play Kentucky for the NCAA title at your home. It was the first time an all-Negro starting lineup won the national championship. What made you remember that?"

"You practically talked through the whole game, but it didn't bother me because I was amazed at your grasp of basketball strategy. It was almost as if you had written the game plan for Texas Western."

Frazier started laughing. "You were so happy for Texas Western at the end of the game that you cried. But you know what, man? I got to know a lot about your soul that day. When Leon Stone told me about you, I thought you were just one of those fake white guys who used Negro boys to win and then forgot about them when they left school, with or without a diploma. But our conversation during that game told me something different. Even so, that isn't what's on your mind now. What's going on, man?"

Marcus looked out the window next to the booth as he continued to speak.

"You know, I love to hear preachers talk about being faithful to God, even when you get a bad report. There's something good about that kind of optimism, and it's quite refreshing."

"What are you talking about, Mickey? You're a preacher now?"

"I just wanted to get that off my chest, but the report thing was on my mind and I had to say it." Marcus began rubbing his face.

"What report, Mickey?"

"A bad report, I have a bad report."

"A bad report? What, did you just check your credit score? You're too rich to have bad credit."

"Caleb, I have cancer."

Frazier stopped drinking his coffee, mid-sip. "Cancer? You, really?"

"Yeah, me, Mickey Marcus, with colon cancer. I shouldn't be surprised because both my father and grandfather died from cancer. I'm not dying, but I'll have to alter my schedule with the team. According to my doctor, I have to make some changes."

"Oh, we can work that out. I can always finish up the practices after you spend an hour or so with the team on what you expect from game to game."

"Caleb, it won't be that simple. I have been advised to stop coaching right away because the treatments will be extremely intensive and I need as much rest as I can get. You are going to have to take the team the rest of the way."

"You can't be serious, Mickey."

"I wish I weren't, but I'm real serious. You are going to have to be head coach of the Weequahic basketball team."

"The school that didn't even want me to be your assistant three years ago, is now going to accept me as head coach? Hell, the principal barely speaks to me and now he's going to trust me with the nation's tenth-ranked high school basketball team? Me, a Negro, taking the place of the great Mickey Marcus? This is unbelievable."

"Slow down, Caleb. I've just been incredibly lucky. Now listen to me, and hear this. You are the only person I can trust with these boys. They know you are loyal; you showed that when you didn't leave to take another job when many people in the city wanted more Negro high school basketball coaches. I've seen your instincts and know you make good decisions. You earned my trust during your first year, when you coached the junior varsity team to the county championship."

"When do we meet with the principal to discuss me coaching the team?"

"Caleb, the team is yours already. That's *my* decision."

"Never in my wildest dream could I have imagined the storied Weequahic High School with an ordinary Negro as head basketball coach."

"You're not ordinary, Caleb. You're highly qualified. Both as a coach and as a man."

Chapter 17

"I do not believe the urban disturbances to be part of a conspiracy. I think them to be rebellions brought on by social and economic ills."

~ U.S. Senator Edward Brooke (Republican-Massachusetts),
as member of President Lyndon B. Johnson's
Commission on Civil Disorders, in 1967

Esquire magazine published a story by reporter, Gary Wills, in 1968, which said, "The second Civil War is not a possibility, but a present reality. Anyone who denies that is certainly not telling it like it is." The article contained interviews with police officials across the country, officers from the National Guard and the U.S. Army, and black and white radicals. As expected, the discourse about whether or not the uprisings during the mid-1960s—Harlem, New York (1964), Rochester, New York (1964), Philadelphia (1964), Watts, Los Angeles (1965), Cleveland (1966), Division Street Chicago (1966), Omaha (1966), Detroit (1967), Newark (1967), Plainfield, NJ (1967), Minneapolis (1967), Tampa (1967)—should have been defined as rebellions, rather than riots, was more than a casual discussion.

"This was an incredible waste of time," Herbert Evans said while sitting with two other Newarkers at a luncheon. They were attending a meeting of New Jersey political activists to discuss electing more African

Americans in Newark. Though the meeting was bi-partisan, there were far more Democrats than Republicans present.

"These people are somewhere in outer space," former New Jersey Assemblyman, Perry Williamson, said to Evans. "Whoever came up with the idea of this meeting is living in the past. The rumors about President Johnson not runnin' this year are real, so what happens after that? Do they think those racist Democrats in the South care about them? And I hope they ain't countin' on Republicans! That damn Nixon is talkin' about a Southern strategy and you know where that puts us Negroes. Heaven help us if he gets into the White House."

Gene Oldham raised his fork and began waving it like an orchestra conductor. "Brothers, you're missing the big picture," Oldham said.

"Oh hell, here comes the 'it's the strategy' lecture," Evans said. "Man, you West Indian Negroes are somethin' else. Are you the ghost of Sam Garvey?"

"Let me make this clear; I consider being compared to Sam Garvey a compliment. But Herbert, listen to me. We could place ourselves in several camps if we talk with some of the people here. After this event, we begin meeting with the Democrats, Republicans, the churches, even the black power groups," Oldham said. "Some of us meet by day with various groups of white folks, then compare notes from those meetings with each other at night. Yes, I learned that strategy from Sam Garvey."

"That's probably what got that fool killed, tryin' to play too many games," Evans said.

"I don't know about you two, but I plan to keep the Democrats on the defensive by making them think I have a group of Negroes who are going to be Republicans," Williamson said. "I already have the leaders of the New Jersey Democratic Party worried about us."

Evans laughed. "In your dreams, Perry. They already showed you they don't care about you and your group because they haven't given you the money you wanted to deliver the Negro vote."

"So, what are you gonna do, Herbert?"

I'm gonna do like my man, Adam Clayton Powell. I'm gonna keep the faith, baby."

PRACTICE WAS TOUGH AS Weequahic was gearing up to play in the Essex County Tournament. As the top seed, the Indians were picked to win the twelve-team encounter for the fifth year in a row. Though the team was energetic physically, the emotional mood remained subdued without the man who had led Weequahic basketball for the last nineteen years.

"Alright guys, this was a good one. Are we ready for Bloomfield?" Nehemiah pumped his fist in the air after practice, speaking about Bloomfield High School, who they would be playing in the first game. "We've been playin' without Mr. Marcus, and Mr. Frazier has led us to four more victories so far. Now we are unbeaten in eighteen games and ranked number ten in the country."

"Hip hip, hooray! Hip hip, hooray! Hip hip, hooray!" the players yelled, led by Billy Stern.

"Thank you, boys; thank you," Frazier said. "I want to let you know that I appreciate the cooperation from all of you during this difficult time. We all miss Mr. Marcus in the flesh, but his spirit is with us at every practice and every game. Now, just like he would tell you, go home, get your homework done if you have any, get a good night's sleep, and make sure you get to school early tomorrow for study hall before homeroom."

"IS NEHEMIAH COMING straight home, Auntie Eva Jean?" Denise asked.

"He normally comes home right after practice. Why? Do you need him?"

"I just wanted to ask him about something in my spelling book, but it can wait."

Reverend Wade was in the living room at Eva Jean's home.

"That little girl is really growing up, Lula Mae. It seems like yesterday when her parents were killed, and she came to live with you."

"That was a tough time for all us. But the Lord has been our fortress. Eva Jean realized it was best to let her come live here so she could go to Peshine. It's one of the best elementary schools in Newark and she's doing well there."

"Lula Mae, I know your heart is heavy over what is going on with Nehemiah," Wade said. Just as he completed his sentence, Nehemiah walked into the house.

"Hi everybody. Good evenin', Reverend Wade. I thought I saw your car. Hey Ma, I smell smothered steak and collard greens."

"Your dinner is on the table," Eva Jean said while wiping her hands on her apron. She kissed Nehemiah on his cheek. "When you finish, come into the living room, okay, honey?"

"Yes ma'am. Are you okay, Ma?"

Eva Jean wiped a tear from her face. "I'm fine, son. My heart is just a little heavy right now, but the Lord is the stronghold of my life."

"Of whom shall I be afraid?" her son replied with a broad smile. Eva Jean turned and walked into the living room.

As she re-entered, Wade said, "I am surprised at the father's attitude," Wade said to Lula Mae.

"Is this blackmail, Reverend Wade?" Eva Jean said as she sat down on the sofa next to her mother.

"It sure is and he should be ashamed of himself," Lula Mae said. "I am glad you talked to him and not me, because I would have…"

"Now Lula Mae, that is not the spirit in which we need to proceed," Wade interrupted.

"I should have stopped this as soon as I heard about it," Eva Jean said. "This is when I wish that Sam was here with me. He would have an answer."

"The Lord will take care of this. He's already told me," Wade said.

Nehemiah walked in. "I'm done, Ma, and I washed the dishes. Can I join this conversation?"

"Certainly, young man," Wade said. "I'm sure you know what we're talking about."

"Yes, I do."

Lula Mae spoke up. "We are not here to condemn you, baby. We just want to let you know that we will respect any decision you make about your future as a father. If you need help as you go along, all of us will be there for you."

Nehemiah continued to stand, clasping his hands behind his back. "I ask all of you to forgive me for placin' you in this position. I did somethin' that I should have given more thought."

"Nehemiah, no one is immune from making mistakes," Wade said. "We will be in deep prayer about this in the weeks ahead, but for right now, the recent development is that Cheryl's father has asked for money."

"And he will not get any from this family, not from one member anywhere," Lula Mae said, waving her hand high into the air. "He is using his daughter's situation to get paid. That is wrong. Pastor, what is his minister saying?"

"Unfortunately, their minister is not taking a position on this."

"The father is probably a heavy tither and the minister doesn't want to rock the boat," Eva Jean said.

Wade breathed deeply. "He's a deacon, been one for nearly twenty-five years; so, you know he's a prominent member. I told the minister that I will deal with the father directly. I will not allow that man to try to hold this family hostage over this situation."

"Reverend Wade, this is my responsibility and I should be held accountable," Nehemiah said.

"Son, your father asked me on more than one occasion that if anything happened to him, would I be there to stand in the gap. You know, it is interesting. Samuel came to me when you were pregnant with this young man," Wade said to Eva Jean as he reached over to hold her hand, "and he asked me to choose a name for your child. When I immediately said Nehemiah, Samuel asked me why. I told him that this child will be a builder, one who will complete a mission set forth by God, a child who will be responsible for building a legacy. The meaning of Nehemiah is comforted by Yahweh.

"In the Bible, Nehemiah was chosen by the Persian King Artaxerxes to help rebuild the walls of Jerusalem. What many people overlook in reading the Scripture is that Nehemiah prayed to God for the assignment, and God made it happen through the king. It was met with great opposition. Does any of this sound familiar?"

"That God chose me to help rebuild Newark?"

Wade shouted, "My God, my God! Thank You for revealing Yourself to this child!" He began to pray. "Thank You for preparing him through the trial facing him at this moment. Oh Lord, please cover him with a hedge of protection, and shower him with Your grace and mercy as he accepts a challenge many men have walked away from with due haste. Jesus, I know You are interceding on Nehemiah's behalf, and I know he will be delivered with great deliberation. Please, God, give this family strength and understanding that only You can provide during this dark time. I ask all this, in the mighty name of Jesus Christ, Amen!"

Denise joined the family and Wade in the middle of the living room as they wrapped their arms around each other. Eva Jean held Nehemiah tightly and gently kissed him on his cheek.

"I've been reading a lot about Newark lately," one of Amir Jali's associates said at a black power strategy meeting in Los Angeles.

Jali peered over his horn-rimmed eyeglasses. "I have as well. I started with confidence that our group there was on board with our master plan, but now they seem to be going in a different direction. They have some high-powered personalities in that tiny place."

"It might be a small city in size, but Newark has a lotta heart. There are some tough brothers and sisters in that city. We're seeing it with the Nehemiah Garvey kid.

"Brother Abasi Chaga is on trial for his actions during the rebellion last summer. He was arrested for illegal possession of a gun. His defense is that the police beat him up and they planted the weapon on him, but they also said he assaulted four cops and resisted arrest. The brother is barely five-foot-two and probably weighs only a hundred pounds soaking wet. How could he beat up four cops?

"There are some brothers from Chicago and Detroit in Newark to watch the court proceedings, so we'll know what to do when we face similar trials in other parts of the country. This is worth watching."

Jali laughed. "That New York Jew-boy lawyer who's working for him is giving the prosecutors a rough time. Yeah, Abasi, that's my man… Now, back to what Newark is doing. Did I hear right, that they're talking about aligning their efforts with Puerto Rican activists to take over the politics in City Hall?"

"That's the rumor. I understand that they are organizing some kind of conference to start the process of choosing candidates for the next city election. And my understanding is that they don't want any outsiders involved."

"Typical Newark, nativist attitude, 'we can do this by ourselves'. I'm not surprised."

"Speaking of outsiders, what happened with that college girl in New Jersey who is supposed to be with our organization?"

Jalil leaned back in his chair and stretched his legs. "Funny you should ask. I haven't heard from her since the holidays. I called her dormitory and was told they would give her my message when she returned. So far, no call. The group she was organizing has not sent a report, either."

"You don't think she's working with the Newark crowd, do you?"

"Nah, she's from Roselle, not Newark. She would be considered an intruder. There's got to be more to it."

"Did you try calling her at home?"

"She didn't give me that number. She just vanished. Poof. Gone."

Chapter 18

"Racism advocated by blacks is no less primitive, cruel, ignorant or dehumanizing than racism advocated by morally eroded and pathetic whites."

~ Dr. Kenneth B. Clark, Professor of Psychology at City University of New York, on blacks who seek to drive whites from the struggle for racial justice, in 1968

WEEQUAHIC, SOUTH SIDE AND Camden were the only New Jersey basketball teams ranked in the top ten of the *Scholastic Magazine* high school poll in February 1968. Northern New Jersey, however, was well represented in the second ten and honorable mention category by Central High School from Newark, along with Newark Tech, Arts High from Newark, East Orange, Bloomfield, Montclair, Hillside, Jefferson in Elizabeth, and Linden. New Jersey had more schools in the national rankings than any other state.

From the beginning of the season, all of the nationally ranked teams had rosters comprised of nearly all black players; except one, Woodlawn High School in Birmingham, which had a roster comprised of nearly all white players.

"We have heard from all the coaches in this year's tournament, and now we welcome the coach of the team that has won the Essex County Tournament the past five years. Let's have a round of applause for Caleb Frazier of Weequahic," Hy Silverman, sports editor for *The Star-Ledger*

158

said. He was hosting the annual luncheon that signaled the beginning of the tournament.

"I think having Frazier as coach is a good thing for Weequahic, but I might be in the minority," Mort Levin, former principal of Weequahic said to Mickey Marcus, as they sat at a reserved table. "I cleared the way at the Board of Education for Caleb to take over for you, but Max certainly had mixed feelings about it." Levin was speaking about Max Steinberg, the principal at Weequahic.

"I have never met a principal who seems opposed to his students' success in sports the way Max is," Marcus said.

"Be kind, Mickey. He did support Nehemiah Garvey during the time when that petition was circulated to get Nehemiah removed from the AP program."

"Mort, that wouldn't have gone as far as it did if Max had kept his ear to the ground around the school. He should have known that the petition was being circulated. I'm not sure if he feels comfortable with the student population at the school."

"Max has strong ties to Weequahic because he grew up in the neighborhood and attended the school," Levin said. "Deep down inside he is not happy about so many Negroes moving into the area. He feels..."

Marcus interrupted. "Hold that thought. Caleb's speaking."

"I am sure you know that Weequahic is going to win the tournament again," Frazier boasted. "Nothing against any of you other coaches, but we are on a roll and we've beaten most of you at least one time this season."

"Yeah, but that was when Mickey Marcus was the coach," one of the coaches in the room yelled out.

"Alright, alright, pipe down. We're not going to turn this into a boxing match weigh-in session," Silverman said as he sat up in his chair next to the podium. "Let's switch subjects. Caleb, I understand you have some news that might make history."

Frazier smiled. "After we win this tournament and before the state tournament begins, Weequahic is taking a trip down south. To play in Birmingham."

"What in the hell is he talking about?" a startled Levin said as he stared at Marcus.

"What? You can't hear?" Marcus laughed. "He said *his* team is going to play a team in Birmingham."

"He wants to go to Birmingham, where Martin Luther King led a number of demonstrations and was jailed at one time. Does he know what's going on in the country about King's criticism of the Vietnam War?"

Frazier continued his speech. "We are going to play the second ranked team in the country, Woodlawn High School, at their gym. By the way, they have eleven white players and one black player. This has never happened."

"Dammit, Mickey, you knew about this," Levin said. "He wants to play an all-white team in Alabama? This hasn't been approved by the Board. And who's paying for it?"

"Mort, calm down. Correction, the team has one black player. Now, this was Billy Stern's idea. He played against one of the school's players in the national Jewish Y tournament when the kid played for the New York YMHA. The boy's family moved him to live with his grandparents in Birmingham so he could go to Woodlawn and dominate the competition down so he could gain attention across the country. The kid is the main reason Woodlawn is number two nationwide, and he is getting recruited by big schools.

"Billy Stern called and told him Weequahic could beat them. Of course, the kid from New York couldn't turn down a challenge from a Jersey boy, so he convinced his coach to agree to a game against Weequahic."

"Since when does a high school boy make policy for a high school team?"

"Caleb negotiated the deal after he discussed the idea with the other players. And guess who agrees with it?"

"Who, the devil?"

"Well, you're close. Larry Gottlieb."

"Gottlieb! How did he get into the conversation? He hates Weequahic."

"Not true. He hates me, but he loves the school. He still believes I convinced Billy Stern and the other players from the Y to leave him and play at Weequahic, but he's been at every game we've played except when we were in LA."

"Mickey, you are playing fast and loose with the rules. There are people, Negro and white, who will not like this. They don't want those boys playing against those crackers. Have you forgotten that just five years ago the nickname for Birmingham was 'Bombingham' after those four little Negro girls were killed in that church bombing?"

"Mort, Mort, I know that. How can I forget it? But we can stop heinous things like that from happening if we reach out and touch each other. I will say this; that board will look mighty bad if they vote against a Negro coach with a predominantly Negro team, which has three Jewish kids and an Italian boy playing important roles, going to the Deep South to play an almost all-white team."

"It seems as if this move was calculated, since going to the segregated south playing a predominantly white team *is* a big deal. But wouldn't you say going to Atlanta would have been better? But Birmingham, Mickey? Where Sheriff Bull Connor turned water on from fire engine hoses and unleashed dogs on children? There's a little smell to this."

"Why, because a Negro will get credit for the idea and not some white guy?"

"Mickey, are you trying to embarrass some people in Newark so they accept Caleb as head basketball coach at Weequahic?"

"What Caleb does as coach will speak for itself. I don't have to force him on anybody. But this I do know. Weequahic is going to the Deep South to play a basketball team with only one Negro player, and a Negro is the one whose name will be attached to the accomplishment. The country will be watching, and I know you and the Board do not want to be on the wrong side of history."

"This was not done properly, Mickey. The Board won't give Weequahic the funds to pay for it."

"I'm paying for everything out of my own pocket—travel, accommodations, and meals for the team. I'm even paying for the families that want to attend the game who can't afford to go. Weequahic or the Board will not have to pay for *anything*."

"Mickey, I have watched you match wits against some of the best coaches in America. I've seen you intimidate referees during games and give your teams advantages in close games by baiting the officials. I've seen you coach teams to championships with players who would have been so far down on the bench of other teams that the coach would have to call long distance to get them in the games," Levin said, "but this is a master stroke of genius. You are using the need to rescue Newark from the rebellion debate to keep anyone from going against you on this move. Are you sure your cancer is slowing you down, or did you fool me on that, too?"

"You're my friend, Mort. You are one of the people I credit for the amazing success of the basketball program at Weequahic. You have tremendous vision when it comes to educating children, especially Negro children. That's something many people in Newark lack, shamefully. The city will eventually rise from the ashes, and when the story is told years from now, your name will be on the page that lists the architects of the movement."

"Mickey, you didn't answer my question. What about the cancer?"

"My last checkup was encouraging," Marcus said with a sly grin. "Very encouraging."

Tongues were wagging all over New Jersey as the news spread about Caleb Frazier's announcement at the Essex County Tournament luncheon. Hy Silverman offered his opinion the next day in his sports column in *The Star-Ledger*.

The 15th Essex County Tournament tips off today at four different high school gymnasiums. The defending champion Weequahic High School Indians have been installed as the top seed and will be hosting one of the games, as will the three other seeded teams. The games will move to Seton Hall University's Archbishop Walsh Auditorium for the quarterfinals, semifinals, the consolation game, and championship game. The tournament is the brainchild of former Weequahic principal, Mort Levin, who in 1953 needed funding for a foundation he organized to help underprivileged children attend summer camp. He enlisted the help of a number of businesses in the county to fund the tournament and help it become a household name across the state. Several other counties in New Jersey followed the lead of Essex County and are now hosting their own tournaments.

This year's event marks the first time that Negro coaches will lead several of the schools. Weequahic is one of four teams that has a non-white coach. Caleb Frazier replaced Mickey Marcus after the legendary coach was diagnosed with cancer earlier this month and advised by his doctors to sit out the rest of the season.

Frazier used his speaking opportunity at yesterday's kick-off luncheon to announce that Weequahic will be the country's first high school basketball team coached by a Negro to play a predominantly white team in the Deep South. The Indians, the nation's tenth-ranked team, will leave for Birmingham after the conclusion of the Essex County Tournament to play Woodlawn High School, ranked second in the country. The national newswires printed the story last night and newspapers in major cities across the country have included it in their morning editions.

One of our writers, Ralph Edmondson, wrote a story in this morning's newspaper that offered the history of the lack of sports participation between Negroes and whites in the South, and why a game of this magnitude is so important. Coaches are talking about it. Politicians of all stripes are talking about it. I am sure that someone close to President Johnson has told him about it. And to think, just seven months ago, Newark was smoldering from an urban uprising.

What a difference commitment makes.

"THIS IS BRAD SHERMAN WITH 1430 WNWK Radio morning sports," Sherman said in his rapid-fire radio delivery known to listeners in the New Jersey-New York metropolitan area. "The world is talking about our hometown and history-making Weequahic High School. The undefeated Indians will make history after they play in the Essex County Tournament, by going to Birmingham, Alabama to play an all-white team. We have a caller on the telephone to talk about this historic event. Hello, caller, you're on the air pad with Brad."

"Brad, this is no big deal. Weequahic is a team with a bunch of Uncle Tom Negroes and Jew boys. They don't represent black people, so who cares if they go down South to play a bunch of crackers?"

"What about the fact that Caleb Frazier coaches the team, which will make him the first black man in high school history to coach against an overwhelmingly white team in the Deep South?" Sherman said.

"It don't mean nothin', because everybody knows that Mickey Marcus is still coachin' the team and Frazier ain't nothin' but a puppet."

"Where you calling from?" asked Sherman.

"South Jersey, where the Camden Panthers are waiting for Weequahic in the state tournament, if they get that far." The caller hung up.

"He's from Camden, so what else would you expect from South Jersey?" Sherman said. "We'll be back next hour with 1430 WNWK Radio Sports. I'm Brad Sherman. Now, back to soul music on WNWK. It's Billy Woods with the morning goods on 1430."

The players were in study hall, listening to Nehemiah's small transistor radio.

"Okay, let's turn off the radio and get your books together," the study hall teacher said. "The bell is going to ring for homeroom."

"Nee, does it make you mad when people call you an Uncle Tom?" Billy Stern asked.

"Sticks and stones may break my bones, but words will never hurt me."

"I wish I could say that, man. I was at the Y the other day and this punk called me a nigger lover. Mr. Gottlieb had to run over to keep me from kicking that kid's ass. I don't like to be called names by nobody."

Nehemiah put his arm on Stern's shoulder. "You better get used to it, big boy. The white folks in Birmingham will try anything to keep us from beatin' their team. We shouldn't be surprised at whatever they might do. Name callin', throwin' trash on the gym floor, maybe even death threats. In fact, we might be gettin' some of that right here in Jersey, you never know. Weequahic represents some things a lot of people don't wanna see in Newark."

FIVE WELL-DRESSED WHITE MEN arrogantly strode into Don's 21 Restaurant on McCarter Highway, close to downtown Newark.

"The back room is ready for you, gentlemen. I will send a waitress to serve you," the host said. The men hung their coats on the rack outside the room.

"That damn Mickey Marcus and that kid are outsmarting us."

"Yeah, they're keeping the spotlight on the city."

"Looks like we can't do a damn thing to take advantage of the damage the riot did."

"The mayor can't help us because he's tied up in some legal issues with that crime family."

"Our boy in the Central Ward is getting criticized because of his support for the hospital that will put a lot of families out of their homes."

"That Chaga son of a bitch might get off that weapons charge and we can't buy his support if he's back on the street."

"The only person who can help us at this point is you know who."

"Do we really want to deal with him?" At that point a tall, nattily attired black man walked into the room.

"Well, if it isn't my good friends from the North Ward. Y'all ready to talk to me now?"

It was Herbert Evans.

Chapter 19

"Riots are illegal, but make no mistake about it, they are not illegitimate. They are the results of legitimate grievances from people who have a legitimate claim upon the society and upon an equitable share of its resources."

~ Reverend Jesse Jackson, director of the
Southern Christian Leadership Conference's
Operation Breadbasket, in 1967

Newark and cities that had similar urban footprints were undergoing radical changes during the 1960s. While huge black populations resided in what was commonly defined as the "inner city" in the middle of the decade, the better educated and upwardly mobile African Americans moved out of those areas into the more comfortable lifestyles of suburbia. However, the cities still had infrastructures that could yield huge economic benefits to whatever entity controlled City Hall.

Herbert Evans, former Essex County Freeholder and unsuccessful candidate for the South Ward City Council seat in 1966, walked into Don's 21 restaurant on McCarter Highway in Newark, crashing a meeting of businessmen who lived in the predominantly white North Ward.

"Herbert Evans. Funny you should be here. We were just discussing your people," one of the men said.

"My people? You mean the people who like to make money?"

"Herbert, you're breaking my heart. We thought you liked black power."

Evans pulled up a chair and sat at the table.

"Let me tell you boys somethin'. Green power can buy black power any day at any time. I've been watchin' white boys like you buy each other since I was a little kid in Pin Point, Georgia. I know how much you boys like money."

"You're different from when you ran for City Council two years ago."

"I ran a stupid campaign back then. I didn't identify how I could help the Jewish businessmen in the South Ward make money if I became councilman. I thought if I reached out to the Negroes in the ward, I would easily win over that white boy with the irritatin' voice."

"So, you figured out race politics can't win?"

"Not without a dollar bill attached. Okay, let's leave the past in the past. From what I saw when I walked in, you boys were in a deep discussion."

"Herbert, we need some help. We have to figure out how we can make money in Newark without having to live here."

Evans sat back in his chair and briefly yet intently stared at each man.

"I used to think you boys were smart, that people like you had all the sense. I actually believed because you went to all white private schools and then to Ivy League universities or other big-name colleges that you actually had functionin' brains. After bein' around you for the last couple of years, I realize that most of you can't spell cat, even if I told you there was a 'c' and 'a' in the word."

"Damn Herbert, you're being mighty disrespectful. There was a time when you could get lynched by talking like that to white men."

"That was then, this is now," Evans said with an arrogant tone. "There was a lotta slaves pickin' cotton back then, so one or two bad ones were expendable. Not true today when there's a Negro who can help you make money. Y'all need me and you know it."

"Sorry about that disrespect, Herbert. The lynching reference was wrong."

"No apology needed. I can tolerate ignorance, even though I don't like it. Now here's the answer to your question. Use your money to put somebody in City Hall who you can depend on when it comes to makin' money at the port and the airport. The deal with New York is gonna bring a lot of money through Newark, but you boys have to find a way to have the money hit your hands before Newark gets it."

"That sounds damn complicated. How do we do it?"

"Commit to supporting me for City Council at large in 1970 and I'll show you."

AFTER HIS SPEECH ON April 4, 1967 at New York's Riverside Church, Dr. Martin Luther King Jr. became a man many people avoided. Titled "Beyond Vietnam: A Time to Break Silence," it was viewed as a betrayal to President Lyndon B. Johnson because of its criticism of the Vietnam War. At the same time, Dr. King was attempting to get support for the Poor People's Campaign scheduled for April 1968, but was encountering resistance from black politicians, black organizations, and surprisingly, from many black pastors.

"I appreciate your invitation to meet, Reverend Wade," Caleb Frazier said. "I understand you not wanting to speak on the telephone."

"Yes, Brother Frazier, I know about the wire-tapping that has been going on by law enforcement around the country and I did not want to be a victim. That's why I asked you to come to the church."

"I'm not trying to be funny, but are you involved with something illegal?"

"Oh no, I'm just being cautious. Are you aware of what is going on with Reverend King?"

"I only know about his criticism of the Vietnam War, which has caused a rift between him and President Johnson. I don't know any more than that."

"Well, Reverend King has done more than that. He's been making speeches across the country about the war being unholy and against the will of God. He has also been accused of being militant and willing to meet with Stokely Carmichael, H. Rap Brown and many others in the black power movement."

"I've been reading those stories, but I don't believe everything I read, unless of course it's in *Jet* or *Ebony*," Frazier said with a laugh.

"It's good that you read, my brother. I know you are an educated young man. You know, Malcolm X once said education is our passport to the future, for tomorrow belongs to the people who prepare for it today. That is so true."

"I'm impressed that you quote Malcolm."

"I'll repeat any quote that makes sense. That includes Booker T. Washington, W.E.B. DuBois, Teddy Roosevelt, Kennedy, President Johnson, Keats, even James Brown. But we are digressing. I wanted to meet with you to personally thank you for scheduling that game for Weequahic down in Birmingham."

"I don't know if you heard, but the idea actually came from one of my Jewish players. It made sense because Woodlawn is ranked second nationally, and so beating them at this point in the season means we could move several notches in the national poll. That is if we win the Essex County Tournament."

"Young man, you have made a lot of us Newarkers very proud. First, one of our schools is making history by playing a *heavily* predominantly white school in the Deep South. Second, a Negro did it. Newark is getting nationwide coverage and all of this is fulfilling Mickey Marcus' quest to bring a good name to post-rebellion Newark."

"Don't forget about all of the work that Nehemiah Garvey has been doing. He brought the Jewish players back to Weequahic, and that hotshot Italian boy is living with Nehemiah's family, which has allowed him to go to Weequahic. Without those boys, we wouldn't be the team we are."

Wade stood up and walked to a table where several pictures were displayed.

"I have been in conversation with the Southern Christian Leadership Conference about Reverend King coming to this church to promote the Poor People's Campaign," Wade said as he picked up a photo of King. "I am asking that you don't discuss this possibility with anyone. Reverend King has been getting a lot of death threats, so I don't want a lot of people knowing about it. I'm telling you because I want you to be here when he comes."

"Your secret is safe with me, and I accept your invitation. By the way, do you intend to come to Birmingham when we play?"

"I have already called my friends in Birmingham about speaking at the high school. I might even preach at a church. Brother Frazier, this is history. How could I miss it?"

WEEQUAHIC CRUSHED ALL OF ITS opponents in the Essex County Tournament, which included a 20-point win over South Side in the championship game. South Side was ranked one spot above the Indians at number nine in the *Scholastic Magazine* high school poll. Meanwhile, fifth-ranked Camden scored a major upset by defeating Dunbar of Washington, D.C., the number three team nationally, at a tournament in the nation's capital.

Mickey Marcus was the guest speaker at the Weequahic victory dinner at Eva Jean Garvey's restaurant. "We are so proud of you boys with this victory in the Essex County Tournament," Marcus said. "Not only did this team win the tournament for the sixth year in a row, but this is the twelfth county championship for the Indians. Well done, boys.

"Now, there are some in this city who want to give credit to me for winning this year, but no, that would be wrong. The man who was on the bench, giving directions to the players was Mr. Caleb Frazier, my friend. Mr. Frazier, come on up to the microphone and tell us how you did it."

"I know you must be extremely proud of what is going on at Weequahic, with all that Mickey Marcus has done and what Caleb Frazier is doing. I know your son wants some of the credit, too," Herbert Evans said to Eva Jean Garvey. Evans had been invited to join Eva Jean and her family at their table by Nehemiah's grandmother, Lula Mae Eleazer.

"Herbert, you know Nehemiah isn't looking for credit. He just wants to get respect for Newark in whatever way he can get it," Eva Jean said.

Lula Mae rolled her eyes in Evans' direction.

"Herbert, with a remark like that you probably need to be seen and not heard," she said. "You are our guest and I would appreciate it if you would act respectable. I know that might be hard for you to do, but please try."

"Lula Mae, I don't deserve your scorn and…"

"Mama, this is the team's night. Don't let this man spoil it," Eva Jean said.

Frazier had already begun speaking. "… and none of this would have been possible without the families of these young men. The Clark family, the Trawick family, the Sterns, the Rashid family, the Rosenbergs, the Cambridge family, the Greenblatts, and how about the Garvey family? And what about the staff and faculty of Weequahic, led by our committed principal, Mr. Steinberg?" The audience stood up and applauded.

"Thank you everybody, thank you so much," Frazier continued. "The next page in the great history of Weequahic High School turns in a few days as we travel to Birmingham, Alabama to face Woodlawn High, the only predominantly white team in the top ten of the national polls. While I am not comfortable tooting my own horn, I will be the first Negro to coach a predominantly black high school against an all-white team with the exception of one player in the Deep South. During these turbulent times, that is a big deal not only for us at Weequahic, but for the whole country.

"That said, I don't want anybody in this room to discount the impact this has for the city we love. I came to Newark four years ago at the insistence of a friend I played with at Johnson C. Smith University in Charlotte, North Carolina. His name is Leon Stone, a legend in Newark high school basketball. Leon competed against Weequahic when he played at South Side. Mickey Marcus said he was the toughest player his team ever faced, and you know Weequahic has played against a lot of great teams during Mr. Marcus' long tenure. Leon set up a meeting with Mr. Marcus and me, and the next thing I knew, I was sitting next to him on the bench after coaching the junior varsity team for one season.

"We won the state championship two years ago with an undefeated record, we won the state championship last season with an undefeated record and were named the number one team in the nation. We are now unbeaten in twenty games, embarking on the New Jersey high school record for consecutive victories. We are on track to win another state championship, and we could be the first high school basketball team in the country to ever claim number one status two years in a row. All of this after the most devastating period in the history of Newark, the rebellion of 1967.

"But none of this is as important as the dream of two men, a white man and a young Negro man. A dream that was shaped from wanting to stop the negative talk about their city, a dream formed from a tiny thought and a simple prayer from each of them in their own small way. Mickey Marcus and Nehemiah Garvey, would you please come to the podium?"

Nehemiah rose from his seat amidst the applause from his teammates who were sitting with him. He met Marcus halfway and they walked together with the confident stride of two gladiators who have battled foes and consistently won. Tears quietly fell from the faces of Eva Jean and her mother, Lula Mae, who grabbed Eva Jean's hand and squeezed it. The moment captured everyone in the room, but not one single person was overcome with more gratitude than Caleb Frazier.

"These two men, yes, I am calling Nehemiah a man," Frazier said as Marcus and Nehemiah stood with him, "are my best friends. Their friendships captured me from the first day I met them, and they have never let me down. That is why I have this verse underlined in my Bible, and on a sign on a wall in my home. It is from Matthew twenty-five, which started out with heaven being likened to ten virgins, who took their lamps to meet the bridegroom, who was Jesus Christ. After much detailed conversation about talents—which can be defined as spiritual gifts—the Lord realized He had someone who knew how to make something out of nearly nothing.

"His Lord said unto him, 'Well done, thou good and faithful servant. Thou hast been faithful over a few things, I will make thee ruler over many things. Enter thou into the joy of thy Lord.' Mr. Marcus and Nehemiah, thank you for doing your part to save Newark."

Chapter 20

"I have to be honest with myself and admit that up until the time I had to make the decision to go to Washington or not go, my liberalism on the race issue had been based to a large degree on the pragmatism: it was simply good business for Atlanta to be an open city, a fair city, a "City Too Busy to Hate," a city trying to raise the level of its poorest citizens and get them off the relief roles…I am certain that at this point I had finally crossed over and made my commitment on a very personal basis."

~ Ivan Allen Jr., Mayor of Atlanta, Georgia 1962–1970

The report from the National Advisory Commission on Civil Disorders concluded that, "The most fundamental matter is the racial attitude and behavior of white Americans toward black Americans. Race prejudice has shaped our history decisively; it now threatens to affect our future. White racism is essentially responsible for the explosive mixture which has been accumulating in our cities since the end of World War II." Meanwhile, the Malcolm X Society, a black separatist group formed during the Detroit Riot in 1967, formulated a plan to move at least three million blacks into Southern states in order to begin the process of a massive separation from the United States. The plan would consolidate Mississippi, Louisiana, Alabama, Georgia, and South Carolina into a union that would seek military and economic partnerships with other black nations with the intention of forging a worldwide federation.

"Nee, you pulled off the near impossible with all of this attention being paid to Newark," Lena Ashby, his childhood friend, said. "I couldn't believe the way you took on that Pan African group in LA when they were trying to get momentum for their cause. You stared down their leader in a way no other sixteen-year old could have done. And then you got all that attention from the newspapers and magazines." The two of them were sitting in the hall outside the gym at Peshine Avenue School.

"I only did what I believed the good Lord wanted me to do."

"You did that and more. You are changing the conversation in Newark from desperation to inspiration. I believe the Lord is taking the trouble from your heart."

Several boys came down the steps to the school's ground floor, then walked toward Lena and Nehemiah. They were athletes from Weequahic, South Side, Central, and West Side. Nehemiah's body language exhibited massive trepidation at the sight of this unexpected encounter, but it turned out to be far different from what he was thinking.

"Hey man, you know we missed you on the football team, but we won the City League anyway," Bernie Boone, one of the running backs from Weequahic said. "But I heard you plan to play baseball. We could use another great hitter like me."

"Bernie, you and that ego. You know I'll be there, especially since we have a shot at winnin' the city title we should have won last year." The other boys began to surround Nehemiah.

"Did it take all of y'all to tell me that?" Nehemiah asked.

"Nee, we came to say thank you for what you're doin' for Newark," the player from South Side said. "I know we been playin' against each other in basketball and baseball since I was at Miller Street School and you played here at Peshine. But I got to know you when we played football for the Newark Bears in Pop Warner."

"Yeah, two undefeated seasons and two state championships," the other players recalled at once.

"We sure worked hard to win. We were little kids, seventh and eighth graders," Nehemiah said. Lena started laughing.

"How hard did y'all really work just playin' football?" she said.

"If you had to run that one hundred yards to the flagpole after every practice at Branch Brook Park you would know how hard it was," the player from Central said. "Mr. Strong believed in bein' in shape and bein' tough."

"He prepared all of us for high school ball," one of the other players said.

Nehemiah pointed his finger at the group. "He prepared us for *life*."

"That's right, man," Boone said. "That's why when we were at my house liftin' weights tonight, I told these guys that we needed to tell you to your face how much we appreciate you for bringin' a good name to Newark. We went to your house and your mother said you were here."

"And there are a lotta other guys that want to say they appreciate you, man. We salute you, Nee. You're a good brother."

"And you got a good South Side sister with you, man," one of the other players said in reference to Lena.

"Nehemiah and I have been friends since we were four years old, and we will be friends for the rest of our lives. I'm glad to know that he has guys like you in his corner. It says a lot about all of you, since you compete against each other so much."

"Oh, we'll still be playin' hard against him, but when he plays against schools outside of Newark, he's our boy."

"Okay, so they'll meet us at the school about forty minutes before we leave? That sounds good," Mickey Marcus said as he spoke on the telephone. "I can't tell you how much I thank you for doing this. Okay, we'll talk later."

"Sounds like good news," Ralph Edmondson, staff writer for *The Star-Ledger* said.

"That was the commander of the New Jersey State Police. He went to the governor for permission to recruit volunteers to travel to Birmingham with the team and provide security. He got the clearance and was telling me that he got more officers than he needed."

"Looks like the whole state is behind the team," Edmondson said as he wrote on his notepad. "You called me about some issues over this trip. What's going on?"

"I wish everybody in New Jersey was behind us, but we do have our detractors," Marcus said. "There are some who don't like the fact that Caleb Frazier is leading the team. If I closed my eyes and somebody read these letters to me, I would swear we were somewhere in the South dealing with the Ku Klux Klan," Marcus said as he handed some of the letters to Edmondson.

"As you'll see, there is some strong language there," Marcus said. "Nigger this, nigger that. Darkie, black s.o.b., plantation jockey."

"Are you going to show them to Caleb?"

"Absolutely not, but not for the reason you might think."

"What do you think I'm thinking?"

"That he might get depressed if he saw them."

"Wrong. Mickey, you know that I'm black, right?"

"That's obvious."

"I know a little bit about this stuff. Do you think I got this job because they like me at the newspaper?"

"Well, you're a superb writer. That should count for something."

"Yeah, and a cold cup of coffee thrown in my face. With spit in it."

"Really?"

"Yep. But I'm neither dismayed nor discouraged. Guys like Caleb and me understand this stuff, and we move on. As professionals."

"That's got to be tough."

"No tougher than what our ancestors went through as slaves and victims of Jim Crow. Now, that's it for the history lesson. Let's get to the story. Can I mention any of these letters in my story?"

"Yes, you can. But please keep it upbeat."

"Mickey, are you a writer now?"

"I just want to stay as positive as possible."

"I know exactly what to do. Mainly, I know what will get past the editors. Ready to start talking?"

"Sure am."

"One more thing, Mickey."

"What's that?"

"I think you are a great example of what a man should be. A lot of people share my opinion. Just thought I would throw that in."

BILLY STERN, STUART GREENBLATT and Lenny Rosenberg sat in one of the booths at the Weequahic Diner on Elizabeth Avenue in Newark.

"I gotta get home and do my homework," Rosenberg said.

"Me too. Billy, did you tell him what time we were supposed to meet?" Greenblatt asked.

"You guys know how he is. *Late* is his middle name," Stern said. "Oh, there he is."

"Sorry, guys. I had something to do and it ran late," Larry Gottlieb said as he sat next to Greenblatt, across from Stern and Rosenberg. "Good place to meet, don't you think? Interesting that it's across the street from a White Castle in an area where Negroes have taken over. This is our diner, but it might go down like the Park Restaurant down the street went after the neighborhood changed. This was a great area for Jews a long time ago."

"Larry, was all of that necessary?" Stern asked.

"I just wanted to put everything into perspective for you boys," Gottlieb said. "Our history, our heritage, all gone because of the changes around here."

"Okay, Larry, we appreciate the community background, as if we didn't already know," Stern said. "Who's payin' for this anyway? You know your reputation about squeezin' Abe Lincoln off the five-dollar bill."

"C'mon Billy. That is so unfair. I'm just fiscally responsible."

"Alright, if that's what you call it. Why are we here?"

Gottlieb started shaking his head. "I'm concerned about you boys. All of the stuff that's going on at Weequahic makes me wonder who's in charge."

"Caleb Frazier is in charge of our basketball team," Rosenberg said.

"That worries me," Gottlieb said.

"You don't care about Weequahic, so why are you worried?" Greenblatt asked.

"I feel responsible for the three of you. You're the only white boys on a team at a school where there's a lot more Negro kids than Jewish kids. Your families are worried. I hear about it at the synagogue, I hear about it when I talk to some of your friends at the Y who have transferred to schools that are friendlier to Jewish kids, especially Newark Academy."

"Uh, Larry, are you sayin' we should be concerned about Mr. Frazier because he's black and not Jewish?" Stern asked. "And by the way, Tommy Caruso is also white. But he's Italian. Does that count against him, since Italy is close to Africa?"

"That's what I'm talking about—the use of the word black instead of Negro. That sounds like you're being indoctrinated by these guys spouting black power and saying stuff like 'kill whitey'. To me and many other people in the Jewish community, that sounds like you're being influenced by Caleb Frazier."

"Oh boy, Larry. Is this your way of trying to convince us to come back to play basketball for the Y?" Rosenberg said.

"At least you'll be coached by your own. And you wouldn't be going to a place where your lives are threatened because of your mere presence with a Negro coach. That wouldn't happen if you came back to the Y. You boys do know that there have been death threat letters sent to Mickey Marcus over this trip to Alabama, don't you?"

"Do my grandparents know about that?" Stern asked.

"What about my mom and dad?" Rosenberg asked.

"And my family?" Greenblatt asked.

"I'm sure they'll soon find out. I understand *The Star-Ledger* will be running a story about it tomorrow."

Stern got up from his seat and stood over Gottlieb.

"Larry, whatever you have against Mr. Marcus is stupid. Jewish people don't act like this, at least that's what my grandfather has told me since I was a little boy runnin' around Keer Avenue. All of us are gonna stay with Mr. Frazier not because of our devotion to civil rights, or somethin' political like that. It's because we believe in that man because he believes in us, and he has a winning attitude. That's all that matters to us. C'mon boys. Let's go home. Oh, by the way, I have black neighbors on Keer Avenue, and they're nice people."

"THIS IS BOB SCOTT WITH 1430 WNWK Radio News. The top story this morning is the article in today's newspaper about the death threats aimed at the Weequahic High School basketball team, which is preparing to travel to Birmingham to play the nation's number two ranked team, Woodlawn High School. The significance of this game is that it will be the first time an all-white team from the Deep South plays a predominantly Negro team coached by a Negro. I have three men in the studio who will play pivotal roles in this game; two New Jersey state troopers who will accompany the team, and Caleb Frazier, the Weequahic coach.

"State troopers John Flowers and Nick Pfeiffer were part of the contingent dispatched to Newark during the riot last summer. They also testified about some of the injustices they witnessed during the riot at one of the hearings of the governor's civil disorder commission. Welcome gentlemen."

"Thank you," all three said.

"First, Mr. Frazier. What are your thoughts about *The Star-Ledger* story that described the death threats leveled at you?"

"I am not pleased, but I am not surprised," Frazier said. "Our country has been blowing up in many corners and it seems that none of us are immune to any of it. I suppose it's the price we pay for freedom. The people who have problems with our trip to Birmingham have the right to free speech, but they don't have the right to threaten people's lives and intimidate those who support our efforts."

"Mr. Flowers, you're from Elizabeth, a city that had a riot before Newark, in 1964. Then you ended up being on the front line as a state trooper in the Newark riot, three years later. What was on your mind when you got the assignment?"

"To do the job right," Flowers said. "I was a police officer during the Elizabeth riot and saw some of my fellow officers do some things that were not right. Unfortunately, I kept my mouth shut. When I was assigned to Newark during the riot, I had a completely different attitude about enforcing the law; regarding both the people who broke the law and any officers who did the same, presumably in the name of justice. That's why I testified at the committee hearing about what I saw in Newark."

"Mr. Pfeiffer, your background is much different," Scott said, "you're from Lyndhurst, in Bergen County. Not many Negroes there, yet you and Mr. Flowers ended up working together during last summer's riot in Newark. You helped some of the victims of the riot after it was over. Could you briefly talk about that?"

"First, I want to say that this man I am sitting next to is one of the finest people I have ever met. I watched him go above and beyond the work of a state trooper when we were in Newark, and after we went back to our normal duties, I called to let him know I was returning to Newark to help with the cleanup. We met up there and worked with the people in those neighborhoods. It was gratifying to support that part of Newark getting back on its feet. I've been driving from Lyndhurst to volunteer at the Boys' Club in the South Ward at least three times a week since September."

"Those are great stories," Scott said. "Now, I understand that the two of you are providing security for the Weequahic High School basketball team with no pay. Why?"

"It's the right thing to do," Pfeiffer said. "I played against Weequahic when I was in high school. I saw Mickey Marcus coach that team. He's a decent man, and then when I heard about what he did for boys in Newark who didn't even play for him, I realized he is a *great* man.

Mr. Marcus picked Caleb Frazier to take over the team, which to me means he believes Caleb is the right person to continue his legacy at Weequahic."

"I volunteered to go because this is a big step for race relations in this country, and I am proud that a black man is stepping forward to make it," Flowers said. "Even though I'm not from Newark, I want to see the city rebound from the riot, just like I want to see the other cities like Cleveland, LA, and Detroit move past their racial problems. I want my name to be attached to the good things that are happening in this country."

"Bob, before you sign off, I would like to repeat something I heard Martin Luther King say," Pfeiffer said. "He said, 'we will have to repent in this generation not merely for the hateful words and actions of the bad people, but for the appalling silence of the good people.'

"I don't know how much good me and Flowers are doing, but we certainly don't want the bad guys to succeed in dividing the country, regardless of their color."

Chapter 21

"He is a black American and damned proud of it. He is an American without apology for not being white. This is the way Americans must take him or leave him, and it is obvious that he is in no mood to be left."

~ Dr. C. Eric Lincoln, professor of sociology at Union Theological Seminary, describing black men in the United States, in 1968

THE BEGINNING OF THE DECADE of the 1960s brought waves of new attitudes toward liberation of massive populations throughout the world. Though some of the freedom rebellions in Africa began in the '50s, the uprisings in the Congo, Cameroon, Senegal, and Mali thrust the names of these countries into American homes via television en masse in 1960, which ran parallel to the fight by blacks for equality in the United States. Some of the tactics employed by Dr. Martin Luther King Jr. during the Civil Rights Era were said to have been influenced by what was televised from the African continent during that time. The faces of Patrice Lumumba, Joseph Kasa-Vubu, Sekou Toure, and Kwame Nkrumah were as common on the nightly network news as those of President Dwight Eisenhower, members of Congress, Soviet Union Premier Nikita Khrushchev, and the Prime Minister of Cuba, Fidel Castro.

The decade had swept in with a wave of optimism when popular Senator John F. Kennedy of Massachusetts competed against Senators Lyndon Johnson of Texas, Hubert Humphrey of Minnesota, Stuart Symington of Missouri, and Wayne Morse of Oregon to win the Democratic nomination for President of the United States. Kennedy won the contest, and then narrowly defeated Republican Richard Nixon, then Vice President, in the general election.

The roots of crusades such as the Civil Rights movement, anti-war movement, feminist movement, and gay rights movement either grew or were planted at the beginning of the decade of the sixties. While hope and change fomented during this time, those aspirations were seriously eroded by the end of this significant ten-year period in America's history. It began with President Kennedy's Camelot, and after his assassination in 1963, the age of innocence went downward toward Armageddon.

"I want you guys to look outside of your windows and take in this scenery," Caleb Frazier told the team. "This is part of the route that the Freedom Riders took to the South in 1964, as part of the fight to allow all people to travel from state to state without being discriminated against."

"Mr. Frazier, didn't some of the students that participated get beat up?" Billy Stern asked.

"Most of that happened in Alabama, and some members of the SNCC got beat up in South Carolina."

"What does SNCC stand for?"

"The Student Non-Violent Coordinating Committee."

"Are they really nonviolent?"

Frazier laughed. "Do you think Stokely Carmichael and H. Rap Brown are nonviolent?"

"Nope."

"Okay. Now, back to the reason I chose for us to take this route to Birmingham. For you juniors, you'll be learning Negro history at Weequahic next school year. What happened along this highway is a major part of that history."

"Mr. Frazier, will you be in the history books because of what we'll be doin' in Birmingham?" Nehemiah asked.

"I don't know, but I won't lose any sleep over it if I'm not. What's important is the well-being of you boys while I'm in charge," Frazier said. "Okay, listen up. Here's the plan. When we get to Birmingham, we will be staying at a place called the A.G. Gaston Motel. All of the people who have traveled from Newark will be there. I need you to go to your rooms immediately, and then come downstairs to the restaurant which is next door. We'll be having dinner there. For now, just relax and enjoy this ride."

Billy Stern leaned toward his seatmate and said, "Nee, I don't know if I told you this before, but I'm glad you came to the Y and challenged us to that game last year. Some people thought we came back to Weequahic because you beat us that day. The real reason we came back is because we wanted to play for Mr. Marcus. But I'll never forgive you for dunking on me three times."

Nehemiah elbowed Stern in the ribs. "Billy, do you remember when I came to Weequahic in the ninth grade and tried out for the JV team? Mr. Marcus was thinkin' about movin' you up to varsity, but he changed his mind after the ninth graders whipped the tenth graders, led by you, in that practice game."

"Oh, do I remember. But I'm glad I didn't move up because I got the chance to play with you and we won the City League JV championship and the Essex County JV tournament."

"And nobody beat us," Nehemiah said. "I have never played for a basketball team at Weequahic that lost a game."

"I heard about you when you were in the eighth grade at Peshine. I also remember playin' baseball against you in the summer league at Untermann Field. Plus, you played football for the Newark Bears in Pop Warner, right?"

"Yep. Won the state championship both seasons, when I played quarterback. But you know what, Billy? I wouldn't trade this season for any of those years."

"Nee, I feel the same way. I thought when we won the Jewish Y national championship last spring it was the greatest feeling in the world, but this is something special. I don't know what, but it's bigger than us, bigger than just this game. We have a chance to make something good come out of all that horror last summer. It feels special."

"We're playin' for a cause, man. We're playin' for our city—the city that your people have worked hard to build, and my people too. Do you know that even though we have beaten the other city teams, they all still cheer for us when we play teams outside of Newark?"

"I don't get that, Nee. We beat some of 'em pretty bad."

"It's because they respect that we set a goal to bring glory to Newark through our basketball team, and we have done it. Look what we did in LA. We beat the top three teams in the country out there. We've been showin' great sportsmanship and class in winnin' the City League title and the Essex County championship.

"And remember, we won the City League in football with no losses and one tie, our swim team is gonna win a state championship; and we have the best debate team in the state. All these accomplishments from people in a city that was written off as dead after last year. Well look at us now. Weequahic is leadin' the rise of Newark to respectability."

"And we are gonna beat the number two team in the country tomorrow night," Stern said.

"Right on!"

REVEREND FREDERICK WADE rode on one of the five buses that was occupied by the Newark contingent. He was sitting next to Mickey Marcus in one of the front seats.

"Mickey, I'm mighty proud of what Caleb Frazier is doing with your team."

"C'mon Reverend Wade, you know the team became Caleb's the first day he had practice with them as head coach," Marcus said. "But remember, Caleb had all of those boys on his undefeated JV team when Nehemiah was in the ninth grade. They all know him and he knows them."

"Alright, you can be honest with me. If you don't come back, is Frazier going to be the coach?"

Marcus looked down at his feet, and then slowly shifted his gaze in Wade's direction. "I really don't know."

"Mickey, I asked Rabbi Seligman the same question. He said he didn't think so."

"Really? Did he say why?"

"Said he didn't think the Jewish alumni of Weequahic would stand behind the selection of a black man as permanent head coach of *their* school's legendary basketball team."

"That's funny. They weren't saying that when so many of them ran for the hills as Negroes started moving into the Weequahic neighborhoods. *Their* school. Yeah, right," Marcus said.

"You and Caleb have been quite a force for the past three years. I find it quite disturbing that a group of people would not see something so obvious. Two undefeated seasons in a row, City League, county and state championships for the past three years and number one in the country last year. This has been a coaching masterpiece by both of you with a team that was thought to be the underdog before this season began."

"Reverend Wade, you don't seem pleased."

"I am, but I'm realistic. I have to acknowledge that people generally support their own ethnic groups. Remember what happened around this time last year? The candidates for the job of the secretary of the Board of Education were a black man with advanced degrees and relative experience, and a white man who only had a high school diploma. The Board, which to this day has only one black member, was going to select the white man because the mayor wanted him, but many blacks, including me, protested at several meetings until the Board pulled the appointment.

"Mickey, this was the second most important administrative job at the Board of Education, and the mayor was trying to use his influence to get a councilman appointed to the post who had not even been to college or gained management experience, over a black man with an MBA from an Ivy League university, who was already serving as Newark's budget director."

"Reverend Wade, you will not get an argument from me. I was accused of waiting until the season was almost over before I disclosed that I had cancer, just so I could open the door for Caleb to get the job."

"Is that what you did?"

"Now really, do I look like that kind of guy? It shouldn't make a difference anyway. Caleb has the job and the team has not lost since he took over. He should get the job when I…"

Reverend Wade interrupted. "When, Mickey? Are you leaving Weequahic?"

"That question keeps coming up. The people at the Board want me to let them know now, so they can look for a qualified candidate to replace me, as if Caleb has not already proven himself to be perfectly qualified for the job."

"I have to keep a stiff upper lip when I hear things like that. Let's call it like it is. Caleb was the one who convinced those Jewish boys to come back to Weequahic, even though their parents wanted them to transfer. Caleb is the one who's been personally working with them to help improve their playing skills and look at the results. They are important players on this undefeated team and their chances to get scholarships to major colleges have greatly improved as a result. Your friends around here know that you turned those kids over to Caleb, and look at what he's done, yet they still want to replace him. And I thought many of your friends are friends to the black man.

"Then again, I shouldn't be surprised. I've seen how many of Martin King's so-called friends have turned their backs on him since he became more confrontational about the poor in this country and his displeasure with the Vietnam War. Some have said that Martin is teaming up with Stokely Carmichael, because he met with him last week.

"I'm watching how people's memories are so short, forgetting what has happened in the cities with these rebellions over the past three years. They forget how certain groups want to form a black nation within the United States because they perceive that many white people in this country don't want to treat blacks fairly. Martin must engage these people in order to learn how he can best present their issues to the government; but people like your friends want him to ignore them. Mickey, it's a different day. Martin King can't do that and call himself working to heal this nation.

"I plan to speak about this Caleb situation to your friends behind closed doors, properly and in order, instead of making a fuss in public. If I did that, it would only fuel the arguments of the black power crowd, and most of us know what they want. I pray every day that nothing happens that will send us back to that dark place of last year, but there are some cloudy skies on the horizon."

"I applaud you, Reverend Wade, and I have always respected you. There are some in the Jewish community who are thinking correctly, especially since the findings from the governor's riot report have been released. Newark is in a big mess, according to what I have read, as are many other cities across the country when you read the federal government's summary of the situation. That's why what happens with Caleb, if I don't come back, is enormously important."

Chapter 22

"America must not become a nation of onlookers. America must not remain silent. Not merely black America, but all of America. It must speak up and act, from the President down to the humblest of us, and not for the sake of the Negro, not for the sake of the black community but for the sake of the image, the idea and the aspiration of America itself."

~ Rabbi Joachim Prinz, then president of the American Jewish Congress, in his speech at the March on Washington, in 1963

"We must develop strength in order that we may be able to back and support the civil rights program of President Kennedy. In the struggle against these forces, all of us should be prepared to take to the streets. The spirit and techniques that built the labor movement, founded churches, and now guide the civil rights revolution must be a massive crusade, must be launched against the unholy coalition of Dixiecrats and of the racists that seek to strangle Congress. We here today are only the first wave."

~ A. Philip Randolph, civil rights pioneer and chief organizer of the March on Washington in his speech at the March, in 1963

A HUGE CROWD FILLED the cafeteria at Woodlawn High School on the day of the Weequahic-Woodlawn basketball game. Reverend Frederick Wade was the keynote speaker at the volunteer recognition breakfast. The attendees included senior officers in the Birmingham mayoral administration, business leaders from a cross-section of the city, a diverse representation of the religious community, and the superintendent of schools. Both teams were represented, though they were seated separately.

"I want to first thank Mr. A.G. Gaston, for sponsoring this breakfast. His high regard for desegregation in this country is noteworthy and legendary, and he should be commended," Reverend Wade said, imploring the crowd to extend a round of applause for Gaston. "This is an historic occasion, for no other schools in the country have the courage to do what will occur tonight. Sure, the University of Kentucky and Texas Western University played for the national basketball championship in 1966, a significant game for civil rights. But their matchup was the result of the luck of the draw. Tonight's contest is due to the collective will of committed Americans.

"I take this time to say 'thank you, Birmingham' for making this event possible. Even though we are living in some difficult days, there are some of us who are winding the clock forward to progress amongst the races. I have to believe it is the intent of many of you who are present in this room to open the doors of equality and opportunity to the masses, even if Woodlawn is still slow walking toward desegregation of its halls." Wade's comment drew a groan from some of the crowd, which included Rabbi David Seligman, who took a flight from Newark into Birmingham to be in attendance.

"That's a gutsy comment, wouldn't you agree, David?" Mickey Marcus said to Seligman, who was sitting at a table reserved for him by one of the city's business leaders. "It would be a good thing to see more than a few black children at this school."

"I am pleased that brother Wade would say such a thing in public," Seligman said. "By the way, he told me at dinner last night about the conversation the two of you had during the trip here. He made it clear that if you decide not to go back to Weequahic, he wants me to support the hiring of Caleb Frazier."

"And you said?"

"I told him I like Caleb Frazier."

"David, that's not saying you support hiring him."

"No, it is not."

"I can tell you that your position could be a problem with Negroes in Newark."

"Why?"

"You're the last man to which I should be explaining this. Are you really unable to see why your non-committal of support for Caleb is troubling? You played a pivotal role in the organizing of the March on Washington in '63, and you were on the stage that day when Martin Luther King talked about his dream. You were in the East Room at the White House when President Johnson signed both the Civil Rights bill and the Voting Rights bill. How can you be on the fence about Frazier?"

"Mickey, please lower your voice. Some of these people are eavesdropping. Look, many Jewish people were distressed over last year's riots. That's a fact. They couldn't believe the pictures of Negroes looting and destroying property, and a lot of them will never forget what happened. I have talked to my friends in Detroit and Los Angeles, and they feel the same way about what occurred in their cities.

"As far as Reverend King is concerned, I have concerns about him meeting with Stokely Carmichael and others who are talking about black power. That same group calls Jewish people robber barons. Those are the people Reverend King has been meeting with. That's not the same preacher we remember from Birmingham in 1963 and Selma in '65. And look what is happening at Weequahic with the children there."

"What, they want to learn about their history, and they want better jobs and better education? And what is wrong about that, David?"

Seligman shook his head. "Oy vey, Mickey, you are sounding like a mensch with some meshugana tendencies. You Jews from the South are a rare breed, with strange ideas about being Jewish," he said with rising anger in a light Yiddish accent. "I am hearing that some of our people feel Negroes are moving too fast, that they are not being patient. Have you heard the talk about the convention being formed to discuss getting more Negroes voting in the next election, so a Negro mayor can be elected? Some people who are involved with that are nothing but a bunch of gonifs. They don't care about their own people, they are just trying to use them to get rich."

"David, I am a proud Sephardic Jew from South Carolina, from the Malka family. I am not ashamed of my particular Jewish upbringing, and I find nothing strange about it," Marcus whispered. "Now with that settled, I would like to add that the name-calling is beneath you. Plus, you don't know what their intentions are with that convention. Maybe they feel that Negroes can do a better job in responsible positions in the city. Newark has had Jewish people in charge, Irish people in charge, and now there is an Italian in charge. The city has gone down under all of them. This mayor is being called a crook because it seems like he is looking the other way while unscrupulous things are happening in his administration. That is not okay, and maybe there needs to be new blood leading the city.

"David, Newark is changing rapidly. I am going to keep doing what I'm doing to help with the change. I urge you to do your best to convince our people to be active in the change and not be bystanders."

"I'm here, aren't I? I still have hope, Mickey, but I am cautious. So too are some of our people. Maybe you should be our next mayor. You're a good man who has done great things in Newark. Why not you?"

"David, I appreciate your confidence in me. Who knows what I might do in the future? As far as caution, I understand. Unfortunately, I understand too well. But let's pray that nothing calamitous occurs anytime soon. Our country is sitting on a powder keg, and Newark is one of the fuses."

While Marcus and Seligman were engaged in their conversation, Reverend Wade was still speaking.

"Proverbs 13:20 says, 'He that walketh with wise men shall be wise, but a companion of fools shall be destroyed.' Our coach at Weequahic, Caleb Frazier, has only been at the helm since February, but he has been working with the legendary Mickey Marcus for close to three years. Mickey is here, by the way. Please give him a round of applause." Nearly everyone in the room stood and showed their appreciation with sustained clapping. Marcus stood and acknowledged the attention.

"Mr. Marcus and Mr. Frazier have guided the young men from Newark in this room to another winning season. Their basketball victories, however, have taken second place to what the Indians have done for the city of Newark. It hasn't been easy to dig out from under the rubble left by the Newark rebellion last summer. Yes, I feel it is inappropriately called a riot, that is why I call it a rebellion. Newark was in a dark place, and the success of this team has raised the banner of the city to national, perhaps even international heights. Mr. Marcus and the captain of the team, Nehemiah Garvey, made it their mission to bring Newark back to respectability. As faithful servants to a cause, they have made key strides to rescue the city from the physical and emotional flames of a rebellion. The coaches at Woodlawn have done their work to bring Birmingham to a better place, and with time, I pray they will be successful. You too have been faithful in your servanthood.

"There's been a lot leading up to this game since Mr. Frazier took on the task of coaching Weequahic after Mr. Marcus was diagnosed with cancer. From convincing his friends in Birmingham to help with race relations, to proving Weequahic could beat the top three teams in the country at the Watts Roundball Classic, Mr. Frazier has pushed hard to convince the Woodlawn coach to play Weequahic. It is truly ordained by God that we stand here now, twelve hours from tip-off, especially with Woodlawn being a previously all-white school which still has an overwhelmingly white faculty and few Negro children as students.

"In Proverbs 13:20, the word 'wise' stands out prominently. How wise it was for Mr. Frazier to heed God's call when he was told to walk with Mr. Marcus, and in the process, he became wise because he walked with a wise man. He was joined by the wise coach at Woodlawn, and the wise people here in Birmingham, and this monumental game was wisely scheduled. Now the nation can see what happens when wise people do wise things to accomplish wise deeds.

"It's funny, though, that the part of Proverbs 13:20, 'but a companion of fools shall be destroyed,' is ringing loudly in the ears of those who have problems supporting wise people because of the color of their skin. It makes me wonder if we will ever get beyond that sickness, or if it is a plague our country will have to live with for eternity. Nevertheless, we are here this morning in brotherhood because some people have not allowed themselves to be blinded by the malady of bigotry and misled by the altered definition of altruism.

"Tonight, there will be a clash of titans and at the end, there will be only one winner on the scoreboard. But the real victors will be the fans in the arena, cheering for their favorite teams while ignoring their physical differences. We must also ignore the regional segregation that has been unfortunately legislated and imposed by our antiquated political system. Add to that, these young men will be able to look back at this day many years from now, and say they participated in something that helped to save America during an unsettling time. May God bless all of us for having the courage to witness one of this country's best days. Hallelujah!"

There was joy in Mudville when the mighty Casey walked up to the plate, but the ecstasy was muted when he struck out. Of course, "Casey at the Bat" is a work of fiction. Not so in Birmingham last evening. It was all fact.

The Weequahic Indians put on a clinic of epic proportions in their rout of the country's second-ranked high school basketball team and gave Newark another reason to believe that its rescue from last summer's rebellion is making progress. Caleb Frazier's integrated squad took the full measure of the predominantly white Woodlawn High School Rebels. The proceedings before the game were substantive, with events sponsored by the Birmingham business community, the city government and Negro businessman A.G. Gaston.

It was a different story at the game, as the Woodlawn team was led on the court by the school's cheerleaders waving the Confederate flag. While the display could have been unsettling to the hundreds of fans that traveled from Newark, other cities in New Jersey and parts of America, Reverend Frederick Wade used his skills of persuasion to convince them to express a spiritual demeanor amidst the hostile atmosphere. It worked, especially when tempers flared on both teams at a time when the game was close.

The nation, including dignitaries from civil rights organizations, closely followed this significant chapter in our country's history, much like it did when Jackie Robinson broke the color line in major league baseball, playing his first game for the Brooklyn Dodgers on April 15, 1947; and when Jesse Owens won four gold medals at the Berlin Olympics in 1936, during the dawn of Adolf Hitler's racist regime.

Although the history books may never place Weequahic versus Woodlawn on equal footing with other barrier-breaking events as helping to cement the struggle for racial equality in America, it will certainly never be forgotten by those whose feet were firmly planted in that high school gymnasium, where the light of brotherhood began to erase the shadows of segregation.

And to think, it happened because Caleb Frazier, a Negro, dared to dream what was once thought to be impossible.

— Hy Silverman's column in *The Star-Ledger* sports section

"Well, Weequahic pulled it off," Gene Oldham said over the telephone to Herbert Evans. "Did you read the column by Hy Silverman?"

"Yeah, yeah, yeah. Big damn deal. They're still not gonna give that Negro the job," Evans said. "Ain't no way they're gonna let a Negro named Caleb coach at Weequahic, it just ain't gonna happen. There are certain people who don't want smart Negroes runnin' things that are made for white people to run.

"Frazier does things that make some people feel uncomfortable, like what he did in Birmingham. White folks and some of us don't like that. Look at all the hell Martin Luther King is havin' over tellin' the whole world that Lyndon Johnson and the white folks in this country are wrong about Vietnam. He even called the country weak because it hasn't beaten the Viet Cong yet. People don't like that kinda talk comin' from a Negro man. White people don't care for uppity Negroes."

"Yeah, some people in Atlanta told me he recently preached about the war at a service at his father's church. I was told he kicked President Johnson's ass with a whole bunch of five-dollar words. But Herbert, you have to give the man credit, he is not backing down about what white people aren't doing for blacks in America. He is not scared."

"I believe he has a death wish the way he's speakin' out, but it's all talk. That non-violent thing is holdin' him back because white people know he will turn the other cheek when it comes to a fight. As long as there's no threat of disruption, those people ain't givin' King no respect. Frederick Douglass said power concedes nothing without a demand, which means the people with the money ain't givin' up a damn thing if they don't think someone will take it from them. If King thinks that a poor people's march is gonna move Johnson and the Congress to go against white people and pass more legislation to help Negroes, he's crazy."

"Okay, Herbert. You're starting to get long winded. I have a meeting to attend. I'll talk with you later."

"Perry, Gene might not be the one we need on our team," Evans said to Perry Williamson, who was sitting in his office as he talked to Oldham on the telephone. "He's too timid, wantin' to go along to get along. Like King."

"You know, Herbert, Reverend King might not be as timid as you say he is. He has been taking President Johnson to task about Vietnam in every sermon or speech he does. I heard he said something about riots being the language of the unheard. He also said that America has failed to hear that poor people have gotten poorer and that white people are only interested in calm, even if it means to keep things as they are."

"Perry, I've been thinkin'. All that might work for us. We might be able to take advantage of people thinkin' that King is militant, anti-patriotic, yet too accommodatin' to white people."

"What's working in that mind of yours, Herbert?"

"King is supposed to be comin' here at the end of the month. He's supposed to be goin' to First Samuel, but Pastor Wade is gettin' a lot of criticism from the mayor and some Negroes about the visit. I guess because they're veterans and they're patriotic. We can go to some of these people and tell them we can help keep King from comin' here."

"And then people will point their fingers at us, saying we are causing problems with people who support King. How does that help us with the next election?"

"We create doubt about why King is comin' to Newark with the folks in those neighborhood organizations around the city and have them plant the seeds of discord. There are a number of Negroes in Newark who don't like King. They will talk to their friends about him and why there might be trouble if he comes here. I heard he got treated rough in Memphis and had to run from some unruly Negroes who didn't want him there. We just plant the seed of doubt about him, and the organizations will water and fertilize the ground."

"Herbert, that's a risky roll of the dice."

"It's a risk worth takin', Perry, especially when you look at the reward. There could be members of some of these organizations who want to run for City Council in '70. We get them to understand that our coalition can make that happen and ensure they will have representation in City Hall after the next election. We then tell the big money boys that we have the Negroes under our control and they need to finance our campaigns when we run for office. If we convince them to support us, we'll have the opportunity to take the ground floor of controllin' Newark, and the money that will flow through this place for decades."

"What about the men who want to run for City Council in '70?"

"What about them? We convince them that we need to take the lead in the next election, and that they should support us for that round. We'll pledge to stay in office for just one term and we'll support them in the election after that, in '74."

"Herbert, my opinion remains the same. That's a dangerous game you're getting ready to play."

"Perry, I've been livin' with danger all my life, why should I stop now? I got out of the South by blowing smoke up the asses of those peckerwoods down there, by shuckin' and jivin', makin' 'em think I was some kind of a Stepin Fetchit. Boy, did I fool 'em. I did it when I was elected Freeholder in '62 and almost pulled it off in '66 in the City Council election. I had those white boys in the palms of my hands when I ran against that slick talkin' Jew boy here in the South Ward, but we had too many Negroes on the ballot and the Negro vote got split. It won't happen like that again."

"So, you don't actually plan to support those people in the neighborhood organizations if they run for City Council after the 1970 election?"

"Hell no! And mess up my good thing? Perry, I have been plannin' this for a long time, and I'm ready to make my move."

"What about the black power crowd?"

"Let those Negroes wear afros and dashikis, with dungarees and dungaree jackets with Afro picks in their pockets, talkin' about speakin' Swahili and all that. I'll play the game with them so I can achieve my goal, but I got my eyes on the prize of controllin' Newark, not some cultural mumbo jumbo."

"Do we have to make it a Democratic Party or Republican Party plan?"

"Perry, you're the one who's pittin' the Democrats and Republicans against each other for Negro support, not me. It's up to you to sell your plan about voting independence for Negroes when we meet with those neighborhood groups. I'm gonna use my time to talk to the Jewish folks about the elections in '70, and what I'm willin' to do for them. They still have money and investments in Newark and we have to get all of that in order to win the next election."

"Sounds like you'll be selling yourself to the highest bidder."

"Perry, Perry, I know how the game is played around here. The Jewish folks don't want to be viewed as enemies of Negroes. Look how they've sold their synagogues here to the Negro churches at bargain basement prices, just to let us know they want to continue to be our friends. They might not want to live in Newark, but they certainly want to have their presence felt here for a long time. I'll be their connection, especially on this side of the city, as long as they pay my freight."

"You forgot about the north Newark crowd."

"Those boys have enough on their plates with the Puerto Ricans and other Latinos movin' over there. And plus, they don't want Negroes around their stuff, so they won't be doin' any biddin' for help from us.

"They also have their hands full with the problems about the mayor's alliances with some mob guys, and that right-wing dude who likes to appear in newspaper photos with rifles and handguns is creatin' problems for my Italian brothers. I'm already workin' a side deal with the people who are controllin' the port and the airport and downtown expansion, the ones who don't give a damn about the mayor and that criminal element. I'm goin' where the money is, with the Italians and the Jews. I love black power, but green power is mighty, baby."

"What about the neighborhood block associations? What are you gonna tell them when they want attention?"

"Once again, Perry, I have the answer. There are about six neighborhood block associations in the South Ward alone, right? Each one is around an elementary school, okay? As a matter of fact, I've already been meetin' with them every so often, so they see my face *before* it's election time. That way they get to know me better and askin' for their support once it's time to vote will be easier for me. Oh yeah, and I always bring food. You know our people love to eat."

"So, you meet with them until election time. What happens after that?"

"I form a civic association, in my case the Herbert Evans Civic Association, made up of people from the neighborhood block associations. They elect a president for my association, with a vice president, treasurer and all that, but I control the flow of the money. I'll find a way to use city dollars to finance the operations. We rent a building in the ward, call it a little city hall and we have community meetings there. We take trips to the beach, some Yankees and Mets games, stuff like that, and they feel connected.

"I find out what they're thinking about city government, help them with solutions and they keep voting for me. State and federal government officials who come to spend dollars in Newark will have me at the table with the mayor because they will want my support when it comes to their re-elections."

"What else? There's got to be some more."

"Perry, my mama and daddy didn't raise no fool. You think I'm gonna tell you my whole plan? Just stay tuned, you'll see it work as the 1970 elections get closer."

"You heard about what's happenin' in Washington?"

Evans rose from his chair. "What's that?"

"Robert Kennedy threw his name in the hat for Democratic nomination, since President Johnson barely won against Eugene McCarthy in the New Hampshire primary."

"Yeah, Kennedy's father is opening up his checkbook for another one of his sons to be in the White House. Kennedy's been tryin' to get Adam Clayton Powell to support him. He'd better be ready, because it's gonna take more than talk for that endorsement. Those Harlem boys know how to play politics for money; they won't be endorsing any white boy for free."

"There's another rumor out there. President Johnson might not be not running for reelection."

"What? Are you serious?"

"As serious as a heart attack."

"Get outta here!"

IN A SPEECH ON March 31, 1968, President Lyndon B. Johnson said, "Believing as I do, I have concluded that I should not permit the Presidency to become involved in the partisan divisions that are developing in this political year. With America's sons in the fields far away, with America's future under challenge right here at home, with our hopes and the world's hopes for peace in the balance every day, I do not believe that I should devote an hour or a day of my time to any personal partisan causes or to any duties other than the awesome duties of this office, the Presidency of your country.

"Accordingly, I shall not seek, and I will not accept, the nomination of my party for another term as your president."

Three days later, Dr. Martin Luther King Jr. said in a speech at a church in Memphis, Tennessee, "Well, I don't know what will happen now. We've got some difficult days ahead. But it really doesn't matter with me now, because I've been to the mountaintop. And I don't mind. Like anybody, I would like to live a long life; longevity has its place.

"But I'm not concerned about that now. I just want to do God's will. And he's allowed me to go up to the mountain. And I've looked over. And I've seen the Promised Land. I may not get there with you. But I want you to know tonight, that we, as a people, will get to the Promised Land. So, I'm happy, tonight. I'm not worried about anything. I'm not fearing any man. Mine eyes have seen the glory of the coming of the Lord."

The next day, on April 4, Dr. King was shot on the balcony of a motel in Memphis, Tennessee, shortly after 6pm. He was pronounced dead at 7:05 that evening.

WEEQUAHIC HAD MOVED TO number two in the *Scholastic Magazine* national rankings during the first week in March 1968, after its win over Woodlawn of Birmingham; but Camden dramatically vaulted to number one in the nation by defeating Boys High of Brooklyn, New York, which briefly sat atop the poll after its win over former number one, Beach High School of Savannah, Georgia.

Both Weequahic and Camden worked their way through the state tournament to the championship game in the New Jersey AAAA classification, which meant the two undefeated teams would face each other in what was billed by media across the country as the "first national championship game in high school basketball history" on the third weekend of March 1968.

Chapter 23

"We need a focused strategy on those communities where unemployment is higher, where poverty is higher. The bigger the headache, the bigger the pill. That means, the higher the unemployment rate, the bigger doses of medicine needed to get beyond unemployment and get back to economic growth."

~ Marc Morial, president of the National Urban League,
in the League's State of Black America report, in 2011

"That is why, with this milestone 40th Anniversary State of Black America, the National Urban League proposes a sweeping and decisive solution to the nation's persistent social and economic disparities. We call it the Main Street Marshall Plan. This bold and strategic investment in America's urban communities requires a multi-annual and multi-pronged commitment of $1 trillion over the next 5 years that would course correct our main streets. As America's urban communities continue to struggle in the slow rebound from the Great Recession, we can expedite the recovery by taking a lesson from the pages of our history books and similarly focusing our efforts with great vision and purpose-filled ambition. Our economy

205

and infrastructure have been shattered, not by bombs and tanks, but by malfeasance and indifference."

~ MARC MORIAL, IN THE NATIONAL URBAN LEAGUE'S
STATE OF BLACK AMERICA REPORT, IN 2016

NEWARK, REPRESENTED BY Weequahic High School, and Camden met in a classic New Jersey state championship game at the Convention Hall in Atlantic City, mid-March 1968. The largest crowd in the facility's history witnessed the first consensus national championship game in high school basketball in the 15-year history of the *Scholastic Magazine* high school basketball rankings.

"Triple overtime. I still don't believe we won that game," Nehemiah Garvey, now 65, said to Chante, the 40-year old daughter of his deceased cousin, Denise. He and Chante were sitting in the lobby of Newark's Robert Treat Hotel, waiting for several of Nehemiah's friends. Together they would attend the 50th anniversary ceremony of the 1966–67 Weequahic High School basketball team that was undefeated and ranked number one in the country. Nehemiah had played on that team as a sophomore. The event was being held at the New Jersey Performing Arts Center—better known as the NJPAC—in downtown Newark.

"You say that every time you talk about that game, Daddy," Chante said. She had been left motherless when Denise passed away at 23. Nehemiah legally adopted her at five years old, immediately after her mother's death.

"I remember how hard your mother was cheering that night. She even started crying when we were losing with two minutes left in the game."

"She used to tell me that story whenever we talked about how her life was so different, back when she was a little girl. She said she followed you around like a little puppy dog."

Denise found out after she became a teenager that she had been adopted by Nehemiah's aunt Elizabeth, which debunked the story that her parents had been killed in a factory explosion in 1959. She relentlessly searched for her birth mother until she met her outside of a liquor store, on Bergen Street in Newark. A woman approached Denise and some of her friends when they were leaving a record shop. She was reeking of alcohol and seemed to be high on drugs. The woman began babbling about knowing Denise and telling her that she was her mother. She said that Denise was taken from her by, "that lady who owned the beauty parlor on High Street," and the family wouldn't allow her to see Denise.

Denise confronted Lula Mae and the rest of the family, asking them about her birth and why they never told her that her mother was alive. The family told Denise that her mother was a superb vocalist, who had attended Arts High School in Newark—the oldest public high school specializing in visual and performing arts in the country. Her mother started singing in local nightclubs when she was only fourteen and began having a sexual relationship with a musician who was in his thirties. She got pregnant a year later, but the man refused to admit he was the father and left Newark before Denise's birth. When the girl started using drugs, drinking alcohol, and neglecting Denise, Lula Mae—who would talk to the girl at the beauty parlor whenever she would get her hair dressed before she sang at the clubs—convinced the young mother to give the child to Elizabeth to raise.

The Eleazer family had treated Denise as one of their own, giving her everything all of the other children received: upbringing in a respected family, a great education and a promising future. All of that began to unravel after Denise's discovery. She became friends with unsavory people, missed school on a regular basis, and was constantly uncooperative and disrespectful to adults. Denise got pregnant at 18, left home soon after she gave birth to Chante, and several years later was found dead in a drug house in Philadelphia. After practically growing up as brother and sister, losing his cousin had left a severe impact on Nehemiah.

"I never considered your mother a puppy dog, but she certainly stayed close to me when she was little," he said. "That girl made me leave my state championship jackets at home when I went to college, the ones with my varsity letters on them, so she could show them off to her friends. Because of our relationship, I refused scholarships from major colleges in other parts of the country and accepted the offer to remain in New Jersey and go to Rutgers so I could stay close to her. I was devastated when she died."

After graduating from Weequahic, Nehemiah had gone to Rutgers University, playing for the varsity basketball team for three years. He was the squad's Most Valuable Player during his senior year, when Rutgers went to the Final Four of the 1973 National Collegiate Athletic Association basketball tournament. He graduated with an undergraduate degree in Business Administration, then worked for Mickey Marcus as chief operating officer for his chain of health spas throughout the country. While he was employed by Marcus, Nehemiah earned an M.B.A., also at Rutgers, and had been awarded a scholarship to law school at the Newark campus of Rutgers.

Mickey Marcus kept his promise to help Nehemiah advance his career; he loaned him money after he completed law school. Nehemiah used some of the money to open a real estate and property development company, while investing the rest in a company which grew to be a well-respected entity listed on Wall Street. Nehemiah became a remarkably wealthy man before he turned forty, largely because of his association with Mickey Marcus.

Nehemiah was singing softly. *"I was born by the river in a little tent, oh, and just like the river I've been running ever since. It's been a long time coming, but I know a change is gonna come, oh yes it will."*

"You really love that song, don't you?" Chante asked.

"If you listen to the words, you hear some powerful emotion. It means a lot to me, especially with all that I saw and went through growing up during that time." Nehemiah draped his arm over Chante's shoulder, his eyes glancing around the room. "Sam Cooke wrote this song after he and his musicians were denied accommodations at a whites-only motel in Louisiana, a practice that was legal in many parts of the South in the 1950s. Many people involved in the civil rights struggle sang that song when they were marching and protesting. Funny though, it seems we're going back to those days in a strange sort of way."

"Still waiting for change, huh? Sounds like a political campaign I heard about nine years ago."

"Even after having an African American president for eight years, we're still waiting," Nehemiah said with a soft tone as he closed his eyes. "Yes, still waiting. I pray not in vain."

A moment later, a group of men walked out of the elevator and across the lobby.

"Wake up, man," Billy Stern said. "It's time for a celebration."

"Billy, what are you doing here?" Nehemiah exclaimed while rising from his chair. "I thought you were vacationing in the south of France."

"What? And miss this? Never."

Nehemiah hugged Stern, then slapped hands and fist bumps with the other men.

"Cecil Cambridge. The Bahamas Man who saved the Weequahic win against Camden in '68, who played on three NCAA championship teams at UCLA, and played ten years with the Knicks. And the heroes from the Woodlawn victory, Lenny Rosenberg and Stuie Greenblatt. You guys didn't tell me you were coming."

"This is special for us," Rosenberg said. "Even though it's for the '67 team, we kept the tradition goin' with what we did the season after those guys left, and then you, Howard Lucas, Cecil, and Tommy Caruso won again in '69. Four straight undefeated seasons, consensus national champions three years in a row, and the longest winnin' streak in the history of New Jersey high school basketball. That was the final achievement for Mr. Marcus."

"Plus, we brought Newark back from the ashes of the riot with the magical year in '68. Can't forget Caleb Frazier and how he took over when Mickey Marcus got cancer," Stern said.

Nehemiah's eyes began to tear up. "As you guys know, we didn't have Mr. Frazier our last season. He wasn't asked to return after '68, so Mr. Marcus came back for one more season. Mr. Frazier went back down south and coached his old high school team in Charlotte, became a principal, and later retired down there. He coached his teams to eight state championships in ten years. I stayed in touch with him over the years, and when he passed away, I went to his funeral. He never got over not getting asked back to be head coach at Weequahic."

"What about Tommy Caruso? He was a tough little dude," Cambridge said.

"He got involved with big money gangsters down in Miami after he finished college," Nehemiah said. "He ended up in California, where he was convicted in a money scheme like that Bernie Madoff dude. He got convicted and sent to prison; he died out there. I didn't find out about that until a few years ago."

"Alright, man, this is getting a little too deep. Let's head over to the center," Stern said. "Wait a minute. Is this Chante?"

"Live," Chante said, striking a model's pose, "and in living color."

"You look just like your mother. I thought for a minute that my man Nee was robbin' the cradle," Stern said. "I didn't wanna say anything when I first saw you after I got off the elevator. You can't be more than twenty-five, right?"

"If you're trying to find out my age, that line won't work."

"Alright, Billy, stop flirtin'. Just because your wife's not here doesn't mean you're not married," Nehemiah said. He and Chante proceeded to lead the other four out of the hotel to the street, heading toward the New Jersey Performing Arts Center, less than a thousand feet away.

More than three hundred people were mingling in the foyer, while a few hundred more were making their way into the venue. A large number of schoolchildren were among the throng, mixing with a strong representation of older citizens, many of whom were high school students when the Weequahic basketball team had its incredible season in 1967. Mickey Marcus—now in his nineties—was being interviewed by a number of reporters inside spacious Prudential Hall, where the ceremony was going to be held.

"I am thankful to have lived this long to see this day," Marcus said. "A lot of things happened to this city in 1967, much of it not so nice. What this team did that year was one of the few bright spots for Newark and I am proud to have been part of it."

"You weren't just part of it, Mr. Marcus, you made it happen," one of the reporters said. "And it wasn't just a bright spot, it was the light that led the path to a couple of more great years for Newark high school basketball."

"Well, the real heroes were the players and their families. The moms and dads, grandmothers and grandfathers who instilled solid values in those young men that kept their minds uncluttered. Did you know that every one of the players and student managers from our team went to college, and with the exception of two, received their degrees in four years? Now, do you still want to lavish all that praise on me? I think not."

Eva Mae Garvey sat in the foyer with a number of her friends from First Samuel Missionary Baptist Church.

"Eva Jean, I know your heart is burstin' with pride, lookin' at all these young people gettin' ready to honor those boys," one of the women said.

"I'm just happy that we got a special invitation from the mayor's office to be here today," Eva Jean said. "A lot of those boys' families were members of our church. In fact, some of those families are still represented there. My mother and Reverend Wade would have been so happy right now," she said, wiping a tear from her cheek, "especially with one of our First Samuel members as mayor of Newark."

A group of men who played at other high schools in New Jersey were standing close to the entrance.

"I got a text from Billy Stern about ten minutes ago," one of guys said, "and he told me that he would have Nehemiah walking in just about now. Now, remember what to do when he gets here."

Stern was play boxing with Nehemiah as they approached the crosswalk in front of the center. Though the light was red, Nehemiah kept walking.

"Whatcha waitin' for, Billy?" Nehemiah asked. "Oh, that's right. You're down there in Florida where they don't jaywalk." Billy and the rest of the group followed as the light turned green.

"It's Nehemiah Garvey!" the men from the other schools yelled as he walked into the center. At that moment, the crowd inside began chanting "Nee" as Nehemiah walked toward his mother and her friends.

"I came from California to pay my respects to this great team," one of the men in the foyer told Nehemiah. He was Stan Johnson, who had played for Central against Weequahic and was considered one of the best players from Newark during those years. "I played against you guys for three years in the mid-sixties. It was a shame that it was the three years y'all won three state championships. Central had some great teams in the same classification as Weequahic and Camden, but we couldn't get past Weequahic to get to the state finals back then."

"As I live and breathe, I am seeing two of New Jersey's greatest basketball players together. Me and Stan Johnson," Smokey Baker said. Baker played on three of Weequahic's state championship teams in the mid-sixties and was on the high school All-American team when the Indians were rated number one in the country in 1967. Baker played for five teams during a 12-year career in the National Basketball Association.

"I'm surprised you're being that humble, Smokey," one of the players from the great 1965 South Side High School team said. "You have argued for as long as I can remember that our team wasn't the best team in the history of the state, though almost everybody I know agrees that we were, including Mickey Marcus." A few more people got involved in the conversation and before anyone could say, "Newark Pride," there was a full-scale debate being recorded by television cameras, smartphones, and other recording devices.

"Ask Mr. Marcus if you don't believe me. The Central teams from '60 to '64 were the best in New Jersey," two women who were cheerleaders at Central, Newark's second oldest school, said.

"I haven't heard anybody mention any teams from East Orange, Linden, Camden or even Teaneck during the seventies, eighties, and nineties. They had some great players during that time," somebody yelled.

"What about the Catholic school teams in Jersey City, Roselle, and Elizabeth?"

Mickey Marcus walked up on the debaters. "Okay, everybody, this could go on forever. It's time for the ceremony. We need to start going inside the auditorium."

Somebody yelled out, "Mr. Marcus, what team was the best in New Jersey? You should know!"

"Who me? What do I know?" Marcus said. "I've only been around here for about eighty years." The people in the foyer laughed out loud.

MORE THAN FIFTY YEARS after the rebellions of the 1960s, Newark and many other cities in America that were defined as urban enclaves, had populations of more than fifty per cent black/African American residents. An overwhelming number of those affected were crowded into neighborhoods that suffered from benign neglect due to economic development targeted for downtown areas. Unemployment and underemployment, health care, and K–12 education were largely ignored. Crime exploded as a result of those maladies, while the law-abiding occupants in those sectors watched helplessly as their pleas for sustained assistance remained unseen, unheard, and un-answered by governments, which on a number of levels were both inept and corrupt.

"I cannot believe I am hearing nearly the same arguments against helping cities with large African American populations as I heard when I was a teenager in my hometown during the sixties," Newark mayor, Lena Ashby Mosley, said at the opening session of the U.S. Conference of Mayors annual meeting. It was being held in Newark for the first time ever, and Mosley was serving as the host.

"I watched Newark get pillaged by desperate people who felt that the only way their voices could be heard was through the destruction of their already economically deprived neighborhoods. After watching what has been happening lately in these same cities, I have often wondered if time just passed them by. Before this three-day conference is over, I pray that we will leave with a plan that the new administration in Washington, DC will make a priority.

"All of our cities in this association have contributed to the writing of this plan and we are committed to seeing it implemented.

"One of the good things happening during this conference is that we will be honoring the former mayor of Newark, who is now the country's Secretary of Housing and Urban Development. As a former educator and high school principal, he understands the connection between intact neighborhoods and well-educated children with lower dropout rates. We all know how desperately we need to restore our neighborhoods. As H.U.D. Secretary, he will oversee the Sterling Neighborhoods program, something that the new administration talked about during the presidential campaign. In closing, thank you for coming to Newark, and enjoy yourselves while you are here."

Lena Ashby Mosley was Newark's first female mayor in its 351-year history. She was elected shortly after the former mayor was confirmed as the H.U.D. Secretary, in February 2017. Though he was instrumental in getting huge numbers of African American voters to the polls for one of the two losing candidates, the former mayor was nevertheless recognized by the new president as someone who could be instrumental in moving his agenda forward as it related to improving the nation's infrastructure.

"Man, it's still hard to believe that our childhood friend, Lena Ashby, is the mayor of our hometown," Jimmy Trawick said. He was in attendance with Nehemiah at the welcome breakfast for the U.S. Conference of Mayors annual meeting. "I hope she realizes it's because of you that she's in City Hall."

"Jimmy, you know I don't believe in taking credit," Nehemiah said. "Lena won because she had a great team behind her. She was helped by the lives that her mother and father touched while they were in the Newark school system and as members of First Samuel. Plus, Lena brought a great reputation back to Newark for the work she did in Virginia after she graduated from Hampton."

Lena Ashby had earned a Master's degree in education from the University of Virginia, immediately after graduating from then Hampton Institute (now Hampton University). She married a man from a prominent Richmond, Virginia family, and gave birth to three children while establishing herself as a dedicated social worker. She later became a nationally recognized superintendent of schools in the county where she lived. Lena's husband passed away when their children were teenagers, leaving her to care for them as a single mother. Nevertheless, she continued her pursuit of education, taking night classes to earn a PhD. in public administration. All three of her children attended college and became gainfully employed soon after their respective graduations. Lena had returned to Newark two years before the mayoral election, to care for her aging parents.

"Lena's challenge is going to be growing the neighborhoods to match the growth of downtown," Nehemiah said.

"That's your specialty, Nee. Look at what you've been doing with your business partnerships across the country."

"Jimmy, Newark is a different kettle of fish. I've been trying for years to duplicate my national efforts here, but the pushback from local politicians has been enormous. Our former mayor seemed to be coming around to my side, but then he went to Washington."

"And you convinced Lena to run. And she won. And now she is lookin' to you to work your economic development magic at home."

"Sounds like what I wanted to do fifty years ago, after the riot."

"You did it, didn't you?"

"Yeah, I guess I did."

"Nee, it's time to go to work again."

"The more things change, the more they remain the same. Looks like it's a throwback to 1967."

Chapter 24

"Abraham Lincoln had to deal with race, George Washington had to deal with race, Lyndon Baines Johnson had to deal with race, how come you are the first president that does not have to deal with race? It wasn't a black president who passed the Civil Rights Bill. It wasn't a black president who passed the Voting Rights Act. It wasn't a black president who passed the Fair Housing Act. It wasn't a black president who dealt with Affirmative Action. If you're going to be like any other president, deal with race."

~ Dr. Michael Eric Dyson, at the State of the
Black Union conference in Chicago, speaking
about President Barack Obama, in 2010

"For too long, we were blind to the pain that the Confederate flag stirred in too many of our citizens. It's true, a flag did not cause these murders. But as people from all walks of life, Republicans and Democrats, now acknowledge—including Governor Haley, whose recent eloquence on the subject is worthy of praise—as we all have to acknowledge, the flag has always represented more than just ancestral pride. For many, black and white, that flag was a reminder of systemic oppression and racial subjugation. We see that now."

~ President Barack Obama, delivering the eulogy for Charleston, SC state senator and pastor, Clementa Pinckney, in 2015

The opinions about how governmental policies improved the lives of African Americans were largely mixed during the eight years of President Barack Obama's administration. The prevailing notion was fairly negative among people who lived in the neighborhoods that experienced higher rates of crime, unemployment and underemployment, and poorly funded K–12 education from 2009 through 2016.

"We are now walking in the neighborhood where my father purchased a home when I was five years old," Nehemiah told the group he was escorting on behalf of Mayor Lena Mosley. The group consisted of a number of officials representing cities that were part of the U.S. Conference of Mayors annual meeting. "Before he went to Washington to serve in the president's cabinet, our former mayor was drawing up a great plan to restore areas like this, which have unfortunately fallen on hard times."

"Yeah, maybe the Obama administration should have made shoring up inner-city neighborhoods a priority when he first took office," someone said. Some local residents were observing the group from their porch.

"Excuse me, sir, are you Nehemiah Garvey?" a woman with a distinctive Caribbean accent asked as she walked toward Nehemiah.

"Yes ma'am. Do I know you?"

"No, I don't think so. But this man says he knew your father. He claims he lived around the corner from your family."

"Your daddy was a fine man. He really cared about this neighborhood," the elderly man said while extending his wrinkled hand. "My name is Gabriel, like the angel who told Mary she was going to give birth to Jesus Christ."

"Okay, Gabe," Nehemiah said as he and the man exchanged firm handshakes.

"No, Mr. Garvey, he wants you to call him Gabriel," the woman said. "He insists he be called Gabriel. He wants to talk to you."

"Ma'am, you can call me Nehemiah. Sir, I would like to find out more about my father, since you knew him. But I'm busy conducting this tour for the mayor right now. Nehemiah looked at the woman. "Can I meet with you later?"

"Yes," she said. "I would also like to talk to you about this neighborhood. You still own some property around here, right?"

"Yes ma'am. I still have a presence around here. I welcome that conversation. Give me your contact number and I'll call you."

SINCE THE FORMATION OF THE United States, large numbers of northern cities overlooked the concerns of communities that were once considered ghettoes. Jewish families, as well as Italian, Polish, and other European clans were crowded into such communities in the beginning, but from 1915 through 1960 black families moved into those areas in great numbers, an era known as the Great Migration. Though property and sales tax revenues were plentiful during part of this period, the dollars were largely spent to develop downtown properties in what were termed public-private partnerships during much of the '70s and '80s. After middle-class families fled to suburban hamlets and more affluent neighborhoods, black home renters and less educated African American, lower middle-class homeowners were left to reside in the vast wastelands of the inner core of many cities.

"We can't be held hostage to negotiate any deals left in place by the former mayor," one trustee of the Port Authority of New York and New Jersey said at a Board of Directors meeting. "We haven't agreed that we owe the city of Newark any money, thus we are under no obligation to purchase the land occupied by the airport and seaport to satisfy that debt."

"You don't think Mayor Mosley is capable of forcing our hand?" another trustee said.

"She's a lightweight. The only experience she has is in social work, and as a superintendent of schools in a small district down south. Newark doesn't have any economic development gurus in the black community, so who is she going to turn to for advice?"

"Well I don't know about that. Her best friend is Nehemiah Garvey. He got her elected. He's smart, shrewd, and he knows how to handle money. I mean, that guy was considered for Secretary of Commerce by the new administration. People in high places like him."

"But she's not him, plus he has no interest in helping with deals in Newark. Absolutely *zero* interest. He's making too much money in other cities."

"There's a first time for everything."

"Garvey is at an age where he just wants to count his money and fade into the sunset. Mosley is on her own, which means we don't have her to worry about."

THE PEOPLE NEHEMIAH MET in his old neighborhood were ecstatic about talking to him. He returned to meet with them.

"Our network of neighborhood block associations throughout Newark backed Mayor Mosley's campaign, and you were the reason," the president of Newark Block Associations United said in her home. "Of course, we want something in return."

"Like the city cleaning up the neighborhoods and making them attractive for people to move into, at the same time downtown is being revitalized?" Nehemiah said. "I'm already on it. Just need to confirm some of the logistics and details."

"We need more homeowners in the neighborhoods, and more projects like the one that grows food and teaches healthy living."

"That's the SWAG Project around the corner in front of the Peshine Avenue School. A good friend of mine is in charge of it. As far as home ownership goes, the owners will need tenants who will consistently pay their rents, which will help owners offset their costs and expenses. My company has helped communities in other cities with revitalization projects, but they only extended the programs to areas close to downtown."

"The block associations wouldn't be happy about something like that."

"I know it, and neither am I. That's why I'm working on something far different. It's loosely based on what Abraham Lincoln and Congress did in 1862, during the Civil War."

"Abraham Lincoln? 1862? Civil War? All of that is a long time ago," the president said. The other members of the group began to murmur.

"Y'all hear him out. Give him a chance to explain," the man named Gabriel said.

"President Lincoln wanted to spread the country farther westward for a multitude of reasons, some of which had to do with stopping slavery," Nehemiah said. "He pushed to get The Homestead Act of 1862 through Congress. The legislation stated that any current or future citizen could claim a homestead of up to one hundred sixty acres of government land for only ten dollars, as long as the land was not in one of the existing 34 states. I'm writing a plan similar to that for more home ownership in areas of Newark where there are large numbers of boarded up homes."

"Our former mayor did something like this. He offered boarded up homes for $1,000. It's not working that well right now."

"I know all about that. As a matter of fact, I thought about investing in that program, but I needed more details, like specific incentives. The program I am writing will not only improve the neighborhoods but minimize criminal activity and rebuild the schools in those areas as well."

"Do you have any ideas to get control of the Newark public schools from the state?"

"The former mayor put that plan into motion before he went to Washington. All Mayor Mosley has to do is continue to move it forward. That should happen this year. Now, do you mind if I change the subject?"

"No problem. We just wanted you to understand our concerns and see if we could work with you. We've lost a lot of ground in the years since the riot, even though the different mayors and city councils each tried to make progress. We are confident that Mayor Mosley will take the best of what the former mayor started and add her own touches."

"I think I agree with you on all of these issues, and I will work with Mayor Mosley to help make those tasks happen. For now, really, I would like to change the subject to something personal, if you don't mind. I'm trying to find out what happened to my father back in '65. Mr. Gabriel, you knew him. Was he having any problems with people in the community?"

"Like your father, I come from Jamaica," Gabriel said with a thick accent. "He and I lived there at a time when the English treated us like slaves, even though we were free. He and I were children in those days. We knew very little about what the English government was doing. But your father grew to be an intelligent man who knew a lot about the world and shared his knowledge with anyone who would listen. I knew no one that did not like him."

"If my father were alive today, he would be more than 100 years old. Mr. Gabriel, how old are you?"

"Gabriel does not know his age," the president of the group interrupted.

"Does he have any identification? Driver's license? Social Security card? Medicare card?"

"Let me explain about him," the woman said. "Do you remember the big fire in the Central Ward in '65?"

"Yes, I do. My grandmother's beauty parlor was damaged, but she was able to do the repairs in a short period of time because she had insurance. Others weren't so fortunate."

"Our home was burning," she continued. "I was a young teenager then and I was trapped inside with my two sisters. Our father was able to get our baby brother out and wanted to go back in to rescue us, but the firemen would not allow it. We were screaming, when all of a sudden, a very large man with big hands picked all three of us up and carried us out of the house. It was as if God paved a path for us and the man through the flames."

"Who did that?"

"Mr. Gabriel did, and he did more. He went back into that house and rescued five old people. But then he ran away."

"What do you mean he ran away? Where did he go?"

Nehemiah looked back at Mr. Gabriel. "Where did you go, sir?" Gabriel stayed quiet, avoiding eye contact.

The woman continued. "He acted as if he did not want anyone to know him and what he had done. But my father and some of the other men looked all over the neighborhood and found him. They brought him back to our home, cleaned him up and fed him. Oh, he was so hungry, and he needed a bath. My father and mother took him into our home and he became part of our family. We gave him the name Gabriel.

"He worked at my father's handyman business and when we moved into the Valley, he came with us. To make a long story short, we never found out his age or where he came from. He has been with me through my teenage years, the passing of my parents and grandparents, then with my husband and now our family. He worked with my father, doing repairs on homes inside and outside of Newark, and they fixed all kinds of appliances for people in the community. As you can see, he is still with me today."

"That is a great story. More people should hear about it."

"No, no. Gabriel does not want that. It's as if he is running from something, or somebody."

"Far be it for me to challenge his right to privacy. I respect his wishes, but I am sure glad to have met him." Nehemiah looked again at Gabriel directly. "Maybe one day you and I will talk about my father. I would love to listen to anything you might know or remember."

THE ANNUAL MEETING OF the U.S. Conference of Mayors received nationwide media coverage, which put the spotlight on the changes in Newark. While a Newark native was in the president's cabinet—the former mayor of Newark was appointed Secretary of Housing and Urban

Development—Mayor Mosley had become a spokesperson for addressing the problems facing depressed areas in major cities.

"Mayor Moseley, there are some people in Washington who are calling you a lightweight on economic issues, saying that your experience as a social worker and a superintendent of schools does not equip you in that arena. How do you address that perception?" The reporter was in the front row at the final news conference for the national mayors' annual meeting.

"Well, first of all, I don't know who 'some people' are, thus I can't address them by name, as much as I would like to," Mosley said. "I do know, however, that the meetings here these last several days have seen a number of energized debates over the processes of partnerships between the federal government and individual cities, either urban or rural. It's been a long time since small towns have felt respected by large cities, and within this organization we aim to respect diverse concerns. As far as being behind the learning curve when it comes to dollars and cents, please tell those people in Washington that I will be leading a team of experts on the economy and then maybe they will understand how much I weigh."

"Does Newark have an advantage with the president since there is a cabinet member from your city in a prominent position?" another reporter asked.

"I will take this time to congratulate the new president for having the foresight to see the kind of leaders that come from my hometown," Mosley said, "but I caution anyone to believe that Newark is by itself when it comes to creative leadership, even though our own Nehemiah Garvey was considered to head the Department of Commerce. There are gold mines of intellectual excellence within many of this nation's underserved communities, but they have been overlooked because of the unbridled partisanship of the major political parties, which blinded Congress and the former executive branch for the past eight years."

"Was that why the black community suffered during the Obama administration?"

"That question needs to be posed to those persons who advised President Obama during that time. My concern is advancing the agenda of the majority of people who don't live inside the beltway of Washington, D.C. I appreciate this time we have spent together this afternoon, discussing what has been accomplished at this annual meeting of the U.S. Conference of Mayors. I will look for many of you at tonight's gala at the Performing Arts Center. Thank you for being here in the great city of Newark."

"GRANDMA, DO YOU EVER WANT to go back to live in the old neighborhood?" Chante asked Eva Jean Garvey. The two of them sat in the living room of the home Eva Jean shared with Nehemiah, within a stone's throw from Weequahic Park in the South Ward.

"I miss living around Peshine Avenue School. That was a special place back in the fifties and sixties, but it began to change in the late seventies when the people who owned homes began to leave and more renters started moving in. Those people didn't care about the quality of life we had there.

"I remember Nehemiah and his friends playing football in the street after it had snowed when they were little boys, about nine or ten. I remember the playground right across the street from our house, when we had the neighborhood carnival every spring."

"Daddy told me about those. That's when white people still lived in the neighborhood, right?"

"Um, hm. But even after they left, we still did special things at that school. Our monthly PTA meetings always had a lot of parents in the auditorium. There were after school basketball leagues, the jump roping competitions. What I miss most is the way we looked after each other. The boys would take the neighbors' trash cans into their backyards after the trash was taken up. The older people would have friendly conversations while they swept the trash from in front of their homes. If somebody was sick, some of the ladies would make sure their children were taken care of with dinner or help them with their homework.

"It was a real village, kind of like what the African proverb says about a village raising a child, except it was our entire neighborhood raising each other. The Peshine neighborhood was special, but I'm sure everybody's neighborhood was special. The same in cities like LA, Cleveland, and Miami. Neighborhoods like Harlem. That's why I'm praying that Nehemiah will be able to convince the politicians to change their ways about helping poor people, so the places where they live will get better and safer. I hope he has the energy to do it."

"Grandma, Daddy did it before. He can do it again," Chante said.

Chapter 25

"The White House is not in the dark on our agenda. The White House knows quite well what our priorities are. Democratic leader, Nancy Pelosi, knows. Speaker of the House and Republican leader, Paul Ryan, knows. But we get overlooked, and that is very unfortunate."

~ Congressional Black Caucus chairman
G.K. Butterfield, United States Representative from
North Carolina, on federal budget spending, in 2015

"The Democratic Party has got to say to working people we are on your side. We are going to take on Wall Street, we are going to lower the cost of prescription drugs, we are going to raise the minimum wage, we are not going to be the only major country on earth that doesn't guarantee health care to all people. Democrats have got to stand with the working families of this country."

~ U.S. Senator Bernie Sanders, Independent from Vermont
and 2016 Democratic Party primary candidate for
President, after Donald Trump won the campaign, in 2016

"I HAVE TALKED TO THE other mayors in the conference and they are comfortable with you as a member of the group that will meet with the congressional leadership from both parties in Washington," Mayor

Mosley told Nehemiah in her office. "They like your style, and most of all, they absolutely love the story about what you did after the riot."

"I wonder how much they heard was fact and how much was fiction?"

"C'mon, Nee, get serious. What you did back then was courageous, especially for a teenager. Remember, I watched you up close and personal when you did it."

"I'll receive that pat on the back, but that was then and this is now. I don't know how effective I was at that time because we took a serious nosedive with the first black mayor's time in office, which was for sixteen years. It got a little better with the next one, quite successful in some areas, moderately successful in others, a failure in others. The jury is still out on the third one, but his record looks spotty. But he is our Senator and one of the people who could be the Democratic nominee for president in three years."

"The man we elected as mayor in 2014 did a great job of catching up in a short period of time," Mosley said. "He put some great ideas on the table, made tremendous strides in implementing them and now the city is on an upward trajectory. Still, those of us who are working to improve the conditions in the other cities are finding that nothing much has changed in any of them.

"That's why we need a clear thinker like you going to Washington to fight to bring money back to these underserved communities. Back when we were teenagers, Congress defeated a bill that would have appropriated money to combat rat infestation problems in Newark and other cities. I actually knew a kid who died from a rat bite; he lived next door to me. Believe it or not, rodent problems are coming back. And do I need to say anything about violent crime? The politicians in Washington just keep saying to please be patient. I say we need to make some noise, like a squeaky wheel, and get some grease."

"Oh, I agree with you. Remember, my company works in cities across the country and I am hearing the same talk that I heard back in the sixties and seventies, that things don't happen overnight. I am just as angry about the current situation nationwide as I was when I wanted to save Newark after the rebellion fifty years ago. You're right about the politicians giving a lot of lip service, both the Republicans and Democrats."

"So, that means you're on board, right?"

"Lena, I mean Ms. Mayor, how can I say no to you?"

"You couldn't when we were kids and you can't do it now. I love you, Nee. Thank you."

"Now that we've gotten all of that out of the way, I have something else I need to mention to you," Nehemiah said. "I am on a crusade to find my father."

"You think he's alive?"

"My mother does, which means I'm leaning in that direction."

"Nee, your father would be about a hundred years old if he is still living."

"Doesn't matter. If he *is* still alive, there's a reason why God kept him here this long. Right now, I need your prayers. I might need more later on."

"Just let me know what I can do and it will be done."

THE REPUBLICAN-DOMINATED Congress and the Democratic minority in both chambers—the House of Representatives and the Senate—consistently bickered over a wide variety of issues during the eight years of the Obama administration. Though relations seemed to be getting better when Wisconsin Congressman Paul Ryan became Speaker of the House in 2015, cities with high percentages of African Americans and Hispanics found themselves getting the short end of tax dollar appropriations. Some members of the Congressional Black Caucus made statements such as "half trillion-dollar handouts to the rich and well-connected" and "giveaways to corporations, special interests, and the richest few" to get the attention of lawmakers on Capitol Hill and President Obama's budget advisors but got no results.

> Mayor Lena Mosley is already shaking things up in
> Washington with her strong advocacy of better treatment
> for cities with large populations of poor people. During the

recent annual meeting of the U.S. Conference of Mayors, hosted by Mayor Mosley in Newark, she let the world know that she is willing to go on the offensive to get more tax dollars for housing, education and economic development in urban areas.

The mayor has only been in office for ninety days, and wisely used her brief time with conference leaders to form a task force comprised of elected officials and business leaders from a number of cities. That task force will aggressively lobby Congress and the new administration in the White House. Mosley strategically worked the conference hierarchy to place someone on the task force familiar to Newark residents: Nehemiah Garvey.

It was fifty years ago when a teenage Garvey forged his well-known crusade to restore Newark's reputation after the devastating riot in 1967. Garvey led his Weequahic High School basketball team to a number one national ranking while making Newark a household name across America. Since that time, Garvey has been a successful businessman around the country, establishing home ownership opportunities for low-income residents in underserved communities.

If Garvey is as determined and capable in this campaign to resurrect America's urban neighborhoods as he was in leading the charge to redeem his hometown in 1967, Mayor Lena Mosley will be viewed nationwide as a trailblazer of inner-city restoration. Her legacy as a leader will largely result from her long-standing connection to Garvey.

Not bad for a place that was given up for dead fifty years ago.

— The Star-Ledger editorial

MICKEY MARCUS WAS SITTING with an old friend, having breakfast in a local diner on Route 22 in northern New Jersey.

"Mickey, I can't believe that you support Mayor Mosley appointing Nehemiah Garvey to lobby the federal government for more funding. Taxpayers in this country have been supporting programs for African Americans since Lyndon Johnson's Great Society, and all we've gotten back is bad behavior, illegitimate children, poorly educated youth in public schools, out of control crime, and crooked politicians keeping down the very communities they purport they want to save. Enough is enough."

"Tell me how you really feel, Harvey. Do you have a problem with Nehemiah, or the funding sources?"

"Both. But not so much with Nehemiah. I think he has good intentions."

"Really? So, let me make sure I have this right. You say Nehemiah has a good heart, but you have a problem with him going to Washington to ask lawmakers for fair treatment of law-abiding taxpayers who play by the rules?"

"Sounds like another power grab by people who claim that racism is the reason that blacks can't make progress. When are they going to take personal responsibility for their problems?"

"First, Harvey, it's not just about black people. It's about *all* citizens who want to get the services from government that they pay for, whether they're black, brown, white, woman, man, gay or straight. I think they were clear about that in last year's election.

"Secondly, you sound like a broken record. I heard this same refrain when I asked you to help with the formation of the Weequahic Alumni Association fifteen years ago. All I heard you do was whine about the school having a student population that is all black, and that there are no white children there, especially no Jewish children."

"I have been supporting that association since day one, just like many of my classmates and other alumni, to the tune of nearly a million dollars, Mickey. Even though our children have been gone from that school since the late sixties. You cannot question my commitment to today's Weequahic community."

"And I thank you for that."

"And Mickey, how much of that money is coming from blacks who went to Weequahic? How many of them still have people there? Oh, I already know that answer. Close to one hundred percent, right?"

"I can't quarrel with you about that. But let's have that conversation at a later time. Yes, I support the inclusion of Nehemiah on Mayor Mosley's task force. He is an incredibly bright man, always has been."

"Even with his support of liberal politicians like Mosley and the former mayor?"

"Yes, and even with his support of moderately conservative politicians here in New Jersey and across the country. Don't forget, the new president was seriously considering Nehemiah for Secretary of Commerce. The president got a lot of heat from his progressive supporters over that, but he was willing to sacrifice political capital for Nehemiah."

"Touché Mickey. So, what would you have me do?"

"Be public about your support of Nehemiah as an important member of Mayor Mosley's task force. Write a letter to the editorial board of *The Star-Ledger* extolling the virtues of the mayor's action; call some of our friends in the Jewish community and tell them to release some of that old hostility against blacks in Newark by supporting the mayor. She is going to need help against the people who have profited since the riot, which by the way wasn't anyone in our circle, despite what people might think."

"You know something, Mickey, you might be an old man, but your mind remains as sharp as it was when you coached all those years ago. And you are still the consummate salesman. Okay, I'm in. I'm trusting your word that Nehemiah will present a plan that offers a hand up for blacks in urban America, rather than a handout."

"Nehemiah has been a faithful servant. He has been working to rescue Newark from the rebellion since he was sixteen years old, and now he's sixty-five. That's almost fifty years. He has proven himself time and again, and I believe he's going to pull off another win now."

DURING THE 1960S, police brutality was articulated by many citizens as one of the top reasons for the unrest in cities where large numbers of blacks resided. In the 1968 *Report for Action* compiled by the Governor's Select Commission on Civil Disorder in New Jersey, cruel treatment by cops was among the top reasons cited for the Newark Riot in 1967, ranking close to overcrowding of Negro areas, lack of job opportunities and breaking of official—i.e., political—promises.

"Why isn't the Black Lives Matter movement concerned about the black lives that are threatened by the bad guys and girls who prey on the black community?" Reverend Frederick Wade Jr. said to a group in his office at First Samuel Missionary Baptist, the same church that had been led by his late father for nearly sixty years.

"We are concerned about all lives and committed to their causes. It's just that people like you refuse to believe that today's politically driven organizational structures are inherently unfair and racist, especially the police," the leading activist of the local chapter of Black Lives Matter said. "Your church member, Lena Mosley, was endorsed by the police union when she ran for mayor, which indicated to us that she will have an open-door policy to them. Our organization has a problem with that."

"Even though she continued the police review board that was put in place by the former mayor?"

"That is simple window dressing by an ambitious politician, just like that Texas racist Lyndon Johnson did with civil rights and voting rights in the sixties. As we see today, those bills have been rendered meaningless to black people by the American system. Our rights are being violated in spite of them."

"The law that opened the voting booths to people who were previously denied the right to vote, though amendments to the Constitution gave them the right to vote right after the Civil War. You're telling me that was window dressing and meaningless? And you're calling President Lyndon Johnson a racist? The fact that a woman has been elected mayor for the first time in this city's history, and is already making an impact with creative legislation, are you maintaining that is window dressing and meaningless too?"

"How many states are changing election laws, making it more difficult for blacks to vote? It was present in the last election. They are in violation of voting rights. What about the black people dying at the hands of law enforcement? Is there anything civil about that? America is standing straight and proud when it comes to fighting wars in other countries, that is true, but it remains racist to the core within its borders. America has to be taken down a few rungs, and it is our job to do it," the activist said.

She continued. "You and the other elements of the religious community should join us in faith and make sure justice is being served to black people. A theologian by the name of Walter Brueggemann said that the church should be modern day prophets as called by God to have an impact on persons, to impinge upon perception and awareness, to intrude upon public policy and to evoke faithful and transformed behavior."

"I hope you realize this isn't the first time I've heard this kind of talk. Stokely Carmichael, H. Rap Brown, Eldridge Cleaver were out there in the sixties and seventies with the same rhetoric. There was even a move to separate from the United States within the country, with a number of the southern states forming a black country. Before that, Marcus Garvey had the Universal Negro Improvement Association, where he wanted black people to leave this country. Your movement sounds like the rebirth of Black Nationalism. Sounds like you're talking about bringing down the United States of America." Reverend Wade was finding it hard to believe after so many years, that he was still having essentially the same conversation as his father had in the fifties and sixties.

"If that's what it takes to stop the police from killing innocent black people, then so be it. We disrupted the presidential campaigns last year and we sent the message that our mission is serious business. The new president should know that if things don't change, we are prepared to do whatever it takes."

"Will you do what was done in Baltimore two years ago, or maybe what was done here in Newark in '67? Are you willing to destroy the black community by burning and looting the stores that employ people who live there?"

"We didn't have anything to do with what happened in Baltimore."

"Did you do anything to stop it?"

"We did our work outside of the media spotlight in Baltimore, so don't try to blame that on us. But I will say this. Our reaction to police violence against blacks will be equivalent to what is being imposed upon us. If the killing of black lives continues, then our response will be evenly matched.

"I don't expect a black preacher to understand, because all you tell your people is to pray and Jesus will make a way when times are tough. But what about the LGBTQ brothers and sisters? Should those who are lesbian, gay, bisexual, transgender and queer just pray and the discrimination against them will stop? What about the ones who pay for their crimes with jail sentences, but can't vote when they've done their time and are released? What about the ones who can't get a job because they have a prison record? Can we depend on Jesus to stop all of that?"

"You're missing the point of the gospel of Jesus Christ, young lady."

"Really? After all of the non-violent preaching and marching in the sixties, did the Prince of Peace, your Jesus, save Dr. King from getting killed by a white man who was a well-known criminal in Memphis? How long did it take to convict the people who killed Medgar Evers in Mississippi? What, thirty-five years? And the people who killed him were supported by the police? And what about the sheriff and his deputies who led the three civil rights workers in Mississippi to their murderers? Did Jesus bring them to justice?"

"We prayed and our God led us to resolution of those issues. My father was on the front lines for more than fifty years to get justice for black people, and he didn't have to break the law to get that done. A voting rights bill, a civil rights bill, fair housing laws, Medicare, Medicaid, Head Start, all done because there was a plan of action without breaking the law. And now a child of the sixties, a member of this church, is working to get better housing, better jobs, and better education for people across the country, starting right here in Newark.

"You may see it as meaningless window dressing, but I can tell you that I have known both Mayor Mosely and Nehemiah Garvey for many years, and they are faithful servants to Newark."

"You mean Mr. Goody Two Shoes, Nee Garvey? The man who tried to save Newark a long time ago and failed? The same man who stands to profit from restoring boarded up buildings with government money and then selling them to black people for more money than they're worth? All in the name of building up Newark's reputation? Yeah, right. Nehemiah is just another wannabe, rich, colored man who is propped up by Wall Street. He is simply another tool of the one percent in this country, just like many of you preachers."

"So, while Newark grows, what does Black Lives Matter do?"

"We will speak truth to power and walk over anyone or any group that tries to stop us. That includes Nehemiah Garvey, you, and your preaching brethren. We feel comfortable with our position because the racism that is being imposed on black people by police is an unpardonable sin."

"I will be praying for you."

"Save your breath, preacher man. Don't waste it on prayers for me."

Chapter 26

"When people tell the story of the American Dream, they talk about the many ways that hard work will help someone transcend class. They talk about hard work. People who earn the minimum wage work hard. People who make ends meet on public assistance work hard. It's not just about hard work. It's about hard work and the hook up."

~ Dr. Julianne Malveaux, noted economist, on African American empowerment, in 2013

"Democrats talk about public policy as though it were always 1965 and the model of the Great Society welfare state will answer our every concern. Republicans talk as though it were always 1981 and a repetition of the Reagan Revolution is the cure for what ails us. It is hardly surprising that the public finds the resulting political debates frustrating."

~ Yuval Levin, author of "The Fractured Republic, in 2016

According to a January 5, 2015 report by *BlackPressUsa*, the 2008 recession that engulfed the world economy began the worst economic situation for black Americans since the presidency of Ronald Reagan from 1981 through 1989. The unemployment rate for African Americans went to 16 percent in 2011, the highest in 27 years. It averaged

14 percent for the eight years of the Obama administration, more than double the rate of white Americans. The percentage of African Americans in poverty was 27 percent in 2015; and according to a December 2014 study by the PEW Research Center, the wealth gap between blacks and whites reached a 24-year high in 2015, stating that the average worth for black households was $11,000 compared to $141,900 for white households.

Public education for African Americans also took a hit, where 42 percent of black children attended high poverty schools compared to 6 percent of white children. The educations of more than 28,000 students in Historically Black Colleges and Universities were interrupted due to drastic changes in loan requirements set forth by the U.S. Department of Education, all during the President Barack Obama administration.

"I say we help Nehemiah Garvey lobby the federal government to start decreasing the opportunity gap around Newark," the Essex County executive director told the Board of Freeholders. "He has some outstanding ideas about making Newark a great city and he is getting support from across the country. Plus, Garvey has the respect of many lawmakers nationwide because of his work restoring distressed neighborhoods.

"Is his plan going to help Newark pay its way, instead of making the suburbs in the county pick up the tab?" one of the freeholders said.

"Are we going to hear that same old song about Newark paying its way? Aren't the taxes pretty high in Newark? We could pay our way if those tax dollars are used properly," one of the freeholders who represented Newark said.

"I didn't bring this up for an argument," the executive director said. "I met with Nehemiah and listened to his thoughts, but I didn't go by myself. Ladies and gentlemen, I yield the floor to the man who accompanied me to that meeting, Perry Williamson."

Williamson was a community activist in Newark during the mid-fifties, using his popularity to win election to the New Jersey Assembly. He represented the portion of the county that was dominated by voters from Newark. As the only black Assemblyman during the early sixties, Williamson was a Democrat who consistently battled the party over fairness to minorities in New Jersey, especially Newark. He was in demand as a speaker to black and Latino groups across the country, challenging the leadership of the Democratic National Committee, much to the chagrin of white Democrats.

After failing to win election to higher offices over a fifteen-year period, Williamson gave up campaigning and became a known figure in the state capitol as an influential lobbyist.

"Thank you, sir. I would like to express my deep appreciation to your director for allowing me to participate in what could be a huge victory for Newark and the county. It's not every day that a party boss of his stature would reach back and bring an eighty-seven-year-old, washed up politician to assist in the potentially explosive growth of the county; especially in the neighborhoods where citizens have been neglected by the federal government over the past sixteen years.

"As a lobbyist in Trenton for more than thirty years, I watched helplessly as cities like Newark, Camden, and East Orange were essentially given crumbs by the rich and powerful from the appropriations table. Yes, there were some big projects that were built, such as the New Jersey Performing Arts Center and the Prudential Center, but I'm not sure if the political prices paid for them were worth it. I've spoken with Nehemiah Garvey and heard his idea for improving the crime-ridden neighborhoods by crashing down on illegal drug activity and underperforming public schools. We all know Garvey's track record and devotion to Newark. I want to do my part."

"Haven't we done enough for the inner city?" someone asked. "Hasn't the country invested enough? Is pouring good money after bad the best solution? What are those people going to do to improve their surroundings?"

"That's what makes Nehemiah's plan intriguing. He is talking about private investment. What government needs to do is what it does for any other community— make sure public safety is appropriately paid for with tax dollars, make sure the streets are clean and well maintained by tax dollars, and treat children in public schools in those areas just like children attending public schools in more affluent areas, whose educations are also funded by taxpayers, might I remind all of you.

"And I would like to add, that hasn't happened in years in Newark, Camden and cities like them across the country," the county executive director said, "and this is coming from me, a man who grew up in north Newark and had a quality public education in a neighborhood that was well taken care of with tax dollars. What's happening in these communities now is just plain wrong."

"Sounds like you're getting a little liberal in your old age, Mr. Director."

"Being conservative doesn't mean you don't have a heart for what's right. Investment in these communities is the right thing to do. Mr. Williamson gave you what he knows about the past, and I am telling you that we cannot keep allowing our inner cities to be dens of iniquity where the bad guys thrive at the expense of good people. With those things in mind, I want all of you to vote on a resolution that says we support Mayor Mosley's task force at the U.S. Conference of Mayors. And remember, this is something that our native son, Nehemiah Garvey, has his fingerprints all over."

"I heard about Mr. Garvey and what he did fifty years ago as a high school athlete to keep Newark from going into the abyss. My question is how do you know he can do the same on a national scale?"

"I knew Nee Garvey the boy when we were boys. I played against the boy as a boy. Now I know the man as a man. I've watched the man as a man. I stake my reputation as executive director of this body on this man. He's a man who can get this job done, just like he did as a sixteen-year old... man."

"IT'S ALMOST AS IF THE people involved were saying, 'I'm sick and tired of being sick and tired.' Now the originator of the statement, Daisy Bates, was tired of fighting the system over voting rights," Nehemiah

Garvey said to a group of community activists and business leaders at a Chamber of Commerce luncheon in Los Angeles. "But she didn't give up until she got what she wanted at the Democratic National Convention in 1964. Neither did the mother of the black teenager who was stopped by the white California Highway Patrolman in 1965 for allegedly driving drunk. She was yelling at her son for drinking, but the patrolman said she was obstructing him from doing his job and he arrested her. She protested the arrest, which probably meant she was sick and tired of mistreatment at the hands of law enforcement in that area. The crowd of people probably felt the same, because they became larger and hostile to the police that night. Then the rebellion in Watts happened, as many of you know.

"What about in Omaha in '66, when a group of blacks were ordered by police to leave a corner. All they were doing was talking with friends. That city experienced a rebellion that cost millions of dollars. Can I say Detroit in '67, where law-abiding black citizens were arrested for celebrating the return of servicemen from Vietnam? That rebellion cost many lives and many more millions of dollars. Same thing happened in my hometown of Newark, where a black serviceman just home from Vietnam was harassed by police, and then arrested and beaten up by several white policemen for allegedly running a red light. Newark is still haunted by that rebellion to this day, fifty years later.

"Those are just a few of the stories that dominated the news landscape at that time. If you search the archives of any media outlet in America, you would find articles and video reels showing what I have described. What's troubling and distressing is that you will find the same articles with the years 2013, 2014, 2015, and 2016 on them. Ferguson, Baltimore, the killings in Chicago with police fingerprints on them, the grand jury verdict in Cleveland over the shooting of a twelve-year old boy brandishing a toy gun, the man killed in Minnesota just for telling the police that he had a gun and a license to possess it."

Nehemiah walked from behind the podium toward the attendees who were seated less than ten feet away.

"Enough of that. For the next two weeks, I am traveling to cities like LA, places that have been working to stop the violence that has plagued their inner-city neighborhoods. My mayor, Lena Mosley in Newark, is leading a lobbying effort by the U.S. Conference of Mayors to urge Congress to appropriate federal dollars for the restoration of areas where people who are unemployed and underemployed live, where public schools are noncompetitive academically and where there are more renters than there are homeowners. She asked me to work with the lobbying team that will be going to Washington.

"I am asking those of you who are Chamber of Commerce members to support the effort when a formal bill is offered. The initial plan is something that our country did during the Civil War, when the country was on the edge of destruction. If you look at the challenges we have right now, both nationally and internationally, we are in a similar position.

"Before I leave you, I would like to read something from the Bible that my grandmother read to me whenever I needed an emotional lift," Nehemiah said as he pulled a piece of paper from his jacket pocket. "It comes from Psalm 91 and it reads, 'whoever dwells in the shelter of the Most High will rest in the shadow of the Almighty. I will say of the Lord, He is my refuge and my fortress, my God, in whom I trust. Surely, he will save you from the fowler's snare and from the deadly pestilence. He will cover you with his feathers, and under his wings you will find refuge. His faithfulness will be your shield and rampart. You will not fear the terror by night, nor the arrow that flies by day, nor the pestilence that stalks in the darkness, nor the plague that destroys at midday.' I have lived by this for much of my life, and I will remember these words as I crusade for those in this country who feel they've been left out and left behind. Thank you for allowing me to speak to you at this time."

Nehemiah answered a number of questions after his speech. As he began to leave the room, he was stopped by an elderly man dressed in a dashiki with a colorful kofi on his head.

"Abaragani, my African brother," the man said in Swahili, a language spoken in a number of African countries.

"Asalamalakum," Nehemiah said with the popular Arabic greeting used by many American-born Muslims.

"Ah, I see you have finally learned to talk like your brothers and sisters," the man said.

"My good friend, Amir Jali," Nehemiah said. "It has been a long time. You've been busy since our last encounter fifty years ago."

"Yes, I have been. Working through difficult obstacles to counter the influence the western culture has on African Americans. We've made some progress, though I see you haven't. I heard from your speech that you have been fully brainwashed by America. That looks like a thousand-dollar Wall Street suit you're wearing. Probably designed by some gay white boy."

"To the contrary. It was designed and sewn by an African from Ghana whose sexual preference I am not aware of, nor do I care to know. As a matter of fact, he custom designs all of my clothes when he isn't too busy designing clothes for many African American professional athletes and entertainers. Interestingly enough, he designs white people's clothes too."

"I see you're the same smart-ass kid you were back in '67."

"Nothing's changed, my brother. Only that I'm smarter today than I was then, which makes me dangerous to people like you. So, what's on your mind and why should I listen to you?"

"I just wanted to say that you're wasting your time with these white boys in corporate America, unless you're going to help them set up more plantations in African American neighborhoods. That's what they've been doing since our people have become Americanized. You know, that gentrification thing, like they've done in Brooklyn and trying to do in Newark."

"There's a method to my perceived madness, my brother. I'll admit that. But it doesn't include uprooting people from their traditional neighborhoods."

"I'm keeping my eyes on you. You could be a dangerous man."

"You mean like you were dangerous with those black sisters? Didn't you do some jail time in the seventies for torturing women? Most of them were black women, right?"

"Yeah, I see you are a tool of the white man, spreading malicious gossip about a brother who is trying to liberate his people. We should have eliminated you when we had the chance."

"God placed his hedge of protection around me and shielded me from people like you."

"I see you're still talking about that white Jesus. Did he shield you from Cheryl Johnson?"

"What do you know about her?" Nehemiah said with a startled tone.

"Ah, you would be surprised, my brother. You would be highly surprised. I will say this. You might want to ask the family of that black preacher in New Jersey what I know about Ms. Johnson. I would advise you to not get comfortable with this plan to change the ghetto. There could be some things revealed about your past that would hurt your efforts."

"Is that a threat, Amir?"

"I don't deal in threats, Nehemiah. I deal in promises. Chew on that for a while."

THE WORD *GENTRIFICATION* became popular in the United States in the 1970s, when neighborhoods heavily populated and maintained by African Americans during the Great Migration from the South became attractive to upwardly mobile whites. Areas such as New York's Harlem community, the New York borough of Brooklyn, Washington D.C.'s Anacostia neighborhood, and Atlanta's Old Fourth Ward were some of the notable targets in the '90s and the early years of the 21st century, much to the dismay of longtime residents of the areas.

"Mayor Mosley, some members of the City Council want to see the plan for neighborhood revitalization before it takes it up in committee," the mayor's liaison to the Council said in a senior staff meeting. "Some of them are worried about Nehemiah Garvey's influence."

"What? They're worried about Nehemiah? Some of them weren't even born when he rescued this city in '67 and '68. He has personally helped some neighborhoods across the country survive for close to forty years, through the work of his property development company. He has been giving back and paying it forward for decades, even though he got no help from the political leadership in this city until about three years ago."

"Ms. Mayor, you know much of that distrust is because of the relationship he has with you. I mean, after all, the two of you were practically boyfriend and girlfriend as teenagers."

"Oh, that sounds so cute. Boyfriend and girlfriend. Yes, Nehemiah and I are close, but that's because we grew up in the same church under the leadership of one of the country's most dedicated and influential pastors, the late Reverend Frederick Wade."

"You know it's more about how you won the election and what he did to help you win."

"He didn't do anything more than what has always happened in politics in this city, or anywhere else for that matter. Nehemiah simply convinced the power brokers all over Newark, including the North Ward, that I was the best choice to succeed our former mayor, and they needed to raise the money to get me elected. What's wrong about that?"

"A lot of blacks in the South Ward and Central Ward don't like the North Ward crowd, mainly because they like to support Republicans, especially our current governor. And because they support the charter school movement, which a number of black constituents do not. In fact, many people who voted for the council members absolutely hate the charter school program. So, the council members from those wards are influencing the other members to give you a hard time about this plan that Nehemiah is writing to present to the U.S. Conference of Mayors. We need to do something to make them happy."

"Let's figure out what they need right now. There are some budget dollars for constituent projects in their neighborhoods, which we can appropriate immediately. Good thing about the former mayor, he left some money that we can use to keep the council calm while we focus on getting what we need from the infrastructure deal from Washington. We'll have to meet with the New Jersey congressional delegation to carve out our piece, then help the other cities get theirs. That's where Nehemiah comes in."

"You have a lot of confidence in Garvey, huh?"

"I consider him a miracle worker sent from God. Just like his father back in the day."

Chapter 27

"Money has changed today's black athletes. Those who have the ability as African men to bring a change in a community that so desperately needs it are concentrating only on their own careers, some charities and how much money they can make."

~ JIM BROWN, LONGTIME MEMBER OF THE PRO FOOTBALL HALL OF FAME, SPEAKING ABOUT STIMULATING GROWTH IN ECONOMICALLY DEPRESSED NEIGHBORHOODS, IN 2013

"These students have big dreams, and I'm happy to do everything I can to help them get there. They're going to have to earn it, but I'm excited to see what these kids can accomplish knowing that college is in their futures."

~ LEBRON JAMES, ON HIS $41.8 MILLION GUARANTEED FOUR-YEAR SCHOLARSHIP TO THE UNIVERSITY OF AKRON (OHIO) FOR NEEDY STUDENTS IN HIS AKRON HOMETOWN, IN 2016

SEVERAL BLACK PROFESSIONAL athletes, led by retired Cleveland Browns fullback, Jim Brown, and then halfback, Curtis McClinton, of the Kansas City Chiefs, formed the Negro Industrial and Economic Union, in 1966. Its mission was to stimulate investment of capital in African American-operated businesses, and to provide technical assistance and loans to such enterprises. The organization received a $520,000 grant from the Ford Foundation in 1968, to help the program expand its reach nationwide.

THE TELEPHONE RANG several times at Eva Mae Garvey's home.

"Hello. Oh, Hi Billy. It's good to hear from you. I haven't seen you since the celebration for the 1967 Weequahic basketball team. How's everything in Florida?" Eva Mae was talking to Billy Stern.

"I cannot tell you how nice it is to talk to you," Stern said. "I want to thank you again for being at my grandfather's shiva when he passed away. He thought very highly of you when he got better acquainted with you and Nee's grandmother, after Nee and I played together at Weequahic."

"Yes, your grandparents were great people, as well as your mother. I really prayed that you would stay here in Jersey and go to Rutgers so you and Nehemiah could have played together. But going to the University of Miami was good for you, especially coming in after Rick Barry had graduated."

"Yeah, the college likes Jersey boys. Rick Barry gave New Jersey a good name while he played there before he went to the NBA. They sold me on the weather in Miami, and I'm sure they got Barry's parents to realize that winters away from Roselle Park was not a bad deal. Mrs. Garvey, would you please ask Nee to call or text me? I have the information he needs to start writing the plan he's going to bring before Congress."

"Are you talking about the urban initiative plan?"

"Yes, that's the one. I am fully behind what he's doing, and a lot of people who supported the new administration owe me a few favors. I don't know if Nee told you, but I supported the president during the election, which meant I didn't support the Democrats or Republicans in the presidential race. The new president's progressive ideas changed my attitude about our two-party system."

"Billy, my husband always told me that people should vote their interests," Eva Mae said. "It's obvious that you were looking for something different in the country during the election, some things that neither the Democrats nor Republicans offered. I find it refreshing and honorable that you're willing to cash in some of your favors for Nehemiah."

"No doubt about it, Mrs. Garvey. You know how I feel about Nee. He's my friend for life. I want him to succeed. The relationship between the two of us reminds me of the song 'Against the Wind' by Bob Seger."

"How so?

"The part that says, 'We were young and strong, we were runnin' against the wind'. Nee convinced me when we were just teenagers that his mission was worthy. Even when our friends and relatives thought we were a bunch of crazy kids, Nee showed us we could do it—not with his mouth, but with his deeds.

"Another part of that song talks about '…being alone, surrounded by strangers I thought were my friends'. Whenever I hear the song I think about Nee's pep talks before those games, how he got us fired up to win one for Newark, and all the other places that went through what Newark went through during those times," Billy said. "I found myself seeking shelter against the wind…I'm older now but still runnin' against the wind. I'm older now but still runnin' against the wind. Against the wind."

Billy began crying quietly. "Mrs. Garvey, I've been through a lot in my life, but my experience during that one season kept me lifted up and got me through some really tough times. I have Nee to thank for that, because it has carried me through the years. Helping him with this project is the least I can do. I love your son."

"You're a good boy, Billy. God bless you."

THE BEGINNING OF THE 21st century ushered in a different kind of philanthropy, chiefly based on the internet and social technology. Many celebrities began to fund charitable foundations that provided more than just money to traditional non-profit organizations, opting to assist the programs with diverse strategies that helped their clients obtain education credentials and training that led them toward self-sufficiency. This was also an era that witnessed more African American athletes investing in restoring neighborhoods in cities with large black populations.

"Do you think Hassan Nelson and his partners will be able to secure the financing for the office building downtown?" Mickey Marcus asked.

"If they do, it won't come from local institutions, that's for sure," Nehemiah said. "The level of scrutiny for the project is amazing, especially when you look at who's involved. The credit worthiness of these men is being questioned beyond anything that I have ever seen." The two of them were having lunch at Marcus' condominium in a Bergen County senior living complex, where he and his wife split their time with their residence in Newark.

"You wouldn't be speaking about yourself, would you?"

"Yes, I am. And I am also speaking for the owner of the largest black-owned funeral home in the state, and for the others on the investment team. All of us have the financial wherewithal to purchase the building, but financiers in the state are giving us a hard time."

"Nehemiah, the problem isn't the purchase. It's what happens after the purchase. Your group wants to control all aspects of the management. There are certain elements in the country that don't want blacks to control anything outside of their neighborhoods, as if your people can't manage anybody but yourselves."

"Mickey, you don't believe that, do you?"

"Sometimes I do, sometimes I don't. I'm an old man and I've seen a lot of things. There was a time when black people could have been running everything in Newark. As a matter of fact, black people could have been running things in a lot of these major cities. In Newark, Philadelphia, LA, a lot of places. I've seen it. But your people suffer from the crabs in a barrel mentality. If a crab tries to climb out of the barrel, the other ones pull it back."

"Mickey, have you ever seen that? I mean, have you ever watched a group of crabs pull another one back into a barrel?"

"No, but the notion is catchy. In truth, I have watched many of your people go out of their way to stop another's progress. Damndest thing I've ever seen. Good people with good ideas getting stopped or held back by their own people. Look at the school superintendents who have come through Newark over the years. Some smart people with great educational qualifications and creative ideas. They had plans that would improve education for the children in Newark. Most of the opposition over them came from teachers who were convinced by their unions that change in the system would have been bad for them."

"Mickey, I would love to discuss the past ills of Newark, but right now I have to come up with a way to get the management contract for Hassan and his partners. I told the U.S. Conference of Mayors task force that a management blueprint for development in the inner cities of America would be the deal breaker for many of these young men and women to be investors. They don't want outside entities telling them what to do with their money."

"Here's what you do, Nehemiah. Since the former mayor is the secretary of Housing and Urban Development, you have someone who knows about proper management of distressed properties, and not to mention, has the attention of the President of the United States. Remember, too, that Billy Stern was a major supporter of the president. One of the guys from your old neighborhood, William Fore, is doing great work with the State of New Jersey land management office. His personal mission is to make urban neighborhoods livable again, like the way they were when you were growing up. He can create private/public management arrangements where they are needed, and he has relationships with major financial institutions because of his position in state government."

"Lena Mosley is highly regarded by the new presidential administration, which helps her standing in Trenton with a number of legislators. Mickey, you have given me some ideas to bring to Hassan and his partners, which will help athletes in other cities who want to copy what he is doing here. You know, you said our time together would be fruitful as the years passed. I must say I've learned a lot from you, more than I did from my father."

"You don't mean that, Nehemiah. Your father taught you a lot before he disappeared. You were a great young man when I met you, and you proved to be a concerned and committed young man when you stepped out to represent Newark after the rebellion. You have been faithful to Newark's cause for more than fifty years, and that says something about the way you were raised by both of your parents. I will never be your father, though I am honored to have my name mentioned in the same conversation as his. For some reason, I believe I am going to meet him one day."

"Maybe in heaven."

"Nehemiah, I pray that it will be before then."

"REVEREND WADE, I NEED to know what your father did about this girl who claimed to be pregnant by Nehemiah," Eva Jean Garvey said to the late Reverend Wade's son, Reverend Frederick J. Wade Jr. They were meeting in his church office, and Eva Jean decided it was time to put him on the spot.

"I only recently heard about that, maybe fifteen years ago," Reverend Wade Jr. answered carefully.

"And you didn't think to talk to me about it?"

"I honestly thought you knew, since your mother was involved."

"Oh, really. My mother? You're saying that Lula Mae Eleazer knew what happened to the girl who said she was carrying my grandbaby? She never told me anything after we met with your father and he said he would handle the situation."

Wade reached into his desk drawer.

"After my father got sick, I was managing his affairs and saw this envelope one day in his safe deposit box. According to his will, I couldn't reveal the contents of the box until after he passed away. I never read this entire document. In fact, I stopped after the first sentence."

"Your father died twenty years ago. It took you this long to give this to me? And I am supposed to believe that you haven't read it? Reverend Wade, please."

"Mrs. Garvey, I felt this was far too much information for me to digest, especially since I heard rumors over the years."

"You mean the ones that said I paid the girl's family to send her down south to quietly have the baby? Or that I paid for an abortion? None of that is true."

"According to my mother, my father had some tense meetings with her family and their pastor, but that's all I know."

"I believe you, I really do. It's obvious my mother kept the details from me and now here I am, six years from being 100 years old, and I'm just getting information that was compiled by the person who supposedly took care of this matter nearly fifty years ago. I pray that I can explain all of this to Samuel."

"Samuel! Are you talking about your husband, Samuel?"

"I most certainly am. Do you have a problem with that?"

"Uh, Mrs. Garvey, your husband disappeared more than 50 years ago, and no one has seen him anywhere since."

"Samuel is alive, and he is somewhere in Newark. Nobody will convince me otherwise. Reverend Wade, Samuel Garvey will make himself known, and soon."

"Does Nehemiah feel as you do?"

"My son says he does, but I don't think he is as certain as I am. I *know* Samuel is alive."

For the second year in a row, New Jersey has been listed as one of the worst states for black Americans. The study, conducted by nationalaffairs.com, used statistics that compared the quality of living between blacks and whites. For example, the numbers state that less than forty percent of African Americans in New Jersey who live in single-family dwellings own those homes, while seventy-five percent of white families own the homes in which they reside. Another number that helped place the Garden State in the top ten in this ignominious poll is the incarceration rate of blacks versus whites. While the poverty rate for African Americans is more than 17 percent nationwide, New Jersey has consistently been over that number. Yet, enthusiasm is lacking in our state when it comes to upward mobility in communities of color.

Of what value is this poll? To tell people who live in under-served communities—and that includes the growing numbers of whites moving into such areas—that they are doing poorly? And why are the target populations only black and white?

The fastest growing demographic in New Jersey is the Latino population, now more than nineteen percent of the state's residents and growing faster than any other minority group. Do they commit crimes? Do they own the homes in which they reside? Is their quality of living important to the fabric of New Jersey? With the new immigration laws set in place nationwide over the past several years, many cities are being impacted by the Latino influx. That's why polls like the one in question should indicate the purpose of its commis-sion and how it could improve public policy. Perhaps these numbers will help cities like Newark, Hillside, and Elizabeth succeed in getting better treatment from the federal govern-ment. The country's new progressive administration is giving hope that things will change for minorities.

Before he left office, the former mayor of Newark set a partnership in motion among the neighborhoods, the busi-ness community, and law enforcement. The alliance has been inherited by Newark mayor, Lena Mosley. As tax incentives for investment in neighborhoods continue for another five years, her push for home ownership in the city's economically depressed areas has taken a major leap forward with the collaboration she forged at the U.S. Conference of Mayors. Camden, Irvington and East Orange are making similar advances in the areas of law enforcement and education; and other cities in our state are focusing energy and resources on improving the environment in which impoverished citizens have languished for more than a half century.

This new poll will serve notice to states that are stuck in the past when it comes to African Americans that they need to accelerate their efforts. New Jersey might not earn a gold star for excellence in the category of African American progress, but there is a spirit of cooperation between the stakeholders that could become contagious across America.

— Ralph Edmondson, columnist, *The Star-Ledger*

"You've made a lot of progress since the mayors' conference," Lena Mosley told Nehemiah at a meeting in her office. "Just one question. How did you get so many pro athletes involved?"

"Through knowing people and having relationships. You remember the Nelson family that lived around the corner from First Samuel?"

"Sure. Their daughter got pregnant right after she graduated high school. But she had the baby and went on to college. The father was a no-account, trifling son of a gun. He used to hang out on Bergen Street doing drugs. You knew him, didn't you?"

"Uh huh. He was younger than us; played for South Side after they had those great teams in the sixties. He graduated in '72 and went down to Shaw University in North Carolina. Reverend Wade Sr. helped him to get into school, but he came back to Newark after one semester because he got kicked out for selling drugs and gambling. He was found dead about ten years after the little boy was born, but he was practically dead before that with all those drugs in his body."

"Well, you know I was down in Virginia during that time, so I didn't see all of those people grow up. Wait a minute. Isn't the basketball star, Hassan Nelson, from Newark?"

"That guy I just told you about was his father. Hassan was born here and raised by his grandparents while his mother attended Essex County College. She started dating a guy older than her while she was in college. He was from Newark and went to South Side. He joined the service after he graduated, got wounded in battle in Vietnam, and was discharged after earning a Silver Star and a Purple Heart. He came back to Newark and began dating Hassan's mother.

"They married before she finished college and moved to Georgia, where he started coaching high school basketball while earning his degree. Hassan became a great high school player under his stepfather's coaching down there, was an All-American at the University of Georgia, played in the NBA for twelve years and got four championship rings."

"What's his deal with connecting with Newark? He didn't grow up here."

"Hassan often came back to see his relatives and saw Newark at its lowest points. He told them he would like to come back and help the city get back on its feet once he became famous. He would always talk about Newark whenever I visited him and his family in Atlanta."

"So, Hassan, whom you've known since he was a little kid, has expressed an interest in restoring neighborhoods in Newark?"

"Not only neighborhoods, he wants to invest in downtown. And he has been talking to his friends about investing their money in the neighborhoods where they grew up; using their personal finances and influence with corporate America to clean up where they once lived. The politicians in Washington will like all of this because of the connection to celebrities in their districts.

"The new president's administration will hopefully support a program that African Americans thought would happen but never did because of the toxic relationship between the Obama administration and the Republican-controlled Congress."

"You know what, Nee? I often wonder what Newark would be if I had come back after I graduated from Hampton. I knew I wanted to be a resource for my community, but I would have never believed I would be managing a school district, much less mayor of a city that is trying to redeem itself from a checkered past."

"I knew you were destined for excellence when we were little kids living in the Valley. Remember when the Sunday school teacher would let you lead the class when she left us by ourselves? And after all, you were president of your sixth-grade class, and you were the first female president of the student association at South Side. You should have been in more leadership positions at Hampton. Still, God prepared you for such a time as this."

"And I thank God for you being in my life. I still remember your visits to Hampton during my freshman and sophomore years, and we had some good times when I came home for the holidays and during the summer. I really enjoyed seeing you play against teams in the Virginia area when you were at Rutgers."

"Then you met Ernest Mosley III when you were a junior, and Nehemiah Garvey became a thing of the past."

"Don't say it like that, Nee. You and I talked about marriage, but you didn't want to leave Newark and I didn't want to come back. I appreciate you for accepting the invitation to be a member of our wedding party, and you did become friends with Ernest. And don't forget, my oldest child is your godson.

"I will always remember you coming to Virginia when Ernest got sick and spend time with him before he died. You've been a friend at every point in my life when I needed one. And what can I say about the mayor's race? You were the architect of the victory."

"I'll receive some of that, but who said, 'I came to represent the left out and the left behind' on the campaign trail? You did, not me. Those words galvanized your supporters and brought voters from all over Newark for you."

"Still, you've been with me for what seems like forever. When my tough times came, I prayed constantly that you would be there for me. And you always were. Thank you, Nee."

"You know what's good about prayers, Lena?"

"What's that?"

"They don't have expiration dates."

Chapter 28

"We need to face some hard truths about race and justice in America. After 250 years of slavery, 90 years of Jim Crow, and decades of separate but equal, our country's struggle with racism is far from over. That's true in our criminal justice system; in our education system; in employment, housing, and transit. And tragically, it's true in the very air our children breathe and in the water they drink."

~ HILLARY CLINTON, DURING HER CAMPAIGN FOR
PRESIDENT OF THE UNITED STATES, IN 2016

"We're trying to create the kind of opportunity society to reignite the engines of economic opportunity, to reconnect people with the American idea, which is the great idea that the condition of your birth doesn't determine the outcome of your life, and that we want to have a dynamic society where everybody is involved, where everybody can participate in an economy of inclusion, so that everybody can reach their potential."

~ PAUL RYAN, SPEAKER OF THE U.S. HOUSE OF
REPRESENTATIVES, FROM HIS BOOK, *THE WAY
FORWARD: RENEWING THE AMERICAN IDEA,* 2014

GARVEY'S RESTAURANT OPENED IN 1945 and over the years became an institution in the tri-state area of New Jersey, New York, and Connecticut. Eva Jean Garvey operated the establishment alongside her husband for twenty years, and practically by herself after he mysteriously disappeared in 1965. Though *Garvey's* is now managed by Nehemiah's adopted daughter, Chante, Eva Jean still dines there on a regular basis.

"Ms. Eva Jean, there's a man who wants to meet with you," one of the servers said as Eva Jean sat at her customary table, eating breakfast. "He says he was a friend of your husband."

"Really? Did he tell you his name?"

"Gabriel. Like the angel, he said." Eva Jean looked in his direction and motioned for him to come to her table.

"How are you, Mr. Gabriel? I'm Eva Jean Garvey."

"Yes, ma'am, I know. I met you many, many years ago."

"That's strange. I don't remember you. And you say you were a friend of Samuel's?"

"I was actually with him when he came to America on Marcus Garvey's ship in 1917."

"So, you were childhood friends in Kingston?"

"Yes, yes. The same Jamaican lady who taught him to read taught me. Samuel and I were in Harlem together when we arrived in America, and we both joined Timothy Drew and the Moorish Temple when we came to Newark. We united with First Samuel Baptist Church here in Newark after we became disenchanted with the leadership of the temple."

"My goodness. Your story is hugely similar to Samuel's. Your accent is just like his. It is amazing. But I'm confused. What was your name and why didn't you change it to Garvey like Samuel did?"

Gabriel gave Eva Jean a dazed look. "I can't remember my name or if I changed it. But I was just like a brother to Samuel Stephenson. We did so much together."

"How can you remember his last name but not your own? I didn't even know his original last name, but you know it was Stephenson.

Gabriel, I don't remember you. Now, if you were so close to Samuel, do you know why he would leave his family when he did?"

"No, no. Samuel was forced to leave his family. That woman was the reason he left you and your son."

"A woman? What woman?"

"Oh, Mrs. Garvey, I cannot tell you anymore. Those men told me that I would be killed if I said anything to anyone."

"What men told you that you would be killed? What did they look like?"

Gabriel rose from his seat, looking as if he was having a flashback. He exited the restaurant in a mad dash, knocking over a table and several chairs.

"Wait, Mr. Gabriel! Don't go!" Eva Mae shouted.

Security was high at the Rayburn House Office Building when Nehemiah Garvey and other members of the U.S. Conference of Mayors Task Force on Urban Restoration entered.

"You are scheduled to meet with the chairs of several committees and we have them listed here," the security officer said. "Mr. Garvey, the House majority leader and the House minority leader want you to meet with them in the office of the Speaker of the House. I have assigned several officers to accompany you to the Capitol."

"I knew you were important, but meeting in the Speaker's office?" one of the task force members said. "As we say in the South, you're walking in high cotton."

"Just pray that I don't make a mess of it," Nehemiah said. "Many of the leadership team in the White House were not happy when I took my name out of nomination to serve in the president's cabinet. But I told Mayor Mosley that I was committed to Newark. Anyway, I'm sure all of you will do well in your meetings."

As Nehemiah walked toward the Capitol, he engaged in conversation with one of the officers.

"How is it around here with the new administration?"

"We're not supposed to discuss anything about the atmosphere around here," the white male officer said. "They tell us to be like paint on a wall."

"I hadn't heard that, so I'll give you my opinion," the white female office countered. "The feeling is more relaxed, in my opinion. I think when President Obama's people were here there was a lot of pressure."

"Yeah it was," the black male officer said. "I worked all over the district and I encountered a lot of hostility during his administration, even from Democrats."

"Get outta here," Nehemiah said. "I heard it was cool to have an African American president as the new sheriff in town."

The white female officer nearly interrupted Nehemiah's statement.

"I didn't say it wasn't cool to have Mr. Obama as president, it was just a little tight around here. Some people seemed to be afraid to speak their opinions when certain issues like health care and same sex marriage were being debated on the Hill."

"And I heard blacks disagreeing quite a bit about what the president should have been doing for the black community," the black male officer said. He looked over at the white male officer. "Dude, you had a lot to say when we worked together at the White House over the past four years. You could hardly keep your mouth shut about your opinion of President Obama."

"I was told to be like paint on a wall, so I will not join this conversation," the white officer said.

Nehemiah arrived at the Capitol within a few minutes and was quickly ushered to the House Speaker's office. The Republican leader and Democratic leader in the House of Representatives were just ending a conversation as he walked in. They both looked up to greet him.

"Mr. Garvey, it is an honor to have you in our midst," the majority leader said with a distinctive Alabama accent. "I'm Len Matthews from the great state of Alabama, and this is my good friend from the loyal opposition, Jerry Wilson of California. I must let you know that it isn't normal for a minority and majority leader, a Democrat and Republican, to meet together with anyone who is planning to lobby the government. That just doesn't happen. But both of us felt that a man of your stature deserves our collective attention.

"Unfortunately, our time is limited, so we're going to get to the point. But I have to say first that the three of us have something in common. We played basketball against each other in our younger days."

"Did I play against you when I was at Rutgers?"

"I didn't play against you in college. I was on the Woodlawn High School team in Birmingham that you beat when you were a junior at Weequahic," Matthews said.

"And I was on the Fremont team from Los Angeles that played against Weequahic in the Watts Classic in '67. You blocked my shot with about two minutes to go in the semifinal game. And you won that one, too," Wilson said.

"Me and the team were on a mission. We needed to win for Newark that season."

"You pulled it off in both ways," Wilson said.

"Well, there were some bumps in the road in the years after that, but Newark is beginning to move on up, thanks to our former mayor. You guys are already getting to know him, since he's H.U.D. Secretary."

"He's a hard ass, and I respect him," Matthews said, "but he can be a sonofabitch. He's pushing us hard on that infrastructure legislation."

"He's a Newarker, what do you expect?" Nehemiah said.

"I don't agree with that assessment because your late congressman was a total gentleman, and his son who replaced him when he died is also mild mannered. Both of them are from Newark."

"Newarkers aren't monolithic, we're tough in our own ways. If you think our former mayor takes no prisoners, wait until you hear about this plan for urban neighborhoods that our current mayor is pushing."

"I heard about it from some members of the mayors' conference. Sounds ambitious," Matthews said.

"It's exactly that, but there's money behind it from private investors. Now you people who advocate the 'pick yourselves up from your bootstraps' theory need to do your part."

"We can get there. I heard you're trying to liken your plan to the Homestead Act of 1862. How?"

"Just like Abraham Lincoln wanted to homestead the west by getting settlers to occupy the land, we want to approach it in a similar way in urban areas. The government gave money to those who wanted to settle the land, allowed them to own the land they claimed and they got protection from the United States military against the original occupants, Native Americans. Plus, they were taught by government agents how to live off the land. Might I add, the settlers didn't pay for the education.

"Conversely, when the Civil War ended and slavery was abolished, blacks were left to fend for themselves without any life skills, and worst of all, with no money or land. That's like telling a baby that once he can talk and walk, he's on his own. The rest of the story is well known, with Jim Crow and all. Those slaves could have become productive members of society if they were allowed to participate in a program like the Homestead Act."

"It didn't happen exactly that way," Matthews said, sounding offended by Nehemiah's take on history. "I'm a student of history, taught college courses on the subject. You and I disagree there. Did you know that the Republican Party pushed hard to help African Americans get out of the South and acquire property in the Midwest, especially in Kansas?"

"Congressman Matthews, as you did, I taught college level history classes as well and yes, we respectfully disagree. I know all about Benjamin Pap Singleton and the Exodusters movement, and truthfully, *that* Republican Party doesn't deserve the kind of credit you're trying to give it. Actually, if Republican Rutherford Hayes had not ended the Reconstruction policy set in place after the Civil War with his compromise to be president in 1876, such a grand movement of blacks from the South might not have been necessary."

"I'm not so sure about that. Some historians might challenge you on the facts."

"Let me tell you something," Nehemiah said as he leaned in his chair toward Matthews, "what I'm saying is what happened then was close enough to have a major impact on today's society. Here's what I do know. All of the social programs that are in place because of guys like the two of you, both Republicans and Democrats, have made a mess of things by giving away too much to too few people, especially rich folks. They gave one segment of the populace an opportunity to secure property while the government completely funded the initiative, but the government freed the slaves and told them they had the same opportunity as anyone else because the North won the Civil War, but gave them nothing to work with. No access to any kind of education, not even the forty acres and the mule that was proposed by Union General William Sherman. That was a false notion, and with all due respect, Congressman Matthews, you know it was.

"Land is the great equalizer in this country and this country paid for the dreams of those who were willing to take a chance, while telling the newly freed slaves that they had nothing to worry about because the federal government had their backs. Do you want me to recount the rest of that story?"

"That might take more time than either of us have," Congressman Matthews said.

"I didn't think so. But I warn you; it will be part of my formal presentation when I come back."

"Let me tell you something, Nehemiah. I guess I can call you by your first name, right?" Matthews said.

"No problem, just as long as you pronounce it correctly. My parents went through great pain coming up with that name for me."

"You seem to be quite a debater and I get the sense that both parties will have their hands full when you present your plan," Matthews said. "I just want to say that I will listen to you as long as you're making sense.

When you no longer make sense, you'll have no audience with me. Or, as we say in the South, that dog won't hunt. What say you, Mr. Leader?"

"I'm in total agreement. Mr. Garvey, your points about the plan seem valid. I'm leaning toward your corner."

"Nehemiah, in listening to you, I don't see any reason I would be against this. I'm looking forward to the presentation during committee meetings. If you do well, I can get our guys on your side, guaranteed, but right now I have to go, sir. Thank you for coming over. I appreciate you and God bless you."

"He really wants this deal. And he will fight for it on the floor if it gets that far," Wilson said as Matthews left the room. "Contrary to popular opinion, that Southern boy wants to get things right up here. That presidential campaign we just went through humbled him, as it did many of us in both parties. The president's policies are far different than anything I've seen from a Democrat or Republican. I guess that's what happens when voters get tired of the feuding between the two parties and cast their ballots for the alternative."

"I'm glad to know that he likes the plan. I'll give my associates the good news."

"I got a question that has nothing to do with the plan. What's your connection with Amir Jali?"

"Huh? Where did that come from?" a puzzled Nehemiah asked.

"The rumor is that you and he are friends."

"We are not friends, but I do know him."

"How well do you know him?"

"I've had two encounters with Mr. Jali, the most recent being about three weeks ago in LA. Why do you ask?"

"He's been sniffing around the Hill, trying to get federal grant money to support his organization. He had it made with the previous administration, but this White House is not interested in working with him. Unlike the previous eight years when he had unfettered access to the Oval Office, Jali now needs security clearance just to walk on the

White House lawn. I'm asking because he is not someone you want to be close to."

"I don't have any affiliation with Mr. Jali. Were you told something different?"

"It's just that he keeps bringing your name up, especially around my daughter. It's as if he wants her to know something about you."

"I don't know what."

"I need to be upfront with you about Amir. His former girlfriend is my wife and we have one child."

"The child wouldn't happen to be in her late forties, would she?"

"Yeah."

"You know, I might need to butt out of this dialogue. But some things are beginning to add up."

"Like what?"

"Like the relationship between you and her mother, while she was with Mr. Jali."

"That's a minor part. There's something bigger than that."

"How much bigger can it be?"

"You don't want to know."

"So, you were just talking to Amir Jali?"

"Yes indeed," Ralph Edmondson said to his assistant after hanging up his mobile phone. "He wants to discuss Nehemiah Garvey's influence in Washington."

"I'm not surprised. Many of the issues that Nehemiah has been speaking about over the years happen to be at the top of the president's agenda. So, I guess in Jali's mind he's been replaced by a smooth operator who can talk the talk, as well as walk the walk," the assistant said.

"That's exactly the road he was taking. He sounded as if he wanted to vent his frustrations. I'm not sure I want anything to do with that."

"Have you lost your mind, Ralph? Can you see the build up to this? Two prominent black men feuding over who will have access to the White House to meet with the president on major issues confronting urban and rural America? You need to jump on this with no hesitation. Amir got used to running in and out of the West Wing so much that even the Secret Service thought he was a member of President Obama's Cabinet. Eight years was enough for that guy.

"It's time for a new black face to have unimpeded access to the president. Nehemiah could be that guy; he's smart, shrewd, and calculating, with no apparent baggage. Seems as if Jali is upset that he is being displaced and doesn't like it. He must have something on Nehemiah, and that's why you need to follow the trail that Jali is laying out. This might have big time implications because of the personalities of these two. Honestly, I see the story of a lifetime."

"I guess my relationship with the Garveys will go down the drain if I pursue this."

"Man, stop worrying. It's business, Ralph, they'll get over it."

Chapter 29

"The late Judith Sklar, a former political theorist at Harvard University, said that what's unique about the United States is that it is the only modern constitutional state that begins with slavery. The issue of racial slavery overdetermines the very notion and nature of citizenship in this country. So, black and white colors and shadows all interactions between these two groups. So, not only whites who feel they are under attack are scapegoating African Americans, they are scapegoating Mexicans, Muslims and immigrants who they believe are eroding white privilege."

~ Eddie Glaude Jr., author, *Democracy in Black:*
How Race Still Enslaves the American Soul, 2016

"To sustain a national conversation about solving problems we have to see ourselves as a unity. We don't. The political parties are at each other's throats, we live in racially and economically segregated communities. There are politicians and leaders in media who literally talk about citizens as if they're traitors, as if their rivals actively want to hurt the country. They talk about the president that way, talk about Congress, elements of the population as if they're actually trying to harm their own country. People talk like that

267

> about the enemy and when you use that about people inside
> your own camp, you are dividing the society.
>
> ~ Sebastian Junger, author, on cable
> network television, in 2016

Reverend Frederick J. Wade Jr. has been pastor of First Samuel Missionary Baptist Church since his father retired in 1990. There had been no debate over selecting him as his father's successor, and he quickly earned respect as a civic leader across ecumenical lines in New Jersey, living up to his family name and legacy.

"I guess my mother was trying to protect my child and me back then," Eva Jean Garvey told Nehemiah's adopted daughter, Chante. A letter was on Eva Jean's desk in her office at the restaurant.

"She should've told you before she passed away," Chante said. "Big Mama was wrong for that."

"What was really wrong was that it took Reverend Wade's son nearly thirty years to tell me about this letter."

"Grandma, you remember Reverend senior lived quite some time after he retired, so Reverend junior couldn't divulge the contents of the safe deposit box. His father's will was clear about that."

"Well, I've read what was most interesting to me. Especially Samuel's fake birth certificate, which Reverend senior obtained for him. I don't even know my husband's real age, or his real name. That man, Gabriel, said something about Samuel's last name being Stephenson."

"Grandma, you mean to say that he never talked about how he got to America?"

"No, not really. He talked about coming here very young and posing as a member of Marcus Garvey's family, but never gave me an age. He said he lived in Harlem for a while, then moved to Newark and that was it. I was about nine when I first noticed him at the church."

"How old was he?"

"First of all, he was cute. I thought he was about eleven, but some of the people in church said he was thirteen. Now I don't know, since Reverend Wade's father admitted that he got an illegal birth certificate for him."

"What about Daddy? When do you plan to tell him about the letter?"

"As soon as he gets back from Washington. I pray that he will get his work done there and get home safe and sound in due time. He'll figure out what we should do."

"Grandma, what about the other part of the letter? About that girl?"

"What are you talking about, child?"

"Cheryl Johnson was in college during all of that talk about black nationalism and black power, right? Daddy told me that he had some encounters with people who had issues with his crusade to save Newark's reputation. Some of them were with the black power crowd in Newark. Reverend Wade's letter gives the impression that she wasn't really who she told Daddy she was."

"Are you saying that she could have been part of a conspiracy? She was, or is, black, so why would she set up a black man? Plus, Nehemiah was only sixteen," Eva Jean said as her voice began to rise.

"I did extensive research about the Newark riot and I read about Tom Hayden and the Students for a Democratic Society's influence in the city at that time. I also read about Amir Jali and Abasi Chaga, the Newark activist, combining efforts to get white radicals like Hayden out of Newark right after the riot."

"Chante, I know I'm an old lady, but I still have a good mind, and I don't understand a thing you're saying."

"The black power crowd wanted to eliminate anyone who might limit their control of Newark. That meant anybody black, or anybody white. That Johnson girl might not have met Daddy by accident. She might have been part of a plan to stop his crusade."

"Honey, you have been reading too many mystery books."

"No, Grandma, this is not my mind playing games with me. Something tells me those people were setting Daddy up back then. I'm almost sure of it. He believed in working together with many Jewish people in Newark, most of all his coach, Mr. Marcus. Chaga didn't believe in working with white people, especially Jews."

"That's what Chaga wanted people to believe. But he got real close with some of the white militants over in north Newark right after Dr. King was killed. Why, I don't know. Then, he and Jali started doing some things together," Eva Jean said.

"That's my point, Grandma. My research said that once Newark elected a black mayor in 1970 and the City Council became predominantly black and Puerto Rican, Chaga figured he would have some power and he kicked Jali to the curb to do his own thing."

"But Newark went deeper into hell after that. Girl, those degrees you have look like they're paying off for this family."

"Can I tell Daddy about my suspicion?"

"Yes ma'am. You have my permission."

THE MOOD WAS FESTIVE in the community meeting room at Newark's City Hall. Members of the U.S. Conference of Mayors Urban Restoration task force were celebrating their progress in talks with Congress on legislation targeted at cities with large pockets of underserved communities. There were a number of professional athletes and noted entertainers present.

"We are on the verge of finishing what Dr. King was doing in 1968 with the Poor People's campaign," Mayor Lena Mosley said to the group of nearly one hundred. "The good part about it is that we didn't have to lodge threats of violence in the streets to move the needle. We combined the efforts of savvy lobbying by the members of our conference and our partners in the private sector."

"I want to say thank you to my brothers and sisters in professional sports and the entertainment community who are committing resources to improve home ownership and business opportunities in places like Newark's poorer sections," former pro basketball player, Hassan Nelson, said. "All of you responded when I called. We are all on one accord when it comes to giving people who live in depressed neighborhoods a hand up, not a handout. And that attitude extends to communities in rural as well as urban America."

Nehemiah was surrounded by a small group in the back of the room.

"I guess you're pleased that the eight years of the Obama administration ignoring African Americans are ending under this new administration in Washington," one person said.

"Are you tryin' to get me to say something negative about President Obama? It ain't gonna happen," a testy Nehemiah said. "He did the best he could, but the fight between the Democrats and Republicans on Capitol Hill was the obstacle."

"Well, according to many black experts, African Americans made no progress in the nation's most important societal categories during his time in the White House. Mind you, I said black experts, not white social scientists," another person countered.

"Look, this is not gonna be a let's beat up President Obama session. He left office on January 20, 2017 and he's enjoying his life. This new administration has appointed a Newarker to a top post in the Cabinet and he is already bringing fresh ideas to the forefront. I am over about what didn't happen from 2009 through 2016. It's old news."

"So, Mr. Garvey, you're not concerned about the Obama legacy?"

"No, he isn't, and neither am I," Mayor Mosley interrupted. She had been making her way toward Nehemiah after her remarks from the podium, and now stood between the two men. "Excuse me, sir, but I need to talk to Mr. Garvey privately. The rest of you please go on and enjoy yourselves at this celebration and stop worrying about Mr. Obama's legacy. What he did will speak for itself and I am sure historians will be kind to him when they tell the story. Our concern is the future of Newark and cities like Newark."

"Thanks, Lena. That guy was beginning to work my nerves," a relieved Nehemiah said. "What's on your mind?"

"I have three things on my mind. First, I want to thank you for all your work in Washington and around the country on behalf of the

U.S. Conference of Mayors. You traveled to fifteen states and forty-five cities on your own money, and our group appreciates it. You did an outstanding job in working with the task force. I can't tell you enough how proud I am."

"Lena, you had the vision for a long time, even before you came back home. None of this is new to me."

"Let's walk outside for a minute," Lena said in a whisper.

"This must be mighty important. I guess this is item number two."

"I got a call from Ralph Edmondson today. He's working on a story about the relationship between you and Amir Jali."

"Me and Amir Jali? Now that's interesting, especially since I have only been in the man's presence two times in my whole life."

"Ralph mentioned Cheryl Johnson's name."

"A blast from the past. Cheryl Johnson."

"Nehemiah, whatever happened to her? It seems as if she was in your life for a brief moment back in '67, and then she suddenly vanished."

"Lena, you just said it. She was in my life for a brief time, and then she was gone. Did Ralph give you any idea of his approach to this story?"

"No, but you know Ralph is the senior columnist at *The Star-Ledger* and he wouldn't be pursuing a story angle if there wasn't anything substantial to write about. I've got to get back inside, but please Nehemiah, be careful. You have become a target again, just like you were fifty years ago."

"Ok. I understand and I'll be careful. But before you go back inside, you said you had three things you wanted to say to me."

"Yes. Number three is that I love you."

The Star-Ledger placed the relationship of well-known black activist, Amir Jali, and Nehemiah at the top of its list for an investigative story. Social media got wind of the newspaper's plan and it was the subject of the blogosphere worldwide. The newspaper was bombarded with calls from media outlets inquiring about the imminent story that could mean political trouble for the new presidential administration.

"Ralph, we have to proceed carefully on this," *The Star-Ledger* city editor said to Ralph Edmondson.

"You're talking to me as if this is my first rodeo. I came to this paper in 1966. I have been an eyewitness to the rise of Nehemiah Garvey, from his teen years to the present day, so I don't have to endlessly sit in front of a computer screen gathering information about him and his journey. I know him well.

"I worked the city beat for a number of years after the first African American mayor of Newark was elected. Newark remained on my radar as I worked at print media outlets from LA to Chicago, Miami, and New York. I went toe to toe with our great city editor, Walt Peters, when I first came to the local beat at this paper, yet he begged me to come back just before he retired ten years ago. I was given the title of senior columnist and my writing is the stuff of legends. Ask any media person of prominence in this country. Ask the chair of any communications school at any college. I've appeared on the major news networks as an analyst on topics that varied from national politics, to international terrorism, to pop culture. The name of Ralph Edmondson pricks the ears of media professionals all over the world.

"Being from Newark, I hold a tremendous amount of pride for where my hometown is going. We have come a long way with three black male mayors, and now with the first female leader in City Hall. But I am still a newspaperman and this is an important story. I will tackle it with more ferocity than Michael Strahan tackled any quarterback in the National Football League."

"Even if it means possibly darkening the reputation of one of Newark's favorite sons? Do you want to be compared to what Woodward and Bernstein did to President Nixon with Watergate?"

"That's being a little dramatic, don't you think? But be that as it may, would you be saying this if I was one of your fair-haired, liberal wunderkinds out of the Newhouse School at Syracuse, or Medill School at Northwestern? Did you say that to the white boys who wrote those unwarranted stories about black leadership in Newark, even though you knew the whistleblowers had suspicious motives? And you need to hold up comparing me to Bob and Carl. They were barely copy boys when they broke the Watergate scandal. In fact, I believe one of them didn't even have a car. My trophy cabinet already had three Pulitzer Prize nominations and two Pulitzers before they had a byline. I had more than five honorary degrees from major universities before Ben Bradlee knew the names of Woodward and Bernstein. You need to zip your lips when you even think about speaking of me and Woodward and Bernstein in the same breath."

"Okay, Ralph, enough. You've made your point. I'm greenlighting this project. You can get whomever you need to assist you. I just hope you don't flush more than fifty years of your life's work down the drain for this story. There's a lot of risk with this one, my friend."

"I'll have to ride into the sunset one day. I don't mind if this is the one that will put me in a rocking chair for the rest of my life."

BLACK ACTIVISM WENT IN A number of directions after the tumultuous decade of the sixties. The Nation of Islam encountered a huge change after the death of Elijah Muhammad in 1975, with his son Warith Deen Muhammad assuming leadership in 1976, leaving erstwhile vanguard, Louis Farrakhan, and other mainstays to explore the formation of another Muslim organization. Earlier than that, in 1956, the director of the Federal Bureau of Investigation, J. Edgar Hoover, began the CounterIntelligence Program (better known as COINTELPRO) to target organizations and individuals deemed subversive and threatening to the federal government. The initiative primarily targeted Communist Party sympathizers but started aiming its work in the 1960s at civil rights groups and African Americans who stood at the forefront of the movement for equal rights, which learned observers said created dissension within the ranks of those organizations.

Dr. Martin Luther King Jr., Stokely Carmichael, H. Rap Brown, along with the NAACP, the Student Nonviolent Coordinating Committee

(SNCC), Congress of Racial Equality (CORE) and similar alliances were at the center of Hoover's disgust, and thus became the focal point for COINTELPRO.

Though the actions of Hoover and the FBI—and those who agreed with their tactics—were deemed un-American, the administrations of Presidents Eisenhower, Kennedy and Johnson allowed the bureau to work without any oversight. Organizations that legally petitioned the government during that time started becoming skeptical of the motives of their once-trusted allies. Activists who had previously worked from storefront outposts in working class neighborhoods, struggling to keep the lights and telephones on, were now operating in high-rise office suites with well-paid staffs, funded with government grants and lucrative, no-bid contracts from various public entities.

"I am the last living revolutionary from the sixties who still has a sound mind," Amir Jali said to one of his associates. "I clearly remember the days of the jean jackets and Afro combs, sitting in my apartment in Watts, smoking reefer and planning marches to fight the system. That's more than I can say for my contemporaries."

"You sound as if you're proud that you've survived," one friend said.

"I am. Those bastards sold me out to the conservative political crowd in Sacramento when Reagan was governor. And to think, I fought to get a lot of them in office after Dr. King was killed."

"Amir, you didn't do it by yourself."

"My name was out front."

"That's because you had the biggest mouth."

"Damn right, because I had no fear of those crackers."

"Are you sure you're not still holding a grudge against the black militants here in LA, who treated you badly when you came from Louisiana?"

"No, but it does cross my mind. They thought I was a little country boy who didn't know about injustice, or how to deal with racists. Then they found out differently. They found out that this Mississippi boy was a lot smarter than them because my parents were educators. They accepted me, made me their leader. I was one of the agitators in the Watts riot and I got respect."

"And then came Nehemiah Garvey, and your life changed."

"That sonofabitch punked me. I lost respect from my peers after Garvey called me out at that meeting in '67. Before that I was getting my due as a black man, and I was determined to do things my way. I couldn't bring myself to cut deals with white people like they did at that time, but I had to take a different course after the encounter with that Garvey boy."

"You really still hold Nehemiah Garvey responsible for what happened to you fifty years ago?"

"Damn right I do. And I am determined to create havoc in his life for what he did to me. *The Star-Ledger* is moving forward on a story I brought to them, and they have Ralph Edmondson writing it."

"Seriously? Amir, you know Edmondson's reputation. He shakes people up when they see a text or email from him. It's almost like when someone heard that Mike Wallace of *60 Minutes* was waiting in the lobby. Ralph Edmondson can be that ruthless."

"Well, I don't feel sorry for Garvey."

"Amir, you're not immune, you know. You have some skeletons in the closet, and some in full view. And have you forgotten about your friend, the congressman from California, and what he knows?"

"He's got too much to lose. He won't utter a word about me."

"From your lips to God's ears."

"C'mon man. What's God got to do with this?"

Chapter 30

"On this day, we gather because we have chosen hope over fear, unity of purpose over conflict and discord. On this day, we come to proclaim an end to the petty grievances and false promises, the recriminations and worn-out dogmas that for far too long have strangled our politics. We remain a young nation. But in the words of Scripture, the time has come to set aside childish things. The time has come to reaffirm our enduring spirit; to choose our better history; to carry forward that precious gift, that noble idea passed on from generation to generation: the God-given promise that all are equal, all are free, and all deserve a chance to pursue their full measure of happiness."

~ President Barack Obama, his first
inaugural address, January 20, 2009

"I don't think it's helpful to pin blame to individuals. I don't actually blame the people who support Donald Trump. There are many people who support Trump who have very real grievances, who have had years of stagnant living standards who fell left behind by the globalized world. And we have failed those people in many ways."

~ Zanny Minton Beddoes, editor, The Economist,
on cable network television, in 2016

Chante Garvey was an exemplary student; had been from first grade through college. She completed her undergraduate studies at New Jersey's Montclair State University, and then earned an MBA from the Wharton School of the University of Pennsylvania.

"Chante, is your friend coming to dinner tonight?" Eva Jean Garvey said to her granddaughter as she was setting the table.

"No. We were together last night and we decided to take a break. Plus, Daddy's coming and we need to discuss the letter, which is none of her business."

"That letter has been on my mind, along with that episode at the restaurant with that man who said he knew Samuel."

"Grandma, you need to let me deal with that man, just like I'm dealing with the letter."

"Hello everybody!" a voice bellowed from the front door. It was Nehemiah.

"Daddy, you're early."

"I thought I would get here before dinner so we could talk about what I've missed. I've been busy these past few weeks working on that project Lena Mosley gave me. Hey Ma, I need a hug. I need one from you too, Chante."

"Oh, my big baby needs to hold his mother."

"That should relieve some of the stress we've had lately," Chante said.

"What stress?" Nehemiah asked as he wrapped his arms around his mother and daughter.

"Daddy, we have something to talk to you about. Actually, we have a few things to talk to you about."

"Hmm, you sound serious."

"It *is* serious. Cheryl Johnson serious."

"Cheryl Johnson. Again? I hear about her in LA, then in DC, and Lena Mosley tells me that Ralph Edmondson mentioned her name. What's up with this reincarnation of Cheryl Johnson?"

"Daddy, reincarnation means the body died."

"As far as I'm concerned, Cheryl Johnson is dead."

"Possibly, literally. But definitely not figuratively."

"Ma, what is this girl talkin' about?"

"That's your daughter. You raised her."

"Daddy, look. Let me get to the point. The older Reverend Wade did some things that were not strikingly religious in dealing with Ms. Johnson. That's what he said in a letter he left behind."

"And my mother was part of it," a somber Eva Jean said.

"No, Ma. Grandma Lula Mae was as honest as the day was long. She couldn't have done somethin' wrong. Not the grandmother I knew. Is this letter authentic?"

"Yes, the letter is real. I've read it at least a hundred times and it makes sense. What I got from it is that your grandmother was trying to protect you," Eva Jean said. "She and Reverend Wade paid that girl's family for many years to keep them from saying anything about the baby."

"But, Ma, couldn't the child and me have been tested at some point in order to prove whether or not I was the father?"

"Oh yeah, and make all of it public once the paternity was discovered? What if you were the father?" Chante said. "Daddy, the two of them didn't see a way out of this, and to keep your reputation clean they did what they did. And by the way, what did you mean about hearing Cheryl Johnson's name in Los Angeles and from Mayor Mosley?"

"I was in LA making a speech at a Chamber of Commerce meeting and ran into Amir Jali. He mentioned Cheryl Johnson and sort of threatened me. Then I was at City Hall and Lena told me that Ralph Edmondson was working on a story about Amir Jali, and Ralph mentioned Cheryl Johnson."

"Why would Ralph Edmondson be interested in Amir Jali?" Chante asked.

"It was somethin' about a connection between Jali and me. As a matter of fact, when I was in DC, the minority leader in the House of Representatives asked me about Jali and my relationship with him. That was a strange conversation."

"Why was that?" Eva Jean said.

"Because he abruptly ended the conversation when I asked about Jali's ex-girlfriend being his current wife."

"What? The congressman is married to a woman that Amir Jali used to date? Wait a minute. Did they know each other before he became a congressman?" Eva Jean said.

"That could be the $64,000 question. I wonder what the history is between those two?" Nehemiah said.

"Daddy, one of them has the answer to the Cheryl Johnson question."

"Yeah, but who?"

THERE WAS A WAVE OF irony that Newark was experiencing a major transformation during the 50th anniversary of the riot that left the city broken in many sectors for nearly four decades. The former mayor, now U.S. Secretary of H.U.D. in the new administration, improved the areas surrounding the New Jersey Performing Arts Center and the Prudential Center along with other parts of downtown as soon as he took office as mayor in 2014. He then aggressively began to clean up the city's neighborhoods with a forceful crime-fighting initiative coupled with strengthening communities through citizen participation. The former mayor had the renaissance of Newark in full swing in three years.

"One year ago, there were questions about whether the next president would have a proactive attitude as it pertained to urban and rural America," Mayor Lena Mosley said in a speech announcing the passing of a federal bill similar to the Homestead Act of 1862, which accelerated the westward expansion of the United States. "Well, while we still aren't sure if the president is fully committed to true urban renewal, we at least have a voice for our interests in his cabinet. In addition, the task force empowered by the U.S. Conference of Mayors grabbed the bull by its horns and worked diligently with Democrats and Republicans in the House and Senate to ensure the passage of the bill that at least gets our interests off the bench and onto the playing field. It is not all we wanted, but our cities are thankful to the White House for making this landmark legislation possible through the power of the presidency.

"I was not in office during the eight years of the Obama administration, so I cannot comment on what was or wasn't done for urban and rural America during that time. Yes, I've heard the complaints from many quarters that other legislation over the past several years held more importance than issues facing Africans Americans. But we have an opening to get something done, especially when we have included rural America in our efforts.

"President Obama said in his first inaugural address that our time of standing pat, of protecting narrow interests and putting off unpleasant decisions has surely passed. Did we get there during his presence in the Oval Office? Only the history books will tell that story. But I, Mayor Lena Mosley, am here to say we are beginning to overcome. Thank God Almighty, we are beginning to overcome."

"I'M KIND OF CONFUSED ABOUT your motivation to get this story out," Ralph Edmondson said over his mobile phone to Amir Jali.

"Confused about my motivation? What's confusing? The poster boy for white America is a fraud and has been for fifty years."

"But Nehemiah Garvey is black, Amir."

"So, what does that mean to me? Clarence Thomas is black."

"You did not just go there, Amir."

"Yes, I did. And I am prepared to go further if I'm provoked."

"Okay, let me put that remark aside. What kind of fraud are you talking about?"

"Africans in America were fighting for independence in '67. We had several rebellions in this country that frightened the hell out of the white power structure. Detroit, Tampa, Milwaukee, Buffalo, all of them got the attention of honkies like President Johnson and those crackers in the South. In Newark, we really shook up America because it seemed as if the rebels were organized. Those brothers were shooting at cops and state troopers from all areas of the city with pinpoint precision, as if they were on the battlefields in Vietnam.

"And then all of a sudden you get this corny ass, Jew loving nigger Nehemiah Garvey who starts talking about saving Newark. Hell, we had them whiteys on the run. That nigger's campaign put a chill on the heat from the rebellions. He acted like that damn Booker T. Washington."

"And what was bad about that?"

"Man, Brother Ralph, I'm so glad you're a reporter and asking these questions from that prism, because if you weren't you would be considered a naïve fool. What was wrong about that was that Garvey, just like Washington did during his day, made white folks comfortable with the injustice they were peddling to people of color at that time. They thought he was perfect. But he was devious, and he messed up a girl's life and had no empathy over how her life would be affected."

"Slow down, Amir. You're all over the place. Let's take one subject at a time. Now, there's talk that you have been holding a grudge against Nehemiah Garvey because he upstaged you as a teenager at a black power program in '67. Any truth in that?"

"Brother Ralph, you know me. Can you envision a snotty nosed teenager upstaging me, a college educated brother with black warrior credentials? And aside from that, are you going to follow up on that nigger messing up that girl's life?"

"We'll get there, just be patient. From the reports that I read, Garvey did eat you up at that conference."

"I beg to differ."

"Well, that's what the major newspapers reported at the time as an irrefutable fact. I've searched the archives. But let's move on. Now, based on our previous conversation, you claimed that Nehemiah Garvey fathered a child when he was a teenager that he has never supported, and has never seen. Am I correct?"

"Most definitely."

"You are also contending that you don't know the woman in question, Cheryl Johnson, right?"

"Correct again, Brother Ralph. You're on a roll, my man."

"Let me ask this question. How familiar are you with the minority leader in the House of Representatives, a white man, who represents the congressional district that covers predominantly African American south central LA?"

"First of all, I know a lot of politicians," Jali said with a bit of apprehension in his voice. "I know him, but mostly as an acquaintance; not any more than I know the rest."

"Amir, when you initially called me about this story concerning Nehemiah, I told you that I would thoroughly research what you were telling me, right?"

"Yes, you said that. I knew you would do your homework on him."

"Amir, a good reporter researches *everybody* on any story. In fact, I have several assistants working on this story and they have been intensely thorough. Amir, remember I told you to be straight with me and not play around with the truth, right?"

"Brother Ralph, I've been around a lot of journalists and I know what you guys do. I'm not stupid."

"Amir, you're not being straight with me."

"What? Are you calling me a liar?"

"I won't use that word, but your statements are not passing the smell test. I talked to some people in LA who know both you and Congressman Jerry Wilson, the minority leader in the U.S. House. You made a lot of campaign calls for him when he ran for a seat on the Los Angeles City Council in the late '70s. You supported him when he was in the California Assembly in the mid-'80s, and you supported him in 1992 against a black candidate for the congressional seat in which he sits today, even though many blacks supported the brother. Is that black power, Amir?"

"Brother Ralph, things changed with black folks over the years and this white man had the best interests of African Americans in his heart. He was not hard to support."

"Let me break it down, Amir. I know the congresswoman's wife was once your girlfriend. Supposedly he met her in LA, but he actually met her in Atlanta, and yet she wasn't from Georgia. She moved there from New Jersey, Roselle in fact. And she was pregnant when he met her. Do I need to continue, or do you want to tell me your version of this story?"

"I can't believe you would take that white boy's word over mine, but I'll tell you this. Not only will I go to somebody else about this story, but I will make sure that congressman will have an opponent in the next election. You're missing a great story by going against me, Brother Ralph."

"Why are you being so defensive? First of all, Amir, Congressman Wilson doesn't even know I'm talking to you. I'm piecing this story together from a number of sources. I have been in this game a long time and I know how to research a story. But I'm not going to go down your road because my credentials speak for themselves. I already have enough for my story to be written tomorrow.

"I know the congressman's wife is the former Cheryl Johnson, who was leading your black power efforts in New Jersey back in '67. At the time she was doing that, she was a student at Douglass College here in Jersey. She set her sights on Nehemiah at your insistence because your good friend Abasi Chaga told you about Nehemiah's fight to restore Newark's good name with the help of Mickey Marcus.

"You needed someone who could slow down Garvey's momentum, which was growing. Who better than Cheryl? She was enamored with the black power movement because of her disenchantment with Dr. King's nonviolent stance in the fight for freedom, plus she was gorgeous and could get any man's attention. Congressman Wilson was part of the Students for a Democratic Society at the time and the two of you became friends right after the Watts riot in '65. You came to Jersey around the Christmas holidays in '67 and began to meet with Cheryl."

"From what you're telling me it sounds like a bit of conjecture and rumor. You don't have a damn piece of concrete evidence."

"Amir, I have more than you might want to know. I know that Congressman Wilson became close to Cheryl during the time you and he were in Jersey. The two of them spent hours upon hours talking about the effects of the riot on Newark, on both the African American and Jewish communities all over Jersey. Though he was white, he understood her frustration about relationships between blacks and whites in America. They decided to stay in touch after he left Jersey, but something happened that caused her not to return his telephone calls after he went back to LA. You want me to go on?"

"I'll listen to this white media inspired crap, even though it is nothing but a bunch of lies. After the black community hears how the congressman is trying to smear my name, he will never be elected in that district again. And you are just as dirty as he is because you have been working with him to destroy me."

"You don't have any facts that can prove I am working against you. I called you to get your side of the story. It seems as if you want to place blame on everybody but yourself. I'll tell you what, though. I'm going to move ahead with this story and I'll let you respond after it hits the newsstand. It will also be on all of our social media platforms. My editor knows the direction in which I'm going with the story and he's already approved it."

"I will sue you and that sorry ass newspaper if you run this."

"Well, you better have a great lawyer. Not only is there damning evidence that I have in my possession, but there are also people who know a lot about you; and trust me, none of them include Congressman Wilson. Let me warn you, too, if you go to other credible media sources to try to shop this story you better believe they'll call me to get my background information."

"Brother Ralph, I should have known that you would try to protect your homeboy from Newark."

"I'm just a newspaperman doing my job."

A GROUP OF NEIGHBORHOOD advocates was touring several areas in Newark. The man named Gabriel was with the entourage.

"I don't know if most of you know our friend Gabriel, but he has some memories of Newark that none of us can lay claim to," the tour coordinator said. "Gabriel was a homeless man who saved a family from a fire in the mid-sixties. Please tell the story, Gabriel."

"I was living in an abandoned house a few doors from this family," Gabriel said in his thick Jamaican accent. "One night, I saw their house on fire and heard the little girls screaming. I go in and get them out, and the family takes me in after that."

"Gabriel is not telling the whole story. He saved the girls from dying in that fire, and after he got them out, he went back in and saved five more people. This man is a hero. He is just like a father to me, because I am one of those girls he saved that night. I love you, Gabriel."

"God put me in place to do what I did," Gabriel said with tears forming in his eyes. "God is also calling me to tell the story about how I got there in the first place. I am having dreams, and my friend Samuel Garvey keeps coming to mind. I am also dreaming of men who are coming after me and will kill me if I tell the truth."

"Are your dreams happening a lot?" one of the tour members asked.

"They become fresher every time I see the lights on a police car. I have no idea why that is happening, but it does."

"You became homeless during the time when large numbers of black men were mysteriously disappearing in Newark after encounters with policemen. Do you think you were one of them?"

"I know I was one of them."

Chapter 31

"I think we do a great disservice by crafting solutions without being cognizant of the history that led us to the place where we are, both in terms of how that history has had an impact on African Americans and other people of color, but also the impact that it's had on white folks in this nation. It's crippled both groups, I think, in a variety of ways. I think there's a fear, even among well-intentioned, good people, that if you speak about something that is heartfelt, but perhaps not politically correct, that you will be labeled a racist. Black people talk about race all the time. I don't know if white people talk about it all the time. I'm not there when they have those conversations. But I suspect they do talk about it more than they do when there are blacks and whites mixed, because it's a difficult thing."

~ FORMER U.S. ATTORNEY GENERAL ERIC HOLDER ON THE IMPACT OF RACE IN THE 21ST CENTURY, IN 2009

"In 1968, President Lyndon B. Johnson convened the National Advisory Commission on Civil Disorders. The commission studied the causes of the 'racial disorders' that had erupted across the country during the summer of 1967. Their basic conclusion was the nation was moving toward two societies, one black, one white—separate and unequal.

287

> Almost 50 years later, historians and scholars look at the commission report as another reminder of how much is still unchanged and needs changing to make the promises of American democracy work."
>
> ~ Marian Wright Edelman, columnist for George Curry Media, in 2016

The dynamics of race were dramatically altered as the decade of the seventies emerged. The most influential players in the theater of Black Nationalism during the 1960s followed the path of forming minority-owned businesses, ascended to places of power within elected political offices (largely due to the establishment of the Congressional Black Caucus in 1971) and assumed policy-making positions in educational institutions on all levels. On the downside, the influx of illegal drug activity in once-proud urban provinces exacerbated the demise of those communities, which created the flight of middle-class African Americans to more accommodating suburban locales. Most notably, African Americans embarked on a second Great Migration in the 1990s, albeit with smaller numbers than the early and mid-20th century, and this time it was back to the South.

Newark Mayor Lena Mosley is living a charmed life after just seven months of assuming leadership of one of America's most-watched cities. Once a place many social scientists had written off after the devastation left from the 1967 riot, Newark is now rising because of the dogged determination of faithful servants who refused to give up on the city they love.

At Mosley's side, along with having her back in professional support and lifelong friendship, is former Weequahic high school athletic superstar Nehemiah Garvey. Though Garvey had ample opportunities to play professional football, baseball, or basketball, he remained in Newark and opted to become a businessman with an eye toward improving his beloved hometown. With the help of his high school basketball coach, the legendary Mickey Marcus, Garvey has been able to carve out a career that has elevated him to multi-millionaire status.

Starting today, in this three-part series about the rise of Nehemiah Garvey and his work to bring Newark to a positive, valued place on the American landscape, we look at his work as a teen-age activist in post-riot Newark, his business partnerships that helped bring modest yet notable attention to Newark's attributes as an economic development hub, and his coziness with black power advocates, including the well-known Amir Jali.

While our coverage will be fair and balanced, we plan to open doors that were previously closed as they relate to Mr. Garvey. It is our intention to get a deeper look into the life of a man whose singular mission has been to elevate Newark to one of the nation's greatest cities.

— Ralph Edmondson, *The Star-Ledger*

"Well, young man, you are a star!" Mickey Marcus said to Nehemiah at their regular lunch meeting in Montclair.

"Yeah, I know. That's what's bothering me, especially when my name is included with Amir Jali's."

"You don't have anything to worry about, trust me. All that baby stuff is dead."

"Baby stuff? What are you talking about?"

"Nehemiah, I know about the baby. I've known since Caleb Frazier told me when he found out. He sensed a problem with you after we won the tournament out in LA."

"My mind was so divided after I got that call from Cheryl Johnson that I entertained the thought of quitting the team."

"I knew something was going on after I talked with Caleb. And I was upset. That's when I went straight to your mother and grandmother about you giving up, and Reverend Wade and I decided we had to go into action."

"How did the two of you get involved?"

"The Johnson girl's family wanted money or they were going to make a big deal about their daughter's pregnancy. They planned to go to *The Star-Ledger* with a story about you and the relationship you had with their daughter. Your grandmother didn't want that, so she was going to mortgage her business *and* her home to get the money. I told her not to give in to that girl's family, but she was determined to keep your name clean. I told her to keep her money and don't worry about you. I paid it. I gave it to your grandmother each month. In cash. Reverend Wade delivered it."

"Reverend Wade didn't say anything about that in his letter. He made it look as if my grandmother paid the family."

"We never told him who gave the money. We didn't tell your mother, either."

"Does Ralph Edmondson know anything about any of this?"

"Only what I want him to know."

"Mickey, what's up with all this cloak and dagger stuff? Just explain why you don't think I have anything to worry about with this upcoming newspaper story." Nehemiah was frustrated.

"First, let me say this. You have an amazing daughter. She loves you with no boundaries. After she talked to you about the letter and you told her about the questions you encountered from Jali, Congressman Wilson, and Lena Mosley, Chante got to work. She called Edmondson and told him that you would not be answering any of his questions, but she would speak on your behalf."

"Get outta here! Chante did all that?"

"All by herself. She also did an extensive background check on Jali via traditional sources and social media, pulled up stories about your encounter with him back in '67, and got information about Cheryl

Johnson's family. Then she talked to Reverend Wade's son and found out that his father often talked about me, saying that I saved your reputation when many in the Jewish community had negative views of you. Once she had all of the information she could gather, she called me. We met, talked about what she had, and then God blessed me with the contact we needed."

"And what was that?"

"A phone call from Cheryl Johnson's mother," Marcus said with relief.

"How did she know to call you?"

"It was all Chante. She set it up. In his letter, Reverend Wade Sr. talked about the conversations he had with the Johnson family's pastor during that time. Chante decided to attend the church in Roselle a few times and get to know some of the longtime members there. She met a lady who knew the Johnsons when they lived in Roselle and was told that they had moved to Atlanta to join their daughter, a year after she left college and moved down there."

"Mickey, I'm gettin' dizzy. This is a lot of information to process."

"Nehemiah, I'm trying to get you to understand why you don't have anything to worry about with this three-part story that's coming out in the newspaper. Just listen to me," Marcus said. "The Johnson girl moved to Atlanta to live with her grandparents and give birth. Several months later, the grandparents told Cheryl's parents that either they come to Atlanta and take care of their daughter and her child, or they were sending them back to Jersey. Of course, Cheryl's parents didn't want to be embarrassed by bringing their daughter back to Roselle with a fatherless child, so they made the decision to move to Atlanta. Your grandmother told them she would pay for the move and give them money to take care of the child. That's when I came in."

"Mickey, you're startin' to show your ninety plus years. You're all over the place with this story. You need to get to the point already!"

"Okay, okay," Marcus said. He began talking slower. "Chante got the mother's phone number from the lady she met at the church in Roselle, called the mother, who is still in Atlanta, and asked about Cheryl. Chante found out that Cheryl is now married and lives in California. But the mother wouldn't answer any more of Chante's questions.

"About a week later, out of nowhere, I get a call from Cheryl's mother. She tells me that your grandmother stayed in touch with her all those years while the child was growing up. Cheryl's mother said she felt guilty because Lula Mae confessed that I was the person giving Lula Mae the money to take care of the child, and Cheryl's mother wanted to say thank you. She added that she wanted to talk to me years ago, but her husband told her she couldn't call me. He died last year, which gave her the opportunity to come forward."

"Thank you, for finally reaching the point. But I still don't see how I don't have anything to worry about. I have a child who is now an adult, whom I've never met. Wouldn't it be a good idea if I establish some kind of relationship with her?"

"Stop right there, Nehemiah. You still aren't getting it. *You aren't the child's father.*"

"Wait. What? What do you mean?"

"I mean you are not the father of Cheryl Johnson's child. Amir Jali is."

"Wait one minute. What? Seriously, what? Amir Jali? How did that happen?"

"When he came to Jersey in '67 to recruit Cheryl to work for his black power campaign, he used his personality and charm to convince her to go out with him. Jali raped her on their first date. Congressman Wilson, who was a student activist at the time and one of Jali's associates in Los Angeles, was also on the trip and met Cheryl. He was immediately smitten with her and took her out a couple of times. Nothing happened between them.

"When Cheryl told Jali she was pregnant as a result of the rape, he told her this would be a good time to take you down, by telling you that the baby was yours. Cheryl kept the rape between her and her mother for years. That is until Cheryl told her husband, the former student activist now congressman, after they were married for a few years."

"Okay, Mickey, what is the timetable on the wedding and the rape confession?"

"Congressman Wilson was told by Jali that the baby was yours and you were paying child support. That was in 1970. Wilson told Cheryl that he didn't care that she had a baby, he wanted to marry her. Against Jali's demands, Wilson came to Atlanta, married Cheryl in 1971, moved with her to LA and raised the child as theirs. Of course, Jali never said anything about the pregnancy to Wilson, and became a major supporter of Wilson's political career.

"Then the child got sick when she was eight, which was 1976. She needed a blood transfusion. It was a rare type and the child's life was in peril. Of course, Cheryl asked Jali about his blood type. He was a match, but he was reluctant to give the blood."

"That sonofabitch."

"Oh yeah, Mr. Defender of Black People not wanting to save his own African American child's life. Don't even get me started. Anyway, Cheryl had to be truthful with her husband about Jali raping her, her agreement with him to keep it quiet, and blame it on you. Wilson went to Jali and told him he knew he raped Cheryl before they got married. He told Jali he would keep his mouth closed about what he did to Cheryl if he gave blood to save his daughter's life. Jali agreed to give the blood, but they had to say it came from his sister, not him."

"How could he do that without the attending doctors knowing?"

"By getting a doctor who was sleazy enough to get involved, which he did. But he also had an accomplice in Wilson, whose political career was on the rise. Jali told him to never disclose what they did, or he would say it was all Wilson's idea. Wilson agreed."

"So Jali knew he had Wilson over a barrel because Wilson wanted to save the child's life. He would agree to anything to make sure that happened." Nehemiah now had a better understanding of what Marcus was saying.

"Nehemiah, you're quick. Better than Columbo," Marcus said. "Fast forward several years later, when Jali saw your rise to prominence across the country. He told Wilson that he felt the need to create some problems for you because he thought you were bad for black people, though he was more troubled about being replaced as a spokesman for the black community with the President of the United States and all the power that came with it. Wilson didn't like that idea, so much that he called Cheryl's mother and started talking about how Jali had orchestrated what had happened to Cheryl."

"You got all of this from Cheryl's mother?"

"I sure did, and it was heartbreaking to hear that woman recall all of what happened at that time. The story Ralph Edmondson has written is going to crush Amir Jali, and rightfully so, because he's a no good schvartze."

"Schvartze? What does that mean?"

"Nehemiah, you don't want to know, but trust me, that's what Amir Jali is."

"What about the daughter?"

"Cheryl told her daughter what happened a long time ago, when Wilson adopted her. She knows about Jali but calls Wilson her father."

"Mickey, once again you've come to my rescue. Saying thanks doesn't seem like enough."

"Don't thank me, thank your daughter. If it weren't for her, none of this would have happened. She took on the task and saw it through. Just like you did after the riot in '67.

"It just goes to show you, Nehemiah, when you live right, good things come your way."

Chapter 32

"He picked his economic team and when the going got tough, his economic team picked Wall Street. Not families who were losing their homes. Not people who lost their jobs. Not young people who were struggling to get an education. And it happened over and over and over."

~ United States Senator Elizabeth Warren of Massachusetts, on President Obama's economic advisers, from the book, *BUYER'S REMORSE: How Obama Let Progressives Down* by Bill Press, in 2016

"Access to a job in the summer and beyond can make all the difference to a young person—especially those who don't have access to many resources and opportunities."

~ President Barack Obama, announcing the Summer Opportunity Project, a $21 million Department of Labor youth jobs grant, in February 2016

It was a mixed bag of opinions that came forth across the country from media, government, and interested parties regarding the economic success of the Obama administration. Many of them believed the president was correct to sign the American Recovery and Reinvestment Act—also known as the *stimulus*—into law in 2009. The same group, however, had negative opinions of the effects of the legislation, because the economy continued to perform poorly in the area of housing and full-time job creation.

A faction in the Democratic Party argued that financial bailouts for Wall Street companies caused a recess in the economic fortunes for middle class families, while a bloc of Republicans argued that national security was at risk because of the ongoing turmoil in the Middle East.

"I NEVER WOULD HAVE thought that we would have those kinds of people in the White House at this time in our country's history," a conservative commentator on a national television talk show said.

"You sound like those right wingers who couldn't find any redeeming quality that President Obama possessed during his eight years," a liberal analyst said with a countering opinion. "He did a lot for the American people and they will soon find out."

"Both of your parties got your oxen gored during the 2016 campaign, because you thought the American people were going to continue to buy the hypocrisy that you have all been working on their behalf," the moderate announcer declared. "Americans heard certain candidates lay out the argument that both political parties were more concerned with international trade agreements and job creation in other countries, than raising working class wages and helping young people right here at home get affordable college educations. I can only hope you have finally seen that doing what's right for our country is not a partisan effort.

"I know some of you are skeptical of what the U.S. Conference of Mayors pulled off with its urban initiative, but you will see it's a major step in the right direction. As a result, the mayor of Newark is a rising star, because she worked with Democrats and Republicans on Capitol Hill to get something done."

"MY FATHER USED TO TALK about the battles between Weequahic and Central all the time," the police captain said. "According to him, Central would have been state champs in '67 if it wasn't for Weequahic."

"Central had Stan Johnson that year and nobody could stop him," Nehemiah said. "It took everything we had to beat them. Matter of fact, I think they were better than Camden High School, who we played in the state championship game in '67 and '68. Those were the great days of sports in Newark. I remember playing against Butch Bryant from South Side. He was cool on the court, with a smooth jump shot. He's in the Morgan State University Hall of Fame, and he played with the Baltimore Bullets in the NBA for several seasons. Ozzie Percy from West Side could shoot the nets off any rim and I had to cover him for three years in high school. He played in the Italian Pro League for a long time and was a legend over there. I played baseball with Pete Wayne when we were little boys. He was one of Newark's most productive baseball players while at Central, was a great college player at Seton Hall University, and he was the first African American to coach a Historically Black College and University in the College World Series.

"I really wish we could talk longer about those days, but right now I'm on a mission." Nehemiah and the officer were sitting on a bench in Military Park in downtown Newark.

"I heard about your mission when our office got the call from Mayor Mosley's chief of staff. We were told to give you all the help you need, right away. I understand you're trying to get information on the missing person cases from 1965. Is that right?"

"Yeah. That was the year my father disappeared. I'm actually doing this for my mother, who believes my father is still alive."

"Mr. Garvey, that's gonna be a hard job. The records at that time were handled by a corrupt group in the police department."

"I'm sure most of that crowd is either physically dead or mentally challenged by now. I'm still determined to solve his disappearance. I couldn't forgive myself if my mother passed away without any closure on what happened to my father."

"I know a bunch of the old guys who still come to the union hall whenever we have get-togethers. You have the recently retired officers there, and then you have the real oldies but goodies, the ones who are in their mid-eighties and early nineties"

"I guess there's not too many of the real old timers left."

"The number is small and they're barely getting around, but there's a few who can still talk about the past with clarity. You know how they roll, talking about how they could arrest people without worrying about somebody looking over their shoulder. Remember, when they started in law enforcement there was no Miranda warning to govern their questioning of suspects."

Nehemiah shook his head. "Yeah, that, and not having to worry about body cameras and being recorded on smartphones by interested bystanders. Plus, they could talk to people any way they wanted when they made a stop."

"Using profanity and calling people out of their names. That was standard operating procedure for some of them," the captain said. "Wait a minute. I just thought about something. One of the old guys has been really mouthy about how he used to deal with the colored people in Newark. *Colored* is his word, not mine. Matter of fact, I've even heard nigger come out of his mouth from time to time."

"Ah, he's one of those, huh?"

"His name is Keller and he's about eighty-five, so he might have been in his mid-thirties around the time your father disappeared. In fact, he testified in front of the governor's task force on the '67 riots. What's interesting is that I heard he had to be subpoenaed to the hearing, that he didn't volunteer to show up. According to my father, Keller's partner testified about their role in roughing up crime suspects in black neighborhoods. He also talked about them taking money from defenseless black men."

"What? And I bet he was part of that group that tried to say there was no police brutality in Newark. Too bad your father is not with us anymore. He could have probably given me a lot of information, since he was part of the Newark Police Department during those days."

"Mr. Garvey, my father used to talk to Gene Oldham a lot. You remember that Mr. Oldham, Perry Williamson, and Herbert Evans were major politicians back in the sixties? They were part of the team that got the first black mayor elected in Newark."

"I worked on that campaign during my first year at Rutgers, in 1970. Mr. Oldham and I got to know each other quite well and worked together on many other projects over the years. I had several negative encounters with Mr. Williamson and Mr. Evans when I was doing that reputation restoration campaign for Newark. After I started my business, Mr. Evans blocked bids on a number of my ventures when he was on the City Council. I guess he was angry because I wouldn't offer him any kickbacks."

"Mr. Oldham has been dealing with bouts of dementia for the past few years; he's been spending a lot of time in Florida, but he still comes up here quite a bit. Here's what you need to know. My father shared information with Mr. Oldham about what was happening behind the scenes in the police department. Mr. Oldham knows a lot about police tactics back then."

"You think he'll talk to me?"

"I'm sure he will, as long as you get him on one of his better days. I pray he'll remember you. Good thing, though, he loves to talk about the old times, and if you get him on one of his good days, you might get a lot of information. I have his cell phone number. I'll give him a call."

"I appreciate it. I've got to find out what happened to my father so my mother can leave earth in peace when God takes her home."

THE PREVAILING FEELING about the Newark Police Department in the 1960s was that the leadership knew it had unscrupulous officers but wouldn't do anything about them. The complaints about law enforcement, however, had a double edge. According to a 1968 report from the New Jersey Governor's Select Commission on Civil Disorder, 70% of Newark's black residents believed their complaints to the police did not receive the same attention as complaints from white citizens.

"Many policemen knew I carried a wad of cash when I got off work, because I told them," Gabriel said at the meeting of the South Ward neighborhood advocates, in Eva Jean Garvey's restaurant. "I had asked them to watch me as I locked my business and walked to my car, so no one would try to rob me."

The leader of the group had a puzzled look on her face. "Gabriel, all of these years I have known you, I never heard you talk about a business. Where was this business?"

"Down there in the Valley. I know I talked to you about that," Gabriel said, sounding aggravated. "Yes, I owned a business. Many of you came there. You talked to me and my wife all the time."

"Gabriel, all of this is new to me. I never heard about a family; you never mentioned a wife."

Gabriel began shouting. "You people are liars! You knew me. You knew my son. You knew that those policemen wanted to take my money. I…" Gabriel clutched his chest and began falling. Chante ran out of her office when she heard the commotion.

"Oh, my God, he might be having a heart attack!" someone in the meeting screamed.

"Call 911!" Chante yelled. Gabriel was still conscious.

"Those men took my money and beat me," he said while writhing on the floor. "They called me an uppity nigger. They said the lady called them." Then Gabriel passed out.

"Police brutality was running rampant all over the country," Gene Oldham told Nehemiah over the telephone. Nehemiah was speaking from his home. "The Watts riot was started because of out of control law enforcement officers. As did the unrest in Cleveland and Tampa. The same goes for the riots in other cities. The difference between those uprisings and the one in Newark, was that the people in Newark fought back with a vengeance, and it seemed as if it was well organized."

"When you look back on history, white citizens often attacked black people because they were jealous of black people having success, whether in gaining freedom from slavery or starting a business empire, like when blacks created what was known as Black Wall Street in Tulsa, Oklahoma," Nehemiah said.

Oldham agreed. "You're so right. That's what happened here. Many blacks in Newark were beginning to get better jobs, open businesses, and clean up their neighborhoods in the sixties. But the power structure in place then didn't want that to happen, just like in many other predominantly black cities. So, they slowed down in providing basic services like street cleaning, timely responses from police and firemen, and better public education. Some blacks, mostly men, began protesting these actions by the government. So, the police began intimidating people in the neighborhoods where many blacks lived to stop them from filing complaints with governmental authorities.

"A lot of this was documented during the governor's hearing on the riots. In fact, one black man was recorded as saying, 'just treat a Negro like a man. It is so easy, but the white man will not stand for a black man being a man. He's got to be a boy.' If you read the entire report, you'll find many statements like that."

"So, the Newark police officers were the enforcers of the intimidation policy?"

"That's right. And that's when black men suddenly started to disappear, as if into thin air."

"My mother has consistently maintained that's what happened to my father. He called her just as he was closing the restaurant, to let her know he was on his way home. He never showed up. That was fifty-two years ago."

"That's a long time, Nehemiah. I'm sure you know I've been having health issues," Oldham said. "But I will do what I can to help you. From what I remember about you, you're a fine young man."

"Thanks, Mr. Oldham. I got some information about an officer who showed some racist tendencies during that time. According to my source at the police department, a man named Keller was subpoenaed to testify in front of the governor's task force."

"I know Keller. Nothing could cause me to forget that name. In my opinion, he hated black people. I know for a fact that he would wait outside bars in the Valley, snatch drunken black men when they came outside, and take their money. If they argued with him, he and his partner would beat them up and dare them to say anything.

"One night, me, Herbert Evans, and Perry Williamson set Keller up by posing as men who had too much to drink. Sort of like a sting operation. When he accosted us, two black police officers came up and stopped him. Keller argued with the officers about our behavior when we left the bar, but the officers had seen the whole incident and refuted his assertion. They told Keller to move on or they would report him. Keller cursed all of us and said the next nigger wouldn't be so lucky."

"Now that you look back, do you wish you had filed charges against him that night?"

"No, because it wouldn't have done any good. The Newark Police Department was riddled with crooks in high places during that time; they weren't going to discipline one of their own. But I did get to meet Keller's son a number of years later, and he told me a lot about his father, who was fired in '68 after he testified at the governor's task force on riots."

"All that's good Mr. Oldham, but how does it help me find out what happened to my father?"

"Keller's son told me his father went on a rampage after we set him up. He believed his father might have brutalized many black men on a consistent basis for almost two years. He told me some things that I have never told anybody, but since my days might be numbered now, I might as well tell you." As the old man was talking, Nehemiah's mobile phone buzzed.

"Mr. Oldham, hold that thought. I have a text message from my mother. I'll be right back."

The message read, "Nehemiah, this is your mother. I'm at Beth Israel Hospital." Nehemiah called her.

"Hey Ma. Why are you calling from the hospital? What's wrong?"

"You know the old man Gabriel from the neighborhood group? He had a heart attack at the restaurant. You need to get over here."

"Why? What can I do?"

"He called your name before he fell unconscious. Your name and the name of the lady who taught him to read in Jamaica. Nehemiah, you need to get here *right now*."

Chapter 33

"I request only that McCallum be granted a full hearing by the Brooklyn conviction integrity unit, now under the auspices of the new district attorney, Ken Thompson. Knowing what I do, I am certain that when the facts are brought to light, Thompson will recommend his immediate release. Just as my own verdict was predicated on racism rather than reason and on concealment rather than disclosure, so too was McCallum's."

~ From an opinion piece by professional boxer Rubin "Hurricane" Carter in the *New York Daily News*, in which he asked for an independent review of a murder conviction, in 2014. Carter himself was wrongly convicted in 1966 for a double murder in New Jersey

In 1967, President Lyndon Johnson's National Advisory Commission on Civil Disorders placed in its report that "the police are not merely a 'spark' factor." According to the opinion of the 11-member commission, "to some Negroes, police have come to symbolize white power, white racism, and white repression. And the fact is that many police do reflect and express these white attitudes. The atmosphere of hostility and cynicism is reinforced by a widespread belief among Negroes in the existence of police brutality and in a double standard of justice and protection—one for Negroes and one for whites."

"Daddy, I'm so glad you got here." Chante wrapped her arms around Nehemiah's neck. They were standing outside Gabriel's hospital room in the Intensive Care Unit.

The attending physician approached Nehemiah. "Hello, Mr. Garvey. Do you know Mr. Gabriel?"

"I just met him about five or six months ago, but he claimed to have known my father for a long time."

"He was a bit disoriented before he passed out. He told me he knew my husband, but I don't remember ever meeting him," Eva Jean said. "He seemed familiar when I met him at my restaurant. He reminded me of Samuel. I guess the Jamaican accent makes them alike."

"We typically don't discuss any patient's case with non-family members, but Mr. Gabriel is struggling to live, and since he said your name along with the woman who took care of him as a child, it is apparent that the two of you have a deep connection. I can make an exception in this case."

Nehemiah walked toward Gabriel's room and looked in through the window. "How do you think I can help?" Nehemiah asked.

"The best thing you can do is sit in his room while he's asleep. If he wakes up and sees you, it might be comforting for him."

The hours passed slowly. Nehemiah never fell asleep during the time he sat in Gabriel's room. Instead, he stayed in constant prayer for nearly five hours, recalling Biblical scripture.

It was about 2 a.m. when Gabriel's eyes slowly opened.

"Good morning, Nehemiah." Gabriel instantly knew it was Nehemiah who was sitting at his bedside.

"It's good to see you, Mr. Gabriel. We've all been worrying about you."

"All of you? Does that include your mother?"

"Yes, my mother, my daughter, and your friends. Most of them have been here since you were admitted."

"I must get up and tell everyone thank you." Gabriel began to climb from the bed.

Nehemiah stood up. "No, no. You need to stay in the bed. They are keeping your heart under observation to make sure you don't get sick again. You almost left us."

"I almost leave? You mean I walk out, or do you mean I was going home to glory?"

The last part of Gabriel's statement startled Nehemiah. "Mr. Gabriel, my father used to say that, just the way you did just now."

"You mean, 'going home to glory'?"

"Yes."

Gabriel's eyes closed and he drifted back to sleep. Nehemiah left the room and quickly walked down the hall to a small room where his mother and Chante were sleeping in chairs.

"Ma, wake up. I have something to tell you."

Eva Jean raised her head. "What time is it, honey?"

"It's early, but you need to hear this. Gabriel said, 'going home to glory'."

"There's nothing special about that. It's a popular expression."

"Ma, he sounded like Daddy when he used to say it. Same inflection in his words and all."

"Nehemiah, I suggest you stay in this room with us. Your imagination is playing tricks on you. You probably need some sleep, away from Gabriel's room."

"There's nothing wrong with me. I know what I heard and how I heard it. I'm going back to his room. I need to be there just in case he wakes up again."

"I'm going to wake up Chante and we're going home. Please call us if anything changes with Mr. Gabriel."

THE DOCTORS FOUND A small blockage in one of the arteries in Gabriel's heart, but decided against placing a stent in the valve after angioplasty surgery.

"Though we are not positively sure about Mr. Gabriel's age, his heart is not strong enough for any procedure beyond what we performed." The attending physician was speaking to the daughter of the family Gabriel had lived with since the mid-sixties. They were talking quietly in his office. Nehemiah waited to enter.

"Can Mr. Garvey come in?" the woman said. "He's been here since yesterday afternoon and he spent the night in Gabriel's room. I don't mind if he hears what you have to say."

The physician motioned for Nehemiah to join them.

"How does it look for him?" Nehemiah asked as he entered.

"If he was younger, it would be a matter of monitoring his heart and prescribing medication. But he's an old man, and anything we do could be a risk."

"How old do you think he is?"

"That's hard to tell, but we did find something interesting. After we performed the surgery, we gave him an EKG. As they were preparing his body, one of the attendants discovered an old scar on his side. We had a skin specialist take a look at it. Here's the chart." Nehemiah's eyes widened as he read the chart.

"It says here that the scar looked as if someone attempted to brand Gabriel, like an animal in a herd," Nehemiah said. "But it says here that it's an old scar, and undistinguishable."

"It seems as if whoever branded him was trying to make sure he could be identified if someone didn't know who he was. Did anyone in your family ever see this scar?" the physician asked the lady with whom Gabriel lived.

"Gabriel never took his shirt off in front of us."

"He was probably self-conscious about it," Nehemiah said. "I'm sure the pain alone was something he couldn't forget."

Nehemiah looked through the doctor's office window and saw his mother and Chante with two men.

"Ma, I didn't call you, so why are you here?" He was irritated as he walked out to meet them in the hall. "And who are these men?"

"This is Mr. Keller and his father. They came to talk to you after your conversation with Gene Oldham," Eva Jean said.

"I called your mother after I talked to Gene Oldham about the conversation between the two of you. Mr. Oldham called me as soon as you got off the phone with him yesterday," the younger Keller said. "He told me you had some questions about my father's time as a policeman."

"My conversation with Mr. Oldham started me thinking about the parallels between what happened to Gabriel and other black men during that time." Nehemiah had a cold stare aimed directly at the elder Keller as he continued. "My father mysteriously disappeared around the same time. Can you add anything to the conversation I had with Mr. Oldham?"

"I can add my father's actions as an officer with the Newark Police Department in the fifties and sixties. He did some things that were awfully wrong during that time and he was forced to leave the department as a result. What Mr. Oldham told me bothered me to the point that I needed to speak to you as soon as I could. I called your office and your assistant told me that you were at the hospital, looking after a friend. I thought I better call your mother before I came here, so I took a chance and called her at the restaurant. Luckily, she was there."

"Mr. Keller told me about what you and Gene Oldham talked about, so I decided that we needed to meet here at the hospital," Eva Jean said.

"Daddy, I think we need to hear what Mr. Keller has to say," Chante said.

"I agree, but first I have to talk to you and Ma alone. Let's go to Gabriel's room and see how he's doing. Gentlemen, please excuse us."

The three generations of Garveys proceeded toward the elevators. They walked past the photos that depicted the leadership of Beth Israel since its founding in 1901. The images displayed the farmland on which the hospital was built in the South Ward in 1926, after it was moved from High Street—now known as Martin Luther King Boulevard—in the Central Ward. There were photographs of the men who financed the first building campaign, and of the metal receptacles known as *pushkas*. The jar-like devices sat on the counters of Jewish merchants in order for people to donate their pennies, nickels, dimes, and quarters to the early

Beth Israel Hospital. There were timelines that spoke about Beth Israel having the first hospital-based blood bank in the state, the state's first successful implant of a nuclear-powered battery heart pacemaker, and New Jersey's first heart, lung and kidney transplants.

"Mr. Oldham was getting ready to give me information about Keller when I got your call to come here yesterday," Nehemiah said. "From what he was telling me, this guy Keller was in the middle of a lot of crime against black men in Newark in the sixties."

"I didn't tell you everything about the conversation I had with Mr. Gabriel that day at the restaurant," Eva Jean said, recalling the day she first met the man who had claimed to know her husband. "He said something about a woman being the reason your father left us, and men killing him if he said too much."

"I have had to process a lot of information in my lifetime," Nehemiah said. "Playbooks in sports, classwork in college, plus getting my MBA and a law degree. But all of this stuff? In a matter of less than an hour? A woman causing my father to leave home and he never contacts us again? Men threatening to kill another man if he talks too much? A scar that looks like a brand put on an animal?"

"Wait a minute, Nehemiah. Slow down," Eva Jean said. "What about a scar?"

"The scar they found on Gabriel's body."

"A scar?" Eva Jean and Chante said in unison.

Chapter 34

"Those who profess to favor freedom, and yet depreciate agitation, are men who want crops without plowing up the ground. They want rain without thunder and lightning. They want the ocean without the awful roar of its many waters. This struggle may be a moral one; or it may be a physical one; or it may be both moral and physical; but it must be a struggle. Power concedes nothing without a demand. It never did and it never will."

~ FREDERICK DOUGLASS, IN A LETTER TO AN
ABOLITIONIST ASSOCIATE, IN 1849

"Donald Trump will be the next president, the 45th President of the United States. And it will be up to him to set up a team that he thinks will serve him well and reflect his policies. And those who didn't vote for him have to recognize that that's how democracy works. That's how this system operates. And you know, what's clear is that he was able to tap into, yes, the anxieties but also "the enthusiasm of his voters in a way that was impressive. And I said so to him because I think that to the extent that there were a lot of folks who missed the Trump phenomenon, I think that connection that he was able to make with his supporters, that was impervious to events that might have sunk another candidate. That's powerful stuff."

~ President Barack Obama, on the
election of Donald Trump, in 2016

Cities with neighborhoods that had housed ethnic minorities for decades began to experience occupation in the mid-1980s by a group described as young urban professionals; they were called "yuppies." While the movement drastically changed the complexion of influential urban centers throughout the country, new leadership teams with diverse members emerged as the 21st century dawned. Their ranks included people of dissimilar education and political backgrounds, members of different lifestyle persuasion groups, and factions of persons with high levels of disposable incomes seeking to change the fortunes of dispossessed communities.

"At this ignominious site, on this day, fifty years ago, a young community activist stood atop a car and pleaded with a group of angry citizens to disperse. A rumor was circulating that a Vietnam war veteran had been beaten and arrested by Newark police officers." Mayor Lena Mosley was speaking outside the building that housed the Newark Police Department's 4th Precinct, the site where the Newark Riot began in July 1967. "As history has told us time and again, the people did not heed that request. Instead, they threw Molotov cocktails through the windows of this building behind me, which started a conflagration that not only burned major parts of this city, but also left haunting memories for those who were smeared with the ashes in more ways than one.

"I saw the destruction firsthand when it happened, and though I moved away a few years later and stayed away for more than forty-five years, I never forgot the Newark of my youth. Today I am here to commemorate the ascent of a new day for Newark. Today I am here to finally bury the hatchet that has been used to divide this community along racial, spiritual, and political lines. Today is the day we take the lemons that soured the reputation of this great city and make lemonade for the committed residents who have waited decades to see their neighborhoods revitalized. Now is the time for increased security, and a return of local control over our public schools.

"Because of the three-point plan focusing on jobs, economic development and security implemented by the former mayor before he joined the new president's administration, Newark is in great shape to gain serious concessions from both the state and federal governments. We still have a tough road to navigate on the education front, but the vision is clearer today than it was yesterday.

"If we had listened to the social scientists, Newark's residents would have believed they had to settle for living in a city not suitable for development, a whole population condemned to urban blight. If we had listened to the social scientists, we would have to accept a future of high crime rates, negative health outcomes, and higher dropout rates among school children. But we are not doing that! That is why I am thanking the people of Newark for your steadfast dedication to this city, and not giving in or giving up. There are generations of Newark families that had the opportunity to flee our territory, yet they took deep breaths and exhaled with positive outlooks.

"Under my administration, their devotion will yield tremendous benefits. Not only will we use the full strength of my office to reduce property taxes, we will ensure that for every dollar of tax breaks we extend for development in downtown Newark, we will match the amount with tax relief designed to restore our great neighborhoods. On the three hundredth fifty first anniversary of our existence, our city is now basking in the glow of being one of the leaders of a new emphasis in urban community renewal. I firmly believe that the toughness of Newark will make us the gentle giant in the fight to treat all of our citizens fairly and equitably."

The admission of guilt by former Newark police officer, John Keller, in the 1965 beating of Samuel Garvey has created headlines across the country for the past two months; trending high on social media for just as long. This episode, however, is only one of many that occurred during the most shameful period in Newark's history. Black men were taken off the streets and violated by duly sworn law enforcement personnel in the worst ways that could be conceived.

Samuel Garvey, the father of Newark businessman and philanthropist, Nehemiah Garvey, and husband of noted restaurateur Eva Jean Garvey, has been missing since that year. The tragic tale of a man named Gabriel, whose disjointed yet plausible story about the last night anyone saw Mr. Garvey alive, was the subject of a front-page story in this newspaper and created quite a stir among people who remember Newark in the bad old days. Talk about the beatings many African Americans suffered at the hands of out-of-control policemen during that era has given rise to possible lawsuits against the city of Newark, but statute of limitations issues might prevent such actions.

There is hope that help is on the way, to stem the current overzealous policing. Two years ago, the U.S. Department of Justice found that the Newark Police Department's law enforcement practices had a "disparate impact on minorities." According to a 2016 report in U.S. News & World Report, a 74-page consent decree from the Justice Department demanded that the city's law enforcement hierarchy institute reforms to resolve allegations of civil rights violations. As a result, a report by the federal monitor who has been appointed to oversee the changes to the department, states that, "the Newark police have developed a positive working relationship with the monitoring team and the U.S. Department of Justice." Still, many Newark citizens get the chilling notion that the more things change, the more they remain the same.

So, can anyone envision that what happened in Ferguson, Baltimore, Charleston, Minneapolis-St. Paul, and Staten Island will lead to a new round of rebellions in racially depressed communities? Did the crises in Harlem and Los Angeles during the early sixties open doors for the long hot summer in 1967, punctuated by civil unrest in Newark and Detroit?

It is amazing that it has taken our federal government more than a half century to find that law enforcement agencies across America are more likely to ignore the actions of the bad characters who are wearing their uniforms. I am, however, one of the people who is pleased that at least Newark is working to create a laboratory of change in crime prevention; on the streets and in the precincts.

— Op-ed article from a professor
of college history in *The Star-Ledger*

"Gabriel has no idea what's going on." Eva Jean looked into the bedroom where Gabriel was sitting on a chair, facing a window. He was at Eva Jean's home.

"I would give a penny for his thoughts," Chante said.

"Me too, but his reaction to me knowing about the scar was unexpected," Eva Jean said. "I really thought he would begin yelling like a madman, like he did in the restaurant that day. But he surprised me. He was quite calm when I told him I knew about the scar."

"Can I see that picture again?" Gabriel said from the bedroom.

"That's what did it. It was the picture of the lady who raised him when his mother gave him up," Chante said to Eva Jean. "He found comfort and peace by seeing her again." Eva Jean walked into the bedroom and placed her hand on Gabriel's shoulder.

"That lady taught me how to take care of myself," Gabriel said as he looked at the photo. "She taught me how to read and write, and she took me back after I ran away from that man who married my mother. She treated the scar that man burned into my skin, and then

I had to run away to keep them from mistreating me." Chante walked into the room.

"Anything you could do to stay away from people who were trying to hurt you, right?" Eva Jean said. "You're starting to remember?"

"You lived on the streets in Kingston, Jamaica as a homeless child, working for food and shelter wherever you could get it," Chante said. "What did you do after that?"

"I followed Marcus Garvey. I came to America. My life changed. I get a job, I find a church, God gives me you." Gabriel stared into Eva Jean's eyes. "This picture of me with Miss Rachel makes me think of Kingston. It makes me think of when that mean man wanted to make me call him daddy. He burned me when I was little."

"Can you remember anything else?" Chante asked. "Did you have a family? Any children?"

"I only remember Samuel Garvey and his wife, this woman," Gabriel said, pointing at Eva Jean. "I remember how beautiful she was."

"Where did you live in Newark when you were friends with my husband?"

"Please, no more questions." Gabriel stretched out on the bed and closed his eyes.

"Grandma, this man is Samuel Garvey," Chante said. "I am convinced of it."

"Let him sleep, honey," Eva Jean said as she walked closer to the bed. "He's been through a lot in his life and he deserves some rest. Let him have time with God."

"But you need to know, Grandma."

"Chante, I am in no hurry. If God doesn't do anything else, bringing this man to me at this time of my life has already been enough."

"That must mean you think he's Samuel Garvey."

"Shh, child."

"A LOT OF LITTLE BLACK BOYS were thought of as property in Jamaica at that time," Mickey Marcus said. "Especially the ones who were living in the street, like your father."

"We can't assume that Gabriel is my father, no matter how similar their stories might be," Nehemiah said. The two men were walking through Branch Brook Park in Newark. "But let me say this. If we never discover Gabriel's true identity, it's okay with me. I am just glad that a really bad period in the history of Newark was uncovered as a result of this being played out.

"If Gabriel steps up and tells what he remembers, and Keller's son reveals his conversations with his father about what he did as a Newark cop, a lot of questions will be answered."

"And there'll be a spate of books written about that era."

"Just like all the books about the Newark rebellion."

"But none about you, Nehemiah."

"You know, Mickey, I didn't do anything for personal glory. I just wanted to save our city, the city I love. I don't mind if I'm a footnote or not; that does not make a difference to me.

"I'm just glad to be alive. There have been days since my father disappeared in '65 when I just wanted to pack up and leave Newark. But the love for my family and friends kept winning the day, and I'm still here and so are they. And what can I say about the relationship between you and me? It's golden."

"I know you don't mind standing to the side and allow people who did the hard work to get the credit. Like the man who coached you and many other young black and white boys with the Newark Bears in Pop Warner football in the '60s. Like the guys who played and coached high school sports in the old Newark City League, many of whom went on to do good things here and in other parts of the country, and in the world."

"Mickey, when the stories are told, they all break down to faith, family, and friendships. I have been given so much in my life. I have a wonderful mother, who had a great mother and great siblings. My cousin was like a sister to me, who God took home to glory when she was a troubled young woman. Her daughter became my daughter, and I have had a wonderful life with her for nearly forty years."

"Son, you have been living your entire adult life for your family and friends. You stayed in Newark to be here for those you loved, which was a lot of people. You walked away from scholarships to major colleges because you wanted to be close by, to make sure Denise grew up to be a responsible woman. You decided against a career in any professional sport because you wanted to ensure your mother's and grandmother's business ventures succeeded, and you felt being around them constantly would make that happen.

"Even though Denise died at a young age, she gave birth to Chante and you adopted her, and that young woman has become the responsible adult you always wanted Denise to be. There wasn't a better nephew for your now departed aunts and uncles. And your great friends everywhere, they are at your beck and call whenever you need them."

"I recently read this prayer by Pastor Rick Warren on social media. 'Dear God, I don't want to go another day without you in my life, controlling every part of my heart. I offer you my body. I dedicate myself to you. In light of all you've done for me, I give myself as a living sacrifice to you as a spiritual act of worship.'

"It's going to be fun watching the streets on which I played, and the parks on which I ran get re-developed and restored for the next generations. I credit all that happening because of many partnerships, blacks and whites, across this giant of a city that spans only 24 square miles. Isn't it amazing that so much greatness has come from such a tiny place? I thank God for His hedge of protection around Newark."

"You had the dream of living and thriving in Newark, even though you've had options to live in the places where you have homes; California, Florida, Georgia, Italy. Yet, you never left Newark as the place where you spent the most of your time. You have acquired a stable of antique cars that you enter in shows all over the world; you have a massive art collection, and a private jet. Yet, you seldom said no to anyone, or any organization, that had a need.

"I've enjoyed watching you grow from a boy to a man. The faith you had that Newark would be rescued one day is something that no one should ever discount. Now, I'm interested in what you'll do with your personal life. As your pastor sermonizes on many occasions, this is your season, Nehemiah. It is your time. You've never been married, so maybe you're ready."

"Alright, Mickey, aside from being a great basketball coach and successful businessman, you now want to be Cupid? May I ask who you are matching me with, sir?"

"Who else but Lena Mosley? She's been your friend for more than sixty years, and the two of you have been there for each other during some tough times. You two were Barack and Michelle Obama before they were Barack and Michelle."

"Mickey, I never thought I could get anything past you, especially when I look at this extremely fit 90-year old, who still completes marathons, works out at his fitness centers on a regular basis, and takes his wife on date nights each week," Nehemiah said. "But you are really late on this. Lena and I have been dating for quite some time."

"You got that one past me, young man. Am I going to hear wedding bells?"

"Only God knows that. But it doesn't really matter, as long as we have each other in some form. Just like you and me. We have walked some difficult roads during this 52-year journey, and we didn't work through any kind of binding contract. The steps we took were ordered by God. Very small and meaningful steps.

"It brings to my mind Matthew 25:23, 'The Master said, 'Well done, my good and faithful servant. You have been faithful in handling this small amount, so now I will give you many more responsibilities. Let's celebrate together!'"

"Mazel tov, Nehemiah."

"Amen, Mickey."

Remembering Philip Roth

In Philip Roth's 1981 book, *Zuckerman Unbound,* the novelist Nathan Zuckerman (Roth's alter ego) encounters a man who criticizes his writing about Newark, New Jersey. "What do you know about Newark, Mama's Boy?" the man says. "Moron! Moron! Newark is a nigger with a knife! Newark is a nigger with the syph! Newark is junkies shitting in your hallway and everything is burned to the ground! Newark is dago vigilantes hunting jigs with tire irons! Newark is bankruptcy! Newark is ashes! Newark is rubble and filth!"

One could reasonably surmise from the excerpt that Roth had a skewed view of his hometown; most likely because the Newark that Roth knew was not the Newark that I knew. One might say that we grew up on different sides of the railroad tracks. He was a member of the Weequahic High School graduating class of 1950; I graduated Weequahic in 1969. Roth grew up in the city's South Ward as I did, albeit in two very distinct neighborhoods. We both left Newark as teenagers with desires to make our marks in a world that viewed us with question marks; Roth because he was a northern Jew who identified more as American than immigrant; me, because I was a young, restless Black man who was skeptical of white liberalism that was carried from the Civil Rights era. Though we traveled along paths that were contextually formed the same way, the fashion in which we walked them were diametrically opposite.

I read and listened with great interest the post-mortems about Roth after his passing in 2018. My eyes widened over the words from his books that linked him to Newark. The Newark Museum (from *Goodbye Columbus*): "I could see it without even looking; two oriental vases in front like spittoons for a rajah and next to it the little annex to which we had traveled on special buses as schoolchildren." Clinton Avenue (from *The Plot Against America*): "We were on Clinton Avenue just passing the Riviera Hotel, where, as I never failed to remember, my mother and father spent their wedding night…directly ahead was Temple B'nai Abraham, the great oval fortress built to serve the city's Jewish rich and no less foreign to me than if it had been the Vatican." Weequahic High (from *Portnoy's Complaint*): "At football our Jewish High School was notoriously hopeless…We were Jews—and not only were we not inferior to the goyim (non-Jews) who beat us at football, but the chances were that because we could not commit our hearts to victory in such a thuggish game, we were superior! We were Jews—*and we were superior!*"

After many conversations about Philip Roth with my author friends over the years, the word *enigmatic* is copiously tossed around. Perhaps it is because he cannot be placed in a single literary category, or maybe some judge his prose a bit too harshly. Others might characterize him as a 'literary hustler'; someone who used his disdain for the Jewish condition in America as backdrops, or his perceived racial intellectualism as it appeared in his writing about a black man passing for a white man in his critically acclaimed novel, *The Human Stain*. It is in those instances that I hail Roth's genius, in part because he claimed those issues as his own and in part because he made no excuses.

Who was Philip Roth? It is according to whom you ask. But for sure, his brilliance informed this second edition.

Thank you, Philip Roth.

THIS BOOK REMEMBERS the people in forgotten enclaves of America who are struggling to find relevance in the 21st Century. As many of them now realize, they are the unwilling recipients of a situation that was not of their doing.

FAITHFUL SERVANTS is a novel that could be written about any underserved community in America: where forces of evil lurk behind smiling faces, and good intentions pave any path that is decent or gracious. The faces of depression don't have a particular color, but their fortunes are shaped by laws and policies designed to build ladders toward upward mobility with several rungs missing. There are far too many stories to quote about the human condition meeting immovable objects and irresistible forces, but one passage from James Baldwin's earth-shaking, mind-blowing essay, *The Fire Next Time,* could sum up a common frustration: "Do I really want to be integrated into a burning house?"

The intent of *FAITHFUL SERVANTS* is to inspire learned people to consider what might have been accomplished, had those in power during the 1960s actually worked to fix the trauma within white, black and brown ghettoes, rather than accept the Band-Aids that were haphazardly applied to blood-gushing wounds of despair and discontent.

This book does not intend to provide a new social science theory about problem-solving in America; nor is it a dissertation on yet another grandiose study of the rich and poor. Rather, it is the story of a group of people who work painstakingly to improve the condition of their lives after a horrendous series of tragic events, with the intent of also saving those around them.

Acknowledgments

ELLA WHEELER WILCOX said in her 1914 poem, "To sin by silence, when we should protest, makes cowards out of men. The human race has climbed on protest. Had no voice been raised against injustice, ignorance, and lust, the inquisition yet would serve the law, and guillotines decide our least disputes." A historical novel weaves truth into a mosaic of made up stories, giving readers the opportunity to think, "What if?"

My protest of what I have seen in my 67 years on this planet is magnified in the storytelling I attempt to convey in each of my books. Of course, no person's journey is taken alone, and I am not an exception. I am grateful to my good friend, "Big" Eddie Taliaferro, for encouraging me to take a deeper walk in Newark, New Jersey to write this book. I cannot thank my childhood friend Ali Rashid enough for lifting my spirits during this literary journey, when my thinking was not what it should have been. My research would have been incomplete without the help of Tom Ankner at the Newark Public Library and James Amemasor of the New Jersey Historical Society. I appreciate the assistance of people from across the country who supplied the profound historical quotes. Beth Kallman Werner, not only were you a superb editor, you inspired me along the way. I must give nods to my friends in Newark, from the Peshine Avenue School neighborhood and my classmates and teammates from the 1969 graduating class of Weequahic High School, as well as my friends from the other classes.

I would be remiss if I neglected to recognize some of my family, teachers and coaches, whose words of wisdom and role modeling I fondly recalled as I wrote this book; outstanding people such as my father Matthew Major Little, Fred Eleazer Lacey, Thelma Eleazer Bryant, Eva Eleazer Wadley, Jean Eleazer Carter, Marion Eleazer Richardson, Grace Eleazer Hopson, David Eleazer, Charles Eleazer, James "Hap" Sumner, Nora Sumner Bauknight, James "Kaboobie" Sedgwick, Leonard Moore, George Geller, Les Fein, David Wright, Artie Johnson, Hal Ginsburg, Seretha Tinsley, Leonard Chavis, Bob Zuber, Pastor Darrell Gilyard, Anthony Chirico, Pastor H.B. Charles Jr., Anthony D'Agostino, Willie Hutcherson, Leo Pearl, Bill Bellott, Ed McLucas, Elsie Cavicchia, Evelyn Crawford, Joseph Nerenberg, Bill Thayer, Don McCall, Seth Hicks, Emma Garrett, Nick Malpress, Daniel Hladney, Tom Slade, and Betty Holzendorf. All of them, in their distinct ways to my mind, were faithful servants.

A lot of inspiration for this book came from having seen, competed against and read about the great high school sports programs at Weequahic, South Side, Central, West Side, Vailsburg, Barringer and East Side in the old Newark City League, and the schools in the former Big Ten Conference, during the 1960s. Essex County had its share of great athletes in a number of outstanding schools during that time, and I had the good fortune to know many of them while growing up in a closely-knit working class neighborhood.

The list of my friends, classmates, teammates and rivals on athletic fields and courts is long, but I would be remiss if I did not mention them in some form or fashion. I start with my teammate on the 1968 and 1969 Weequahic baseball team, Larry Felton, whose life met an untimely end at only 18 years old. The Dykes brothers, Petie, Jimmy, and Wayne played on our neighborhood baseball teams that represented Peshine Avenue School from 1964 through 1968. Also, on those teams were Ronald "Stan" Staley, Lamont Williams, Thurman Perry (now known as Akbar Muhammad), my younger brother Duane, Gary Harris, Allen Bailey (now known as Ali Rashid) Frank Patterson, Titus

Patterson, A.D. Thorpe, Rod Twyman, Keith Guyton, Ronnie Felton, Butch Trawick, John Mosley, Desmond Russell, Dennis Childs and a number of others. We had an outstanding after-school basketball league where the competition between friends became very intense at times, and many of us old-timers still talk about the games. "Big" Mike Johnson, Joe Powell, Skip Jones, Greg Boone, "Little" Lenny, John Milbourne, Greg Milbourne, Larry Wright, Clarence Hawk, Bruce Branch, Alfred Hutchinson, James Armstrong, Calvin Britton, Michael Boss, Darrell Stevens, "Big" Bill Evans and many more. We had our legendary touch football games in the St. Charles Roman Catholic Church playground and our tackle football games behind the statute at Weequahic Park. Bo Pierce, Stanley Bell, Al McCoy, Fred McGill (now known as Malik), "Black" Sam Jackson, Ed Garvin, were outstanding players on those fields.

Going to Weequahic High School from 1965 to 1969 provided a new level of education in both the classroom and in the arena of athletics. I met and associated with people who were blessed with marvelous academic skills. Now I know I risk neglecting to name some, but I have to mention Lois Flagg, Paul Blake, Scott Seligman, Nancy Sheffey, Ivan Finman, Douglas Farrar, Howard Feldman, Denise Clark, Regina Clare, Dorcas Clark, Ivory Wise, Leonard Rosenhand, William Mantell, Deborah Davis, Harvey Mantel, Patricia Douglas, Steven Levine, Deborah Waters, Myra Walton, Larry Williams, Marc Grodman, Linda Gibson, Maureen Portee, Evora Thomas, Allan Terry and so many more. The mixture of members of the National Honor Society, high achievers in advanced placement classes and participants in the myriad of extra-curricular activities was my circle and my life has been blessed because of its existence.

The competition was keen among my contemporaries on the various sports teams at Weequahic and I interacted with many of them. My friends on the two-time Newark City League champion football team in 1967 and 1968 included Luther Howard, William Southerland, Frank Green, Ernie Barron and Dennis Mosely (also my teammates on the Newark City League champion baseball team in 1968), Mickey Coppock, Lanny Ferguson, Greg Scercy, Ronnie Smith, Marcus Hinton, Larry Hockaday, Rob Poteete, James Phipps, Willie Johnson, Fred Sly, Reggie Phifer, Brooks Burroughs, Willie Lewis, Norman Mann, George Davis, and Harold Hooper. As student manager of the varsity basketball team for all four of my years in high school (two of which the team was a state champion and number one in the country), I made friends for life with Charles Talley, David Wright, Larry Bembry, Dennis "Moe" Layton, George Watson, Dana Lewis, Phil Hickson, Rob Gaskin, Dwain Talley, Leroy Cobb and Gerry Gimelstob. As captain of the school's soccer team during my senior year, I shared a locker room with Mike Nicolau, Jean Hunt, Ed Trujillo and Ray Chojnowski, along with our other teammates.

I had many friends in other sports at Weequahic; Billy Twyman, Leonard Cisco, William Faulk and George Marshall on the track and field team, Marshall Cooper and Alan Stephens on cross country, Ralph Steele and Rodney Jones on wrestling, and Ronald Hale on the swimming team. My fondest memories, however, are reserved for the baseball team. The time I spent with Ronald Staley, Ron Howard, Jorge Menendez, Willis Bradwell, Greg Clark, Ralph Harkness, Roger Kinard, Larry Miller, Mel Holloman, Ronnie Hawkins, Ron Knight, Ernie Barron, Sid Haynes, Billy Jacobowitz, Luther Howard, Dennis Mosley, Paul Blake, Danny Morheim, and Bo Harkness was priceless. Playing on a championship baseball team as a high school junior, and serving as captain of the same team that was one game away from being a champion as a senior were experiences that I will never forget. Memories are as Barbara Streisand said in *The Way We Were*:

"Memories light the corners of my mind

Misty water-colored memories of the way we were

Scattered pictures of the smiles we left behind

Smiles we gave to one another for the way we were

Can it be that it was all so simple then

Or has time rewritten every line

If we had the chance to do it all again

Tell me, would we?

Could we?"

While practically nothing is ever final in acknowledging offerings, the benediction has to be read at some point. I am grateful for the Scriptural education provided from the pulpit and the blogosphere by people of faith. Their divine words helped shape the spiritual messages embodied in the book, bringing to mind 2 Timothy 2:15, 'Study and do your best to present yourself to God approved, a workman tested by trial who has no reason to be ashamed, accurately handling and skillfully teaching the word of truth.' I know that none of this book could have been written without the intercession of my Lord and Savior, Jesus Christ.

MARC CURTIS LITTLE is the award-winning author of five novels, including the critically acclaimed *After Obama*. He is a former journalist who frequently debated issues on radio and television during a 35-year career. Little also served as a public relations counselor, campaign strategist, and speechwriter for politicians and business leaders.

A native of Newark, New Jersey, Little resides with his family in northern Florida.

www.ingramcontent.com/pod-product-compliance
Lightning Source LLC
Chambersburg PA
CBHW070057120726
47909CB00002B/413